Praise for
DragonFire

"*DragonFire* is a soaring adventure. But I wouldn't expect anything less from Donita K. Paul, as she always gives us a delightful read: intriguing, challenging, and full of blessing."
　　—KATHRYN MACKEL, author of *Vanished* and *Outriders*

"A rich, fantastical treat—*DragonFire* lights the imagination with every turn of the page!"
　　—ROBERT ELMER, fantasy/sci-fi author

"*DragonFire* is not only a book for the young of age, but also for the young at heart. Donita K. Paul possesses a unique talent for instilling deep wisdom and spiritual truth in a story that is engrossing and satisfying for adults and children alike. She is one of my favorite authors."
　　—HANNAH ALEXANDER, author of the Hideaway series

"In *DragonFire*, Donita K. Paul has outdone herself! Though all of her dragon tales enchant, entertain, and inspire, this latest entry reveals even more profound depths in her characters—and in her magical winged creatures. This story will touch your emotions—and your soul."
　　—JIM DENNEY, author of the Timebenders series
　　and *Answers to Satisfy the Soul*

"*DragonFire* is 'predictable'—in the very best sense of the word! Breakneck pacing. Plot twists aplenty. Spiritual truths that inspire. And a powerful ending that—here we go again—leaves you wanting more."
　　—TAMARA LEIGH, best-selling author of *Perfecting Kate*

"*DragonFire* is a worthy continuation of the endearing series begun by Donita K. Paul. Lovable, admirable characters, entertaining adventures and misadventures, and breath-stealing plot twists—all deftly woven with sustaining strands of spiritual truth. Youth and adults alike will find these books impossible to put down until the last page is read."

—JANELLE CLARE SCHNEIDER, author

"Another enchanting fantasy starring the Dragon Keeper, Kale. Even when she thinks she's failed those she loves and who trust her, obedience and Wulder's love guide Kale. Inspiring."

—LYN COTE, author of *Blessed Assurance*

"Donita K. Paul has created another delightful tale featuring Kale, Bardon, and their enchanting friends. *DragonFire* takes the reader inside a wonderful world of fun and fantasy, with spiritual truths lighting each pathway. I loved it!"

—PEGGY DARTY, author of *When the Sandpiper Calls* and *When Bobbie Sang the Blues*

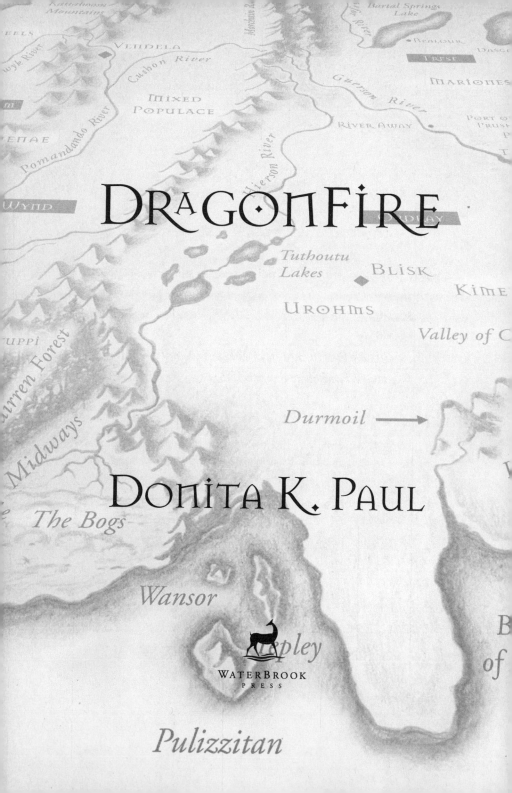

DragonFire

Donita K. Paul

WaterBrook
PRESS

DRAGONFIRE
PUBLISHED BY WATERBROOK PRESS
12265 Oracle Boulevard, Suite 200
Colorado Springs, Colorado 80921
A division of Random House Inc.

ISBN 978-1-4000-7251-4

Published in association with the literary agency of Alive Communications Inc., 7680
Goddard Street, Suite 200, Colorado Springs, CO 80920, www.alivecommunications.com.

Library of Congress Cataloging-in-Publication Data
Paul, Donita K.
    Dragonfire : a novel / Donita K. Paul.
        p. cm.
    ISBN 978-1-4000-7251-4
    1. Dragons—Fiction. 2. Religious fiction. I. Title.
    PS3616.A94D723 2007
    813'.6—dc22
                                        2007012652

Printed in the United States of America
2007—First Edition

10 9 8 7 6 5 4 3 2 1

This book is dedicated to these first readers,
who "test" my work for me:

Mary Darnell
Hannah Johnson
Alistair and Ian McNear
Rachael Selk
Rebecca Wilber

Contents

Acknowledgments

This time you went beyond writing help and helped me live!

Evangeline Denmark
Jani Dick
Michelle Garland
Dianna Gay
Cecilia Gray
Jack Hagar
Sharon Hinck
Beth Jusino
Krystine Kercher
Paul Moede
Jill Elizabeth Nelson
Shannon and Troy McNear
Stuart Stockton
Faye Spieker
Case Tompkins
Elizabeth Wolford
Laura Wright

Cast of Characters

Alton—purple and black riding dragon, friend to Sir Kemry Allerion

Ardeo—white and gray minor dragon, glows in the dark

Armin—marione from Trese, in the employ of Paladin's army

Bardon—o'rant and emerlindian knight in service to Paladin

Becca-ree—blue minor dragon, a messenger

Leetu **Bends**—emerlindian in the service of Paladin, recently undercover in Creemoor

Benrey—a rare, red fire dragon and a riding dragon belonging to Sir Kemry Allerion

Botzy—female marione innkeeper in Black Jetty

Farmer **Brigg**—marione who befriended Kale at the beginning of her journeys

Brite—wolf friend of Granny Noon

Bug—male ropma collecting dragons for Crim Cropper

Wizard **Burner Stox**—evil female wizard, married to Crim Cropper

Wizard **Cam Ayronn**—lake wizard from Trese

Celisse—Kale's black and white riding dragon

Clive—one of Kemry's many major dragons

Colly—marione musician in Black Jetty

Wizard **Crim Cropper**—evil male wizard, experiments with genetics, married to Burner Stox

Sir **Dar**—doneel diplomat and statesman

Dibl—yellow and orange minor dragon, reveals humor in situations, lightens the hearts of his companions

Dobkin—a slow-witted major dragon, friend of Kemry

Doxden—cook at inn in Black Jetty

Wizard **Fenworth**—deceased bog wizard from Wynd

Filia—pink minor dragon, enthusiastic about all things, collects knowledge, some of it quite trivial

Gilda—meech dragon, lives in a bottle to keep from dissipating because of a spell Risto put on her

Greer—Bardon's riding dragon, purple with cobalt wings

Gymn—green minor dragon, heals

Hollen—one of Sir Kemry's major dragons

Lord **Ire**—another name used by Pretender

Izz—female kimen living in Trese

Sir **Jilles**—Bardon's uncle

Sir **Joffa**—Bardon's father

Kale Allerion—o'rant wizard and Dragon Keeper, married to Bardon

Sir **Kemry Allerion**—Kale's father, also a Dragon Keeper

Granny **Kye**—Bardon's emerlindian grandmother

Lo **Kyl**—soldier in Bardon's camp

Latho—bisonbeck spy

Leemiz—cook in army camp

Librettowit—tumanhofer librarian in Kale and Bardon's castle

Lyll Allerion—Kale's mother

Lo **Mak**—soldier in Paladin's palace

Merlander—Dar's red and purple riding dragon

Metta—purple minor dragon, sings

Magistrate **Moht**—judge in Paladin's court

Wizard **Namee**—Paladin's right-hand man at court

Mistress **Nidell**—housekeeper at Paladin's palace

Granny **Noon**—emerlindian, friend of Kale, Bardon, Regidor, and Gilda

N'Rae—Bardon's emerlindian cousin

Paladin—ailing leader of Amara

Pat—chubby brown minor dragon, fixes things

Poe—one of Kemry's many major dragons

Prattack—Cropper's servant

Pretender—ruler of the evil populace of Amara

Rain—Bug's wife

Regidor—meech dragon, in search of a colony of lost meech dragons, likes fancy things

Wizard **Risto**—evil wizard killed by Fenworth

Sho—philosopher and genius observer of ancient times whose mostly lost works have accrued legendary acclaim

Grand **Sorn**—emerlindian in charge of Paladin's health

Streen—one of Sir Kemry's major dragons

Granny **Toe**—curmudgeon emerlindian living in Trese

Toopka—doneel child, under guardianship of Kale and Sir Dar

Traysian—chambermaid assigned to help Bardon when he contracted stakes

Veryan—one of Kemry's many major dragons

Leecent **Voet**—man assigned to be Bardon's batman while the knight recovered

Wardeg—one of Kemry's many major dragons

Wulder—the creator and one true, living God of Amara

Yent—kimen from Trese in the employ of Paladin's army

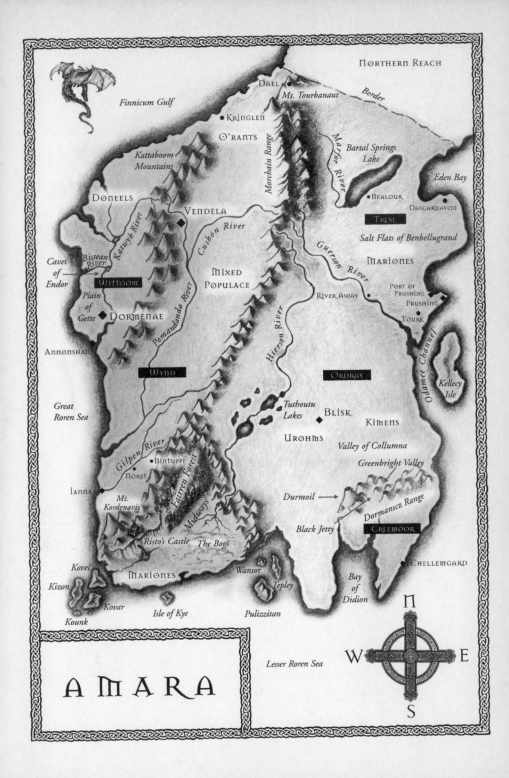

NORTHERN REACH

Dael

Mt. Tourbanaut

Border

Finnicum Gulf

Kringlen

O'RANTS

Morchain Range

Marfor River

Bartal Springs Lake

Eden Bay

Kattaboom Mountains

BEALOUR

DASCARNAVON

DONEELS

VENDELA

TRESE

Salt Flats of Benbellugrand

Katuyk River

Cushon River

MARIONES

Caves of Endor

Bissean River

WITTOOM

Guerson River

PORT OF PRUSHING

Plain of Gette

DORMENAE

Pomandundo River

MIXED POPULACE

RIVER AWAY

PRUSHING

TOURK

Annonshan

WYND

Hieron River

ORDRAY

Odamee Channel

Kellecy Isle

Great Roren Sea

Tuthoutu Lakes

BLISK

KIMENS

UROHMS

Valley of Collumna

Gilpen River

Bintuppi

NORST

Fairren Forest

Greenbright Valley

Durmoil

IANNA

Mt. Kordenavis

Midways

Dormanscz Range

Black Jetty

CREEMOOR

Risto's Castle

The Bogs

CHELLEMGARD

Kovel

Kizon

MARIONES

Wansor

Tepley

Bay of Didion

Kovar

Kounk

Isle of Kye

Pulizzitan

Lesser Roren Sea

N

W   E

S

A M A R A

†REASURE

Sir Bardon gripped his struggling wife in his arms.

"You're not rushing into that battered building, Kale." He lowered his voice to a more soothing tone. "Come on, lady of mine. You can control this urge."

With his arm encircling her waist, he felt her take a deep breath and let it out slowly. He loosened his grasp but remained wary. In this state she couldn't be trusted. Her talent sabotaged her judgment. Perhaps words of reason would override her compulsion.

"Remember, Kale, we must find Regidor and Gilda before it is too late."

Kale's body tensed, and he reacted by tightening his hold just before she tried to lunge out of his arms toward the inn.

"Bardon, please." Her voice broke on the last word.

"I'm just as determined to keep you here as you are to go. Relax, Kale. Think."

He scanned the building she wanted to enter. One end had collapsed under the barrage of a recent battle. The other smoldered sullenly.

The muscles in Bardon's face tightened. *Fire dragons. I wonder how many?*

A drenching rain had doused the flames. *How long ago? Where are the people to answer my questions?*

The rain had finally stopped. The villagers had collected their dead. But still the acrid smells of war permeated the air.

"I have to go in, Bardon." Kale's voice shuddered as she pushed ineffectively against his hold.

"Yes, I know. All I'm asking is that you think first. That you plan."

She leaned her head back against his chest. Her skin smelled of citrus. He inhaled, relishing the fragrance, and rubbed his cheek against her hair. The brown locks in curly twists bounced against his face, tickling his nose.

Bardon regulated his breathing, willing Kale to fall into the same pattern, to draw from his reserve and strengthen her own.

She ceased twitching. "I'll take Ardeo to light the way."

"Good," said Bardon.

Six minor dragons roosted on the saddle of Kale's horse. Their varied colors distinguished them as belonging to a special species both intelligent and willing to work with the seven high races. Ardeo flew from his companions and landed on Bardon's shoulder.

On this cloudy day, the dragon's pale skin looked mottled. In sunshine, his coloring resembled old pasty porridge. But in the dark, the dragon glowed with a moonlike aura.

Kale quivered within Bardon's arms. "I'll take Pat to help me pick the safest route."

Another of the minor dragons flew to roost on her shoulder. He snuggled his plump brown body under her ear, rubbing his head against her chin with affection.

"Good." Bardon approved. The fix-it dragon would analyze the danger in the weakened building. Still, Bardon didn't much care for Kale going into the inn.

Her muscles stiffened, and he tightened his hold. He spoke to focus her attention. "What else? Think."

"I'll wear my moonbeam cape. That'll protect me some against splinters and scrapes."

"Fine." Bardon relaxed his grip. "You'll move slowly, with caution? You'll listen to Pat?"

"Yes." Kale nodded, her eyes fixed on the charred front door.

Pat and Ardeo flew into the air and circled above the yard. Bardon dropped his arms to his side, and his wife took a step toward the shattered inn. Quickly, he placed a hand on her arm and turned her toward the horses.

"The cape," he said.

"I forgot."

He positioned himself between her and the building until she pulled the garment from her saddlebag and draped it over her shoulders. He grasped the front lapels and pulled her to him, fastened the tie at her neck, and kissed her forehead.

"Stay out of trouble."

He watched her eyes focus, knowing her thoughts had finally settled on him, just him. A twinkle brightened the hazel gaze, replacing that distant look.

She mocked a curtsy. "Yes, my knight."

Without a doubt, his wife was a winsome creature.

"Remember, you are *my* fair wizard."

She tipped her face up with a saucy smile. Then he watched the awareness of him fade from her expression to be overtaken by the compulsion to enter that dangerous inn.

He sighed and tenderly, but reluctantly, turned her away. She stepped forward without another word.

"Kale, don't be long. We haven't time." Bardon gestured to the two small dragons she had chosen to accompany her. "Pat, Ardeo, take care of her."

⊹⟞⟝⊹

Kale passed under a tilted entryway where the large beamed framework threatened to crash down around her. An ominous creak caused her to hop over the mantel. Inside, a splintered door lay across piles of rubble. Most of the south wall had crumbled into a pile of rock and plaster. Above her, clouds provided a roof for the front third of the building. She zigzagged around broken furniture and rough boards that might have been part of the upstairs flooring.

With cautious steps, Kale made her way to the back. Pat and Ardeo darted through the air. Pat chirred his displeasure at the lack of stability in the building.

The ceiling sagged, and she ducked under a half-fallen beam. A cascade of bed linens flowed from a hole in the ceiling. Ardeo and Pat flew to the second story, circled, and returned. The light dragon twittered.

Kale nodded. "Not a living soul in the ruin. Fine."

No one to interfere with her mission. Pat's thoughts bombarded her with vivid details of the devastation to the inn. She wasn't interested in what remained above, except that she preferred no loose flooring fall on her.

She braced herself against the pull of her talent. Downward. She must move downward. She *must* find the steps to the cellar.

Stepping on a small pile of debris, she slid. Her foot landed on more secure flooring, and she steadied herself. A reminder. She must take care. She had made Bardon a solemn promise. Pat uttered a series of shrieks, another reminder.

In the kitchen, pottery, dishes, and cutlery had rattled from the shelves. A broken sack of flour spilt over a sturdy table. But the walls stood upright, and only a few piles of plaster from the ceiling showed the beating the structure had taken.

Pat's stomach rumbled. Kale glanced his way, expecting him to swoop to forage the table, but he took no notice of the scraps of food and concentrated on what he could see of the studs and braces. Kale stepped forward before he reported on their soundness, and he hissed a warning she ignored.

She moved along the wall, heading for a door that most probably hid the pantry or the steps to the cellar. As she passed the hearth, she wrinkled her nose at the smell of old green stem vegetables in a pot. An unrecognizable boiled-dry mass lined the bottom of another kettle. Cold ashes lay in the fireplace.

The details of her surroundings helped her focus, helped her restrain the impulse to press forward. But her eyes locked on a door, and she felt a surge of urgency rush through her.

The cellar.

She stumbled across the room, one hand stretched ahead, ready to raise the latch.

Pat chirruped.

A mixture of words and images came from the small dragon's mind, urging her to change directions. Kale hesitated, then veered off to another door and swung it open, expecting to find a stairway. She jerked back, repelled by the foul odor of spoiled food. Pickled cucumbers, beets, and cabbage poured from broken crocks littering the floor. She lifted her arm to cover her nose with the moonbeam cape. Slamming the door shut, she glowered at the brown dragon sitting on a wooden counter.

"Pat! What in all of Amara were you thinking?"

The message came to her clearly. The dragon wanted her to slow down and be more cautious. He'd tricked her into opening the wrong door to demonstrate his point.

"All right. I understand your concern." She used cleansing breaths to help her focus. Standing still took effort. Even as she inhaled for the third time, her feet started moving toward the other door.

"I promised Bardon."

She managed to open the door slowly. The dark passage led downward over stone steps.

"Ardeo," she called.

The dragon flew around her and downward. His skin glowed like moonlight as soon as he descended into the shadows below.

Forgetting caution, Kale plunged down the steps. Pat landed on her head and dug his claws into her scalp.

"Ouch!" She winced and batted at him with her hands. "All right. All right."

She stopped on the last step and surveyed the crates and barrels, then pointed in the direction of the pull.

"That way."

Ardeo flew ahead. Pat remained with his feet planted firmly in her hair.

Kale hurried, barely realizing that she had doubled back under the most damaged part of the inn. Pat sent her frantic messages to watch where she stepped, to avoid debris hanging from the sagging ceiling, and to slow down.

Kale moved with determination to a row of baskets hanging on ropes along one wall. The woven containers of various sizes reached across the space like clothes on a line.

Only one attracted her. She grabbed a creel-like storage bin and pulled it toward her. The rope gave way, and all the other baskets tumbled to the floor. Heedless of the spill, Kale plunged her hand beneath the covering cloth and pulled out a handful of onions. She threw them over her shoulder and reached in again. More onions. She turned the basket upside down and shook it. Nothing but onions. She dropped the basket and stared at the wall.

Placing her hands against the dirt, she felt energy swell within her fingertips. With her teeth gritted and her breath held, she tried to order her thoughts. To think instead of acting on the compulsion caused sweat to bead on her brow.

Move the dirt. Dig. With what? A spell. Pull. Pull.

The dirt crumbled into her hands. She concentrated.

Pull. Pull.

The hard-packed soil came apart and fell out of the wall. She brushed more away and reached in. Another basket. She tugged it free and held it tightly to her chest. She'd found the treasure.

Ardeo landed on her shoulder. His soft glow illuminated a dirty cloth stuffed in the narrow neck of this peculiar container. The woven creation of straw and reed looked more like a gourd than any basket she had ever seen.

Kale pulled the disintegrating material from the top and looked inside.

"Four eggs," she whispered. "Four dragon eggs."

Pat slid down her hair to perch on the other shoulder.

"Minor dragon eggs. It's been so long since I found any, I almost forgot what the lure felt like."

Pat chittered.

"Yes, I know," she answered. "We have to find Regidor and Gilda. We should be asking for news of them in occupied taverns."

Pat and Ardeo chorused another warning.

Kale gazed at her find lovingly.

Pat put tiny teeth on her earlobe and pinched.

Kale jerked. "All right! I understand. The building is unstable. We'll leave now."

She transferred the precious eggs into the pockets lining her cape.

She crossed the cellar space and climbed the stairs. Now that Kale had her prize, she couldn't wait to get out of the inn. The urgent need to find Gilda resurfaced, and she almost ran to where Bardon waited. Pat flew in her face and batted his wings against her cheeks.

"I'll be careful. You're not helping, you know. I can't see where to put my feet."

Pat settled on her shoulder.

The pillars creaked. The walls bulged. The heavy rain of the days before pressed against the swollen seams of the building. She feared the whole structure would collapse before she reached the inn's yard.

She came back into the front room. The clouds above had thinned, and a ray of sunshine broke through. One of the horses outside nickered. Kale smiled and stepped cautiously through the debris.

"I found them," she called to Bardon. "And I didn't get into trouble."

He didn't answer.

"Bardon, I found them."

Still no answer.

"Bardon?"

2

Batting Flies

As soon as Kale reached the yard, Dibl, the most lighthearted of her minor dragons, swooped down from a perch in the tree and bombarded her with his thoughts. Ardeo and Pat, in a frenzy of excitement, joined him as he circled her head. She closed her eyes against the dizzying sight of their chaotic flight and concentrated on deciphering Dibl's chatter.

A small military unit of bisonbeck had marched into the inn yard.

Kale screwed her face in distaste. She didn't like bisonbecks—burly, bad-tempered bullies. She'd never seen a bisonbeck who didn't swagger his huge frame nor one who had an ounce of courtesy.

Dibl informed her that Bardon had taunted the five warriors and led them into the woods. The other minor dragons flew off to help in the skirmish.

She shook her head. *Didn't want me to enter a fight as soon as I came out, right, Sir Knight?*

Shifting her attention to her spouse, she located him, feeling the energy that emanated as he battled the muscle-bound henchmen of the evil wizards. She also realized the ease with which he engaged the soldiers. He didn't need her to vanquish the foe, but she had no intention of becoming a widow due to some bisonbeck's lucky strike.

Twirling in place, she changed her outfit from a comfortable riding habit to a close-fitting ensemble she'd copied from her mother. "Wear pink!" her mother had said. "It confuses the enemy." Kale tended to think that their invisible swords did more to bewilder their opponents.

She took a moment to glance at the horses' reins and mentally unwound them from the fence rail. She wanted the horses to be free to come to her if she called.

"Now, try to be sensible and stay here," she addressed them both. *Horses certainly don't have the intelligence of an average dragon.* Kale preferred traveling on the back of her ebony and silver dragon, Celisse. For the hundredth time since she and Bardon started this search, she missed the riding dragons.

She sprinted through the woods, zigzagging around bushes and leaping over old fallen timber that rotted beneath the canopy of sturdy armagot trees. Slowing, she surveyed with her mind the site before her. Bardon battled two bisonbecks in a clearing. Two had already fallen to his sword. One knelt at the side of the open space, rubbing his stinging eyes. The minor dragons spit caustic saliva into the faces of their opponents. A well-directed shot of spit incapacitated even the mightiest warrior.

Dibl flew into the battle, but Kale waited until a soldier's broad back presented itself for her assault. She picked up a rodlike branch, ran a few steps, dug the pole into the ground, and vaulted into the air. She hit the bisonbeck with both feet, right between the shoulder blades. He toppled forward.

The action distracted the other man facing Bardon, and her husband used the advantage to deliver a knockout blow to the man's temple. The soldier Kale had downed grunted and pushed up with his arms. Kale frowned at him, and he flattened out.

Quick and efficient always, Bardon wiped his blade clean on one of the downed men and sheathed it. "Came to help me bat at these bothersome flies?"

"They're rather big flies." Kale strolled to his side. "Thanks for drawing them off. I suppose you did it to keep them from distracting me."

He put an arm across her shoulders. "Something like that." He nodded at the immobile but conscious soldier. *"What did you put on him?"* asked Bardon without speaking aloud.

He thinks a pair of grawligs is sitting on his back.

Bardon laughed softly and hugged her. *"So, you found the eggs."*

Yes, no problems. She examined the soldiers scattered over the clearing floor. *I don't recognize their uniforms. Who do these men fight for?*

"I don't recognize them either. Perhaps we can ask one of the two still conscious. I don't want to waste the time. We need to get on with finding our two meech friends."

I keep getting this niggling feeling that we have ignored the world outside The Bogs for too long.

"I have a dread building the more I see of the devastation the fire dragons have created. I'd rather leave these men in the dirt and go about our business, but I can't deny it's important to uncover some particulars as to this different army."

Kale tilted her head toward the man rubbing his eyes, and Bardon nodded. She reached into her moonbeam cape and brought out a small pouch. With care, she selected a seed and threw it down at the man's knees. It instantly took root and shot up a green tendril that stretched, thickened, and put on a leaf. It grew at an astonishing pace, and Kale directed it to wrap around the injured warrior. When the vine secured the man from any attempt of escape, the phenomenal growth stopped. Kale gestured to the green minor dragon.

"Heal his eyes, would you, Gymn?"

The dragon landed on the bisonbeck's head, and after a moment, the man quit clawing at his face. The vine kept him from lowering his hands. Kale waited another moment. She felt the healing energy flow through her to the dragon. It passed from the small creature through the man and back to her. With each cycle the flow felt cleaner. When satisfied that the man's discomfort was bearable, Kale nodded to Bardon.

He stepped forward. "Sir," he said in an even tone. "You must forgive us, for we have been residing in the middle of The Bogs these last three years and have somewhat lost touch with the outside world. We do not recognize your uniform as representing any of the provinces of Amara. Kindly tell us to whom you have pledged your allegiance."

The soldier growled.

"Oh, beg pardon." Bardon used the tip of his sword to slice through a bit of vine covering the man's lower face.

A word came out of the man's mouth that fouled the air. The purple dragon, Metta, trilled indignation and fluttered her wings as if clearing a rancid odor.

Bardon tilted his sword upward and brought the hilt down with a resounding thud on the coarse warrior's head.

"Just a reminder that there are ladies present."

The soldier grumbled in an undertone, and Bardon sighed. He pushed the point of his blade between the broad leaves of the vine and touched the man's jugular vein.

"We have already been delayed. I would appreciate quick answers. Your master?"

"Crim Cropper."

"And Burner Stox?"

"Nay. They no longer fight side by side."

"Excellent news. A falling-out among villains." Bardon stepped back and looked the man over. "Tell us where Crim Cropper has his head-quarters."

"I can't. I don't know."

Bardon looked to Kale. She nodded. The soldier told the truth.

"Where are your forces located?"

"At the bottom of the Dormanscz Mountain Range near Geest."

"How many?"

"Eight hundred troops."

"What is your directive?"

"Spoil the land so that it is not valuable to Stox or Pretender or anyone else."

Bardon ground his teeth and walked away from the soldier. "I want nothing further from you. The vine should release you sometime later today."

Kale smiled. "And your eyesight should return tomorrow at the latest. If you have any trouble, call on us. Our residence is in the center of Bedderman's Bog. Anyone in the neighborhood can direct you to Fen's castle."

She hooked her arm through Bardon's as he passed. The yellow and orange Dibl set down on Bardon's head, his favorite place to perch. Metta and Gymn landed on Kale's shoulders. Ardeo settled on her hair, a curly mop, disheveled as always. Filia flew ahead, and Pat rummaged through the undergrowth for food.

Bardon patted his wife's hand as it rested at his elbow. "It might have been fair to warn him that none of our immediate neighbors speak the high tongue since they're all animals."

He pushed aside a branch so they could pass. "And you might have mentioned that we won't be home anytime in the near future."

She nodded.

"And there are mordakleeps in the swamp."

"Oh, but we've almost eradicated them all. Surely there are less than a dozen now." Kale shrugged. "Besides, he will be quite well and won't need us." Worry wriggled its way into her thoughts.

"This dodging of soldiers and stopping to aid villagers is taking up a lot of time. Not that I begrudge the people our aid." She frowned at the clouds. Couldn't they just blow away and let the sun dry this soggy land? "No one gives us any pertinent news when we question them, Bardon. Do you think we'll find Regidor before it's too late?"

"We're close to Granny Noon's. Let's stop in and ask her if she has any suggestions."

Using her talent, Kale summoned the horses, and they came trotting through the trees. By the time the horses reached the riders, she had whirled once more, changing her clothes to the brown riding habit.

"You're going to wear the cape?" asked Bardon.

"Yes, Granny Noon made it." She ran her hand down the luxurious fine cloth of her habit trousers. "But it's the wrong color for this rich brown."

"Change the color of the cape."

Kale rolled her eyes. "Even I can't do that. Moonbeam cloth has a very uncooperative base." She snapped her fingers as an idea occurred to her. The color of her clothing faded and darkened and faded again until she wore lavender and amethyst attire. The grayish moonbeam cape looked much more appropriate.

"Mother would have thought of that much sooner," Kale complained.

Bardon laughed. "So would have Sir Dar. I like the way you dress. Isn't that enough?"

She made a face at him. "It would be if you didn't wear mismatched socks from time to time."

"No one notices but you."

Bardon hoisted her into the saddle. She didn't need the help, but it made her feel good to have her husband act the gentleman.

Riding west, husband and wife followed a long mountain ridge and then turned north. A stiff breeze greeted them. The clouds broke up and sailed away, revealing a startling blue sky. The sun sent waves of comfortable warmth through her body. Her spirit rose, and Metta, picking up Kale's mood of eagerness, sang a tune filled with hope. Few people lived on this part of the mountain range, and the animals scampered through the woods with a joyful freedom.

The track led them around a bend to the first view of the mountainside where Granny Noon resided. Across the valley, a blackened forest covered what was once a verdant ridge. Kale gasped. Metta ceased her song. Fire had scourged the beauty of the forest. Somberly they rode on, coming to a river and following it downstream to a bridge.

"New," said Bardon, looking at the fresh wood. He pointed to the charred beams at the waterline. "And there's the old."

The planks echoed under the horses' hooves as they crossed. On the far bank, each strike of a horse hoof against the scorched ground sent up an acrid smell of burned vegetation. Bardon pulled his mount up, and Kale stopped beside him.

He reached across and put a hand over hers. "Can you find the entrance without familiar landmarks?"

Kale shook away a fear that threatened to overcome her. "Do you think Granny Noon's still there? Do you think she survived?"

"Yes," he answered with a decisive nod.

Kale battled tears, then squeezed her lids tight. She wasn't so sure. As soon as she opened her eyes, she saw a yellow flower.

"Look." She pointed. Nestled in the charred debris, a few green, spindly leaves pushed toward the sun. In the center, a delicate, feather-petaled bonnie nodded its head. Farther on, an owlwing fern had broken through the desolation. "It must have been a while since the burn."

"Yes," agreed Bardon. "We'll find Granny Noon, Kale. And she'll help us find Regidor."

3

Unexpected Help

On purpose, Sir Bardon and Lady Kale rode right past the burned bower that camouflaged the entrance to Granny Noon's underground home. They needed to find her quickly, but not at the expense of exposing her dwelling place. The fire had stripped the mountainside of the foliage that would have hidden their entry into the burrow from prying eyes. Filia and Dibl, acting as scouts, guided them to a deep ravine left unscathed by the forest fire.

Kale felt as though she'd been in the saddle for weeks instead of five days. Her soreness and fatigue passed to Bardon through their special bond, and she in turn received an impression of his attitude. His sense of urgency to find Regidor was every bit as keen as hers. He stewed over the inconvenience of being restricted to the ground instead of soaring above the hazardous landscape. In his thoughts, he expressed his frustration by calling the beast under him all manner of derogatory names.

His head turned her way when he became aware that his wife found his tirade amusing. She smiled smugly at Bardon's chagrin and couldn't suppress a bubble of mirth. It tickled her each time he realized that she coped with discomfort with less internal griping than he did.

And she always knew what he was thinking. That was one of the beauties of their strong connection. Many times she didn't have to explain her viewpoint. And his unique way of looking at things popped into her head just before she was about to express total bewilderment over his actions. Her husband outshone her in so many areas, but she was the better rider when it came to horses.

The self-satisfied smirk on her face melted into a warm glow when he winked at her and she heard his next thought. He would never expect her to call an animal a string of unflattering names.

"You are so definitely a lady."

She blushed and then heard his inward laugh. It settled within her, padding the fierce love she felt for him with a comforting amiability.

Shaking her head, she gestured toward the untouched strip of vegetation. "What happened here?"

"The fire jumped the gorge."

"Is it safe to leave the horses?"

"If you can convince one of the woodland creatures to stand guard and come get us if there's trouble."

She turned her mind to exploring the life around her. The area was sparsely populated. And of those animals she found, not many possessed the intelligence to do her bidding. They'd be willing but would get distracted too easily.

A presence lurked at the edge of her consciousness. She stilled and concentrated. A wolf! The minor dragons caught her delight and chittered.

Hush! she told them. *Don't scare him away.*

Cautiously, she approached him with her thoughts.

"Will he help?" asked Bardon.

Shh! I don't mind your eavesdropping, but he might. He's nervous.

She closed her eyes and got an impression of the wolf's surroundings. He lay in the bushes close enough to observe the strangers in his territory.

Would this animal be helpful? Did he know her friend? Kale sent one thought. *Granny Noon?*

No response. So he didn't know her by name. Kale tried again, forming an image of the emerlindian in her mind. The old woman's skin was as dark as coal, her eyes deep brown, and her straight black hair hung almost to the floor. Small and wiry, Granny Noon looked as if she were made only of bone and muscle. But Kale knew from experience that the wise woman had a comforting embrace, gentle and soothing. Granny Noon's image filled Kale with peace, and she was not surprised when the wolf echoed her reaction.

Aha! The wolf socialized with the emerlindian granny. She called him Brite.

Is she all right? Where is she?

Kale breathed a sigh of relief at his answer.

"She's in her home," she said aloud. The communication from the wolf could not be interpreted by Bardon without her assistance. "The fire did little damage below. It moved swiftly over the ground."

Kale returned her attention to the wolf. After a moment, she expressed her gratitude and dismounted. "Brite says he'll watch over the horses while they're hidden here."

She and Bardon took the horses into the ravine, then unsaddled, tethered, watered, and fed them. The rich greens in the shade of the crevasse not only gave relief to their eyes after the stark mountainside but also filled their nostrils with a pleasant fragrance. Here the horses would remain hidden from unwanted notice. Kale and Bardon would hike back to the entrance of Granny's home.

Satisfied the horses were safe and comfortable, they climbed again to the ridge. To the best of her ability, Kale determined no one was spying on them. The surrounding mountainside seemed to be deserted of high and low races. Her talent did not reach to the forests covering the other slopes.

The sun beat down on the open area, highlighting the black expanse. She and Bardon must stand out like huge, colorful blotches on the dark backdrop.

"Is the area safe?" asked Bardon. "You're uneasy."

Kale scanned the surrounding area, hoping she could see with her eyes any danger that her inner sense did not pick up.

"I'm afraid I'll make an error in judgment and bring evil to Granny Noon's home. Before this fire, the entire forest camouflaged her front door."

"What we need is a farsighted bird of prey."

"Exactly!" Kale scanned the skies with enthusiasm, then wrinkled her brow.

"The fire killed or drove off many of the small animals," Bardon explained. "The large birds followed them." He glanced over the sooty skeletons of trees. "And there's precious little roosting around here."

Her shoulders drooped.

Bardon turned back to the protected ravine. "We'll wait until dark."

The horses nickered nervously.

"One moment, Bardon." Kale lowered her voice. "The wolf is coming out."

Bardon came back to stand at her side.

The black nose on a silky tan muzzle poked through the undergrowth. Kale and Bardon breathed softly and did not move. The wolf's golden eyes peered at them, then he retreated into the bush and moved away.

"Oh, marvelous creature! Thank you." She started after him. "He's going to show us a back way into the burrow. No one will see us."

They followed but at a distance. Brite still didn't care for their company.

The ravine deepened. The wolf trotted ahead and remained out of sight. Kale trailed him by her sense of his being, knowing his direction without seeing him. Bardon, in tune with his wife's instincts, kept pace. A mountain spring appeared, and the gorge changed directions, cutting back down the mountain. The wolf quickened his speed.

Bardon helped Kale over crumbling rock terrain. "Not afraid of leaving us behind, is he?"

"He's hurrying to see Granny Noon. He's almost forgotten about us."
They scrambled to catch up.

Kale squeezed Bardon's arm. "She's there! He's seen her."

They pushed through the last thicket and saw the slight emerlindian stooped over a huge wolf, stroking his head and neck.

Startled, Kale realized Brite had suffered burns in the recent fire. His legs and underbelly displayed patches of pink, scarred skin. Singed fur and bare hide covered one flank.

The wounds had healed much more than one would expect. As Kale watched the wolf and the emerlindian interact, she knew Granny Noon must have found Brite on her doorstep and nursed him back to health.

The wolf pressed his head into the granny's hand, bouncing on his feet and knocking against her legs.

"Easy, Brite." Granny Noon giggled. "You'll push me over." She looked up and gestured to Kale and Bardon. "Come, I've been expecting you."

Brite backed away and sat on his haunches. With his tongue lolling out, his expressive face looked happy.

Kale ran into Granny Noon's embrace. "Oh my! You are so tiny." Kale laughed. "I'd forgotten. Librettowit says emerlindians come in one width and two heights, always lean, but either five feet high or over six."

Granny Noon's arms tightened around Kale. "The librarian is right as usual. And I prefer to be shorter. My life in my lovely underground burrows would be complicated by a stretched-out frame."

Her attention returned to the wolf. She gazed into his eyes for a moment, and then Brite bounded off the way they had come.

"He'll go now to guard your horses," she said and leaned back to get a better look at Kale. "You have grown, girl. When I first met you, you were a mere child. Now you're a woman and married. Seven years? Yes, seven years since you first came to my door." She patted Kale's arm.

The seriousness of their mission descended upon Kale. "Granny Noon, we must find Regidor and Gilda."

The old woman smiled serenely. "Surely finding a meech dragon and his lady should not be so hard. Although Regidor dresses to minimize his more startling features, he does tend to make a stir wherever he goes."

"And he usually keeps in touch with us," Kale said. "He drops in to visit. He sends messages. Gifts are delivered from all over the country. Librettowit receives rare books Regidor has stumbled across in his research. But we haven't heard a thing from him in six weeks."

Granny Noon tugged Kale gently toward the opening of her abode. "Coming, Bardon?"

"Yes."

Kale continued, worry lacing her tone, "The last time I saw Gilda she was lethargic and a mere shade of her former self. I feared she would expire before too long. But we've found the cure, Granny Noon. And now we can't find her!"

They passed through earthen tunnels with steps made out of roots, lit by blue lightrocks in lanterns attached to the wall.

"I would think," said Granny Noon in a deep, soothing voice, "that Regidor would choose to spend the last days with his beloved somewhere safe and secluded."

"Yes, but where?"

Granny Noon pushed the door to her rooms open. "Perhaps here."

4

Tea, Daggarts, and a Miracle

Kale ran into the room. It hadn't changed much since her last visit. Earthen walls, wood furniture, colorful cushions, bright rugs, smells promising sweet treats, candles, books strewn around, and Regidor unfolding his long form from a two-seater sofa. Of course, Regidor had not been there before.

As familiar as she was with his appearance, the elegance of her former protégé never ceased to amaze her. At first glance he looked like a tall o'rant, but his leathery skin held a green cast, and he had no hair and no outer ears. His squarish nose was long, and his mouth was thin-lipped and wide. His smile looked either beguiling or sinister, depending on how comfortable one felt with this rare species of dragon. Kale's heart filled with pride and love.

She hurled herself across the room and dove into his embrace. Her head rested against his broad chest. His arms encircled her and squeezed gently.

Bardon spoke from the doorway. "I'd tease you about manhandling my wife, but we really have come on urgent business."

Kale pulled back from Regidor and looked frantically around the room.

"Where is she? Where's Gilda?"

"In her bottle." Regidor's voice rumbled in his throat. "She hasn't come out yet today."

Kale reached into the hollow of her cape, a small portal to another dimension that she used for storage. She pulled out an ancient book.

She heard Regidor's sharp intake of breath and saw the arrested look on his face.

He let out a question on a hiss of air. "Is that Sho?"

She nodded and extended her hand, offering the book as if it were the key to all wisdom. "Librettowit found this. It's the original, third century, recorded in Sho's own hand." Her hope swelled, bringing tears to her eyes. "I've experimented, and we can do it, Regidor. We can save Gilda."

Regidor did not take the book. Kale pulled it back, resting the heavy tome against her waist as she opened it to a place marked by a purple ribbon. With force, she thrust it into Regidor's hands.

He frowned at her before allowing his eyes to examine the book. The meech dragon scanned down the page. His expression changed. "Cohesion!"

He called out the word Kale had finally latched upon after hours of study. Kale grinned, not at all surprised that her friend recognized the significance in a fraction of the time.

His hairless brow furrowed as he concentrated, and he mumbled as he read. "Yes!" He tapped the page with a clawlike fingernail. "Why didn't I see this before? It makes perfect sense." A growl emanated from his throat. "Wasted time. So simple."

Kale bounced on her toes. *It's going to work. If Regidor thinks it will work, it will. Librettowit and I were right. Gilda doesn't have to die.*

Regidor placed the open book on a plain wooden table. He crossed the room to a bookshelf and retrieved a blue glass bottle inlaid with an intricate silver design. He held it to his chest for a moment, his expression shuttered, then brought it to Kale.

His green eyes twinkled as he removed a cork from the top. "My dear Dragon Keeper, I don't believe I've introduced you to my wife."

Kale blinked at the unexpected announcement and then grinned. A thin stream of vapor rose from the small opening and floated to the floor. The column retained its misty quality for a moment and gradually began to define the form of a tall female dragon who matched Regidor in exotic magnificence.

Still watching Gilda emerge from the cloud, Kale reached for her husband's hand. He came to her side.

Bardon, do you see how long her transformation takes? When Risto first cast this spell upon her, she shifted back and forth without any apparent effort.

"She's tired."

She's almost dead.

"We're in time, Kale. Don't despair."

Why did she have to suffer so? And for so long?

He brought her hand up and placed his other hand over her tense fingers. *"Risto held her in his palm, and when she decided to switch her allegiance to Regidor, he wanted to punish her. Nothing he could do would destroy her love for our meech friend, but Risto determined she would not enjoy that love. Of course, he underestimated both Regidor and Gilda."*

Why didn't Paladin intervene? The only two meech dragons in Amara, and they couldn't live normal lives.

"You know the answer to that."

I do?

"Wulder had a plan."

Another voice entered Kale's mind. Gilda's deep, almost sultry tones whispered in her consciousness. *"I'm listening, Kale. Or did you think I would politely refrain from eavesdropping?"*

Kale growled in her throat, a very tolerable imitation of Regidor's choice means of displaying his displeasure. *Gilda, I would never expect you to comply with rules of etiquette, if by doing so, you would be excluded from any information.* She tried to sober her expression and failed. Her smile grew larger instead.

The translucent appearance of the female dragon's face held a mocking air. *"Ha! Compared to Regidor and Librettowit, you read nothing heavier than* Tales of the Times.*"*

A court gossip sheet! Kale took a step forward, arms lifting, and stopped. She sighed. "I would love to hug you."

Sadness fell on her friend's demeanor. Gilda tilted her strange and exotic face and looked at Kale through thoughtful eyes. "And that embrace is impossible in my present state."

Kale's throat tightened, and tears pushed at the back of her eyes. What if the information they'd found didn't work after all?

I mustn't think like that. She gestured toward Regidor, who had moved to stand close to his wife. "You married Regidor? How imprudent. He must be a beast to live with."

Gilda brightened. "Indeed. Paladin himself performed the ceremony." She set her eyes upon her husband. "It was a simple affair. I wore a cloud. Regidor wore white court dress with silver and gold trim."

Bardon choked on a laugh. "Simple? Silver and gold?"

Regidor nodded and allowed a small smile to part his lips. "With a touch of amethyst. Gilda's cloud varied from elegantly understated cirrus to vibrant sunset hues."

"Oh, you're jesting." Kale looked from one to the other. "Surely you can't be serious?"

Bardon cleared his throat. "That was cirrus, as in wispy and ethereal. Not serious, at all."

Regidor groaned. "Perhaps you shouldn't have developed a sense of humor, Sir Bardon. It doesn't wear well on you."

Gilda perched on the edge of the table where Regidor had set her bottle. "I tire easily, dear friends. Why have you come? To pay your last respects?" Despite the gravity of her questions, her beautiful features flashed with a slight mischievous sparkle.

A nervous chill ran through Kale. She looked from Regidor to Bardon, then to Granny Noon. The old emerlindian offered her a tilted smile. "Don't doubt your good news now. You may tell her, Kale."

She took a deep breath and released it. She almost preferred to continue the pointless banter. Before she saw Gilda, she was confident of the cure. But now…

The expectant look on Gilda's face pierced Kale's heart. She had to speak. "We think we have found the process that will reverse the effects of Risto's spell."

Gilda spun around to Regidor. "Now?"

He inclined his head. "If you are ready."

"What do I have to do?"

"Go back into your bottle one last time. When I call you out, you will form into the solid composition Wulder originally created."

Gilda asked no more questions. The mist that imaged her body thinned and swirled upward, then poured into the blue bottle.

Kale and Regidor moved to the table, standing opposite each other. Gymn came to perch on Kale's shoulder while the other minor dragons settled on Granny Noon, Bardon, and Kale. Granny Noon stood behind Regidor and placed a hand on his shoulder. Bardon stood close to his wife and encircled her waist with his arms. Regidor looked into Kale's eyes, and she nodded.

"Wulder, guide us," whispered the meech.

Without discussing the matter, Regidor took the lead and Kale gladly followed. He formed images in his mind of the smallest particles in Gilda's system. With malformed properties, these elements whirled out of synchronization with the others. Fragments repelled each other. Slowly, Regidor realigned the configurations. Upon occasion he isolated a unit and totally annihilated the foreign substance.

Kale assisted by keeping the images sharp. Her cooperative efforts allowed Regidor to concentrate on minute parts, while Kale sustained a larger picture. The others provided a flow of energy. With Gymn's presence in the circle, the healing aspect of the procedure progressed swiftly. Filia delved into Regidor's deepest memories and pulled out any information that would aid him in his task.

Finally, Regidor scanned through the work he had done and tweaked a few minor segments. One last sweep through the whole process, and the meech dragon was satisfied with the natural cohesion reestablished in Gilda's composition. He pulled his thoughts back from the others.

They broke connection, both mentally and physically, stepping back from the table and exhaling.

Granny Noon sank onto a stool and clasped her hands in her lap. All eyes focused on the blue bottle.

Regidor cleared his throat. "Come out, my love."

The moment stretched. Kale fought back a surge of panic.

Oh, Wulder, please!

Smokelike billows erupted from the narrow opening of the bottle. Kale held her breath. This did not look like Gilda's usual controlled, and somewhat staged, entrance. The pillar of cloud speedily descended to the floor. Everyone stepped back as it roiled in place.

Metta burst into song, breaking the silence. Pure, sustained notes in a soothing melody vanquished the tension. The turmoil within the cloud quieted. The mist thickened, coalescing into a recognizable form. Gilda looked as she had before she entered the bottle the last time.

Kale blinked.

No, I can't see through her. She's truly solid. It worked!

Gilda's eyes roamed from one face to the next.

Ignoring her training not to pry into others' thoughts, Kale plunged into the meech's mind. Gilda looked for some difference in those who watched her, as if her transformation would be mirrored by them. Kale laughed and spoke to her friend, "We haven't changed. *You* are different, Gilda. You're whole."

A slow smile spread across her lovely features. She lifted a hand to Regidor. He jumped forward and took it. Gazing into her eyes, he raised it to his lips.

She giggled, a sound that seemed inappropriate for the stately Gilda. "The first time you've kissed me, and you missed my mouth by a yard."

He jerked her forward and into his arms. The next kiss did not miss and made up for years of being unable to touch.

"Well," exclaimed Granny Noon, placing her fingertips on her throat and giving a shiver. "I'd say this calls for a celebration. If we can get the attention of our two lovebirds."

Regidor threw back his head and howled in jubilance. He swept Gilda up and swung her around the room.

Bardon and Kale laughed, clapping their hands. The minor dragons soared and chittered, adding to the merriment. Regidor paused before Kale and allowed the two women to hug before he twirled Gilda around the room once more.

"Tea and daggarts," said Granny Noon and moved to her cupboard.

"It's a miracle," said Kale.

Regidor put his bride down on the floor but kept an arm around her. "A miracle? Yes, it is! No less a miracle because Wulder used us to perform it. No less a miracle because the answer was already written in His design of the universe. A miracle!"

Granny Noon's offer of tea and daggarts expanded to a lovely spread of nordy rolls, oaten honey bread, cakes, tiny sandwiches, a pot of stew, and candies made from mordat. The party lasted all afternoon and into the evening. Gilda took delight in touching things, stroking the minor dragons, holding a spoon, and sipping from a delicate teacup.

Kale gasped as she watched Gilda raise a brown nordy roll and sink her teeth into it. Gilda paused and tilted her head, sending the Dragon Keeper a look of inquiry.

"I never thought," said Kale. "I mean, it never occurred to me. How did you eat? What kept you alive? All those years in the bottle. You should have starved to death."

Gilda smiled with the serenity that heightened her beauty. "Regidor kept me alive. His research was divided between seeking ways to sustain me and ways that might cure me."

Regidor patted her hand and then, with obvious pleasure, intertwined her fingers with his.

After Kale cleared the table and Bardon helped her wash up, they moved into Granny Noon's comfortable den area. Kale settled on the floor and rested against Bardon's legs as he sat in an overstuffed chair. Gilda snuggled in Regidor's embrace on a sofa.

The warm room exuded comfort and peace. Granny Noon, sitting in her favorite chair, took up her knitting, gave the rocker a little shove with her foot, and took a stitch. "My dears, you've been ensconced in your self-absorbed bubbles for too long. I'm afraid it's time to come out and see where Paladin needs you. We all have work to do."

5

Night Talk

Bardon stooped to keep from hitting his head on the roots woven into the ceiling of the small bedchamber. On his shoulder, Dibl dug in his claws to keep from slipping and let out a chortle. Bardon ignored the minor pest and gazed at Kale, already sitting in the tiny bed under one of Granny Noon's homespun blankets. She pulled her knees up to her chest and did little to hide the mischievous smirk on her face. With the good humor dragon influencing his mood, Bardon edged sideways around the wall without grumping.

He nudged the bright minor dragon from its perch and shrugged out of his shirt. "It's a good thing we're not urohms."

Kale imagined a giant husband and wife bumbling about, trying to fit into the bed. The mental image invaded Bardon's thoughts and caused the corners of his mouth to lift. Dibl did an aerial somersault but bumped into the wall. The six minor dragons chirred their amusement.

Contentment filled the room, and Bardon treasured the moment. He knew his loved ones would soon face war, and that made the peace surrounding him all the more worth cherishing.

The sleeping chamber dimmed as he covered a lightrock with a cloth left beside it. The minor dragons sat up at attention. Bardon grinned slightly, thinking it rather absurd to have obtained the submission of these marvelous, tiny creatures by way of a technicality. He was the master of their home. Although they owed first allegiance to Kale, they paid him the honor of dutiful respect. With a signal, he could banish them to the comfortable pocket-dens within Kale's moonbeam cape, thus affording him and his wife some privacy. But some nights, he allowed them to lounge around the room, sleeping where they chose.

Three years ago, he hadn't fully understood what an integral part these little creatures would play in his life. Now he did. He had married a Dragon Keeper. Dragons popped up at the most unexpected times, sometimes annoying him, but more often entertaining him and coaxing his better nature to the fore.

He ducked under a low-hanging root. "Do you think she put us in this room by mistake?" he asked Kale. "Surely, this is a room for kimens or doneels."

"Granny Noon isn't known for making mistakes. I think she has only one large room and one small besides her own. When I was here before, we slept in the front room on the floor. Since both Regidor and Gilda have tails and wings to deal with, Granny Noon probably thought the bigger room would be better for them."

"I would suggest I sleep on the floor, but there isn't more space between the bed and the wall than there is on the mattress beside you."

"I could shrink you."

Not sure if she was teasing, he cast her a speculative glance and saw her overly bland expression. She guarded her thoughts as she often did when wanting to rib him.

He covered two more lightrocks. "It would be more helpful to enlarge the bed."

"I already did! I've used up most of the floor space."

One small blue rock remained, illuminating the room with a soothing azure hue.

Kale scooted over and nestled into the soft bed. Bardon slipped in beside her. Gymn landed on Kale's shoulder, and Bardon shooed him away. "Oh no, you don't. There isn't room for a bedbug tonight."

Pat snored on a cushioned chair. Gymn and Dibl settled on the same chair, one on the arm, and one on the back. Metta, Ardeo, and Filia crawled into the cape, seeking the comfort of their pockets.

"What do you think of all this?" asked Kale.

He didn't need to ask to what she referred. His thoughts churned over the events of the day and all they had seen since they emerged from The Bogs. He stretched out, and both feet pushed beyond the end of the bed to dangle over the floor. With a sigh, he put his arm around Kale as she snuggled against his side.

" 'Man chooses his path and finds Wulder has walked the way before him, laying the stones of each road.' "

"A principle! Now, that's the knight I know and love." She sighed. "So what does that mean for us?"

"We determined to locate Regidor and deliver the information we found about Gilda's condition. Wulder brought us out of The Bogs to accomplish that mission and join another."

"It wasn't wrong for us to be secluded for three years? To ignore the state of Amara as we dealt with our little piece of the world?"

Bardon shifted, and his leg shot out from under the too-small covers. A draft of cold air hit his thigh where it lay half off the mattress. He twitched the blanket back over his leg.

"Paladin could have sent for us, Kale. We would have answered the call. Don't wallow in guilt that is not valid."

"Surely there's a principle that states that more eloquently."

"When given a bridge to cross the marsh, don't bemoan the lack of mud on your shoes when you get to firm ground."

He felt her tense against his side, and he held his breath, willing her not to delve into his thoughts.

She traced a circle with her fingertip over his ribs. "I don't believe I've ever read that one in the Tomes of Wulder."

Bardon fought the bubble of mirth that would give him away. "Obscure reference," he managed to say in a reasonable tone.

Silence. He waited.

"You made that up!"

He couldn't dodge the finger poked in his side, but he could retaliate. He tickled, and Kale writhed beneath his fingers. Her squirming nudged him off his precarious perch, and he fell the few inches to the floor. That did not deter him from torturing his ticklish wife.

"Stop! Stop! Stop!" she gasped, trying not to screech and wake Granny Noon and her other guests. "Be serious, Bardon."

He stopped, and she regained her breath. A torrent of mixed emotions flowed from his charming wife. Bardon climbed back between the bedding, wriggled into an almost comfortable position, and cuddled Kale. He lay still for two reasons, to keep from landing on the floor again, and to try to sort out Kale's emotions.

"All right, lady of mine, why am I getting this mishmash of feelings from you?"

"I'm excited to see Paladin again and worried by Granny Noon's report of his illness."

"It does sound serious." He thought about shifting more to his side, but that would also shift the blanket and result in one of them being exposed to the night air.

Kale appeared to be more comfortable. At least she was following one line of thought. "That he's sick at all is serious. He's two thousand years old! I assumed he would live forever. Can he die?"

"Yes. He's not Wulder, but Wulder's representative. But I've seen him bone weary before, and he revived." Bardon carefully rolled toward Kale and put an arm over her stomach.

"Granny Noon said his health reflected the attitude of his people. What did she mean?"

His face nestled into her curly hair. He slid back a bit on the pillow to prevent the locks from teasing his nose. "The indifference of the Amarans to the threat of evil has weakened him."

"Ah!"

Tangled thoughts still emanated from Kale's mind, roiling in a senseless rumble of emotions. Bardon waited until her inner turmoil subsided, and he could again understand her mindspeaking.

Unable to move, he squeezed her hand. "We'll do what is before us, Kale."

"I don't understand the politics of all this. This war isn't about Amara! Why did Pretender and Cropper and Stox decide to fight? So many innocent people are getting hurt!"

"I doubt they take into consideration the lives of those who get killed along the way. They don't respect life."

Kale's head turned swiftly on the pillow. Her large eyes stared at him. "Why don't the Amarans fight back?"

"Fight back? They don't feel like the attack is aimed at them, and it isn't, really. The battle is for power. Who's in charge. Who rules. Pretender wants to beat Cropper and Stox into submission. Cropper and Stox want Pretender's position of authority."

"And they certainly don't care that a lot of Amarans are hurt in their grandiose schemes." She jerked her head, facing upward, to glower at the ceiling once more. "Authority? Wulder is the supreme authority. They're fighting for a figurative throne that possesses no glory."

"Yes, but the evil ones refuse to believe that the right to rule can't be snatched into their grubby hands."

"They can kill Paladin?" Her voice sounded small, more like a child than his wizard wife.

He tightened the arm that lay over her and pulled her closer. "Yes, but Paladin is more likely to die from a weak heart."

"And he is in danger of that because his people don't cherish the privilege of his rulership under Wulder."

"Exactly." Bardon distinctly felt the edge of the soft bed sagging. He tried to wiggle more onto the mattress.

"But the people…?"

"The people of Amara are only concerned when the battle between the two evils touches their community." He moved his leg and lost the blanket. He growled. "And then, they hope it will pass over in a short time."

"Three evils, it would seem, if Cropper and Stox have truly fallen out."

"Yes, three."

Bardon waited for Kale to speak. His own apprehension of the future wound around the cord of anxiety emanating from his wife. He didn't feel any more secure in the ultimate defeat of such powerful enemies than she did. His knight's training told him to choose good over evil and fight with all that was within him, to thank Wulder for his strength, and to trust Him for the outcome. In his heart, he wanted to take his wife, her dragons, and their friends deep into the safety of The Bogs. He let out a heavy sigh and almost slipped over the edge.

"Kale."

"What?"

"Fix this bed, please, lady of mine. Make it larger. Let it fill the whole room."

He felt the mattress extend under his feet until the cold air no longer breezed against his toes. The sides of the bed moved outward until they bumped into the wall.

"The covers?" he asked.

The blankets also stretched out. Bardon relaxed, allowing his limbs to savor the new comfort of enough space. Being married to a wizard definitely had a few advantages.

He kissed her forehead. "Thank you."

"How is this all going to end, Bardon?"

"Only Wulder knows, lady of mine."

6

DRUDDUMS

Granny Noon led the procession through tunnels lit by blue lightrocks. Bardon followed, third in line, behind Kale, with Regidor and Gilda straggling along at the rear. Sir Bardon didn't like the feel of this trip.

A frown had deepened the old emerlindian's face all morning. Grannies did not frown, nor scowl. Serenity was their hallmark, yet Granny Noon's expression bespoke apprehension. Where was the peace that normally cloaked the old lady like a garment?

With cheerful calls to his siblings, Dibl dived, combed his talons through Bardon's hair as he passed over, and darted on ahead to circle the newlyweds.

At least the minor dragons liked caves and underground tunnels. Ardeo's glow dimmed and brightened as he flew. When he went by a cluster of lightrocks, his luminescence faded, but his pale skin reflected blue. The other minor dragons flitted around like disoriented bats.

Kale wouldn't appreciate Bardon's likening her little friends to unintelligent flying pests. They landed on her shoulders or in her hair, carrying on conversations that she understood readily. In her presence, he could usually interpret all the chatter through the mindspeaking link with his wife. But for the most part, he didn't bother to keep up with their nattering.

Bardon glanced over his shoulder. The meech dragons strolled together, Gilda's arm tucked in the crook of Regidor's.

"It's a wonder they don't fall on their faces," he muttered.

Kale sneaked a peek at the couple. She snickered and shook her head at him. "They're newlyweds. You can't expect them to watch the path in front of them when they can gaze into each other's eyes instead."

Bardon looked back again, this time studying the two dragons. He couldn't decide who wore the sappier expression. Regidor looked positively besotted.

"We never carried on like that."

Kale said nothing.

"Well, we didn't." Bardon took Kale's arm and guided her past a pile of rubble. Several pieces of shiny metal stuck out of the debris.

Kale nodded ahead toward Granny Noon. "She isn't particularly friendly this morning. And last night, she actually scolded us. The 'self-absorbed bubble' hurt. Of course, she meant all of us. Regidor obsessed over finding a cure for Gilda. We honeymooned in The Bogs. Still, I've never heard her speak in anything but a calm and kind tone."

"She had a statement to make. One we weren't hearing on our own. 'A pointed word spoken by a friend can open the eyes of an endangered sleeper.'"

"She aimed to burst our bubble with her point?"

Bardon's eyes crinkled as he smiled. "Right. She knew we'd respond as she expected. 'A few heavy words will not crush the hearer. The fool won't listen, and the wise man will place the words on the scale of righteousness.' She trusted us to hear the words and act as Paladin's servants." Bardon's eyes narrowed as he watched Regidor and Gilda. "On the whole, our meech friends don't look especially crushed by Granny Noon's reproach."

"Not listening or using the scale of righteousness?"

"I'm not sure they've decided whether to heed the instruction or shelve it for a more convenient time."

Kale spared them a fond glance. "Considering the miracle of Gilda's recovery, who could blame them for not wanting to face a harsh reality?"

"'Consider the circumstances in which a man reacts before you think you can predict his action.'"

"That's enough principles for one morning, Bardon."

He chortled and bit down on the next maxim that had sprung to his lips, but Wulder's principles still streamed through his consciousness. He had no doubt that one would answer the unease he felt.

A druddum barreled through the tunnel. The small furry creature ricocheted off the walls and around their legs in a frantic effort to avoid crashing into them.

Gilda squealed, causing the creature to jump in the air before it careened around the next corner.

"They're harmless," said Regidor. "Their only vices are an obsession with speed and the collection of shiny objects."

Gilda's voice returned to a deep, lazy drawl. "They look a bit too much like rats."

Kale chuckled, but Bardon sensed she, too, suffered from a strange mood.

He came up beside her as they passed into a wide stone corridor, placing his arm around her shoulders. She leaned into him for just a moment before they continued on through the tunnels, still following Granny Noon. Kale's sense of security grew from the interchange, and because of their connection, Bardon experienced the same surge of well-being. Of all the gifts Wulder had bestowed upon him, Kale was the best.

He sought to lift her spirits further. "Neither Paladin nor Wulder is angry with us. We were establishing a new order in The Bogs, Kale. We were doing just what Wulder had assigned as our responsibility."

"And now we have a new direction?"

"Yes."

Although the sob did not come through her body, Bardon, nonetheless, felt her shudder of despair. Her soul whispered to him. *I want to go back to my safe home.*

I think the point of what Granny Noon was trying to tell us is that soon there will be no safe homes in Amara.

Kale didn't answer but kept her eyes on the smooth black hair of the emerlindian she followed. The path narrowed, and Bardon let Kale go before him.

A second and third druddum scurried through the tunnel, making Gilda squeak and causing Kale to let out a shaky laugh.

He admired his wife. Her purposeful stride and straight posture revealed her determination. At fourteen, she had answered a call to serve Paladin. On that first quest, she discerned her own strengths and weaknesses.

The next quest brought her, now a beautiful young woman, together with him, a rather solemn lehman. At the time he'd thought her undisciplined, clumsy, and inept.

Her next thought interrupted the pleasant memories he had of the adventure that taught him what a treasure Kale was.

"We're always learning our strengths and weaknesses, aren't we?"

He grinned. Whether she had done so consciously or not, she had picked up a phrase from his musing.

He answered her question. *Every day.*

She giggled. *"Don't you have a principle to quote on that?"*

A dozen. But he didn't quote them to her. He glanced over his shoulder at Regidor and Gilda. The husband seemed overprotective of his clinging wife. The two whispered with each other. "What's going on with them, Kale?"

"Gilda is tired. That's all. Remember, for many years she escaped that bottle for only short lengths of time. And conversely, she feels claustrophobic in this tunnel. She longs to be out in the open."

Bardon didn't respond. But he didn't dampen soon enough the frisson of apprehension that shivered through his soul.

"Why are you worried?" Kale asked.

"Gilda may not be an asset on this quest. Whatever it is that Paladin wants us to do, I'm sure it will be arduous. Gilda has always been pampered."

Kale turned to study Regidor. Bardon felt her emotions well up, but not a muscle in his wife's face betrayed her turmoil.

Bardon whispered. "Regidor appears strong, sophisticated, intelligent, and unflappable."

"Yes," Kale agreed, "but his vulnerable spot walks beside him."

Gilda fussed over a smudge on her dress. Bardon and his lady exchanged a look.

Bardon sighed. *I'm not sure Gilda's loyalty to Wulder is stronger than her love of self.*

Pat flew from some distance ahead of them and circled Kale's head, chirring a distress signal.

"What is it?" asked Bardon.

"Druddums."

"Druddums?"

"A lot of druddums."

Granny Noon stopped and turned to face them. "I hear them," she said and came back to clutch Bardon's arm. "We need to get out of their way."

"Get as close to each other as possible," Bardon ordered. "Kale, a shield!"

Regidor hurried to join them, pulling Gilda with him.

She joined hands with her meech wizard colleague, and within a second, they had thrown up a barrier as clear and hard as glass but unbreakable. The six minor dragons flew in circles around the top of the protected questers.

The noise increased. A stampede of small, dark creatures hurtled through the tunnel. Some slammed into the protective sphere, but most of the steady stream of animals separated, ran around the obstruction, then merged again as a treacherous torrent. The glistening shell vibrated against the disturbance but did not shatter.

Kale and Regidor maintained the shield after the inundation of druddums subsided.

"My," said Granny Noon. "I've never seen the likes of that before. Whatever do you suppose got into them?" She patted first Kale's arm and then Regidor's. "Thank you for your quick action. That could have been quite unpleasant. But we're all safe."

Regidor started, and the protective bubble expanded and contracted as if with a hiccup. "Where's Gilda?"

Bardon looked around in amazement. The female meech was gone. "Where is she?" he repeated.

"She was inside the shell." Kale, too, peered from side to side as if hunting for a lost child. "She was here. I saw her!"

Regidor dropped Kale's hand and touched the inside of their haven. "She couldn't get out any more than those druddums could get in."

"Then," asked Kale, "where is she?"

7

Another Danger

Kale and Regidor released the shield. Although Regidor moved slowly, examining minute details of the walls, ceiling, and floor of the tunnel, Kale felt the growing panic in her friend.

She turned to the wise emerlindian. "What do you think has happened, Granny Noon?"

"Gilda was startled. There's no telling what a meech dragon of a skittish nature will do."

"I've always thought of Gilda as languid, not skittish."

"Under the draining influence of that horrible spell, of course she lacked vigor." Granny Noon gestured toward the tall dragon as he ran long fingers over a fissure in the limestone wall. Ardeo hovered close by, providing as much light as possible.

"Try to imagine Regidor without his enthusiasm for life. Most meech are insatiable in their exploration of nature. They abound with vitality. In Gilda's case, since her release from the spell, I've discerned an unsettled inclination. She's as edgy as she is eager."

Kale's eyes widened as she realized Granny Noon spoke as one who possessed knowledge of the mysterious dragons. "You know about the meech? I thought little but legend was known about their race."

Granny Noon's expression wrinkled in wry amusement. "My curiosity was aroused when I met Regidor."

"And where did you pick up the knowledge? Librettowit and I scoured Fenworth's library."

Granny Noon smiled. "From emerlindians older than I am. They remember the sudden influx of meech. Long ago meech dragons freely interchanged ideas with the elite."

"What happened?" asked Kale.

"They became wary of our races and segregated themselves."

Kale studied the cool façade Regidor maintained. *He's going to explode if we don't find Gilda soon.*

From the same direction the druddums had disappeared, they heard Gilda's tremulous call. "Regidor!"

The meech rushed to his disheveled bride's side. Her peach-colored, wide-brimmed hat sat at a precarious angle on one side of her head. Numerous veils twisted around her neck and hung in a tangled mess under her chin. Her wings peeked out of the voluminous cape, the delicate cream material shimmering as if it were as indignant as its wearer. Gilda's long green tail swished back and forth.

Regidor put a comforting arm around her shoulders. "What happened?"

"I went poof!" She gestured with fluttering hands and then went back to pulling the veils out of their snarl. She straightened the folds of her skirt, twisted the waistband, and then pulled at the short, matching bollo jacket.

Gilda looked as though Regidor had rescued her from a dustbin.

She's not hurt. That's the main thing. Kale turned her attention to her husband. *But what happened to her? Poof? She went poof?*

Bardon shrugged.

Regidor guided Gilda to a seat. "Start at the beginning," he urged. "When did you feel yourself losing substance?"

Gilda sent an accusatory glare at Bardon. "Our young knight called for a shield." The glare transferred to Regidor. "You hauled me into the circle with considerable, and I think unnecessary, force." She shuddered. "I felt myself stretching then."

Her eyes moved to the old emerlindian. "Granny Noon looked away from the group toward the oncoming stampede. She reached behind her and right through me to grab Kale's hand."

Kale remembered Granny Noon's clammy grasp. She'd thought it unusual for the wise woman to have such a physical reaction to the threat of druddums. The moisture had not been nervous perspiration but droplets from Gilda's essence.

Gilda straightened as if making a monumental effort to control her emotions. "I felt myself scatter, and certainly not in the way I'm accustomed to. I've always drifted toward my destination, which was most often the exquisite bottle Regidor acquired for me. This time there was no destination. And I did not dissipate in an orderly manner, but I poofed!" Again, her hands fluttered. "One second I hung on to my physical form, the next I was completely disassembled and being carried along with the flow of those dreadful little beasts."

Regidor cleared his throat. "I would have thought you'd be above them."

"I sank." The tremble of her lower lip belied her indignant tone. "I had to force myself to rise and reconnect." She looked around at her audience. "It was quite an unpleasant experience."

Petite Granny Noon stepped forward and embraced the broad shoulders of the shaken meech female. Even standing, Granny Noon barely came up to Gilda's chin as she sat on the rock. The emerlindian cooed, "I'm sure it was, dear."

Gilda leaned her face onto the emerlindian's shoulder and sobbed. "Are there more of them? Do we have to stay in this awful tunnel much longer?"

"Well, yes, there would be more druddums," answered the granny truthfully, "though it is very unusual for them to run in such a large mass. But it is only a short distance to the gateway we need." She made a clucking noise with her tongue. "I shouldn't think we will encounter another flood of druddums."

Bardon's hand rested on the hilt of his sword. "I'm thinking there's more to this than just a random collection of misguided rodents rampaging through the tunnels."

Kale peered into the dark recesses of the stone corridor before them. "They were running from something?"

"That would be my assumption."

Granny nodded to the path. "What do you sense, Kale?"

She closed her eyes and opened her mind to what might lurk beyond in the darkness. She detected something. Nothing solid, but something more like the scent of an animal that had recently roamed the tunnels.

"I can't say what was there, Granny. Only that it is gone now."

The emerlindian stood quietly for a moment with an air of concentration about her. She shook her head slightly.

"Try again. This time, examine the physical makeup of the tunnels. Search for something that seems out of place."

Puzzled, Kale again explored the area beyond their sight. Many hardworking hands of the high races had formed these passageways. Sharp tools had chipped away the porous rock, exposing clumps of the luminescent crystals. In some places the glowing lightrocks were tiny but scattered in a swathlike vein running through the less dense composition of the walls.

Her perception coursed along the tunnels, distinguishing bumps and cracks and a sparse scattering of debris along the walkway until she came to a rock of a startling different composition. Heavy, dense, and recently formed.

She clenched her teeth for a moment before uttering the phrase she knew would help her uncover the mystery of this oddity. "I search for truth under Wulder's authority."

Her mind explored the polished surface and discovered a large box without seams.

"What have you found?" asked Bardon.

"I suspect a hiding place for something nasty." She turned to Regidor. "What do you think?"

The meech nodded. "Shall we break it open and face whatever is within? Or shall we creep past and hope it doesn't want to come out and play?"

"Oh," said Bardon, drawing his sword. "I'd rather make its acquaintance formally than have it pouncing on us later."

Regidor lifted one eyebrow. "An informal meeting?"

Bardon nodded. "Informal, and at our enemy's discretion."

Regidor smiled at Kale. "Shall we go knock?"

"Yes, let's."

Kale held one hand in the air, and her minor dragons flew to circle her head.

"Gymn, you and Metta stay with Granny Noon and Gilda. Pat, go ahead and analyze that stone structure. See if you can find a point of entry. Filia, go help Pat."

"Why send Filia?" asked Gilda.

"She has a wealth of knowledge stored in that thimble-sized brain of hers. Between Pat and Filia, they will come up with an answer."

Dibl and Ardeo landed on her shoulders.

"Dibl, you accompany Gilda. Ardeo, light our way. I'd rather not depend on the uneven glow of lightrocks on this visit with our peculiar host."

She opened her moonbeam cape and reached into a hollow to secure a weapon. She held the invisible sword in front of her and nodded to the others. "Ready?"

Bardon and Regidor both winked at her. She grinned at their eagerness and wished her bravado was more than show. No amount of training would ever ease her anxiety when it came to a fight. She depended greatly on the skill and calm that transferred from Bardon to her through their unusual bond.

Regidor led the procession down the cool stone corridor. Bardon followed with Kale beside him. Granny Noon and Gilda walked two dozen paces behind.

Kale's curiosity welled as they approached the stone box. Her first sight of it confirmed what her mind had perceived. The structure stood on end like a coffin. A big coffin. What was inside?

Kale raised a hand as if to touch the box but kept her palm an inch clear of the surface.

"A lot of heat," she observed. "This coffin materialized recently and is unstable."

"Coffins usually contain dead bodies," said Regidor, raising his sword to a ready position. "This box contains one very agitated bisonbeck, who is wondering why his great deception is not working. What are Pat and Filia telling you?"

Kale tilted her head as she listened to the mindspeak of the minor dragons. Their communication consisted of phrases and images.

"They say that it is a wizard's ruse, a mere illusion to provide concealment. One that we can easily shatter."

Paladin's three warriors positioned themselves at a prudent distance around the stone structure. With a glance to either side, Bardon noted his wizard companions' readiness and nodded.

"Kale, Regidor, kindly divest this enemy of his shield."

The two wizards focused on the stone. In only a moment, the appearance of a solid mass faded into a transparent form that exposed the bisonbeck warrior inside. He raised his weapon, a two-edged battle-ax, and roared. The last vestige of the shield disintegrated, and the beast within charged.

"Capture," Bardon ordered.

Regidor passed him a disgusted grimace.

Kale laughed. She agreed with her husband and preferred avoiding bloodshed. Regidor favored an all-out fight.

From one hand she poured a slick substance on the floor at the warrior's feet, and she thrust out the other arm aimed at his shoulder. An invisible force left her palm and set the bisonbeck to spinning.

Regidor dropped his sword, whirled in place, and stopped with his arms extended toward the bisonbeck. From the meech wizard's fingertips, sticky cords blasted to entrap the burly soldier. The wizard wrapped him from chin to toe like a spider would wrap a bug.

The trapped warrior continued to roar. The bellow expressed his rage and frustration as the rate of his spin decreased and he began to tumble.

Kale, Regidor, and Bardon stood back. The web-encrusted, spinning-top soldier gyrated off the slick surface provided by Kale and promptly fell to the ground. There he grunted and struggled against his binding.

Bardon sheathed his sword. Regidor picked his weapon up from the floor and brandished it as if confronting an unseen enemy. He sighed and placed the shining blade in its scabbard.

"So, Paladin's chosen leader," he addressed Bardon. "What do you desire us to do with this captive?"

The struggling man stilled, his expression wary.

"I want information," said Bardon.

Regidor wiggled his fingers in the air. A small flame appeared at each fingertip. "Anything in particular, or just general torture-induced babble?"

"I'd like to know where he acquired a wizard's trick."

Bardon turned to look at Granny Noon. "Have you known a bisonbeck to master the complicated procedure of substance manipulation?"

"Never."

"Regidor?"

"Never."

"Kale, does Filia know of any instance?"

She listened and replied, "Never."

Bardon looked the bisonbeck in the eye. "Explain."

8

Information

The bisonbeck rolled toward Kale, and she thrust her hand in front of her. Now the outside of his wrappings stuck to the floor. He narrowed his eyes at her and growled.

"Tsk, tsk." Regidor waggled a claw-tipped finger at the soldier. "Not smart. Not smart at all."

Bardon cocked his head to one side and pointed at the angry prisoner. "You don't seem to understand. Lady Kale and Sir Regidor are two of the most powerful wizards in the land."

The bisonbeck's eyes widened a bit at this news, but still, he kept his teeth clenched.

Bardon motioned toward Regidor. "We don't need to ask you politely to tell us what you know. We don't have to wait until you make up your mind to cooperate. Sir Regidor can enter your mind quite easily."

The meech dragon grinned, and the sight of his gleaming white teeth inspired a slight shudder from the soldier.

"Unfair!" Regidor presented the knight with a fierce scowl and stepped closer to the imprisoned bisonbeck. "You mislead the man, Bardon."

"How is that?"

"True, it is easy for me to gain access. But for the poor person whose mind I explore, it's not comfortable." He arranged his features in a look of mock sympathy and bestowed it on his intended victim. Then his expression cleared and he spoke to Bardon. "Perhaps you should let Kale do the honors. She is less experienced than I am, but she might proceed in a gentler manner. I would find 'gentle' exasperating. I imagine Kale does exceptionally well with 'gentle.'"

"Sorry to disillusion you," Kale piped up. "I never got that explore thing down. I seem to bump into bits and pieces and dislodge them. Nightmares, childhood traumas, scenes of mass destruction.

"My last attempt at extracting information left the man incapacitated. Of course, it was mostly his fault. He struggled so violently that he broke the chain securing him to the wall. He then rushed off madly, found a window, and jumped. He survived the two-story fall but never gave us any information."

She looked at Bardon as if he had accused her of negligence. "I maintain that the gibberish he spoke afterward was due to the blow to his head, not any terrors that I jogged loose in his memory."

Gilda stepped around Kale, looking almost immaculate after the repairs she had managed during their walk. Dibl left her shoulder and flew to Granny Noon. He chirred, and the old emerlindian held her hand out for him to land.

"I know," said the granny. "It's an unpleasant business, and I, too, would rather have nothing to do with it. But evil men do not understand daggarts and polite conversation."

"Lady Kale's lying, you know." Gilda sashayed to the wrapped man and gazed down at him. An enigmatic smile touched her exotic features. "She's a good wizard." The smile broadened. "And compared to me, Regidor is a good wizard. But I was trained by Risto himself."

The man renewed his struggles. Gilda gestured to Bardon and her husband. "Lift him to his feet. I find it disconcerting to converse with a prone cocoon."

The men placed the bisonbeck on his feet. With a gesture from Regidor, the wrappings fell away. The warrior tried to bolt but fell again to the ground.

Bardon sighed as he and Regidor lifted him once more to a standing position. "Just because the visible instrument of your entrapment is gone doesn't mean you are free. I do wish you would remember you are dealing with first-class wizards. Our interrogation would be so much easier for you to endure."

Regidor and Bardon stood back. Gilda's husband made a sweeping court bow, indicating she was at liberty to examine the prisoner. Sir Bardon crossed his arms over his chest, leaned against the stone wall, and relaxed with an amused grin upon his face.

The female meech slowly circled the bisonbeck, appraising him from all sides before coming to stand directly before him. Her confident attitude shone in her countenance, inches from his.

"My talent is persuasion," Gilda cooed.

The soldier made a disparaging remark, cut off by a glance at her face.

Her odd eyes held the imprisoned bisonbeck's. His expression grew wilder as some force from Gilda penetrated his mind.

In a soft, purring voice, she gave a one-word command. "Speak."

The soldier's tongue thrust forward and seemed to stick to the roof of his mouth. He made a few unintelligible noises until Gilda's lip curled in a sneer, and she repeated her command.

"Speak."

He opened his mouth, and his tongue twisted to and fro, but still no one could comprehend his utterances. Filia trilled. Then Metta and Gymn flew to sit on his head. Gymn wrinkled his nose but stretched out on the unkempt warrior's hair. Metta began to sing.

"Ah," said Kale just as Regidor said, "I see."

"What?" demanded Gilda.

Kale answered. "Gymn and Metta have initiated a healing. The poor soldier has been given a 'suggestion' by his commander. His commander is Burner Stox."

At the mention of the wizard's name, the bisonbeck fell forward and writhed on the ground. Gymn and Metta fluttered in the air for a moment and then came to roost on Kale. The minor dragons huddled close to her cheeks, and Gymn rubbed his chin against her face.

"A very ugly sickness, indeed." She stroked Gymn's wing. "Implanted by evil, the malady will be hard to dislodge."

"Well," said Gilda, kneeling beside the man, "I'm rather good at suggestions myself."

She clasped the soldier's head between her two strong, slender hands and forced him to gaze into her eyes. His struggling ceased.

"You are no longer under Stox's authority. You are mine. I command you. The thought of answering to Stox sickens you. I free you from her and offer you a place of honor among my followers. You accept with pride."

The soldier's expression relaxed, and he nodded. "As you say, Mistress."

"How were you able to use the shield?"

"Burner Stox, that foul and evil wizard, has selected a few of her best warriors and endowed them with special abilities. Crim Cropper—"

His speech broke off, and he resumed the fierce shaking and moaning.

Gilda grabbed the hair on his chin and brought his head around. "You are no longer under the authority of Crim Cropper. You are mine!"

Again, the soldier calmed.

"Now tell me Crim Cropper's part in this."

The bisonbeck gulped, his eyes bulged, and his body trembled, betraying the depth of his subordination to the husband of Burner Stox.

Gilda snarled. "Mine! You no longer fear Stox or Cropper. Your allegiance is to me."

He nodded.

"I'm waiting," Gilda reminded him.

"Crim Cropper." He licked his lips. "Cropper, that foul and evil wizard, used potions to enhance our memories. Stox recited the words that would conjure the images she implanted in our thoughts. The shields hide us from the enemy." He stopped, and a confused expression crumpled his features.

"Cropper and Stox are your enemies." Gilda sighed her exasperation. "I am your commander."

His brow smoothed. "The enemy cannot detect the shields with mind, eye, or touch."

Gilda glanced at Regidor, who winked at her. "In theory, but not in fact. I could even smell the bisonbeck supposedly hidden in the box."

Kale nodded. "Using Granny Noon's advice, I easily found the shield."

Granny Noon shifted so she could get a better look at the prisoner. "Is he saying that Stox and Cropper have been able to give their warriors a shield, much like Fenworth once gave Dar the shell he uses in battle?"

"Yes," said Bardon, "only it doesn't seem to be very effective."

"That will make Burner Stox unpleasantly irritable." Kale summoned the rest of her minor dragons. They settled on her, decorating the moonbeam cape like large, colorful jewels.

Granny Noon crooked her arm through Kale's. "I have something to say to you, my dear."

"Uh-oh." Regidor snickered.

The emerlindian raised her eyebrows at him. "Don't pretend you haven't had your share of lectures, young man."

The chagrined look on Regidor's face surprised Kale and almost made her giggle.

"Yes ma'am," he said. "We'll just ask this prisoner a few more questions while we wait for you to have your little talk with Kale."

His eyes shifted to Kale's. *You're going to wish you were being interrogated by us rather than being exhorted by our Granny Noon.*

Don't be ridiculous. I haven't done anything, have I?

Granny Noon patted Kale's arm and tugged her away from the others.

"I'm in trouble?" asked the o'rant wizard.

"I want to caution you against using falsehoods. First, you are not very believable. Second, your talents are eroded by deception."

"You didn't like the story about my causing a man pain by messing up his mind."

"No, I did not." Granny sat on a boulder. "But let me ask you something more important."

Kale waited.

"Do you like that image of yourself? Does using your power in that manner appeal to you?"

Kale held her breath as she contemplated the question. The feeling of power did hold some allure.

Granny clucked her tongue. "Don't you find that odd, Kale? You have been given more talent and power than most of Amara's citizens, yet you would use this talent to feed a hunger for controlling others. In Wulder's Tomes, there is a principle about the inward enemy defeating the soul with a surprise attack. Don't let your own desires cause your fall into disgrace."

"Yes, Granny Noon. I understand, and I will keep a vigilance against this enemy."

"You understand this enemy is yourself?"

"I do."

"Good."

9

Paladin

Granny Noon still led the way through the tunnels. Bardon and Kale marched behind her while the minor dragons napped in their pocket-dens inside Kale's moonbeam cape. Except Ardeo. He supplied the light needed where the scarce lightrocks shone dimly.

Next in line, the bisonbeck soldier trudged sullenly. Gilda marched behind her new subject. His forced loyalty would most likely slip. Regidor brought up the rear.

When Bardon glanced over his shoulder, he noted that the newlyweds had lost their affectionate demeanor. In fact, from his three years' experience as a husband, he'd say a difference of opinion had surfaced between the silent couple.

Cross passageways riddled this section of the tunnel. Bardon wondered how Granny Noon kept from losing her direction. She turned right or left without seeming to examine her surroundings. He saw no markings on the walls to indicate their location. They followed the granny straight through the next intersection. Behind him, he heard a trample of footsteps and an exclamation from Gilda. He turned just in time to see the female meech facing the cross tunnel with her arm extended. Her fingers formed a fist with her wrist toward the ceiling. As her fingers uncurled, a bright ball of light formed against her palm.

Regidor shouted. "Gilda!"

The blaze rolled out of her hand, across the fingertips, and soared into the side tunnel. A flash of intense light and a popping noise from within the shaft followed.

At Bardon's elbow, Kale gasped. "The bisonbeck."

Gilda lowered her arm and turned as if to continue her trek to the gateway.

Bardon and Kale passed her to peer into the lightrock-illuminated passageway. Ten yards into the tunnel, a lazy haze of smoke drifted above a pile of black ash.

"Gilda!" Bardon barked.

With deliberate nonchalance, she turned and gazed back at him.

"Yes?"

"Why did you kill him?"

"He deserted."

"Could you not have commanded him to return?"

"Maybe." She shrugged. "Without eye contact, it was uncertain."

"He accepted allegiance to you."

She shrugged again and reached up to smooth one of her many veils. "I demanded he follow me. The darkness still held his heart. It was only a matter of time before he turned against us."

Granny Noon came to stand before the meech wizard. "Wulder values life."

Gilda snickered. "Even a life created by Pretender?"

The emerlindian's expression saddened. "Pretender cannot initiate life. That is a misconception. He can, however, twist life."

Gilda looked incredulous. "Pretender did not create the seven low races?"

"Pretender distorted the seven high races." Granny Noon turned abruptly and strode away. "We must see Paladin."

A few more steps took them to the shimmering gateway. Granny Noon passed through without comment, and the others followed. They entered a magnificent palace courtyard, where a sentry greeted them and inquired after the nature of their business. A nod from Granny Noon informed Bardon he was their spokesman.

"We've come to see Paladin. I am Sir Bardon. This is my wife, Lady Kale Allerion. Granny Noon is our advisor. Sir Regidor and Lady Gilda accompany us."

"Three wizards?" The man bowed as he spoke. "Then news of the wizards' conclave has reached you. We weren't sure our messengers would pass through the enemy lines."

Kale glanced at Regidor, who shook his head.

"We've had no news of a meeting," she said.

"Tomorrow night." The sentry pointed to one large tower of Paladin's castle. "At eight. Since you did not receive the summons, it must be Wulder's providence that brought you. Eleven have already arrived."

"Will we be able to speak to Paladin?" asked Kale.

The man's expression turned solemn. "A physician will greet you at his bedchamber. He will decide if you can enter. Do you know the way?"

"Yes." Kale felt a warm, soothing glow spread through her body as she thought of Paladin. "I've known where he is since I walked through the gateway."

The sentry smiled wryly. "I've given up offering escorts to wizards. They always seem to know where they're going."

Gilda stepped forward. "I would like an escort to our chambers. I am tired and would also like some nourishment."

"Yes, Lady Gilda." The sentry raised a hand. A young boy dressed in livery came to his side. "Summon Mistress Nidell." The boy scooted off. "The housekeeper will be here shortly. Please be seated."

Around the courtyard, spots of greenery shaded comfortable benches. Flowers in pots and arranged in colorful beds decorated the open space. A minstrel strummed his instrument while sitting in a stone and wrought-iron gazebo.

Kale tugged at Bardon's sleeve. He looked down at her upturned face. "Maybe my parents are here."

He took hold of her hand. "Maybe."

Kale called the minor dragons out of their dens to enjoy the splendor. Briefly she thought about the unquickened eggs. Would Paladin want her to hatch them now?

The travelers spent several minutes benefiting from the sunshine and the beautiful surroundings, and enjoying the songs of the small birds that inhabited the trees. After traveling in underground tunnels, the elegant gardens relieved some of the tension that had built up between them.

She and the others hadn't yet seated themselves before a bustling marione matron came to greet them. She had two maids in tow and sorted out the guests so that Granny Noon received an escort, Regidor and Gilda were led off by the other maid, and Mistress Nidell took responsibility of Bardon and Kale.

"We'll go straight to Paladin's room and ask if you can be admitted."

"How is he?" asked Kale.

"Not well, but he's perked up a bit with all this company. He does love people, you know."

"Yes, I know," Kale murmured as she followed.

Sensing her distress, Bardon put his arm around her waist and sought to distract her. He pointed out a plain vase stuffed with common bonnies.

I'm surprised by the humble décor of Paladin's palace. Simple rugs carpeted the corridor, landscapes hung on the walls in unadorned frames, and the basic architecture of the building emphasized an unpretentious style. *Have you ever been here before?*

"No. It is different from the other castles we've been in... Certainly different from our castle made of hollowed-out trees."

Kale giggled.

The housekeeper cast a puzzled look over her shoulder at the sound of Kale's amusement. To her, the small laugh had come out of nowhere.

Kale merely smiled and, when the servant turned away, made a face at Bardon.

They traveled to a wing of the castle far from the bustle of activity. A tall, dark emerlindian responded to Mistress Nidell's knock at a heavy wooden door.

"Grand Sorn." She curtsied. "We have visitors to see Paladin. Sir Bardon and Lady Kale."

The grand stroked his chin. "Our leader is weak. But I think seeing his Dragon Keeper would raise his spirits." He addressed Sir Bardon. "Would you mind if I admit only your fair lady and her minor dragons? We must maintain a careful balance, encouraging Paladin, but not tiring him."

"Of course." Bardon kissed Kale's cheek. "Tell him that we petition Wulder for the return of his health."

┼╾━╼┤

Kale watched Paladin from the chair by the window. Late afternoon light filtered in through gossamer curtains. As the breeze stirred the soft material, a shadow danced over Paladin's pale features. The trick of the light turned his complexion gray, then green, and last, a mottled ash.

She pulled Gymn out of her moonbeam cape, but when she placed him on her friend, the healing dragon slinked over the sleeping form, emitting low moans and distressed whimpers.

"Can you do nothing, Gymn?"

The small green dragon settled, curled up on Paladin's chest, directly over his heart.

Kale spent the time reliving every moment she had spent in Paladin's company, every tale she had ever heard of his exploits, and each time she had seen him in action. The stories brought images of vitality to her mind, a direct contrast to the scene before her.

Wake up! Wake up!

She leaned forward. "Please, Paladin, wake up. We need you. I need you."

Gymn lifted his head and blinked at her, then chirruped. Paladin's chest rose as he took a deep breath. His eyes opened, he sought her face, and he smiled when his gaze caught hers.

"Kale, my Dragon Keeper."

He reached out a hand. Kale took it and moved to sit on the side of the bed.

"You look so frail," she said. "I'm afraid for you."

"Afraid for me? Surely not. If I die, I go to be with Wulder. I will dance and sing with those who have gone before me. I think you fear for yourself."

Kale nodded reluctantly. "Yes, and for Amara. What will the country do without you, Paladin?"

"The people of Amara can do very well without me, but not without Wulder. I am just a conduit, a link to Wulder. But the high races, for the most part, have abandoned looking up to Wulder, and therefore I am not needed."

The room darkened. Kale looked to the window to see if a cloud had come between them and the sun. A mist hung over the countryside where a moment before the hills had sparkled with sunshine. She looked back to Paladin and saw him fingering a string. He handed the end to her. As soon as her fingers wrapped around the thin cord, Kale felt herself caught up in an illusion. She stood on a knoll surrounded by grassy plains. A kite sailed above her, tugging at the string.

She heard Paladin's voice, strong and vibrant, unlike the wheezy tones of his sickbed.

"What do you see, Kale?"

"A colorful kite dancing in the sky, reaching higher and higher."

"What do you hear?"

She listened. "The sound of a breeze rustling in the tall grass, crickets, birds. I hear life all around me."

"What do you smell?"

She took a moment to sort out the fragrances. "Flowers, moist earth, the sun-heated, green plants."

"What is the kite telling you?"

This was harder. She pondered what he could mean, but as she watched the bright bit of paper and slender sticks bob and sway against the backdrop of blue, she understood.

"It tells me which way the wind blows and how strong the wind is."

"And if a storm should approach, what would you do with your kite?"

"I'd wind up the string. I'd bring it down. I'd hold it close and run for shelter."

Black clouds gathered over her head, and Kale fought to pull the fragile kite from the sky. When she had it in her hand, she pressed it against her chest and raced to a gully. Her feet tangled in the cloth strip that served as the kite's tail. Stumbling forward, she managed to twist and land on her back in a depression in the hillside. Large, icy raindrops pelted her face.

The kite sprang from her arms, expanded, and changed from sodden paper to a tough, slick material that repelled water. It snapped and crackled above her, then stretched taut over sturdy poles that must have been the cross-supports of the kite moments before. The colorful cloth, now a tent, sheltered her from the storm.

The sound of a raging river reached her ears. She crawled to the opening of her tent and peeked out a flap. A torrent of water roared down the gully she had intended to use as a safe haven. Debris tumbled past and disappeared.

She caught her breath and whispered, "Thank you, Wulder."

Her ears popped as the scene around her flashed into oblivion, and she refocused on another field. This time she saw Paladin walking hand in hand with a young boy. Slowly, Paladin's form changed into a diamond shape, his arm stretched and narrowed until it appeared as a string. Paladin became a kite flown by a small child.

The boy ran and laughed, tugging on the kite, watching the looping antics in the air and enjoying his day in the sun. But a rabbit hopped by, and the boy turned his attention to the small, furry creature. He chased his prey, still pulling the kite along. Keeping hold of the string encumbered his pursuit of the rabbit. After he had missed catching the small animal a couple of times, the boy let the kite go. Into the heights of the heavens, the graceful bit of paper soared away, unnoticed by the rabbit chaser.

Paladin's rasping voice brought Kale back to the bedchamber. "You see, my dear Dragon Keeper, Amara has let go of the string."

✦ 10 ✦

An Evening Diversion

Kale left Paladin's quarters as the sun dipped behind the nearby hills. A maid escorted her to chambers where Bardon sat reading a book. He jumped to his feet as soon as the door opened, and she was in his arms before it closed again.

"Was he able to speak to you?"

She nodded against his chest.

Bardon hugged her, and all the impressions of the meeting flowed from her mind to his. When her thoughts slowed and trailed off, he kissed her forehead.

"Wulder," he whispered against her skin. "Kale, you must latch on to Wulder, not Paladin. We must see past our dependence on Paladin for leadership to Wulder, who provides wisdom to us all."

Kale pushed him away. "You sound like you don't care if Paladin dies."

"That's not it at all, and you know it." He walked over to the window and stood with his hands on his hips, looking out at the crimson sunset. "Your mother and father are here."

Kale's countenance brightened. "Did you see them? Did you speak to them?"

"Your father." Bardon gave a perfunctory nod. "I spoke to your father. We will sit with them at dinner tonight."

"Oh good. I haven't had a nice talk with Mother since they visited last spring. I wonder what they've been doing all summer."

Bardon shrugged and turned to face her. His eyelids drooped as if he were too weary to look wide-eyed upon the world around him. "My father is here as well."

"Oh, Bardon." She wondered what she could say. What question was appropriate under the circumstances? But he answered one that hadn't come to her mind.

"No, I didn't have a chance to talk with him. He was occupied, comparing notes with other knights. Amara is in a perilous state. The cry of the people has changed from 'Don't do anything to call attention to us' to 'Why haven't you done something to prevent this calamity?'"

"And your father?"

"Is angry. What else? The conclave tomorrow night is to involve only the wizards, and you know how he feels about wizards."

Her shoulders drooped in spite of her determination to be encouraging to her husband. "Oh yes. I know how he feels about wizards and dragons and magic."

"I'm sorry, Kale." He came back to embrace her.

She leaned against him. "I'm sorry, too. I know you care whether Paladin recovers or not. I also know you always look at a bigger picture than I do."

She felt him nod as his chin touched the top of her head. His deep voice rumbled under her ear.

"It would be hard without Paladin, but it would be impossible without Wulder. If we manage to remain true to Wulder, then He will raise up another Paladin to guide us."

He gave her a squeeze. "Now, change into something beautiful. We sup tonight in the dining hall of Paladin's palace. A very grand place, indeed." He tilted her chin up with one finger and winked at her. "And I'm sure your mother is most anxious to see you."

Sir Kemry and Lady Lyll Allerion met Kale and Bardon in the reception room before the doors swung open to the dining hall. As the young couple approached the older, Kale mindspoke to her husband. *She's so young-looking and striking. I wonder what I will look like at her age. So far, when I am idle, nothing much happens.*

"I find leaves on you all the time."

Only because you hide them on me to tease me. I know I don't produce those flowers, and twigs, or even the ladybugs you pretend to find in my hair.

"You are the bog wizard."

An inherited title from Fenworth. He was no blood relation. I could be anything.

"My goodness," said Lady Allerion with a small shake of her head. Several hairpins fell out, and her elegant coiffure began to droop. She snapped her fingers, the errant pins hopped back in her hand, and she deftly returned them to their places. "Such a scowl, Kale. What are you thinking about?"

"What kind of wizard am I, Mother?"

Her father kissed her on the cheek. "A bog wizard, my dear. Why the puzzlement?"

"Oh, she doesn't mean her title, Kem." Lyll took her daughter's hand and patted it. "She wants to know what her element is. As she ages, will she find herself waking from a nap with a stringy moss beard on her chin, or will she be dripping lake water from her elbows?"

"Humph!" said her father. "A beard? Highly unlikely. As to your element, no one knows ahead of time. Your knowledge will evolve out of what you experience."

Kale cast a worried glance at Bardon and asked her father, "Then it doesn't pass down according to your lineage?"

"That belief is an old wives' tale. Some people believe one's element is determined by where you are raised. Your surroundings influence what you become. Some believe your destiny is in your heritage. I believe your element is what you choose more than anything. If you choose to appreciate lakes like Cam Ayronn, then naturally you are predisposed to drip."

A trumpeter announced the opening of the dining hall. Servants pushed seven carved panel doors into the walls. Across the huge room seven heavy wooden doors led to the area devoted to preparation of meals. These highly polished doors swung in and out as busy people brought in large trays and tureens. The closed doors blocked any clatter of pans from the kitchen.

The crowd drifted toward the evening repast.

Lady Allerion put her arm through her husband's and started to stroll off. "I think it's an interplay of all three aspects, Kem."

Bardon offered his wife his arm and winked. "You're gorgeous when you're flustered. I do plant the leaves and things to watch you react."

"I know. It's hard with our bond to fool each other." She grinned up at him. "But sometimes you nearly have me convinced." She took in a deep breath, loving the smell of her husband and the very essence of his strength as he stood beside her. "You've gotten very good at tricking me."

He reached behind her ear and pulled out a small ivy leaf, one just like the plant that decorated the hallway. With a flourish, he presented it to her. "You put up with my pointed ears. I guess I can endure your elemental state, whether it be bog or mountain or sky or fire."

He jerked his chin toward an old female wizard who had nodded off. A page stood next to her, puzzling how to wake up the woman who had taken on the shape of a blue flame, although she did not burn the chair she sat in.

"Thanks," said Kale. "I hope in one way or another you always see me as the flame of your life."

Bardon chortled. "Bad pun, Kale." He took her elbow and guided her toward their dinner.

Elegant dishes covered massive banqueting tables. Rare golden light-rocks shone about the room, casting everything in a soft glow. Delicate chandeliers adorned the ceiling with tiny lightrocks reflecting off the shimmering surfaces of cut glass.

Kale learned from her mother that every inhabitant of the castle ate in the same room and from the same fare. Everyone chose their own seating, so it was not uncommon to find a magistrate sitting with a stable boy, or a lady beside a scullery maid. Everyone, however, was required to bathe before entering the dining hall. Quite unobtrusively, The Sniffer escorted offensively odiferous persons to the public bath. Only the staff involved in meal preparation and serving did not sit at the tables. And this entourage of people rotated with others so that all had the opportunity to be served as well as to serve.

The delicious food and her mother's commentary about the people around them kept Kale captivated. Servants whisked away empty dishes, refilled their goblets with nectar, and replenished serving trays with assorted delicacies. Kale followed her mother's example of taking small servings of almost everything.

One dish held a brown-looking sludge with a bright orange swirl through it. Although the man across the table from her smacked his lips as he devoured a hearty portion, Kale decided to skip the thick porridge.

She reached for her engraved goblet and realized the servant had not been out from the kitchen for some time. Her empty glass should have been full. Glancing around, she noticed many of the knights had concerned expressions, and some had even risen from their seats to consult with others. Her father spoke to a wizard near the wall of doors that led to a balcony. He hurried back to the table, touched Bardon on the shoulder, and signaled him to follow.

With her mind, Kale explored the hall and the kitchen. At first she detected nothing but an unusual quiet. The hush in itself convinced her something was wrong. The likelihood of an artificial covering to hide the usual backdrop of noise from people's minds occurred to her. And why would that be necessary?

Reciting the words to petition Wulder to help her see more than her normal senses would reveal, she glimpsed a flash of evil that vanished in a fog.

"Mother?"

"Yes. I can't put my finger on it either."

Kale called with her mind to her minor dragons. *Find the source of this evil.*

"The kitchens," she said to her mother as soon as she had an impression from Pat and Filia.

"Take my hand," instructed Lyll. "It will increase our effectiveness."

As soon as Kale's fingertips rested in her mother's palm, she felt the presence of warriors.

Kale and her mother stood as one, crying out with their minds to all those present in the hall. Bisonbecks! Grawligs! Attack!

The kitchen doors burst open, and bisonbeck soldiers along with slovenly grawligs poured into the room.

Steel whispered against leather sheaths. Shouts rose in warning. Outrage answered with bellowing challenges. Boots clattered on the stone floor. Those peace-loving souls who never fought more than persistent weeds in their gardens scrambled for safety.

Bardon and Sir Kemry fought together. With their backs to each other, they confronted the first onslaught of invaders as they surged into the hall. Kale sent up a quick petition to Wulder, asking for their protection.

Her mother squeezed her hand. "Focus, Kale. We aren't spectators in this fray."

She and her mother twirled, changing their attire to more suitable costumes for fighting. The outrageously pink matching outfits startled the three bisonbecks close by. They soon recovered their belligerent demeanor and charged the two women. The mother-daughter team stood ready.

Each held one hand out in front of them, holding invisible swords. Entering the melee, Kale and Lyll confronted the enemy with as much expertise as their husbands.

To her right, Kale saw a pulse of orange light. She had only a moment to observe the old woman wizard, who earlier had sat as a flame, throw a fireball at the enemy. Unfortunately, a plowman moved between her and her target. But the ball of flame hit the man square in the back, rolled around his body, and continued on its course to splat against a raging grawlig. An explosion left the mountain ogre a pile of cinders on the floor. The maid he had been strangling fell to the floor, landing on her rump. She gasped for air and then began to cry.

Get under the table, Kale ordered the girl. Kale only took a second to register the young woman's confusion as she unexpectedly heard a command not spoken. *Move. Now!*

The maid shook her head as if to rid her ears of a ringing and crawled to safety.

Kale's six dragons, tiny and swift, nipped in and out of the battle, spitting in the eyes of the enemy. Dibl preferred landing on the head of a soldier, briefly digging in his claws, and then flying upward, pulling what hair he could snare as he took off.

Dibl landed on the small of a grawlig's back and with one bite severed the belt holding up the enemy's pants. Pat and Ardeo then jerked on the loosened garment, causing it to fall to the floor. After stumbling, the grawlig shook his pants from his ankles, roared, and swung his club at anything in his way.

They tried the same tactic on a bisonbeck. The soldier pulled his pants up and fought one-handed while grasping the waistband. The three dragons met in the air above his head and chastised him with sharp chirps. With determination of purpose, they all spit their colorful and bitter saliva on his head.

An older bisonbeck with tattered war ribbons across his chest claimed

Kale's attention. He jumped back when her sword tore open his jacket sleeve and roared when he realized she was armed. A blow to the back of his head crumpled him to the floor.

Kale looked to see who had come to her aid. A mountain wizard nodded to her from across the room. Kale looked down at her would-be opponent and saw a jagged rock protruding from his skull. She waved a hand of acknowledgment to the wizard and turned quickly to help a stable boy in his fight against a young grawlig. If she looked too closely at the blood around her, she knew she would be sick.

Regidor danced from one opponent to the next, wielding his sword with grace. While the elegantly attired meech managed to kick soldiers into oblivion as if it were part of a choreographed performance, Gilda picked up her cup and sipped tea. She had not bothered to get up from her seat. She sat, watching the fracas around her and only lifted a finger when someone threatened to disturb her peace. She then picked up an item of food before her and threw it with uncanny accuracy at whoever approached. A bowl of soup left her hand and landed on a grawlig. Only the contents of her missive had altered. The liquid became a green cloud that choked the mountain ogre. He collapsed in an unmoving heap on the floor.

In a matter of minutes, the fighters in Paladin's dining hall subdued the more than a hundred-strong band of marauders. Grim news came from the kitchen that all the servants there were dead. More investigation found a trail of bodies all the way to a breached entryway where goods were delivered from nearby towns.

"This is outrageous!" exclaimed the lady fire wizard. "Crim Cropper and Burner Stox dare an attack inside Paladin's palace?"

Bardon's father spoke up. "It comes from trusting wizards and magic words to protect us. The ordinary man has hidden behind false walls instead of every man drawing strength from Wulder."

"I hardly think this is the time for one of your rants, Sir Joffa," said a meadow wizard as she bent to offer comfort to a young marione woman.

"It's past time you listened to me," he bellowed.

Granny Noon walked through the shambles to place a hand on his arm. "Put away your sword and your anger. Neither one is appropriate in a discussion between allies." She patted his hand, the one still clenched around the hilt of his bloodstained weapon. "I believe what you have to say is valid. Let's do what is needed this moment." Her gaze swept over the devastation left by the attack. "And then, Sir Joffa, we will hear your opinions."

⇥ II ⇤

Distinguished Visitors

The next day Kale, her mother, and Bardon walked among the nervous visitors. More wizards and dignitaries arrived through the gateway. Some bubbled with excitement at being summoned to the palace. They seemed unaware of the gravity of the reason they were called until they heard of the slaughter of servants that had taken place the night before. Others predicted doom for the country and blamed anyone who came to mind for the state of emergency. These responded to the invasion of Paladin's palace with a grim attitude. "Inevitable," said a prickly desert wizard. "Proves my point," said a cold wizard from the North.

The formal gardens, with groomed paths and ornamental flowerbeds, buzzed with disgruntled Amarans. They congregated in small knots and hissed their displeasure. Some had strong opinions of what should be done to rescue the failing country. Others only nodded their heads to support those who pontificated their analyses and predictions.

One marione voiced his opinion loudly as Kale, her mother, and Bardon passed his small audience. "Paladin has no right to claim a sickbed at this point in our history. It's a ploy to avoid his obligations. Why fall ill just when we need him most? It's irresponsible."

"That's unfair!" Kale's voice shook as did her hands as she raised them to call attention to her outrage.

Bardon took her arm and guided her away from the group. "Not all tongues that wag cohabit with a brain."

"Did you make that one up?" Kale demanded, not at all pleased that Bardon could be jesting at such a time.

"No, I didn't." He linked his forearm around hers, laced his fingers between hers, and raised her hand to his lips, kissing it with affection. "I did paraphrase."

Lady Lyll giggled but did not offer a comment.

Bardon led them to a decorative waterfall. "There is another principle that is not being heeded during these rambling and unproductive talks."

Lyll glanced her daughter's way and frowned. *"Kale, you look like you have a teller-twig clamped between your teeth."*

I do. I am trying very hard not to speak my mind.

"Keeping your tongue still is to very little effect when your face is shouting your disapproval."

Kale's features relaxed. Her mother nodded her approval and turned her attention to Bardon. "And the other principle being ignored is?" she asked her son-in-law.

"'A wise man's words travel from heart to mind, or mind to heart, before leaving his mouth.'"

"It seems to me," said Kale, carefully wording her statement, "that these people are expressing thoughts, not from intelligence or compassion, but from their fear."

An unexpected trill of joy rippled through her negative thoughts, causing them to disperse on tiny waves. She sought to capture the feeling as if it were a butterfly fluttering past. The next time it swept through, she focused on its pattern and flight.

"Dar!" she exclaimed. "Dar has just come through the gateway. He's here!" She dropped Bardon's arm to leave.

"I like that," he complained. "She's rushing off to meet another man."

"The man who released your sense of humor," Kale called over her shoulder. "I owe him a lot."

Kale scurried through the walkways, dodging around the groups of people who had so annoyed her a moment before. She rounded the curve that led to the gateway courtyard and squealed.

Dar faced her with his usual aplomb, then his face broke into the wide grin that characterized doneels. She ran to greet him, but as she came into the quadrangle, she glanced around and located a bench. She veered off from a direct path to her good friend and sat, spreading her skirts around her and folding her hands in her lap.

Seated as a proper young matron should be, she awaited Sir Dar's dignified approach. She was glad she'd chosen to wear yellow today. Dar particularly liked yellow. And she was pleased with herself for choosing feminine frills. Dar liked her to look ladylike. Bouncing on her perch spoiled her picture of gentility, but she didn't much care. It was only a little bounce, and she subdued her outward show of exuberance quickly.

Dar drew near and presented her with an elegant court bow.

"It's been such a very long time!" His whiskers quivered while his eyes twinkled, and only Kale's eyes beheld the kiss he blew from pursed lips.

She held out her hand, and he kissed it. Not at all like Bardon, but a peck that missed her skin and truly reflected an aristocratic manner.

Kale burst out laughing, clapped her hands, and grabbed Dar by the tufts on his cheeks. She pulled his head forward and landed a smacking kiss right between his furry button ears. "I have missed you tremendously."

Unruffled by her forward behavior, Dar hopped up on the bench beside her. "And I, you!"

His gaze took in the few people lingering in the gateway courtyard. All seemed too busy to be bothered with a young wizard and a doneel dignitary. "It's a good thing our people have finally come together." Dar sighed. "I trust that it's not too late to recognize the threat. This evil has been with us for years, subtly undermining the foundation of our country. It's high time Amarans arose to deal with Pretender and his enemies."

"There are many who feel that way," Lyll Allerion said as she came near.

She walked beside Bardon to the bench adjacent to Dar and Kale. After seating herself, she patted the space next to her, inviting Bardon to sit.

"It's ghastly." Kale faced her furry friend. "I almost think it's too late to save Amara. We had heard rumors even in the depths of The Bogs. But what Bardon and I saw when we went seeking Regidor and Gilda was shocking." She shook her head, with tears in her eyes, and mumbled, "Shocking."

A raised voice penetrated the serenity of the sculptured garden behind them. Kale tilted an ear toward the source of the disturbance. A mixture of dismay and outrage flitted through her emotions. In spite of her mother's admonition earlier to guard her tongue, she spoke of what most disgusted her.

"And the people!" she exclaimed. "How can these people make rational decisions? They act like rabble-rousing ruffians. They're disrespectful and disregard Paladin as if he were no longer with us." Her eyes went involuntarily to the stone walls where their leader slept.

"Don't panic, Kale," said her mother. "There will be formal meetings starting this afternoon and going long into the night. Paladin is not so far out of touch as we might think."

Bardon nodded. "His decree, delivered at breakfast, has eased much tension."

"What has been decided?" asked Dar.

"An uproar arose over the wizards' conclave." Bardon gestured toward the sound of more angry voices. "Much objection was made over a perceived imbalance of power. Paladin has called a meeting in the throne room prior to the conclave this evening. Representatives of the high races will give reports as to the state of their homelands. Dignitaries will propose strategy to combat the opposing armies that play their battles out upon our land."

Lyll waved her fan to indicate those around them. "They will be allowed to voice their opinions before the wizards meet tonight. Paladin has seen a way to smooth most of the ruffled feathers."

A ruckus drew their attention. Two palace guards came down the path from the castle keep with a loud, angry emerlindian held captive between them. Kale took in a sharp breath and looked at her husband. Bardon's mouth took on a grim line, and a muscle twitched in his jaw just below his ear.

Sir Dar's ears perked up, and he jumped from his seat. Taking a few steps, he positioned himself to block the men's progress. One guard bore the square, solid build of a marione. The other was a young urohm, bigger by half than both men he accompanied but undoubtedly a callow youth.

"Excuse me, guards." Dar held up a hand. "What has Sir Joffa done to deserve this treatment?"

"Magistrate Moht has asked for his removal from the grounds," said the spokesman, the marione guard with a lo insignia on his lapel.

"Your name?" Dar inquired.

"Lo Mak, Sir."

"I am Sir Dar of Wittoom."

The man nodded, without a doubt aware of the importance of the doneel who waylaid him. Performing his duty would be difficult with his interference.

Dar arched an eyebrow at the struggling emerlindian. "Joffa?"

Bardon's father ceased his resistance against the men who held his arms and glared down at the doneel. "They don't want to hear what I have to say."

"It is more likely they don't want to hear the way you are saying what you have to say."

The emerlindian squinted his eyes and blew air out of his cheeks before he bristled, puffing up his chest and speaking loudly. "It is past time for dainty words and delicate tones."

"On the contrary, now is more the time for diplomacy than ever before."

"Bah!" Sir Joffa threw his chin out as if pointing to some figure they could not see. "No diplomacy will alter the minds of Cropper and Stox. And diplomacy can never achieve anything with the likes of Pretender."

"I'm not speaking of diplomacy aimed at our enemies, but diplomacy employed in negotiating with our allies."

Dar turned to the higher-ranking guard. "Lo Mak, I'll take this man into my custody."

The marione hesitated.

Dar spoke calmly. "I intend to return to Magistrate Moht's court with him. You may accompany us."

The lo considered the personage before him for a moment, then nodded to his subordinate. They released their hold on the prisoner.

Bardon's father tugged on his cuffs, straightening his sleeves. He bowed to the doneel. "Sir Dar."

Dar bowed in return. "Sir Joffa."

The two knights turned and walked side by side back toward the castle.

Lyll Allerion put her hand on Bardon's stiff arm. "Your father has always been passionate about his causes. He's frustrated by those who don't jump to do what needs to be done."

"I have very few memories of my early childhood."

Bardon stared at the four men departing. Kale reached into his mind. *Bardon?*

"Two knights and two guards. Four different races. People as different as my father and Sir Dar? How can this work?"

Lady Allerion spoke softly, bringing Bardon back to their conversation.

"Your memories before coming to The Hall are foggy?"

"Less than foggy. In fact, for many years, I had none. Vague recollections have come back to me since the sleeping knights awakened. The most distinct memory I have is of my father uttering 'Fools!' under his breath, over and over again, as I sat before him on a dragon flying over miles and miles of grassland."

"Have you asked him to tell you of that day?"

"Yes."

"And?"

"He cannot recall one particular day out of so many where he found those around him to lack common sense."

Lady Allerion smiled at Bardon. "And let us be frank, Sir Bardon. You have often thought the same. You have little patience with people and their selfish demands."

Bardon looked startled and started to protest. But the words caught in his throat. "I hope you don't think your son-in-law to be a self-righteous boor."

Kale mentally called to one of her minor dragons. All of them were cavorting in the gardens and eating their fill of insects. But her husband needed a dragon's help right now.

"Only in your core, dear boy. Sir Dar, my daughter, and Paladin have managed to help you minimize that horrid flaw."

Dibl swooped in, a yellow and orange streak, and landed on the knight's shoulder.

Bardon's face showed a struggle, but when he looked down into the loving eyes of Lady Lyll, he gave up.

A bark of a laugh preceded his remark. "You are exasperatingly correct, Lady Lyll."

Kale relaxed, but only a little. Underneath Bardon's calm exterior, his feelings still clashed. She felt the turmoil set off by his father's bristling attitude. Bardon's ideal knight conducted himself with dignity at all times. In a debate, he reasoned and did not rant. Bardon wanted to love and respect his father after years of separation. But in his heart, he found it hard to accept his parent's thundering personality.

◄──═──►

Bardon felt a tug on his sleeve. His wife's familiar touch anchored him, making him feel normalcy had suddenly returned.

Her wide eyes made his heart thrum. Once, with his hands cupped around hers while she held a quickened dragon egg, he'd been able to feel the rhythmic drone from the creature within. The ticklish, vibrant hum of that new life was much like what he experienced when those special moments came upon him. Out of an ordinary situation, he would step into the realization that Kale Allerion was his wife, his partner, and he thrummed. This was one of those unexpected special moments. His very being responded.

He turned his attention to Kale, studying her enchanting, upturned face. Her curls had lost the shape she'd given them this morning, a dignified hairstyle, befitting a wizard in Paladin's service. Bardon smiled to himself. The wizards never achieved a sophisticated image, and most gave up trying.

Concern shaded the vivid color of Kale's eyes. The brown, green, and gold flecks pooled together in a worried hazel. She clutched his sleeve. "Dar wants you to come with them. He says to hurry."

He didn't question his wife's reception of a message from Sir Dar any more than he questioned his need to respond. Dar had trained him from a rather inflexible squire to a successful knight. If Dar called, he'd go. Even if it meant the uncomfortable presence of his father.

Bardon left the women in the courtyard and followed his mentor. Dibl went along, riding on his shoulder. Even with his mind on serious matters, Bardon felt the influence of the little dragon enjoying the view and the hurried pace of his knight. Therefore the knight stepped more lightly upon the path leading to his parent and his mentor.

When Bardon caught up with them, Dar had his father laughing. *Laughing! How does Dar do it?*

"Joff," said Sir Dar. "You are an intelligent, passionate man. Which adjective do you think best describes your effectiveness as a knight?"

Joffa rubbed his hand over his beardless chin. "An offhanded lecture, Dar?"

"Yes, but my desire is to see you achieve the purpose in your heart. Please, answer my question."

Bardon walked behind the two men and in front of the two guards, who seemed nervous about allowing their prisoner to stroll through the gardens. Bardon chuckled at the image of his father hightailing it for the castle wall. His father tended to be loud, but he was a staunch knight, dedicated to the code of chivalry.

Sir Joffa turned and acknowledged the presence of his son with a scowl. Bardon wiped the grin from his face, and Sir Joffa returned his attention to the diminutive knight by his side.

The emerlindian gestured as he spoke. "Intelligence is required to recognize and analyze the situation."

"So intelligence is the most important." Dar nodded.

Joffa barked, "Let me finish." He cleared his throat and continued. "Passion is required to invigorate the soul. One must care enough to risk all to achieve an end."

"So passion—"

"Enough, Dar. If you want me to answer, then let me!"

Dar nodded again, and Bardon saw his mentor's ear tilt forward. He imagined the pleasant expression on the diplomatic knight's face. Dar could soothe the most irate opponent in a debate, and Bardon felt sure this ability sprang from the doneel's amiable countenance.

His father harrumphed several times, and Dar waited. The doneel's face showed no impatience.

"It's balance that gets the job done." Sir Joffa halted abruptly and turned to his friend.

Bardon stopped in time, but one of the guards did not. The urohm jostled Bardon from behind as the inexperienced oaf ran up on the young knight's heels.

Ignoring the commotion behind him, Joffa shook a finger at Dar. "That's what you want me to say, isn't it? You want me to acknowledge that my blundering passion makes my intelligence diminish in the eyes of my comrades." They resumed walking. "You've made your point, Dar."

"No," Dar chuckled. "You made my point."

Joffa harrumphed again. "True. But it'll take Wulder's hand, hard and heavy, to keep me from destroying any fine intentions I develop to control my temper."

"He's capable," said Dar.

"I'm willing," returned Joffa with blustery enthusiasm.

Smiling, Dar turned to wink over his shoulder.

12

Talk

Kale watched as her husband, her father-in-law, and Sir Dar ate with enthusiasm. The food smelled delicious. But the memories of the recent battle in this very room upset Kale's stomach. She excused herself and went searching for Granny Noon. She hadn't seen much of the emerlindian since their arrival. After several inquiries, she found the granny in a nursery where a dozen small children of various high races were playing. Among the attendants to the occupants of the room, a ropma sat on the floor with two crawling babies. The infants patted the creature's tangled fur and scrambled over her as if she were a soft climbing toy. If ropmas didn't look so much like shaggy dogs, their near-nakedness would be embarrassing. This ropma wore the traditional cloth tied around her waist, hanging down to her knees. In the next room voices raised in excitement as some older children played a game.

Granny Noon sat in a rocker by a window and held a sleeping babe. She smiled when she saw Kale enter the room and weave her way through the little people playing on the floor.

Kale leaned over to kiss the granny on the cheek and then peck the dozing infant on the top of his bald head. In response, the child made nursing motions with his lips, then sighed with contentment. Kale settled on a hassock beside Granny Noon's chair.

"You are distressed." The emerlindian's warm voice soothed Kale's agitation.

Yes.

"Rock a sleeping baby, build a tower of blocks with a toddler, sing with the older children in the next room."

Why?

"To rediscover what life is supposed to be."

Granny Noon, these children may be enslaved by the evil of Pretender.

"And that is why we will fight."

Kale blinked back tears and picked up an infant who was using her as his handhold as he struggled to stand. "You want to walk, big fella?"

The little tyke grinned with only four teeth in his gummy smile.

"I'll help." Kale placed him on his chubby, bare feet and put her forefingers in his tiny grasp.

Walking behind him, she kept him upright as he took tentative steps. He laughed, and so did she. Kale stayed in the nursery, playing with and nurturing the young of all seven high races, until duty called.

⊦═⊸═⊣

A trumpet sounded, and the doors opened on two levels. On the first floor of the castle, servants ushered dignitaries into the vast throne room. On the second, wizards seated themselves in a balcony that ran around three sides of the solemn chamber. Paladin already sat on his throne in the vast hall. Gymn, green and gleaming in the light, lay draped over his shoulder as if painted on the plain, but elegant, court cutaway. The jacket looked too large for the one it adorned. Kale wondered if Paladin had walked on his own or if he had arrived in an invalid chair, one with two large wheels and a handlebar across the back.

Gymn answered. Paladin had been transported in the special chair that sat just out of view behind the dais curtains.

The large throne, carved with twisting vines and large, open blossoms, swallowed Paladin's gaunt frame. He sat with one elbow on the armrest and his hand cupped over his jaw as if that were the only way he could keep his head propped up. Solemn blue eyes peered out from under black eyebrows as he regarded his people.

They came in with a staid and sober tread. All the fuming, festering acrimony that had characterized interchanges in the garden and the halls dropped away under the importance of the hour. Each person carried a wooden baton. During the meeting, if they wished an opportunity to speak, they would raise the rod and wait to be recognized.

Representatives sat in straight-backed chairs grouped according to regions. Sir Dar sat with delegates from Northern Wittoom. Lady Allerion and Sir Kemry did not sit with Outer Amara, which was a name given to those who resided outside the country but were citizens pledged to Paladin. The wizard couple's home in the Northern Reach qualified them for seats in this segment, but their status as wizards removed them from the floor. Kale sat in the gallery with her parents, while Bardon, who represented The Bogs in Southern Wynd, sat among the high races from that area. Sir Joffa stood behind those in the Inner Amara group. These people claimed no specific homeland but served Amara in general.

In the gallery above, the wizards sat listening carefully but not participating in the meeting below. Paladin had instructed them to attend, in order to take note of the input of the populace, and then take into consideration the temperament of the people when they held their own meeting that night.

When all seats were filled and the rustle of moving bodies ceased, Paladin sat back in his throne and placed his hands together, steepling his long fingers.

Kale held her breath. First he would pray to Wulder.

But he did not.

He pointed to a counselor from Trese. The man stood and lifted his voice in praise of the Creator and petitioned for wisdom and harmony.

Next Paladin signaled Magistrate Moht to come to the front of the hall. He stood beside Paladin and conducted the meeting, calling on individuals to report and analyze and make suggestions. From time to time, he stooped to consult with Paladin, but the leader never spoke so that anyone other than the magistrate could hear.

Kale's concern for Paladin took precedence over the arguments presented by the citizens of Amara. She watched her beloved leader. Her heart ached as she realized how very little he moved. She used her talent to increase her ability to observe him. At certain interludes, she thought he had ceased to even breathe. As the time and the endless talk went on and on, Paladin closed his eyes more often. Just when she thought he slept, he'd open them again and raise a finger. Magistrate Moht bent over, and Paladin conveyed something to his deputy in quiet tones.

Her beautiful healing dragon moved from one position to another as if he could not find a place to settle. Gymn gave lethargic answers to her questions. She sensed weariness from her healing dragon and knew he expended all his energy to do what little he could to sustain the sick man's health. Her attention remained riveted on Paladin.

Kale did note, in the back of her mind, that none of the representatives raised a voice. Even Bardon's father spoke calmly, without belligerence. She gathered from the little she heard that the leaders had repented of their former attitude.

For three years, since the first signs of animosity between Pretender and his underlings had surfaced, the people of Amara had chosen to remain as uninvolved as possible. Now the situation made it clear. They must participate in securing the safety of the land. This would require fighting not one, not two, but three evil forces.

A voice Kale recognized penetrated her concentration. Farmer Brigg stood among citizens from the foothills of the Morchain Mountain Range.

"Aye, some of us 'ave caught on to what's gonna 'appen if we don't pull our 'eads out of our own feedbags. But a lot of folks just don't want to see the danger. They aren't going to be wanting to send their good workers off to war and leave the weaker ones to tend the fires at 'ome."

Farmer Brigg sat down to a murmur of assent on his observation. Kale smiled from her place in the gallery with the other wizards. But her old friend did not look up. The talk went on, this time centered on what response the populace would have to the call to arms.

After hours of debate, Paladin held up his hand. Those who had a wooden baton raised lowered the rod.

A mountain wizard and a sky wizard both rose from their seats and exited the balcony. They soon appeared in the hall below and went to stand on either side of the throne. Unaided, Paladin rose to his feet.

"I...," said Paladin, his voice wispy but audible and distinct through some machination of the wise men beside him. "I do not know if I will remain with you until the final days of this conflict. I do not know the outcome of our struggle."

He swayed. The two wizards at his side took hold of his arms. Gymn wrapped his long green body around Paladin's neck. The leader inhaled and exhaled, slowly and with great labor. With a softly spoken word, he instructed the wizards to allow him to stand on his own.

"I do know"—his voice echoed in the still room—"that it is not my time to lead. To observe and perhaps consult, but not participate. I am content with Wulder's directive for my life. I will return to my more strenuous duties if He ordains."

He struggled for his next breath, and the wizards took him by the arms. He did not reject their aid.

His head drooped, but his voice came strikingly clear to all who listened. "Let this be known. This is a time for each Amaran to seek Wulder. Go directly to His ear with your petitions. Listen only to His voice for guidance. This is not...tragedy, but...opportunity." Paladin slumped, and the wizards lowered him onto the throne.

As a servant wheeled the invalid chair across the dais to Paladin's side, Magistrate Moht stepped forward. "We will suspend our talks until after our evening meal. At the sound of the tower eventide chimes, we will gather with our own to further discuss our situation. In the morning we will again meet in the throne room to put forth plans."

The two wizards supported Paladin as he moved from the throne to the wheeled chair. Kale turned to look her mother in the eye.

"Can we avoid war?"

"No, I think not."

13

WIZARDS' CONCLAVE

Kale entered the Wizards' Hall behind her mother and father. Everyone wore their most elaborate finery. Lyll Allerion had helped her daughter fashion a long shimmering, deep rose dress. She added a jeweled collar to the moonbeam cape and fastened it around Kale's neck. Then she draped the material over one shoulder so that the subtle gray of the cape contrasted with an array of starlike gems that bedecked the bodice of the gown.

"I'm wearing something a bit more matronly," Lyll had declared.

Kale laughed when she saw her parents dressed in attire that matched in material and color. She couldn't help but examine the cloth by tracing the embroidered design of vines with her fingertip.

Lyll's gown of harvest orange fitted tightly in the sleeves and bodice and then exploded in voluminous swirling fabric for a long, elaborate skirt. The same dramatic orange accented her father's basic deep green attire.

"Hardly matronly, Mother," Kale said as she stroked velvet leaves scattered over a lengthy train.

Lyll patted the rich sunset sheen of her sleeve. "Soft fabric is becoming to a woman of my age."

Sir Kemry embraced his wife. "I appreciate not having to worry about my clothing. Lyll always dresses me for these formal affairs." He adjusted the gold and vibrant green braid that accented his collar. "I suggested the emerald mingling with the gold. A nice touch, don't you think?"

Kale examined the trim that brightened his jacket and one leg of his pants. He did look arresting. "Yes, Father. The braid accents the orange in a dashing way."

"Dashing?" He put his arm around his wife's shoulders and gave her a squeeze. "Do you hear that, Lyllee? Our daughter thinks we still make a dashing couple."

Lyll coaxed him toward the door. "We don't want to be late, and she didn't say we were a dashing couple. She said the braid on the velvet is dashing."

"How can braid and cloth be dashing? She meant that we are dashing in the apparel you designed." He touched the braid on his lapel. "With my help."

The conclave gathered in the wizards' room, a large chamber, similar to the throne room, except located in a remote area of the castle. Indeed, when they passed through the entrance, they also passed through a gateway, so that the structure could hardly be said to be part of the palace at all.

The splendor of the room reflected the oddity of its inhabitants. One wall resembled a canyon with different colors of rock strata enhancing the natural beauty. Even a thin waterfall cascaded from the ceiling and created a stream that ran through the room. Several bridges of different designs crossed the creek.

A second wall looked like an outside view of countryside with a star-studded, nighttime sky. The third looked as if one could walk into a forest and leave the wizards' room behind. And the last looked just like the palace wall on the other side of the gateway.

Seating included rocks, logs, elegant chairs and couches, and a boat. Depending on where one stood, the flooring could be grass, cobblestone, sand, rug, or hardwood planks, waxed and polished.

But the clothing of the wizards astonished Kale more than the surroundings. The fire wizard's dress flamed but did not burn. One wizard's robe appeared to be a waterfall, the image flowing from shoulder to hem without leaving the wizard's body and causing a minor flood. The current disappeared in a mist at the man's feet. A lady wizard wore more tiny, fragile leaves than a ten-foot hedge, fashioned in a gorgeous and delicate frock. Feathers bedecked another pair of wizards. Kale at first thought they were husband and wife, but their features were so similar, she decided they were brother and sister.

A wizard dressed with small shells adorning his robe clattered by, smelling fishy, and trailing seaweed. Kale wrinkled her nose, caught her mother's disapproving glance, and schooled her features not to reflect her thoughts.

"Look at your own gown, child, before you cast aspersions on someone else's choice of attire."

Kale's eyes dropped to the material her mother had fashioned an hour earlier. Miniscule streaks of lightning dashed hither and yon. The small beads of starlike gems twinkled and had multiplied to cover the entire dress. She looked up and noticed that a wizard approaching her squinted against the light she cast.

"Light wizard," said her father. "I have suspected as much."

Her mother beamed at her. "Yes, I thought so too, but I didn't want to influence her with my interpretation of the signs. There's nothing special in the cloth, dear. Your element is showing."

Her father harrumphed. "So we have a light wizard, a weather wizard, and a mortal wizard in the family."

"Mortal?" Kale looked at her mother, for it had been obvious for a long time that her father rained when he rested.

"Don't look so concerned, dear," answered Lyll. "It merely means my body is more apt to reflect time and wear than another's."

"But how is that a talent?"

"Healing, like Gymn. I thought for a while that you would have that talent as well, but it is only through Gymn that your ability to heal is intensified enough to manifest."

Sir Kemry patted her shoulder. "Of course we all have a tad of each of the talents."

Kale noticed he had donned spectacles with dark lenses in order to be able to look straight at her.

"Come, dearest daughter," he said. "We've been standing too long. In the future, we must work on your facility to control your light. For now, we will just move to dispel its grandeur."

Kale followed her parents around the room, being introduced to wizards she knew only by reputation or not at all. She had met a few of them since she and her friends had come through the gateway and now struggled to remember their names. Besides her parents, she knew Regidor and Gilda and the lake wizard, Cam Ayronn. Bardon had counted the wizards in the gallery the night before. Twenty-one. Her father said that was the sum total of all known wizards in Amara. He amended that to specify wizards in Paladin's service. It had been centuries since Stox or Cropper attended a wizards' conclave.

Much visiting took place. Refreshments appeared and disappeared. Music played and some of the wizards enjoyed dancing. Intermittently, Kale worried that the conclave didn't seem to be interested in addressing the serious issues at hand. But the company was stimulating and the festive atmosphere invigorating. She sometimes wondered about the passing of time. But no timepiece of any kind could be found in the chamber. When she thought she might be weary and ready for bed and she knew for a fact that she could not put one more delicacy in her mouth or swallow one more mouthful of delicious punch, a bell rang.

The wizards instantly ceased their chatter.

A male wizard robed in cloudlike material rose into the air above the others.

"Namee," Lyll whispered the man's name in Kale's ear. "Sky wizard."

"So we have come to some conclusions that I will present to Paladin."

The others in the room nodded and murmured affirmations.

The knowledge that decisions had been made astonished Kale for only a second. The minds of these great thinkers had been mingling for hours. Of course, they had resolved issues and made plans. Now that she was conscious of the fact, she realized she had participated in the process.

Namee held up a finger. "First, we must engage the enemy to keep them from deterring the progress of the real warriors."

Everyone nodded, including Kale, who had a sudden hard lump in her stomach.

"Second," said Namee with another finger uplifted, "we must unite the populace and solidify their purpose."

Another round of approval, and the knot in Kale's stomach twisted.

"Third, we have decided dragons will be that unifying force. After all, who can resist the attraction of these winsome creatures?"

A cheer. Kale felt sick.

"Fourth, Sir Kemry and Kale Allerion will be the ambassadors to collect the dragons, train them, and present a mighty fighting force behind which the populace will rally."

"And fifth!" Namee paused. "Harrumph! Was there a fifth? Imm? Perhaps not. Oh well, and fifth, we offer good wishes as the old Dragon Keeper and the new Dragon Keeper seek to save all of Amara."

Kale found her father's arm supporting her. She leaned heavily against him and gazed up at his face. He looked out over the cheering crowd with his other arm raised in salute. His countenance glowed with enthusiasm. Her mother appeared at her other side and also offered an arm around her waist to keep her from falling.

"Mother," Kale pleaded, "tell me I am dreaming."

Her mother's words came out between lips frozen in a smile. "Hardly, dear, and do something with that face of yours. I swear a blind illiterate could read it like a book."

The people around them started up a chant. "A quest! A quest!"

Kale tried to relax the muscles around her mouth, but she could not muster a smile. She leaned toward her mother's ear.

"Are you coming as well?"

"What did you say, Kale? Mindspeak, dear, it's the only way."

I said, Are you coming as well?

"Oh no! It's your father's turn to have some fun."

14

FIGHT!

Kale held Paladin's hand as they sat together on the balcony outside his chambers. The early morning sun sparkled on the dew-covered hills beyond the castle walls. Quartz embedded the white stone of the palace, glistening as rays of golden light struck the edifice. Cool, fresh air put color in Paladin's cheeks, and Gymn scampered over him, leaping from the invalid chair to the balustrades and back to Paladin's shoulders. Metta perched on Kale's shoulder and sang in harmony with the birds heralding the sunrise.

Paladin's eyes twinkled at Kale as he patted her hand. "So tell me what troubles you."

"I shouldn't bother you with my troubles. You've been ill."

He threw back his head and laughed, and although it wasn't as hearty as she knew his laughter could be, the merry sound made her smile.

"I'm glad you're better, sir, but why are you better? Will you get well now?"

The o'rant leader scooped Gymn into his hand and rubbed a finger over the sensitive spot behind the minor dragon's neck frill. Gymn closed his eyes and stretched, enjoying the caress.

"My health ebbs and flows as our citizens invest their lives in Wulder." He lifted his hand to the sky, and a songbird dived from a parapet to land on his finger. Kale expected him to say something wise, something she would have to puzzle over to get more than the surface meaning. But

Paladin listened to the bird's notes blend with Metta's for a moment and then shooed the feathered creature off to its more natural perch.

He cocked an eyebrow at his young visitor. "I think you avoided my question, Kale. Tell me what these plans are that so distress you."

"Bardon, Regidor, Gilda, Mother, and Dar are to lead a force against the armies of Pretender."

"They will be in danger, and of course, this is alarming."

"That's not it!" She shook her dainty handkerchief and then deliberately placed both hands in her lap. She couldn't help but lean forward to deliver her plea. "Bardon and I have practiced together for three years. We're really exceptional, Paladin." She drew in a steadying breath. "Together we're almost unbeatable. We fight as one. It's the training and the special bond we have."

Even though she couldn't bring herself to voice her defiant demand, she knew Paladin would grasp the underlying message. One of the unique traits about him was his ability to pick up on subtleties. She could count on Paladin to rectify this awful situation. Everyone listened to him. She almost let out a sigh of relief when she saw him nod.

"Your concern for your husband is understandable, but he can fight without you, and Regidor and the others are just as capable."

"Oh, you're missing the point." She dropped his hand, stood up, and at once sat down again. "I don't want to go look for dragon eggs, to hatch them and build a fighting force. My father can do that. He's the original Dragon Keeper. I want to go to the front with the others. I want to be where I can do some good."

Paladin tapped his lips with one finger as he considered her words.

Kale waited, holding her breath and wondering if this would be the time Paladin lost patience with her. As far as she knew, she was the only one who had the audacity to complain and make an objection to their exalted leader. His eyes narrowed just before he spoke, and she thought it looked as if he winced against the pain of having to rebuke her.

"Kale, you have been chosen to do a job. If there were someone else who could assume that duty, I would excuse you."

"I already have six eggs to tend, and my father—"

Paladin held up a hand to stop her protestation. "By all means, quicken the eggs in your possession. But neither you nor your father could accomplish this task alone. If the task is unpleasant for you, my suggestion is that you put your heart into the gathering of these eggs and work with your father to train the dragons that hatch with due speed."

Kale's eyes widened as she listened to the stern tone of Paladin's voice. Now she bobbed her head. "Yes sir."

She left Metta and Gymn with Paladin. The farther away she walked from his room, the more her feelings surfaced. It seemed no one understood her position. She stormed through the palace to find her husband. He'd been asleep when she returned from the wizards' conclave just before dawn. She'd gone to stand on their balcony, and there she had heard Paladin's summons.

Now she hurried down the corridor, away from Paladin, who could, but would not, change the orders. She sent her thoughts ahead and discovered her parents having breakfast with Bardon in the suite of rooms between their bedchambers.

Did they tell you? She mindspoke to her husband to let him know she was coming and intending to inform him of Paladin's stubborn decree.

"Yes. A good plan."

A good plan? Kale felt Bardon take a step backward from her outrage if only in his mind. *You don't see that we will be separated? Perhaps for years?*

"Well…"

The scope of her husband's anticipation hit her. *You're eager to go fight bisonbecks, blimmets, grawligs, quiss, and whatever. You never once gave a thought as to where I would be.*

"Now that's not true. You'll be with your father—"

And would you rather be with your father than with me?

"And that's not fair."

"Children, children," her mother's voice interrupted the argument.

Her father's voice chimed in. *"Are you saying you don't want to go on this quest with me?"*

"Of course, she wants to go," said her mother, *"but with her husband, not with her father."*

"That doesn't make sense," said her father at the same time Bardon's thoughts clamored, *"I'm not a Dragon Keeper. I'm a knight."*

Her father harrumphed. *"I'm a knight."*

"Of course," Lyll's soothing tone came through as another interrupting thought. *"Bardon meant he is just a knight."*

Another harrumph. *"No such thing as* just *a knight."*

Lyll answered, *"I didn't mean it that way."* Kale imagined her mother patting her father's arm. *"I meant he is only a knight as opposed to being both a knight and a Dragon Keeper."*

Both men mindspoke at the same time. Kale covered her ears and straight away realized how futile that was when all the parties of the conversation were not speaking aloud and weren't even where they could see her gesture. She heard her husband, father, and little comments by her mother as she turned a corner and raced down the hall.

Regidor, with Gilda on his arm, approached from the other direction. Kale took her hands from her ears and waved aside her friends' concern as she sped past. She opened the door to the suite and saw her mother was, indeed, patting her father's arm.

Kale glared at Bardon. "You want to go fight."

"Of course I do." His voice held a note of umbrage. "That's what I was trained to do. Defend and protect."

She took a few more steps into the room, vaguely aware that Gilda and Regidor followed. "I was trained to fight too. A woman belongs beside her husband. Doesn't anyone understand that?"

Lyll moved away from Sir Kemry. "Well, I certainly do."

"And I," said Gilda.

Kale felt a wave of relief at being supported by the two other women.

"But," added Lyll.

Kale's heart sank. No question about it. Her mother enthusiastically glowed with youth and vigor. A sure sign Lyll was going to be right in whatever she decided to say, and right now, right was not what Kale wanted to hear.

Lyll's chin went up, and her eyes seemed to focus on an exquisite scene beyond their ken. "There are times when we are required to put our personal preferences aside in order to achieve a greater good."

"Hear! Hear!" said Sir Kemry.

"Bah!" said Gilda.

Regidor clapped, a sardonic look twisting his handsome features.

Kale burst into tears.

⊰ 15 ⊱

Preparations

Granny Noon's hands stilled as she stopped midstitch in her knitting. "Are you expecting a little one?"

Kale sat up straighter on the short footstool by the rocker. "No, I'm not."

"Are you sure?" The emerlindian's eyes wandered around the nursery. She sighed. "I do cherish these sprouts."

A marione toddler chose that moment to spit up his milk. A ropma nursemaid rushed to clean up the tyke and the floor.

Granny Noon giggled. "Although having them around is not always convenient...or clean."

Kale tried to smile as the emerlindian turned an experienced eye back to her, a confused o'rant sitting at a wise woman's feet. She hoped Granny Noon would give her comfort as she faced this difficult separation from Bardon.

"Kale, sometimes young women get a bit teary-eyed when they're carrying a child."

"I am not! I know for sure. And I'm not crying."

"Not now, but your eyes are red and puffy." Granny picked up her stitch, and her needles clicked at a steady beat again. "You cry because you didn't get your way. Because Paladin didn't agree with you. And Bardon didn't stand up for you and change everyone's mind so you could do what you want."

"That's not why I've been crying. That's childish, and I'm not childish." Her lower lip had somehow managed to stick out in a pout. She pulled it in.

Granny Noon rocked and knitted, her eyes fixed on the stitches gliding from one needle to the other. Kale glanced around the room at crawling babies and small children tottering with ungainly steps.

The swoosh-creak, swoosh-creak of the rocking chair provided a counter beat to the rapid clicking of Granny Noon's needles. "You know, all aspects of life are like those infants learning to move. They pull themselves up to the starting position, struggle to stay balanced, and fight to toddle in the right direction. We tackle each challenge in life in much the same way."

Kale looked up at her mentor. "And this applies to me?"

"Yes, in that you are entering a new relationship and a new task. Don't expect to immediately be able to work side by side with your father. You'll stumble around a bit before you find a rapport. This new quest is under different circumstances, as is every quest. You have old knowledge to blend with new. You will grow and mature. Kale, although it will seem uncomfortable, in the end, you will be blessed."

Kale turned her face away and scrunched up her nose. "I really do know all this, Granny Noon. I've heard it before."

The emerlindian's chuckle eased the tension in Kale's shoulders. "I know you do, my dear. But I don't see evidence that you're applying the knowledge."

Kale sighed and turned her sour expression to the granny so she could see. Granny Noon laughed out loud.

Kale allowed her face to relax and giggled. "What should I do, Granny Noon?"

"You already know. I think Paladin himself once told you."

Contentment filled Kale at the memory of Paladin's tender words and encouragement. "Just what is right ahead of me."

"That's correct." Granny put her knitting in a basket and stood. "Let's go down to the herb room and replenish your supply. You never know what you might need in your hollows when out seeking lost dragon eggs."

They went down winding stone steps to the lower level of the palace where the cool rooms stored perishable produce. Herbs in glass and ceramic jars on shelves lined the walls from floor to ceiling. Lightrocks were embedded in the wooden beams above their heads. A preparation table stood in the middle of the light, dry room. In each corner stood a porous rock column that absorbed moisture. Lady Allerion hummed as she mixed a compound at the table.

"Hello." Kale hugged her mother. "I think we have come to do an identical task."

After Granny Noon and Lyll exchanged a greeting, they got busy. Kale found herself being the one to fetch different ingredients. She pushed the wooden ladder around the room and scooted up and down the rungs to reach jars on the upper shelves.

She set a ceramic pot on the table in front of her mother, who thanked her.

Wiping the dust from her fingers, Kale waited for another request. She watched her mother dip out a clear, sticky substance. Kale passed her a scraper to transfer the goo from the dipper to a bowl. "When I lived in River Away, I thought magic would be to snap my fingers and things would appear in front of me."

"Unnatural," said Granny Noon.

Lyll tapped her scraper on the edge of the bowl. "Defying Wulder's order."

"Or sleight of hand," said Granny Noon.

Lyll pointed at a jar on the table containing thin rods. "Hand me a…" She shook her finger, indicating the rods. "Oh, that thing. No, a shorter one."

Kale handed her the stirring rod. "I saw a magician once at the tavern in River Away."

Both Granny Noon and Lyll stopped what they were doing and stared at Kale.

Kale shrugged. "He pulled doves out of a man's cape and poured water into a lady's bonnet."

"Sleight of hand," said Granny Noon. "Visual deception, meant for entertainment, not for the gaining of power. This is more like a puzzle. Everyone watching knows that it is a trick, and the pleasure is in the amazement of the sight and the wonder of how the magician manages to fool us."

Lyll's face still held a frown. "But there's also dark magic, Kale. People and things that none of us should ever have anything to do with."

"I know." Kale shuddered. "Wizard Fenworth took me to a place where women talked to spirits of the deceased. And a man made a dead man walk." Kale quickly asked Wulder to protect her. Even the memory of the place made her skin crawl. "Fenworth wanted me to see their depravity in the ugliest form so I would know what dabbling in the fringe elements could lure me into." Shivering again, she avoided bringing to mind the immoral activities she'd seen in the darkest corners of the rooms.

Her mother patted her arm. The touch of a loving hand dispelled the dirtiness the image of the dark room had smeared across her heart.

Sir Kemry entered the room. "Found you! Found you both. I came to kiss my wife good-bye and whisk my daughter off on a grand adventure."

He went first to Granny Noon and gave her a bear hug and a kiss on her forehead. "I'll miss you, too, young lady."

The old emerlindian giggled. "Put me down, you big ox."

With tears in her eyes, Kale leaned toward her mother. "How do you stand being away from your husband?"

"Away? He's part of me. I am never truly away as long as he roams through my heart and mind." She kissed her daughter's cheek. "And the time together is so much more pleasant for the time spent apart."

"That's a principle."

"Yes, not worded quite as it is in the Tomes, but the meaning is the same."

"I thought that referred to our future time in Wulder's presence."

"It does, and it is also referring to any separation from a loved one."

"I love Bardon."

"And he loves you. Quick, find him and tell him so. I'll keep your father busy for a while."

The twinkle in her mother's eye reminded Kale that her parents would probably enjoy a private good-bye as much as she and her husband.

Kale hurried to the door. "I've something important to do before we leave, Father. I'll find you later."

"How much later?" her father bellowed after her.

Kale didn't bother to answer. She trusted her mother to make her father comfortable with the wait.

16

Missing

Kale sat on a log and watched her father roam the periphery of the meadow one more time. He meandered, examining the vegetation as if the trees and flowering bushes hid something important. Of course, according to him, they did. She and her father had come through one gateway moments before, and another gateway, her father claimed, existed within a few feet.

Her father beat at a prism bush with his staff. The multicolored blossoms refracted the light and sent rainbows dancing around the clearing. "Gateways don't dissolve into nothing." He moved on to push aside a fragrant bush's heavy branches.

"No, not usually," agreed Kale. She stared at the band of gold encircling a finger on her left hand, then glanced over her shoulder, half afraid the gateway back to her husband would disappear too.

Sir Kemry cleared his throat. "Well, send your dragons out to help in the search, Kale."

"Oh, of course." She stood and spread the front of her cape open.

Six dragons crawled out of their pocket-dens and took flight. Kale put her hand on the blue scarf she used as a belt around her waist. Under her tunic, six more dragon eggs rested against her skin. They would quicken and hatch within a month. Now she had other things to attend to.

Her father might not be able to pick up on her instructions to the dragons. Kale wasn't sure how much he followed her mental conversations with the little beasts. She addressed the dragons aloud, even though she knew they understood her mindspeaking more accurately. How could they confuse the word *gateway*? And it was important her father understand what she was doing. "Help us find the second gateway. It's around here somewhere."

They circled her head, chittered at one another, then proceeded to swoop and careen around the forest's edge.

Kale gestured at the smaller trees and waist-high bushes. "Pat says this is new growth."

Her father stood and put his hands on his hips. "Yes, the clearing seems somewhat smaller than when I was here last. We shall step into the foliage a few feet, search for the gateway once around, and then step another foot deeper into the forest for another round of examination. Methodically, we should be able to locate the gateway." He started into the forest. "Kale, you take that side, and I'll take this."

Kale clutched her skirts close and then released the material. Poking around the woods would be easier in a different outfit. She spun and attired herself in soft boots, leggings, a blouse and tunic, much like the uniforms of Paladin's servants. Inside the fringe of the forest, she moved counterclockwise and bumped into her father within moments.

Sir Kemry laughed. "We're going to have to develop our teamwork skills. Let's start again. You go clockwise, and I will go counter. We'll meet on the other side."

Kale pushed down the first thought that came to her mind. She and Bardon would not have been so inept. Every move they made was synchronized. One barely conjured up a thought before the other knew it. She could pause for a fraction of a second and pinpoint his location. Bardon did the same. On the verge of such an important enterprise, why did Paladin expect her and her father to form a new bond? Wouldn't it have been more efficient to use talent that was already meshed?

The minor dragons buzzed her head as they passed. Clearly, their cheerful moods were not diminished by Kale's morose thoughts. Pat, she noticed, walked at her heels, chomping on bugs she stirred up from the undergrowth. Kale took care to avoid stepping on her small, round friend.

She and her father met on the other side of the clearing without uncovering anything resembling a gateway. They both stepped farther into the woods and made the second sweep in the older and thicker vegetation. Pat still foraged around her feet, and several of the other dragons passed her, occupied by their own search. She met her father again after pushing through the denser foliage.

"Right," he said, awkwardly patting her shoulder. "Well then, the next round should uncover the hidden entry."

Kale offered him a weak smile and started once more to search for the elusive gateway. Again Pat kept her company, but only two of the other dragons zoomed by. She felt a tremor of apprehension as she noted their frantic flight. With her mind, she scanned the area. She located her father and three of her little friends.

Father!

"*What's wrong?*"

Three, no four! Four of the minor dragons are missing.

"*What do you mean missing?*"

Missing! Not here! They're gone!

"*What do the two who are with you say?*"

Kale consulted Pat, who knew nothing. When she reached for the one remaining dragon, dismay wrenched at her heart. The last dragon in the air had disappeared. Pat flew to her shoulder and called out in a series of high-pitched squeaks. No response came from his comrades. He stamped his feet and called again. No answer. He spread his wings, and Kale caught him before he took off. "No, whatever has happened to them might happen to you too."

Father, only Pat is with me now, and he doesn't know where they went.

"I do." Her father's voice sounded in her mind with a deep tone of caution. *"To your left, only a few yards away, is a creature cloaked against our discovering it. I can't tell if it is ropma, bisonbeck, or grawlig."*

Kale sought the creature with her mind and found where it stood by the emptiness of the spot rather than by its presence. She waited, wondering if her father had a plan. With Bardon, she would not have had to wonder. She bit her lip, angry with herself for wasting thought on what couldn't be helped. Her dragons were in danger.

"He's moving."

Yes, I know. Kale sensed the creature edging deeper into the forest. She stealthily followed and knew her father inched closer from the other side. *We've got to catch it.*

"I suspect it's leading us to the gateway."

The dragons are more important than that gateway.

"Calm yourself, Kale. Of course, they are. But I think if we follow our visitor, we shall find both the dragons and the gateway. Cover yourself with your moonbeam cape so it doesn't know where you are."

Kale took the necessary precaution and slipped as quietly as she could through the brush. Her father had also done something to obscure his presence. She had no idea where he was but assumed he advanced on their target from the opposite side.

The creature's shield slipped and resettled around it. Kale thought she detected a ropma, but why would one of those gentle creatures snatch the minor dragons? It moved more quickly now, careless and nervous. The shield flickered as if the fugitive could not hold it steady.

Again her father surprised her. A surge of energy emerged out of seemingly nothing and covered their target. The faltering shield melted into a puddle on the ground, exposing an enormous ropma carrying a cloth bag. A vine sprouted at its feet and quickly trapped it by wrapping the ropma from chin to toes. The captured creature squealed and trembled, tears running down its hairy, unkempt face.

"No hurt. No hurt," it begged.

Kale saw a claw slitting through the bag and knew her dragons would soon be free by their own efforts. As soon as the holes grew a bit bigger, she heard their indignation.

She nodded at the ropma, indicating the sack it clutched. "Bounty carter. You are supposed to soak the material every night to keep it from getting brittle. Your bounty carter still contains the sounds and scent of your prey, but it is not strong enough to keep them from breaking out." She stepped forward and placed a soothing hand on the distressed ropma's arm. "Who gave these to you? Who told you to catch dragons?"

The ropma shook his head, matted tresses of hair swinging wildly about. "No, no tell. Mean woman kill."

"Kill you or kill the dragons?"

The ropma ceased all movement while it considered this question.

A smile lifted his lips, indicating he had come to the answer of the puzzle. Then he frowned. "Me."

Sir Kemry spoke. "We are mighty wizards. We offer you our protection."

Startled by the sound of his voice, the ropma stiffened, with eyes widened and fists clenched. The creature's face folded into a hideous scowl.

Kale patted the ropma's shoulder. "We'll help. We'll keep you safe. Mean woman no kill."

The ropma relaxed, and with a distrustful glare at Kale's father, handed the friendly young woman his prize bag.

"Little dragons pretty, but no want. Bite. Bite hard. Hurts."

"Yes, they do."

"Spit. Bite and spit. No want."

Kale tore open the hole in the cloth carter, making it easier for the disgruntled dragons to climb out.

"Does the mean woman have lots of dragons?"

The ropma's head bobbed with vigor. "Lots. Big. Little. Lots."

"Well," said Sir Kemry. "It looks like we shall have to turn aside from our quest to perform a rescue."

Kale snuggled Metta under her chin. She totally agreed.

17

Bug

"I'm going to let you go." Sir Kemry waved a hand at the ropma. "But stay here. I want you to answer some questions."

The vine loosened around the ropma's legs. As soon as the binding fell away, the beast darted toward the deeper woods. Kale and her father grabbed its arms. It gave up without more ado and whimpered.

"Go home," it pleaded. "No take little dragons."

Sir Kemry stroked the agitated beast's back and guided it out into the clearing. Kale followed with several of the dragons perched on her as the others flew ahead.

"Here, sit," said Sir Kemry and pressed the ropma kindheartedly onto a large boulder. "I have something to eat I think you will like."

"Eat?"

"Yes, a treat."

The ropma watched intently as Kale's father brought out a small package and unwrapped a dark brown hunk of bread.

The creature took it and turned the morsel over in his hands, smelled it, and then stuffed the whole thing in his mouth. It chewed with a smile on its face.

"Good. Sweet. More?"

It ate the second piece of molasses laced soft bread offered without even a brief examination.

"Good. More?"

"No, that's all I have for now."

The ropma frowned and started to rise. Sir Kemry put a hand on its shoulder and kept it on the rock.

"What is your name?"

"Bug."

"Bug, are you a male or female?"

"I Bug."

Kale smiled at the ropma. "Will you be a da or ma when you have little ropmas?"

"I be da. I be da now. We have many bas." He shook his hairy head. "There is woman. Woman no ropma. Woman no good. Mean to bas."

Kale looked suitably shocked. "That's horrible. Very bad. I don't like no-good woman."

Sir Kemry patted the ropma's knee to regain his attention. "What is the name of the no-good woman?"

A puzzled look came over Bug's face, and he didn't move for almost a full minute. He smiled when he remembered. "Stox. She leave becks to watch dragons. Becks say, 'Stox is gonna getcha. You obey.'"

Kale wondered what a beck could be, but then saw a huge, militant warrior in the ropma's thoughts. She shivered at the exaggerated image of a bisonbeck.

Sir Kemry nodded. "Stox is no good."

Solemnly, Bug nodded in agreement. "Becks no good."

Kale pointed to herself and her father and to the ropma. "We are friends. We want to help the dragons."

Bug frowned. The more he thought, the more sour his expression became. "No help dragons. Make becks mad. Becks tell woman. Woman be bad. Hurt ropmas. Hurt bas."

Kale shook her head. "No, we won't let them."

Bug eyed Kale and her father, then stood. "No. Bug go home. No friends you."

"Wait," said Sir Kemry. "I understand your fear. We won't make you help us. Just answer some questions."

The ropma looked longingly toward the woods and the gateway.

Metta sat up straight on Kale's shoulder and sang. The tune caught the beast's attention. Dibl flew over and sat on the creature's shaggy shoulder. Bug cringed, but when the yellow dragon did not bite or spit, the gentle beast relaxed. He turned back to watch Metta as she swayed and occasionally spread her colorful wings.

Kale spoke softly. "When we go through the gateway, are the bisonbecks and dragons there, right next to the gateway?"

"No," answered Bug, his attention on Metta.

"Where are they?" asked Sir Kemry.

Kale focused on Bug's thoughts, knowing his words would not be able to express clear directions. She saw a range of mountains, stark and unfriendly, a river lined with grassy banks, a narrow pass, and a wide meadow in a high country valley. In the meadow, dozens of dragons of all sizes wandered about aimlessly. Among these captured creatures, many ropmas worked. Some carried feed. Others groomed the bigger animals. Among the rocks surrounding the area, bisonbecks stood on guard. Tremors of fear shivered through Bug each time his memory touched on one of the armed soldiers.

"Do you see what I see?" asked Kale's father.

The valley?

"Yes."

She could feel her father's interest in the different views presented in Bug's mind. She could almost understand Sir Kemry's analysis. But not quite. She studied the many dragons and wondered at their docility. *Why don't they just fly away?*

"There has to be some sort of deterrent, but since our friend, Bug, does not understand it, we most likely won't find the answer until we are there."

There seems to be more than an adequate guard on the area. Can we accomplish a rescue on our own?

"A decision we must make after we have seen for ourselves what the situation involves."

Kale watched the ropma's memory of a dozen bas clambering over a full-grown major dragon. The dragon did not even look annoyed. *Are the dragons bonded to their captors?*

"That would make our job more difficult, but again, we won't know until we are there."

Kale marveled at how many dragons there seemed to be, and at the great variety. Was Bug's mental accounting to be trusted? Did he unwittingly show them the same dragons repeatedly but in different settings? From the details of the images, Kale would guess the ropma was, indeed, familiar with a great variety of dragons.

How long has Stox been gathering the dragons? she mused.

"I've no idea. Perhaps—"

We'll find out once we are there.

"Exactly."

Then I guess we'd best get going. "Bug." She smiled and extended a gentle hand to smooth the hair on the creature's forearm. "We want to go back with you through the gateway."

The ropma shook his head in dread. "No, no. Bug bring dragons. Bug bring food. No people. Becks no say bring people."

"Oh, we don't like becks, either. We won't let the becks see us with you." She turned to Sir Kemry. "Will we, Father?"

The older man pursed his lips and made a show of thinking. "No, I don't think we will, daughter. But I would like to see all the pretty dragons."

"And," said Kale, "maybe if one of our dragons would go with you, you would have something to give the becks to make them happy."

"Becks never happy." But Bug eyed the singing dragon and reached up to pet Dibl, who still sat on his shoulder. "Good to bring dragons to becks. Becks no yell, no hit."

Kale furrowed her brow. "Do the becks yell at the dragons? Do they hit the dragons?"

"No. No hurt dragons. No-good woman scream, yell, kill. No-good woman want all dragons. No hurt dragons."

Sir Kemry took Bug's arm and eased him toward the woods. "We best be going now. Don't want to be late for supper."

"Supper?" Bug resisted the knight's efforts to move him.

"Night food," said Kale. "We don't want to be late for night food."

"Rain make good food," said Bug with a grunt and shuffled into the trees.

"Rain is the ma to your bas?" asked Sir Kemry.

"Yes. Good ma. Good cook." He pushed ahead, plowing through the underbrush.

Kale and her father hurried to catch up but froze when they heard a loud voice in front of Bug.

"Well!"

Kale easily identified the growling tone as a bisonbeck. She and her father silently lowered themselves behind the thick foliage. Using her talent, she looked through Bug's eyes to see two soldiers standing beside a gateway almost obscured by vines.

The taller bisonbeck grimaced. "I don't like having to come look for the scavengers." He frowned. "What have you got on your shoulder? Where did you get that little beauty?"

He reached forward to grab Dibl, but the small dragon hopped into the air and flew to a tree branch. Five angry minor dragons swooped at the soldier as he leapt up in a vain attempt to catch Dibl.

"Look at this," said the second man. "This ropma must be a Dragon Keeper or something."

The bigger bisonbeck stood with his fists planted on his hips, staring up at the tree, now serving as a perch for the colorful dragons. The little beasts chattered angrily from their safe roost.

"Nah, I know this ropma. He's Bug, and there isn't anything special about him."

Bug wagged his head back and forth, a sorrowful expression pulling down the corners of his mouth. "Bug no Dragon Keeper. Dragon Keeper in woods."

Kale saw both soldiers jerk around to stare at the ropma. She glanced over at her father, and he shrugged.

"Under the circumstances, my dear, he couldn't have kept it a secret."

The bigger bisonbeck pulled his sword and stared into the trees. "Where?"

Bug turned and pointed right at the clump of bushes where Kale crouched. "She's there…" He searched the forest, his head swiveling. "Man no."

The large soldier started toward Kale's hiding place. "There's two? Or are there more? How many, Bug?"

"A dozen. A hundred. Maybe seven."

"Argh!" complained the second man with his battle-ax held ready. "Fool question. Ropma can't count."

"To be on the safe side," said the first, coming to a stop, "let's drag Bug back through the gateway and get reinforcements. Stox will give a reward for catching Dragon Keepers as well as dragons."

Sir Kemry straightened and strode into the small space in front of the two soldiers, coming to a halt beside Bug.

"Just a moment. Bug does not want to be dragged off. I have no wish to meet Stox at this time. And my friends in the forest have decided you two are a nuisance."

The large bisonbeck raised his chin and pointed his sword at the old knight. "I'm not so sure you have friends. I'm willing to bet you are all alone."

Sir Kemry laughed. "A bet you are about to lose." Without taking his eyes off the warrior, he spoke over his shoulder. "Gentlemen, show yourselves."

18

A Dragon History

Bardon cringed as a servant dropped a loaded tray of dirty dishes. The clang reverberated through the tavern and bounced back from the plastered walls. Sir Dar's ears turned back and down. Bardon wished his ears could block out the clamor. Gilda and Regidor didn't even look up from their conversation in a high-sided wooden booth for two. Bardon thought of the hundreds of couples who must have declared their love in the secluded alcove. He wouldn't mind a quick chat with Kale right now in a private room where he could hold her as well as speak words of devotion.

The image of Kale in his mind brought a smile to his lips and then a frown. He didn't have his wife as a traveling companion, but rather her mother. Who would want to go into battle with his mother-in-law? Lyll Allerion was all right in her own way, but she had a tendency to be bossy and headstrong.

Bardon smiled again. *Just like my wife.*

A marione gent in farmer's homespun garb opened the common room door, letting in a stiff draft of cold air. A kimen followed him. The diminutive man's clothes now appeared dark purple, his hair stood on end, and his lips were set in a grim line. They paused, and their gazes searched the crowd. The marione spotted Sir Dar, and they weaved through the other customers to reach him.

"News," the marione said as he sat down at the table with the two knights, "and it isn't good."

Lady Allerion hurried from where she had been visiting with several local women. She took the chair between Dar and Bardon. The new men gave her a wary look.

"She's with us," said Sir Dar. "Lady Allerion, this is Armin and Yent." He pointed to the marione and the kimen in turn.

Armin stood and took off his hat, making a short bow. "Pleased to meet you, m'lady. And thankful we are that you and the others have come to our assistance."

The kimen stood on his chair and bowed. "I've met your daughter, Kale, and pray she is well."

"Thank you, gentlemen," Lyll answered. "My daughter is hunting with her father. She was well when last I saw her. Please be seated."

Armin sat and kept his hat in his hand. "The rumor is that the wizards are gathering a great army of dragons to defend us."

Lyll Allerion sighed. "I wish that were true, my friend. But there is not a great number of dragons."

"Why is that, m'lady? If you don't mind my asking."

Sir Dar lifted his hand. A maid came to the table, and the doneel ordered a variety of treats and hot tea to be served. When she left, he addressed the marione. "I will tell you what I know."

Bardon, curious to hear again the tale he knew so well, leaned forward. To hear the history from someone gifted as a storyteller would be different than reading it out of a textbook or hearing a dry lecture by a professor.

Lady Allerion surprised him by taking his hand. Her somber face reminded him he must look eager as he waited for Sir Dar to begin.

"It's a sad tale," she said. "One that shames the high races."

Bardon nodded. He knew.

"Why?" asked Armin. "Because they were cruel where they should have been kind? Did they do harm to the dragons when the dragons were every person's friend?"

She shook her head. "No, ours was a sin of omission. We did not regard our dragon companions as we should have. We did not honor their camaraderie. And we took advantage of their generous nature."

Dar agreed with a nod. "First, the meech dragons grew tired of dealing with us." He let his gaze fall on Gilda and Regidor at their isolated table. Anyone giving them a cursory glance would think they were tall o'rants. The clothing they wore with hats and capes disguised their dragon features. "The meech race is intelligent, moral, and conscientious. Those who have memories of when these rare dragons mingled with the high races say they grew tired of making excuses for our people."

"And disgusted," added Lyll. "They withdrew, limiting their contact with us."

"And the other dragons?" asked Armin. "Did they shun the high races as well?"

"No." Lyll looked at Dar, raising her eyebrows. "Not exactly."

The maid came back to the table with mugs, platters of daggarts, bread and jam, and a pot of tea. Lady Allerion poured the hot brew and passed around the treats, making sure everyone had what they wanted.

When the busyness of serving had passed, the kimen, Yent, spoke up. "Continue the history, please, Sir Dar."

The doneel bit into a toffee daggart, sipped the mint tea, and smacked his lips. He placed his mug on the table but cradled it with his hands as if to garner its warmth.

"It wasn't a matter of segregation that led the other dragons to dwindle. They didn't forsake the company of men. While they co-inhabited Amara, they ceased to trust the high races. The scarcity of dragon eggs is the manifestation of this distrust. It is a mystery why the dragons reacted so strongly. I believe there is more to the story than history records."

Bardon shifted in his seat. He wondered if Kale had heard this saga of the dragons from Fenworth, Librettowit, or Cam. The old librarian Librettowit would be the most colorful in his descriptions. He'd also be the most thorough. If Kale knew of this history from one of her mentors, she had never mentioned it. He wished she were here.

Sir Dar enjoyed the rest of his daggart and picked up another.

"Please, sir," said Armin, "the tale."

The doneel took a long slurp of his cooling tea and held the mug as he spoke. "For a dragon egg to hatch, it must be quickened by someone of the high races. Dragons do not nurture their young. The hatchlings are self-sufficient within a day of breaking out of their shell. But dragons do care for the overall welfare of their offspring."

The kimen's clothing faded, the light dimming as if covered with a gray haze. "So they hid the progeny from us to protect them."

"In a manner of speaking," said Sir Dar. "When the majority of the dragons became cautious of us, their former comrades, they began nesting in places where we would not find the eggs. Instead of proudly presenting their eggs to those to whom they had bonded, they didn't mention the laying of eggs."

"Some say," said Yent, "that some of the older dragons made the arduous journey across the sea to the continent south of Amara."

Sir Dar and Lady Allerion nodded.

Bardon closed his eyes and pictured Kale with gem-colored minor dragons flying in to land on her, scampering to claim their favorite perches, and adorning her clothing like living jewelry.

"So the population of dragons has dwindled," he said.

"To our sorrow," said Sir Dar.

"To our shame," said Lyll.

The marione's face reflected the hopelessness of the situation. "Will we be able to win the support of the dragons who remain? Will they join with us against Pretender, Stox, and Cropper?"

Lyll squeezed Bardon's hand. "There are dragons who have bonded with members of the high races. These dragons would do anything for their comrades. Whether they can be persuaded to fight for Amara, for the whole of civilization, rather than just the individuals they care for, I don't know."

"I think they will," said Dar. "But not for the high races. For Paladin. For Wulder."

Bardon nodded. The kimen stood straighter in his chair, and the marione lifted his chin, a new look of hope in his expression.

Dar shook his head. "The point is they don't have to. Legend says the gateway that brought them from their world to ours still exists, and they know where it is. They could leave us in our own muddle, rightly declaring that the tight spot we are in is of our own making."

The marione's brightened countenance faded.

Bardon folded his hands together as they rested on the table. "We shall have to hope their devotion to Wulder is stronger than ours has been."

"Now tell us," said Sir Dar to Armin. "What is your bad news?"

"The fishermen north of Prushing report a swarming of quiss in the sea."

"Is it time for their overland migration?" asked Bardon.

"Narg," snorted Armin. "More like their overland feed. Eden Bay is stuffed full of the monsters. When those two appendages stiffen and they crawl up on shore, there will be thousands more than we've ever faced before."

Lyll sighed. "Crim Cropper's work, I'm sure."

Sir Dar poured himself another mug of tea. "It's amazing how that evil wizard makes us all suffer, when he rarely comes out of his experimenting chambers. I don't know anyone who has ever seen him."

"He has Burner Stox to represent him," said Lyll.

Armin groaned. "And spread his abominable filth among decent folks." He bit into a bread and jam sandwich and spoke as he chewed. "What's this about him and his wife fighting each other?"

"It's true," said Bardon.

Sir Dar laughed ruefully. "Their domestic quarrels have not made life easier for the people of Amara. They throw pots and pans at each other, and dishes on the shelves break, pictures fall from the walls, and furniture is smashed into pieces. Only their pots and pans are armies, and the house being destroyed is our country."

"What are we going to do about the quiss?" asked Armin.

"Destroy them," said Yent. "We know something we did not know before when they last attacked three years ago."

Armin cocked an eyebrow at his tiny friend. "That is?"

"Salt."

"Salt?" questioned several voices around the table.

"Quite by accident we discovered when sprinkled with salt, the body of a quiss reacts in the same way as a slug when doused."

Lady Lyll wrinkled her nose. "I hope we don't have to be too close when this happens."

"I don't understand." Sir Dar scratched the hair along his chin. "Quiss live in saltwater. Why would salt kill them?"

"Because their bodies try to absorb the salt all at once," answered the kimen. "Remember when they come on land, they are in some kind of starvation status. They tear through fences, crawl over walls, swarm and crush buildings. The only homes that remain somewhat unscathed are those we've built into the ground. All because they seek to devour everything edible, both animal and vegetation."

"How are we going to get close enough to shower them with salt?" asked Lyll.

Yent grinned. "The salt can be dispersed from dragons flying overhead."

"Wait." Bardon pushed his chair away from the table and put his hands on his knees. "What type of creatures are these?"

"They're quiss, man!" The marione jammed his hat onto his head, glanced at Lady Lyll, and pulled it off again. He waved it over the table as he spoke in a controlled whisper to the young knight. "They pour out of the ocean as a mass of ravenous flesh, eating everything in sight. The beasts overpower any resistance by sheer number. They look like a walking octopus, but not as pretty. They smell like a sewer, but not as sweet. And they eat like pigs, but not nearly as persnickety as the plump porcine on my farm."

Bardon held up both hands and shook his head. "My cousin N'Rae and I came across a quiss in Southern Wynd on the Gilpen River—"

"Are you completely daft?" interrupted the marione. "Quiss live off the northeast coast, and they abhor fresh water except during their rampage."

"Exactly," agreed Bardon. "Most quiss. But this one had been altered by Cropper. If these quiss are like the odd one we encountered, then we can't slaughter them. He had a mind. He thought. He felt great sorrow. He regretted his life."

"Regretted his life? Then I see no hindrance to our wiping the whole lot out. Do them a favor and exterminate the monsters."

"I see your point," said Dar, facing Bardon. "We fight face-to-face with a creature who reasons. We obliterate a plague if we can. The question is"—he paused and looked each one around the table in the eye—"are we up against intelligence or pestilence?"

"How do we find out?" asked Yent.

"We get close and examine one," said Lyll.

"You're all mad," said Armin.

19

BUG'S BOX

Sir Kemry deftly inserted the image of a dozen young knights into the minds of the two bisonbeck warriors confronting him. Kale followed the imaginary combatants' movements by invading her father's thoughts. She chafed at having to make an effort to interpret Sir Kemry's intentions but also admitted the task was easier than it had been even twenty-four hours before.

"It's an illusion," grumbled the larger soldier. He stepped forward, threatening one of the visions.

Kale realized her father wanted her in that position. The bisonbeck's sword would pass right through the image and ruin the illusion. Kale whipped behind the bushes and stepped into the figure just before the bisonbeck swung his weapon. She bent over and pivoted on one foot, swinging the other leg into the bisonbeck's midriff. The soldier staggered back, regained his balance, raised his sword, and bellowed.

Kale knew exactly what the bisonbeck was thinking and almost felt sorry for him. From his point of view, the knight stood upright and grinned, apparently at ease with the situation. The soldier preferred to have his opponents shivering in outright terror before him. He clenched his teeth and advanced once more.

Kale, in the guise of the knight, pulled out her sword. The image of a gleaming broadsword sheathed her smaller, real, but invisible, blade. She made a figure eight with the point, listening to the whisk of air caused by the thin edge. The sound did not match the look of her weapon, and the experienced soldier hesitated. Kale felt his confusion and the surge of caution.

"Fight me, you coward," cried Kale, her voice rough and deep. She hoped that did the trick. *Don't stand there thinking, soldier-man. I need you to move.*

The bisonbeck lunged, his sword pointed at Kale's heart. She sidestepped and slapped him on the back with the broadside of her blade as he lurched to catch his footing. The impact of blade across the soldier's leather armor resounded as if she'd struck a gong. Her sword triggered a transformation designed to end the evil intentions of the one she struck. The bisonbeck fell on his face, unable to move. As a ripple flows outward from the spot where a pebble hits the water, waves of change passed through the warrior's uniform and protective gear. With each successive undulation the material stiffened until it became a peculiar metal. The soldier lost consciousness, encased in his attire.

Kale blessed Librettowit and Wizard Cam for the work they had done in devising an automatic process for just such an occasion. This being the first time Kale had used the procedure in a fight, she watched with fascination as the transformation took place. An unexpected phenomenon puzzled her. Little sparks of light snapped into being and faded on the man's body until the last moment of alteration. Kale wrinkled her brow in thought but did not waste time. She would report the anomaly to Cam and Librettowit.

"It's a good thing I had your back covered." Her father spoke from a few feet away.

Kale's eyes swept the area. Bug crouched with his arms wrapped around his legs, looking much like a huge, hairy ball. The visions of knights faded as she watched. The other soldier was gone.

"He escaped?"

"No." Her father pointed to a boulder. "That's him. He is a rock from now until Wulder deems him something else."

Sir Kemry moved to put an arm around his daughter's shoulders and nodded at the fallen bisonbeck. "You're handy with your weapon, Kale. But what have you done here? I've never seen the like."

"It's a new process similar to the calcification spell of old. Librettowit and Wizard Cam perfected it and imbued my sword with the catalyst. He's encased in his own clothing. After a few days of imprisonment, the metal will rust away to nothing, leaving the victim unclothed."

"Not a very pleasant experience for him."

"When he awakes, he'll only have the vaguest of memories. He won't return to his duties."

"Perhaps with no ties to his old way of life, he may turn away from evil."

"That's my hope. I much prefer knocking the wind out of his sails to sinking his ship."

"What?"

"I prefer not to kill every enemy I meet."

"Well, that's good to hear. You seem to have developed some noble instincts."

Kale ignored the opportunity to say she'd pretty much been left to raise herself and focused on the downed soldier. "Circumstances might guide him to a more peaceful life. But to be realistic, I know he's likely to tread a path similar to the old one."

"Well, that's up to the man's reaction to Wulder's influence. At least this soldier has a more immediate chance of change than the bisonbeck I turned to stone."

Sir Kemry walked around the prone figure, considering him from different angles. He looked up at his daughter. "You didn't use this trick when the enemy invaded the banquet room at the palace."

She shook her head. "It's too slow. I cannot use my sword again for several minutes, so the procedure is not good in the midst of a melee of any size."

"You have much to teach me, daughter." He sheathed his weapon. "I hope I have a few old tricks that will help you as well."

Kale smiled. For the first time, she felt a longing to spend time with her father. She examined his features—strong chin, prominent nose, gentle eyes. His gray-streaked brown hair was gathered in a warrior's braid that fell between powerful shoulders, halfway down his back. Even at his age, his lean body and long, muscular legs spoke of formidable vigor. It would not be so bad to partner with this man after all. She looked again at his nose and smiled. Her own nose looked just like her mother's.

Merriment sparkled in her father's light brown eyes. He laughed. "And it's a good thing. You're a pretty widget, and with my beak, you'd have been a crone."

He strode over to Bug and clapped him on the shoulder. "Come on, friend. The becks are dispensed with, and we want to see this valley of dragons."

The ropma slowly uncurled his stocky frame and looked with wary eyes around the area.

"Bug go home," he said and made two long strides toward the gateway.

"Wait," ordered Sir Kemry. "I'll go first, just to make sure there's no danger on the other side." He pointed to Bug. "You follow me, and my daughter will bring up the rear. That way, we know you will be safe."

Kale let her mental laughter project to her father. *And we will know he won't escape before showing us the way to this "valley of dragons."*

"That, too."

They passed through the gateway with no incident. Chilled, thin air greeted them along with the visage of barren black mountains that looked as though they had been sliced from onyx. Green splashes brightened the landscape where vegetation had managed to take hold. Only the Dormanscz Range looked so stark, ominous, and yet beautiful.

Sir Kemry nodded at Bug. "You lead, friend."

The ropma stood with his feet planted on the hard black rock of a mountain in the Dormanscz Range. "You no friend. Bug go home. Bug go home alone."

Sir Kemry used a low, calm voice, hoping to persuade the reluctant ropma. "Just take us close to where the becks are keeping the dragons."

Kale appreciated her father's tactics. It would do no good to bully the creature. She could imagine Bardon's father blustering and scaring poor Bug. "You point the way, and we will go into the valley without you. You can go home alone."

With great sadness, the ropma shook his head.

Kale placed a hand on his shoulder. "You are very brave, Bug. You want to protect your family."

He nodded.

Kale continued. "You go through gateways. I don't know of any other ropma who would be so brave."

Bug's chin came up a bit, and he puffed out his chest. "Bug and Rock and Bee and Frog all go through gateways. Many ropmas can't. Bug and Rock and Bee and Frog are brave."

Sir Kemry stepped closer. "Bug, you are special. When Wulder gives anyone something special, like being brave, Wulder wants them to do special things."

Kale gasped at the sudden change in Bug's expression. Great sorrow pinched his features and tears ran down his cheeks.

"Wulder no like ropmas. He hate ropmas."

"That isn't true," Kale protested. "Who told you that?"

"No-good woman. She say Wulder make seven high races. Wulder no make ropmas. Ropmas bad. Wulder hate bad."

The minor dragons, who were foraging, stopped their pursuit of treats and trilled their displeasure. Pat stamped his feet and didn't even pounce upon the grasshopper he stirred up. Metta and Dibl flew to perch on Bug's shoulders.

"Humph," said Kale's father. "This no-good woman's information is distorted. Pretender did not make ropmas from nothing. He cruelly altered an existing race. So you are kin to a high race. All things come from Wulder's hand, and all things are under His authority."

Bug turned a dazed look at Kale. She tried to think what would be the best thing to say to reassure the beast.

She whispered the words close to his ear. "Wulder does not hate you."

Kale watched the confused emotions on the ropma's face and listened in on his jumbled thinking. A point came at which this simple mind could no longer dwell on his twisted thoughts. He gave up, relaxed, and smiled at his two o'rant companions.

"Fine. I go home now."

"Wait." Kemry kept a hand around Bug's arm. "I have one more question."

The ropma sighed heavily and looked down at his toes.

"It's just this, Bug. I'm curious as to how you pulled off that clever trick of disappearing."

Again the beast's face relaxed into a smile, and his chest expanded. "A box. A little box." He stuck his pawlike hand into one of his carters and pulled out a hinged, wooden box carved with intricate symbols. He held up the prize for them to inspect, but when Sir Kemry reached for it, Bug snatched it back.

"I'm sorry, Bug," he said. "I only want to see it better. I won't touch this time."

Bug held out his hand and uncurled his fingers so the honey-colored wood gleamed in the sunlight that hit his palm.

"Pretty," said Bug.

"Very," agreed Kale. "Where did you get it?"

"Stox give it to becks. Beck give one to Bug, Rock, Bee, Frog. Go through sticky gateway. Get box."

"I understand," said Kale with a smile of approval. "If a ropma is brave enough to go through the gateway, he gets a box as a reward."

"Bee is she."

Kale nodded. "If a ropma is brave enough to go through the gateway, he or *she* gets a box."

Bug's head bobbled in enthusiastic agreement.

Sir Kemry cleared his throat. "I've never seen such a fine box, Bug. What does it do?"

"Bug hide in box."

Both Kale and her father gazed at the box in Bug's dirty palm, then looked at each other.

I don't know, admitted Kale. *Do you?*

"I wasn't lying. I have never seen such a device. I do know what I detected when I first found our new friend, but I do not understand how it works."

We can't take it from him.

"No, that wouldn't be right. Not even to have Cam and Librettowit examine the mechanism."

Isn't it just like Crim Cropper and Burner Stox to overdecorate the exterior with meaningless runes? Kale tilted her head to one side. *Still, I'd like to see it work.*

"Me, too." Her father smiled at the ropma.

Now, don't take advantage of him, Father.

"Me?" He arched an eyebrow in her direction then turned his attention solely on the beast.

"Bug," said Sir Kemry, "will you show us how you get in the box?"

His head dipped. "I open box."

With one bulky, hairy finger, the ropma undid the latch and separated the top from the bottom. When the box lay open in one hand, he placed his smallest finger from his other hand inside. One moment, the ropma stood beside Kale and her father. The next, only his rather earthy smell remained.

"Amazing," said Kale. "What natural law do you suppose it works upon?"

"Zoic displacement?"

"Very likely, or light refraction?"

"Another possibility." Sir Kemry put his hands on his hips, stretched his neck first one way and then the other. "I'm tired of this inactivity. Ever since that stint as a statue, I stiffen far too easily. We'll turn the problem of Bug's box over to the thinkers. For now, let's set our minds on finding this valley of dragons."

"Right." Kale surveyed the area. "Bug?" She used her talent as well as her eyes to examine the area a second time. The minor dragons chittered in the trees. Dibl rolled across a broad branch, giggling. "Father, if I'm not mistaken, our ropma guide has skipped out on us."

"I was just coming to that same conclusion." Sir Kemry reached toward the sky and extended one arm and then another in a generous stretch. "Daughter, it is time we enter into an agreement for the benefit of both of us." He bent in half and bounced with his fingertips brushing the tips of his boots.

Kale threw her father a skeptical glance. Was this sudden activity to distract her? She didn't know. His thoughts were shielded. "What is this agreement?"

"I shall not tell your husband, and you shall not tell my wife."

She wrinkled her brow. "Tell them what?"

"That you and I were outwitted by a ropma."

Kale grinned. "That would be shameful."

"Girl, we would never live it down."

☞ 20 ☜

BOTHERATION!

A wisp of cloud obstructed Bardon's view of the ground for a moment. Squares of fertile land exhibited the colors of various crops. Farmhouses sat at uneven intervals. Bardon knew he and his comrades had flown many miles, and Yent, who rode behind him, said that he planned for them to land at a place not much farther.

Bardon glanced over at the riders on Merlander's back. Lyll Allerion leaned toward Dar and talked. Bardon couldn't hear the conversation, but he surmised the communication was chatter. He did not do well with social banter. Dar, however, would enjoy the interchange. The kimen never said a word.

We're better off, just the two of us, Bardon told Greer, his riding dragon and comrade for a half-dozen years.

Bardon listened to his companion grumble. The vibration of the dragon's displeasure jostled the rider's legs where they rested against the purple scales on his sides. *What's that? You'd rather have Dar and Lady Lyll in your saddle? I shouldn't ask, but why?*

Bardon squeezed his knees tighter in the hooks of the saddle. *I do know amusing stories. I just don't think that this is the time to be prattling on about the peculiarities of life. We are on a mission.*

He absorbed Greer's retort, feeling the chagrin of the dragon as well as hearing dragon thoughts in his mind.

Yes, I wish Kale were along too, and I know she is a better conversationalist than I am. On the other hand, I am relieved she's gathering eggs rather than fighting quiss.

"Heads up!" he shouted and pointed east, attracting the attention of Merlander's riders. "I see a blue line at the horizon. It must be the waters of Eden Bay."

In twenty minutes they landed on a promontory over the water. They dismounted and walked to the edge. Below, the surf pounded against the cliff and scattered fallen rocks into the inlet. Beyond the breakers, where the sea should have swelled in gentle waves, the water teemed with ugly, pinkish, fleshy bulbs.

The men stood with their fists planted against their hips. Lady Allerion folded her hands tightly in front of her.

"It's an impressive sight," said Sir Dar, raising his voice to be heard.

"Terrifying," shouted Lyll.

Bardon folded his arms across his chest. "I've been thinking."

The others gave him their attention, gathering nearer in order to hear over the ocean's roar.

"When a quiss dies, his body deteriorates rapidly, giving off a toxin. If we pour salt on them in the ocean, the water will be polluted. In past invasions, countrymen piled mounds of dirt on the quiss carcasses wherever they died."

"I see what you're getting at," said the kimen. His voice carried without his straining to be heard. "Even if we slay every last one of these invaders, their bodies will contaminate our land."

Bardon nodded. "You say this horde outnumbers the past figures by ten to one. The poison will be too much for the dirt to absorb and neutralize."

A sea bird flew over them, gray and white against the blue sky. His stark cry sounded lonely as it faded in the wind. He circled once, then winged along the cliff toward scrubby bushes clinging to the rocky soil.

Sir Dar turned to Lady Allerion. "Are these animals intelligent?"

She shook her head. "I have not detected a reasoning thought among them."

"A trap, then, for the quiss," said Sir Dar. "Suppose we dug a ditch along the shoreline, lined it with salt, and as they cross the trench, we shower them with more salt. They die before they realize their invasion. We cover them with dirt as has been done in the past. And…"

"And?" asked the kimen.

"And we hope that the one strip of barren land is all that we have to remember them by."

Lyll twisted her face in a distasteful grimace. "I should like to consult other wizards first."

Yent hopped and waved a hand over the sea. The light of his clothing flickered. "We've very little time."

"Are there gateways nearby?" asked Bardon.

"Not many were built in Trese," answered Yent.

Lady Allerion put her hands over her ears and turned her back on the ocean. "Let's get away from this roar. I can't think."

Sir Dar looked to Yent for a suggestion.

"There's a granny emerlindian living a mile or two inland," he said. "I think I can find his front door."

They walked the distance. Yent wasn't sure he could spot the granny's home from the air. When they passed a copse that smelled of cinnamon and cloves, he gave a whoop. Before Yent raised his fist to knock on the camouflaged wooden door, they heard a yelp from within.

"Go away," a masculine voice pleaded. "I tell you, leave me alone. Go! Go!" A scream followed.

Bardon drew his sword and yanked the door open. He plunged inside. Sir Dar rushed in behind him, wielding a knife in each hand.

Lightrocks illuminated the down-sloping corridor dug out of the earth. Bardon and Dar charged through the tunnel toward the sounds of distress. They entered a chamber well heated by a roaring fire, dim in comparison to the entryway, with walls draped in live roots, and occupied by one dark emerlindian.

He wore yellow robes with blue trim. He'd chopped his dark brown hair off in short and uneven yanks. He was one of the tall emerlindians, standing almost six feet. But he stooped, either from an ailment of old age or from living underground where the ceilings hung too low.

The granny twisted his hands together and complained, "Didn't you hear me? I said go away. I don't like company. Company brings bother. I hate bother. Would you like a cup of tea?"

Sir Dar slipped his knives back in their hiding places and bowed to the old man. "I beg your forgiveness for me and my friend. We thought someone was in here threatening you."

The emerlindian sat down in a tattered but comfortable-looking chair upholstered in a red and blue flowered cloth. "There is now," he said. "Before, there was someone at my door, threatening to come in. Now they're in. I don't suppose you're alone. You probably have a half-dozen others with you. Worse! You probably have a half-dozen children with you."

"No," said Bardon, his sword safely back in its sheath. "No children. But we are accompanied by Lady Lyll Allerion and Yent, the kimen."

"Yent! I know Yent. He came to visit me once before. I thought he understood I don't like company. Where is that scalawag?"

"Here, sir." He stepped into the room, removed his hat, and made a deep bow. "May I present Lady Lyll Allerion?"

"What's the use of asking me? You've done it already. What are you doing here? I told you not to darken my door for at least half a century."

"It's been that and more," said the kimen. "There's a quiss invasion imminent, and we needed a place to plan."

"Plan?" barked the old man. "What is there to plan? You hide in your hole and wait until they are gone. I've done it for years, centuries, maybe longer." He bestowed a rather frightening grin on Lady Lyll. "Please, m'lady, have a seat. It isn't often I have such a gracious personage as yourself visiting." He gestured to the only other chair in the room, a wooden straight-back that wobbled when Lady Lyll sat down.

"Why are you traveling with this collection of vagabonds?" continued the granny. "They say there is an invasion of quiss. I'd never have noticed, because the quiss are polite enough to stay above ground. Unlike some people who don't knock and come in, and I have to give them tea because it's polite. Would you like some tea, Lady?"

"Yes, that would be nice."

The old man harrumphed and stared at his fire.

"But let me make it," said Lyll, getting to her feet. "We don't want to be any bother."

"Bother! I told you," he said to Sir Dar, "company is always a bother." He pointed to the kitchen area. "There's what you need, and if you'd mix up something sweet like cake or daggarts or pudding or something, that would be nice as well. I do like to put tasties before my visitors when they come."

"I'll help," said Sir Dar. "I enjoy cooking. But first, would you honor us with your name?"

The old emerlindian screwed up his face as he thought.

"No," he finally spat out the word. "No, I won't, and here's why. I don't remember it." He glared at Yent. "Do you remember? You were here just the other day. What's my name?"

"At the time you said your name was Granny Toe. You explained that you had 'the aches' in your big toe, and it helped you to remember your name."

"Granny Toe?" He scratched his head. "That doesn't sound right. My toes have been fine, without pains of any kind, for decades." He jerked and lifted one foot off the floor. "Ouch! A bother! That's what you are. Botheration to bothers who bother me. You reminded me, and now my toe hurts. Ow! Ow! Ow!"

Lady Lyll came to pat Granny Toe on the shoulder. "There, there. It's a good thing we're here. I'll brew up a tea that will relieve the pain."

He looked at her askance. "Do I stick my foot in it or drink it?"

"Drink it," she assured him.

"That's good, 'cause I don't hold with doing strange things with my food. Mashed fruit stuffed in your ear does not cure an earache. I can tell you that one from experience."

"Oh my! I shouldn't think it would," agreed Lady Lyll.

"Smashed and squashed and mangled fruit in your ear is what comes of having visitors." He drummed his fingers on his knees. "Are you going to fix that tea? I offer you a treat, as well, and dinner to boot, and a place to stay out of the cold and wind. Also, sanctuary should the quiss arise. I'm a generous host from all the practice I've had over the years."

Sir Dar called from the kitchen. "Would you have any salt?"

"No, I put that in front of the door. Do you say you cook with it? What a novel idea! I use it to discourage visitors. You stepped right over it coming in."

Yent looked Granny Toe in the eye. "You use the salt to kill the quiss?"

"Of course! Everyone knows they bubble up and crawl away to die when they come across salt."

Yent took in a deep breath and let it out slowly. "How long have you been doing this?"

"It was one of my chores as a lad."

"You never thought to mention it."

"Why would I? Common knowledge. Same as you put only one sock on each foot. Why would I be telling people that? Everyone knows."

Dar interrupted. "Where do you keep your sugar, Granny Toe?"

"What? You didn't bring some with you? See? Botheration."

He steepled his fingers and frowned so that every wrinkle on his face deepened. He squinted as if reading something on the opposite wall. Bardon followed his gaze and saw a picture of two young emerlindians in wedding attire. He picked the picture off its hook and brought it to the old man.

The granny's hand shook as he held it. "My bride," he said. "She was Nell and I was Mel. Granny Toe, indeed. Why would a lovely young thing like her marry someone named Toe? She wouldn't, of course. Had good taste, she did. She picked me. And she would have wanted me to help you, so I will."

"Thank you, sir," said Bardon, though he couldn't remember asking for more than a place to rest and plan.

"It'll be a bother, though," said Granny Mel. "Mark my words, a bother."

⊷ 21 ⊶

A Tavern in the Town

Sir Kemry picked up the ropma's trail quickly with the help of Pat, who spent more time on the ground, where there was plenty to eat, than in the air. They tracked the beast down the mountainside and through a canyon, then up a ridge. Bug traveled at great speed.

Sir Kemry shielded his eyes from the glare of the sun and scanned the harsh mountains. "I doubt that we will catch up to him before he makes it home."

"Then we shall meet Mrs. Bug and the little bas." Kale grinned at the prospect.

"I'd suggest we stop and eat, but look over to the east. That looks like an unpleasant storm."

Kale followed his line of sight and saw black, brooding clouds billowing above the profile of the next range.

She pointed to the base of a cliff. "That looks to be a town. Should we seek shelter?"

"Shelter and information, I think." Sir Kemry tapped his walking staff on the ground. "Let's make haste. I prefer not to sleep this night in the open."

"I could send Pat and Filia to follow Bug and then join us in the settlement."

"Good idea. Tell them not to expose themselves to the storm, though."

Kale sighed but made no retort. "Yes, of course."

She sent the two minor dragons on to catch up to Bug and keep an eye on him. They knew not to take chances and how to find her when their mission was completed. Pat's and Filia's personalities wrapped tightly around practicality. The little dragons flew up the mountain path while Kale and the others turned downward. Sir Kemry removed his cloak and pulled out a thin sweater that he pulled over his head.

"Your mother knitted this."

"Then it must be warmer than it looks."

He smiled. "Toasty, like sitting at home by the hearth." He swung the cloak around his shoulders and fastened it from the neck to midway down his chest, then raised the hood.

The wind picked up before they reached the floor of the ravine, buffeting them from all sides. The minor dragons took refuge within Kale's cape. But once the travelers entered the narrow chasm between steep rock walls, the gusts only came from behind and hurried Kale and Sir Kemry on their way.

The rift opened out on a flat mountain valley. They stayed close to the cliffs at the edge, avoiding most of the wind. The clouds obstructed the sun, and thunder rumbled. The lightning illuminated the clouds from behind, but so far had not touched the earth with its powerful, pointed fingers. When the rain began, the torrent fell as if a giant hand had tipped a bucket over their heads.

Sir Kemry's encouragement entered Kale's mind. *Keep the rock wall to your right shoulder, and we will run into the town. Can't miss it. We'll be all right.*

Kale blocked the thought that would have proclaimed her unafraid and capable of finding shelter. But the tone of her father's voice penetrated her prickly pride. He cared for her comfort. Bardon often smothered her a bit with concern. This demonstration of affection should soothe her, not irritate.

She addressed Wulder but kept her thoughts from the man who led the way. *I suppose if I accepted the fact that my father loves me, I would be less defensive. Right? If I took his care as a blessing, instead of a hindrance, I could tolerate his coddling. The man is clumsy in his efforts to be a father to me, but I suppose I am just as clumsy at being a daughter. This isn't an easy relationship You've given me, Wulder. He's been gone most of my life, and all my training has been at someone else's hands. But I suppose I will learn a lot during this quest and be better for it. Sometimes it appears to me that reading a tome and taking a written test would be a lot less painful way to learn life lessons.*

She trudged on for a few minutes, struggling with a principle that she couldn't quite recall. A clap of thunder shook the ground under her feet just as she remembered the wording. "A word read, a word spoken, a word acted upon, finally learned."

"What did you say?" shouted her father.

"How much farther do you think it is?"

"I've just seen the light in the window of the first house. Shall we go on to the tavern or try to find shelter in a private home?"

"The tavern."

"My choice as well."

The uneven ground next to the cliff gave way to the smoothed stone of a street. Houses could be seen only by the square lights of their windows and looming shadows. Small homes gave way to bigger residences. Shortly thereafter, the buildings squared off and looked more like businesses, closed now, after dark and during the squall.

Kale used her talent to survey the street ahead of them. No one roamed the market square. No one lurked in the shadows. One building, far ahead, held people, noisy and full of fun. This would be the local tavern. She started to point it out to her father but realized he already knew where to go. She moved closer to his back, allowing his tall form to block the wind-blown rain. Her cape kept her warm and dry, but the force of the storm made her tired.

They heard the music and laughter when they stepped up on a covered boardwalk. The last building on the block lit the street in front of it with a golden glow from huge windows.

"It looks welcoming," said Sir Kemry. "I hope the crowd is not too rough."

"I spent my youth in a tavern, Father."

"A remarkably inappropriate place to raise a child."

"I didn't have much choice."

Sir Kemry stopped abruptly, so that Kale almost ran into him. "I regret that I was not there for you, my child. But there are times when parents must make the best decision they can and then rely on Wulder to do the rest. You cannot say that He abandoned you as well."

"No sir." She paused, looked down at her feet, and then back at her father. "I've come to believe you and Mother did not abandon me either. At first I knew it by what you told me. But now I know it in my heart, not by facts."

He placed a heavy hand on her shoulder and gave her a little shake. His face looked tight in the glow of a lamp mounted beside a merchant's door. He pulled her to his chest and embraced her. The hug nearly squeezed all the air out of her lungs.

Releasing her, he turned toward the tavern. "Let's find out if this innkeeper has a fire that is warm and a bowl of stew that is tasty."

He strode with confidence through the massive door. Kale followed with her heart filled with joy. A woman bustled forward.

"You've arrived late and been soaked for your trouble." She raised her voice to be heard over the small band playing. "Hang your wet things on that wall where there's pegs aplenty. You can put your boots by the fire to dry as long as you take away what you leave there and no one else's. I'll bring you hot cider and a bowl of Botzy's Best Beef Stew and bread hot from the oven. I be Botzy."

Kale's father bowed. "Thank you, Botzy. We would like a room for the night."

The old marione scowled and squinted at Kale. "She looks young to be your wife. I have two rooms I'll be giving ye."

"She's my daughter. And I'd prefer one room so I know she is safe."

"This is a respectable establishment, and the locks are strong. You'll have two rooms or none at all."

"Very well, and what is the price of these rooms?"

"Twelve ordends for each room."

"That's highway robbery."

The marione matron's brown eyes twinkled. "There isn't a highway anywhere near the town of Black Jetty."

"This is Black Jetty?"

She nodded.

"Jetty is a peculiar name for a town not anywhere near water."

"They say that an eon ago there was a lake in this valley, but one of the volcanoes erupted, the ground shifted, and the lake disappeared."

Sir Kemry merely pursed his lips and looked at the woman.

She laughed. "You'll be taking the rooms, then. The meal and fine music go along with the lodging."

"A bargain, indeed," said Sir Kemry and peeled off his wet cloak to hang on a peg.

Kale did the same and then followed him to the fire, where they lined their boots up with a dozen other pairs. In thick socks, they wove their way between many filled tables to an empty one across the room from the door, too far away from the fire, but not far enough away from the loud music. If constant mindspeaking didn't zap her energy, she would have foregone using her vocal cords.

"Brrr!" Kale shivered. "I may go back and get my cape. It'll be dry in a trice and keep me warm." She started to get up, but a splash of color on one of the walls caught her attention. "Look!"

Sir Kemry glanced at the mural. "As art, it doesn't seem to be well executed."

"I've seen murals like this in taverns twice before."

He shrugged.

"I've been sent on two quests. This will be the third. Before the first two really got started, I saw paintings on the wall that looked like the same artist did them." She pointed again to the other side of the room. "During the quest, something would happen that mirrored the artist's image."

Kale got out of her seat and went to examine the picture. Too much of it was in shadows, so she took a lantern down from where it hung on a post and moved closer.

The musicians played an old ballad of tragedy and lost love. The baritone had a good voice, and shivers ran up Kale's back as he sang of the wind carrying away the dreams of two lovers. The haunting melody made her think of Bardon, and she purposely turned her attention to the wall and the mural.

Come see, she called to her father and summoned him with a gesture.

When he was beside her, she pointed to two figures sitting on a log. "That's you and me."

"What do you mean? That's a male and female o'rant, but why do you say it's us?"

"It is. I'm sure. The other murals I saw reflected an exact scene in a quest that came to pass. There's a gentleman, maybe Paladin. Over here, next to the fire, are two meech dragons and a doneel."

"Why Paladin?"

"He's well dressed and has that air about him."

"Even in this crude drawing?"

"Yes!"

Sir Kemry leaned forward and peered at the figure in question, then straightened. "Paladin is too sick to be traipsing about the countryside."

Kale put her hand on her father's sleeve. "He is now, but he could get better."

Sir Kemry frowned down at her and then looked back at the picture. "Why meech dragons?"

"Their height."

"Could be urohms."

"Too short compared to the gentleman."

"Short urohms or a tall gentleman."

"No, Father." She pointed to a patch of colors she had first thought was a blooming bush. "Look. Minor dragons. Lots of colorful dragons."

He squinted at the wall. "Those flowers?"

"No, I think they're dragons. The murals before have been indistinct too."

"Humph! Sounds like coincidence to me."

"You'll see."

"Well, just what is in this drawing that might 'come to pass'?"

"Let's see. A camp in a forest. You, me, Paladin, probably Gilda and Regidor, the little dragons and…"

"And?"

"Does that look like a grave to you?" She pointed to a shadowy spot beneath a bentleaf tree.

"Yes, it does."

Kale swallowed the lump in her throat. Who was not in the mural? Bardon, her mother, Leetu Bends, so many others. It could be any one of them, or the grave might hold a stranger. She glanced over at the figures she thought she could identify. The forms were indistinct, ambiguous, hazy. "Well, Father, it's probably a coincidence like you said."

Sir Kemry nodded. "Most probably a coincidence."

22

JUST ONE DANCE

Kale retrieved her moonbeam cape and returned to sit with her father. Botzy brought two tall tankards of hot, spiced apple cider.

"Do you have any poor man's pudding?" asked Kale.

"I could find some, I suppose." The matron cocked her head. "Do you want it before your stew?"

"With, please." Kale smiled and hoped her next revelation would not get them booted from the cheery, crowded room. "I've minor dragons with me, and there's nothing they like better than poor man's pudding."

Both eyebrows on the woman's square face rose an inch.

"Dragons, you say?"

"Minor dragons." Kale opened the front of her cape. Ardeo, Dibl, Metta, and Gymn crawled out, stretched, and moved to their favorite perches on their Dragon Keeper.

Botzy gasped with her eyes wide and her lips in a perfect O. She closed her mouth with a snap. "I'll be getting your dinner—stew and puddin'."

Her skirt twirled in the speed of her turn. She darted away. Even over the lively tune played by the band, Kale heard a strident, "Doxden!" as Botzy stepped through the open kitchen door.

"Perhaps Doxden is the innkeeper and the owner of the establishment," said Sir Kemry.

"Are we in trouble?"

"I think not. I detected no ill intent from our hostess."

"I'm blocking so much of the chatter from the minds of all these people, I missed her reaction. Other than what I could see, of course."

"This is a varied populace, is it not?" Sir Kemry studied the crowd. "I see at least two of each of the high races. I wonder what's the attraction of this out-of-the-way town." He paused for a minute or two and looked as if he was listening.

Kale kept quiet, content to rub the scales of the little dragons and exchange pleasantries with her friends.

"Trade routes," her father said. "This is the crossroads of three main trade routes. Three-quarters of these people are travelers, and the remainder are townsfolk who love to hear of their journeys. This place is a gold mine of information."

Her father's face took on a pleasant expression, and she knew he was unabashedly eavesdropping on one conversation after another. Kale had been taught that listening in on others' thoughts was rude. She still found deciding when it was acceptable and when it was offensive to be ambiguous territory. Her father didn't seem to have any such problem. He bent his ear and stretched his mindspeaking ability to satisfy his curiosity.

Their food arrived, and Sir Kemry ate without a word to his daughter. Kale's scruples strangled her pleasure. She wouldn't probe her father's mind nor listen to the most easily heard conversations around her. She concentrated on the music, the delicious, steaming stew, and the artless interchanges with her dragons. She noticed the look other patrons of the tavern cast her way. Obviously, minor dragons were not common hereabouts.

Dibl finished off his portion and flew to perch in Kale's hair. Metta came to sit on her shoulder and sing. The purple dragon enjoyed the entertainment of the evening.

At one end of the large room, several people played instruments and sang lively songs. Sometimes, the tunes escalated into noise rather than music, depending upon how many of the customers joined in the singing.

Metta, of course, knew all the words. She sang in trills, but Kale heard the lyrics Metta sang in her head.

When the current song came to a rousing end, Botzy yelled to the leader of the small band, a man playing a stringed instrument that lay in his lap.

"Colly, there's a singing dragon here tonight. I've heard more about dragons than seen 'em. Ask the young woman to let her friend entertain us."

"A singing dragon, you say?" The burly marione hollered back. "Have ye been drinking something stronger than your cider, Botzy?"

"Nay, look beyond your own nose and see what's before ye."

Botzy bustled over to the table with a lantern and plopped it in the middle of the empty dishes. "Here they be. Four dragons with a father and daughter traveling through Black Jetty."

The minor dragons fluttered their wings, pleased with the attention.

"Singers?" asked Colly.

"Showing what you don't know," said Botzy. "The purple one's the singer. The others do…" Botzy stalled over a lack of information. "Well, they do other things, of course."

Laughter rippled through the room. A woman shouted, "Maybe one of 'em is a dancer."

Sir Kemry stood. "We have derived much pleasure from the jolly company we've shared tonight, and we'd be glad to entertain you."

He extended a hand to Kale. Equal measures of fear and anger flowed through her veins, with a dash of embarrassment spicing the mix.

What are you doing? she demanded.

"We're going to dance."

Dance? Kale looked around the room to see if anyone had heard the thought she had shouted at her father.

"Of course no one heard." Sir Kemry's pleasant, calm voice in her mind did nothing to slow the rapid beat of her heart. *"Come on, Kale."* He held

his hand out to her. *"And try to make your face look like this is a delightful experience."*

Kale stood and plastered a smile on her face she was sure wouldn't fool a drunken porcupine.

Her father led her across the room to where the band waited for them. Metta flew to perch on his shoulder.

You can't be in favor of this scheme. Kale fussed at the dragon while trying to keep her eyes from straying to the door. Her heart wanted her feet to bolt. However, escape into the storm didn't seem to be a good plan.

Sir Kemry addressed the gathering. "If you would enlarge this dance floor. Double it if you can." Men dragged chairs and tables away from the open area. "Yes, that's good. Now, Metta, let's introduce these good players to a rollicking Meerzanian folk tune." He eyed the fiddler. "May I borrow your instrument for a minute?"

Father, I don't know how to do any but the most simple folk dances.

"You can do this, dear. Be confident."

I can't do this, Father. Be reasonable.

Sir Kemry addressed the musicians. "Have you worked with a singing dragon before? No?" He responded to the negative shakes of their heads. "You're in for a treat. I'll play the tune for you once, but by the aid of this marvelous little beast, you will never forget this song as long as you live."

Kale watched her father tuck the fiddle under his chin and pull the bow across the strings. A burst of energetic music filled the room. She knew enough about melodic form to know the tune had a one-two-three rhythm and that the refrain had an emphatic beat. Her old friend Fenworth would have called the song a toe-tapper.

In her mind, she saw two dancers stamping, twirling, and kicking their heels in fancy, complicated steps.

That's you and Mother.

"Right."

I can't do that.

"Watch closely, Kale. You do these movements when you go through your fighting forms."

Kale concentrated on the vision she caught from her father as he played the music. *Yes, I can see the similarities, but forms are certainly not that fast.*

At the sound of her father's laughter, she fought the urge to march out of the room and leave him to his folly. The sprightly music drove her irritation to the back of her mind. The wild and wonderful dance her parents performed in her father's memory fascinated her.

The music rose to a resounding conclusion, and Kale found her breath coming in short gasps as if she had been doing the steps with her father instead of watching a mental image.

Sir Kemry handed the fiddle back to its owner and turned to his daughter. With a genial smile on his face, he bowed before her with all the courtly elegance of a knight.

He is a knight. What am I thinking? Of course, he looks dashing, even in travel clothes. She had kept her thoughts to herself, but she had an inspiration and consulted her father.

Should I change? Shall I twirl myself into a fancy dress?

"I think the locals might be overwhelmed. They don't know you're a wizard, and wizards are as uncommon in this part of the world as our minor dragon friends."

Disappointment dampened the urge to try this dance with Sir Kemry.

"Be a good sport, Kale. Dance with your father."

She looked into his eyes and saw a sparkle of fun she could not resist. She placed her hand in his. They both turned to the musicians and nodded their heads. The fiddler put the bow to his instrument. The first note exploded into the room, and Sir Kemry swept his girl into a whirlwind series of twists and turns. Kale felt as though her feet barely touched the floor. She realized her father had subtly changed the heavy socks each had been wearing for dancing slippers of a dark fabric with slick soles. He hadn't let her dazzle the crowd, but he had provided for her comfort and given her an advantage she needed to perform well. She threw back her head and laughed. Even distracted by the comfortable feel of a perfect shoe, she didn't miss a step.

She danced with her father and matched his movement as he spun her away, then pulled her back to his side. The ease with which she kept pace reminded her of the way she could fight beside Bardon, knowing before he moved where he wanted her to be and what would be expected of her next.

The fights could be exhilarating, and this dance with her father certainly had her blood pumping. But in this three-beat, energetic romp, she felt joy as well as the spine-tingling thrill of staying alive and unhurt. They came to a place in the dance where her father lifted her into the air and spun her in a circle before touching her feet back to the floor. At that moment, she felt as though she had come out of his heart, was a part of the strength in his arms, and would be safe as long as she could see his rugged face.

The spectators stamped their feet and clapped the rhythm. Three of the minor dragons circled and swooped in the air around them. Metta sang in her peculiar vocalization that sounded almost like another wind instrument.

The music stopped. Kale and her father landed on the last note, facing each other at arm's-length with their hands entwined. The room erupted in clapping and stamping as the crowd hooted and whistled their praise.

Kale stared into her father's eyes. They both panted from the exertion. They both grinned with undiluted delight.

Sir Kemry let go of one of her hands and spun them to face their audience. He bowed, and she curtsied. The minor dragons came to roost on their shoulders. Kale and her father dipped once more to acknowledge the applause. The dragons fluttered above them, coming to rest on their shoulders when they again stood upright.

Sir Kemry pulled his daughter closer and tucked her arm through his. He nodded to the crowd as he escorted her to their table.

Botzy brought them two tall glasses of fruity punch, cold and tasty. Kale sipped and then beamed at their hostess.

"What are ye?" the matron asked. "Some kind of minstrels? Stage performers? Do you do an act at one of those fancy places in the big cities? What do they call them? Auditoriums?"

"No, no," said Sir Kemry with a chuckle. "We're emissaries for Paladin, and we seek information. We represent good, and we wish to vanquish evil. Right now we are following the trail of a ropma, hoping to find someone who has been using the gentle beasts as slaves and imprisoning what few dragons remain in Amara."

A dark cloud descended upon Botzy's friendly face. She leaned forward and whispered just loud enough for them to hear above the noise of the room. "Then you're in the wrong valley."

"Do you know which valley we should travel to?"

Botzy shook her head and leaned closer. "But I'll send you someone who does." She gathered up the dirty dishes and hurried out of the room. "Doxden!"

23

THE QUISS
ENCOUNTER

Bardon spent a more comfortable night in Granny Mel's underground dwelling than he expected. One passageway led to a dozen rooms, so everyone had their own accommodations. Thanks to Lyll's wizardry, the bedding smelled clean, not stuffy from disuse.

When asked why he had so many rooms, Granny Mel replied, "Nell liked company. So do I. Keeps one sharp. Keeps one from turning into an old curmudgeon. You won't be staying long, will you? 'Pot stew and company should be chucked out in seven days.'"

"I don't believe that's one of Wulder's principles," said Sir Dar.

"It isn't," agreed the old man with asperity. "It's common sense. You can add to Wulder's Tomes with words of common sense."

Bardon opened his mouth, but Sir Dar took hold of his sleeve to keep him from jumping in with a retort. With reluctance, Bardon swallowed the words of instruction he longed to bestow upon the old man.

Of course, the diplomat was right. Correcting Granny Mel should be left to someone older and with more than a passing acquaintance with the gentleman. The emerlindian's erroneous statement would not damage the man's ultimate security in his position as Wulder's servant. It would hinder his quality of service. But that was an obvious problem already, one that needed more work than the correction of one misconception.

In the morning, Lady Lyll fixed breakfast with Dar's help.

Granny Mel expressed his pleasure at having food on the table when he got up. "The both of you together are almost as good a cook as my Nell."

Lady Lyll and Sir Dar exchanged a look of amusement.

"Would you like more tea?" asked Lady Lyll.

"No," answered the old man with his head tilted to one side. "My companion is coming, and she's a mite upset. She's going to be surprised to see we've company."

He rose from his comfortable chair and shuffled up the corridor to his front door. He came back a few moments later with a blue minor dragon on his shoulder.

"Becca-ree says," he announced, "there are big ships, run by bison-becks, with nets gathering up the quiss and hauling them off to the south."

Bardon, Sir Dar, and Yent jumped to their feet, ready to go see for themselves.

"Sit down," ordered Granny Mel. "I told you I'd help you, and I will. I've been listening to you stew and plot and speculate on what to do." He shook his head at Lady Lyll and gave her a wink. "It's amazing what these young folk don't know, isn't it?"

"I don't think I'm quite as old and learned as you are, kind host," said Lyll.

Her face reddened as she spoke, and Bardon tried to discern whether the color indicated anger, embarrassment, or suppressed laughter. Knowing his mother-in-law, he guessed she was choking down a giggle.

"Sit down, I said," repeated Granny Mel. "There're some things you don't know. This deplorable ignorance shocks the socks off my feet. You don't know things everybody knows. Isn't that right, Lady?"

Lyll nodded her head but said nothing. Bardon suspected she had no idea what the man was getting at any more than he did. He cocked an eyebrow at her, and she nearly went off in a fit of laughter. She covered the snickering with a series of coughs that he didn't think sounded realistic at all. Granny Mel squinted at her.

"You drink a swallow of tea," the old man advised. "See if you can't get that tickle in your throat under control. I sure hope you folks didn't bring me the plague to die of after you're gone on your way. And you'd better be leaving today. I'd go with you, but I don't like inflicting my presence on people who don't want the company."

He looked each of the men in the eye but avoided looking at Lady Lyll, who obviously had not gotten her "tickle" under control.

"Here's what you do. You fly your big dragons down to the salt flats of Benbellugrand and scoop up as much salt as you can carry. Becca-ree says those bisonbeck sailors have the quiss trapped as if they were going to deliver them someplace. You dump the salt on them, and they'll die. It'll make a bubbly mess for a while, but there's no helping that."

"We prefer not to poison the water," said Sir Dar.

The old man shook his head again, his short black locks swinging back and forth. He glanced at Lady Lyll, and when he saw she had recovered herself, he said, "See what I mean? These young people don't know a thing. Tell them, Lady. Tell them what they don't know that makes all the difference."

Lyll's eyes widened. She searched Sir Dar's face as if she hoped to find some enlightenment and instead saw his mischievous grin. Her lips pressed into a line, and she addressed Granny Mel.

"You're so much better at explaining things, sir. You tell them."

He frowned at her. "Are you feeling all right?"

"I'm fine."

"Don't have any spots coming out or anything? Are you having trouble with your eyes? Blurring or double vision? Have you kissed a rodent lately?"

"No, no, and definitely not."

"Good! Maybe you've escaped the plague."

"Please, sir," said Yent. "Please tell us what we don't know that makes all the difference."

He scowled at his small guest. "You're that pesky kimen who keeps visiting me, right?"

"Yes, I am. And if you tell us your secret, I promise not to return for a century."

"It's the salt."

Yent sighed. "We know about the salt."

Granny Mel chuckled. "You don't know everything about the salt."

The kimen squinted at the emerlindian and answered with a measured tone. "I suppose we don't. Are you going to tell us?"

"The salt in the water is what keeps the quiss alive. That's why they don't just stay on land. After their march—happens every three years, you know, or maybe you don't, 'cause I've been surprised time and again about what you don't know—they return to the sea. The ocean water neutralizes their poison. Those beasts are so full of venom, they'd poison themselves if it weren't for the salt. So when you pour salt on them, and they absorb it too quickly, they die and…" He held a finger up to emphasize his point. "*And* their poison is done away with at the same time."

Bardon, Sir Dar, and Yent exchanged glances.

"Well," said Granny Mel, "what are you waiting for? Go exterminate those vermin before those wicked bisonbecks deliver them to someplace where they mean to do evil. Because I'll tell you one thing about bisonbecks I know you know, even being as young as you are. Bisonbecks never, never do anything without a wicked purpose behind it."

"Yes sir," said Bardon as he stood. "We're on our way."

Granny Mel's visitors rushed to the bedchambers and collected their belongings.

"I'll not go with you," called the emerlindian. "But I will send Becca-ree along."

Bardon and Yent appeared with a bag each. Granny Mel nodded at them and pointed to the blue dragon sitting on the back of his chair. "She likes adventure. And she knows where everything is—the villains, the salt, and the shortest route between the two."

"We appreciate that," said Sir Dar as he came out, a cape swirling around his shoulders and a hat with a feather perched upon his head.

Granny Mel grimaced when he looked at Dar's finery.

Then Lyll dashed into the room wearing a form-fitting outfit of leggings and underblouse plus tunic. Granny Mel's face expressed outrage at the sight of Lyll without her elegant lady's wear.

Bardon examined the shades of blue she wore and grinned. "She usually wears pink," he told the emerlindian.

"That's only for hand-to-hand combat, Bardon, my dear."

He raised his eyebrows. "I didn't know."

She smiled and tugged on sky blue gloves.

Granny Mel slapped his hands against his sides and scowled. "I hope one of you can communicate with Becca-ree."

"I can," said Yent and Lady Lyll together.

"Good, then take care of her. She's my connection to the outside world."

⊁—⚬—≺

A three-hour flight to the south brought the party to the salt flats. The flying dragons rested and hunted for food while Sir Dar, Sir Bardon, Lady Lyll, and Yent coped with the logistics of collecting the salt, packaging it, and figuring out how to transport it.

Lady Lyll had sacks in her hollow, but no shovel. Yent knew of workers who could be paid to dig salt and load the sacks. He ran the short distance and brought back three strong-backed mariones.

"They'll work for free," said Yent as he introduced the men. "They have no liking for quiss, although strangely, the invasion rarely reaches this far before the horde turns back to the sea."

"And now we know why," said one of the burly men. "But I have family up north who take a hit from those sea beasts every three years."

The second marione pushed a wheelbarrow filled with sacks and shovels. "Yent tells us the sacks you brought are not sturdy enough to hold the salt."

"We thank you, friends," said Dar, making a court bow. "You have lightened our burden and saved countless of your countrymen."

The men went to work, Bardon and Dar taking turns, as well, with the shovels. Night fell, and still they worked, while Yent and Lady Lyll prepared a meal.

"We can fill more bags," said one of the men when Sir Dar called a halt for the night.

"Yes," said Bardon, motioning toward the pile of cloth sacks, "but our dragons can't fly with any more weight than this."

Merlander and Greer came back sometime during the night. They had had to go far to find a wild flock of turrich, a huge bird that cannot fly. Greer liked the taste of them well enough, but Merlander insisted they fish in the lake nearby to satisfy her appetite.

Dar and Bardon welcomed them back. Riders and dragons slept better once the pairs were reunited. Distance from their riders always made the dragons edgy.

They ate breakfast at first light.

Sir Dar divided the tasks. "Lady Allerion, you will ride Merlander with Becca-ree guiding you. I'll be the one to clamber over the tied-on sacks and slash them to release the salt."

She nodded.

"Sir Bardon," Dar continued, "you and Yent will follow us on Greer. Yent will slash the cargo sacks."

Both men assented with a nod.

"Becca-ree has told Lady Lyll that there are six ships in two lines, three abreast. Since we don't have enough salt in this load to annihilate all six nets full of quiss, we'll have to make more than one trip.

"On this first attack, I want Greer to fly over the middle ship of the back line, and Yent will dump the salt on the quiss. Lady Lyll, Merlander, and I will see to the middle ship in the front row. Needless to say, we shall have to fly low. Bardon, do you have enough arrows and lances to cause sufficient diversion?"

"Yes. Greer's packs were loaded for battle when we left the others behind." He raised his eyebrows. "Regidor is going to be displeased that he was left out of this scuffle. Our reconnaissance mission was not supposed to involve fighting."

Sir Dar chortled. "We will have to listen to him bellyache when we get back."

Yent lifted his head from his work of tying sacks to Merlander's cargo apparatus. "Who is this Regidor?"

Lady Lyll laughed. "A swashbuckling meech dragon who likes to be in the thick of things. I agree he will be quite put out that he wasn't included in our raid."

In addition to the riding saddles and the cargo contraption, the dragons carried a lightweight netting that Dar and Yent would be able to crawl over. The net provided something for them to grip with their hands and wiggle their feet into for secure footholds. Bardon knew Regidor wouldn't mind clinging upside down to a dragon's belly while in flight, but he'd rather ride on top. He was glad the nimble kimen and doneel were on hand to do that tricky maneuver.

"Are we ready?" asked Sir Dar.

Yent said, "Aye."

Sir Bardon gave him a salute. Lady Lyll smiled as she climbed onto Merlander and hooked her knees into saddle guards.

The marione who seemed to be in charge of the others said, "We'll bag up more salt for your second run. It'll be ready when you get back."

"Thank you," said Sir Dar. "It is imperative that we strike fast. After the first hit, the sailors will be expecting us and may have a defense arranged to complicate our delivery."

Becca-ree sat on Lady Lyll's shoulder and directed them to a stretch of water just south of Eden Bay. Six large barges plowed through the water at a slow speed. The two dragons circled at a high altitude.

"At least these heavy boats won't outrun us," said Yent.

Bardon agreed and looked to Dar for a signal. The doneel crawled out of his safe seat and, with a knife between his teeth, crept to a place where he could open the bottom of the sacks. Yent followed his example. When the two small men were in position, Greer and Merlander swooped toward their perspective targets.

Bardon held on with his knees. The wet, cold sea air rushed around him as they descended. He had a dozen thin-shafted lances in a scabbard at one knee and his bow and arrows at the other.

He heard a bisonbeck shout as he raised the warning of attack. The sailors took up arms, crossbows.

That's interesting, he thought. *Sailors equipped for battle like a land militia.*

Greer's take on the situation was more pragmatic.

You can fly as fast as you want, dragon friend, Bardon answered. *I have no wish to see you poked full of holes, either. Fortunately, the nets are dragging a good distance behind the barges. These sailors will have to be very good marksmen to hit you.*

"I'm ready," Yent hollered from behind Greer's wings.

Bardon couldn't see the kimen, but he took him at his word.

Now, Greer. Dive as low as you can to give this brave little warrior a good chance at hitting his target.

He grinned at his dragon's response. *Aye, aye, Captain? Since when have you acknowledged any authority I might have over you? And where did you pick up the "aye, aye" bit?*

Greer didn't snap back a reply. He banked over the swarming mass of quiss trapped in the net. Yent sliced through the cloth, and the sacks emptied into the target. Only a small amount of white grains fell beyond the rim of the net as Greer soared upward.

"Good work!" Bardon exclaimed and glanced over to see how Merlander and her crew had fared. "Our comrades have made a direct hit as well."

Yent climbed to the top of the saddle and sat behind Bardon.

"Greer tells me," said Bardon over his shoulder, "that Merlander is relaying a message from Dar." He paused. "Dar wants us to observe the effect of our drop. We won't fly back immediately."

The quiss in the targeted traps ceased movement at once, but their bodies bubbled as the carcasses disintegrated.

"Look at that," yelled Yent. He pointed to the nets being pulled by the four other barges.

The quiss in the hammocklike trawl nets pulled by the outside boats panicked. Squeals and screeches filled the air. The frantic quiss threw their many arms over the edges of their confinement. The ropes from the nets to the barge became a bridge, and the sea beasts piled one on top of the other as they fled the water. Their appendages had not stiffened, allowing them to walk, but they dragged themselves across the ropes, over the rails of the ships, and onto the decks. The quiss slithered across the vessels with great speed and captured many of the men.

The military discipline of the sailors on the barges collapsed. Each man tried to save his own skin. Many climbed into the rigging.

Bardon turned to the kimen. "Dar is wondering if the panicked quiss will go ashore. He wants me to set you down so you can warn the people and tell them about using salt to deflect any attack. We'll go back and get the prepared bags of salt to deliver to the coastal people."

"I agree," said Yent. "The normal rhythm of the quiss invasion has been disrupted. But we're better prepared than we've ever been in the past. What will be the outcome of today's events?"

24

†HE DOҤEEL'S S†ORY

Kale leaned forward to touch her father's arm, nodding toward the back of the tavern. "Not the innkeeper or the owner. Doxden appears to be the cook."

Her father twisted in his seat to watch the man approach. Doxden couldn't be missed. The quick-stepping doneel fairly hopped across the room, his bright clothing dusted with flour and a baker's cap sitting jauntily on his head, covering one ear. Waving a hand to the men who pulled tables and chairs back into place, he climbed into an empty chair. His shoulders only reached the edge of the table, so he tucked his feet under himself to give some additional height.

He squinted one eye at Sir Kemry. "You're going to Greenbright Valley?"

"We might be," answered the knight. "Is that where the dragons are?"

"That's where the dragons are rumored to be."

"What can you tell me?"

Doxden looked around the room. "Botzy," he called, "bring me a drink."

The woman waved a hand at him and yelled, "In a minute." She went back to her conversation with a well-dressed urohm and two kimens aglow in shades of pink roses.

A few of the customers had left the room, seeking their warm and cozy beds. Others were quietly talking. The musicians stood around talking, having packed up their instruments for the night. The lateness of the hour called the villagers to leave the pleasant tavern, brave the storm, and return to the comfort of their own hearths.

Doxden jumped down from the chair. "I'll be right back. Do you want your drinks refilled?"

"No, thank you," said Sir Kemry.

"My glass is still half full," said Kale.

The doneel cook dipped his head in acknowledgment and trotted off. *What do you think? Can he help us?*

"He hasn't decided yet if he wants to. But I think if he is willing, he can tell us precisely where this valley is located."

Gathering information with disregard for a person's privacy troubled Kale's sense of ethics. Life had been simpler when Bardon directed their paths. She'd chafed against his strict adherence to principles from time to time, but she never fretted over their direction. Her husband certainly had a clear picture of right and wrong.

Fewer customers sat at the tables. One man snored while his wife continued an intense conversation with another woman. The well-dressed urohm gentleman carried on a quiet debate with the kimens. The atmosphere of the room had changed after the band shut down and the room began to clear. The people here in Black Jetty had a comfortable life and just wanted to live day to day without complications. A big complication existed in Amara when one considered the war being waged between evil forces. The citizens of Black Jetty were a part of the world whether they wanted to be or not.

Kale and her father desired to do good. The wizards' conclave ordered their quest, and Paladin backed them. But did she and her father have permission to gather information unscrupulously? What would Bardon do if he were here?

Her father watched the other people in the room. After the dance, Kale felt more allied with him, but did she really know how closely he walked within the guidelines of Wulder's principles?

She ached to know exactly what he planned. *You could get the infor-mation you want by invading his mind,* she suggested.

"And I will if he remains reluctant. But let's give him the chance to aid the cause."

That statement didn't wholly dispel her doubts. Perhaps she should be more direct.

Father?

"Yes?"

Is it wrong to pry into the minds of these good folk, taking what we want without their by-your-leave?

"Many times in life, the answer to hard questions is 'That depends.' Sometimes you have to test the waters, so to speak."

I don't understand.

"If you are ever mindful of what causes Wulder pleasure and what dis-pleases Him, then you are better able to judge whether your motives line up with His desires."

Kale said nothing. Her father's answer did not give her freedom to dive into other's thoughts, nor did it give her permission to ignore the quest she and her father had undertaken. His words did nothing to help her make a choice.

Her father sighed. *"Kale, sometimes the answer is either yes or no. You will know without a doubt."* He spread his hands in a helpless gesture. *"Even when we have clear direction, we do not always choose the correct path. It is the nature of us all."*

He rubbed a hand across his head, smoothing his graying hair. *"And then there are the times when the answer is not clear."* He held up his hand with his index finger extended. *"In those cases, your first consideration is to not harm anyone. Not physically, not mentally, not in any way."*

He put his hand back down in his lap and surveyed those around to see if any were watching. His serious voice continued to speak within Kale's mind. *"Your second consideration is to not harm yourself. You must not pollute your mind or body with even a taint of evil. Your third consideration is to achieve your goal. Achieving your goal must never be first."*

He studied her for a moment, his eyes probing hers as if to uncover her soul. She hid her thoughts. He looked away, apparently not happy with what he'd determined.

"My advice cannot be any more obvious. If you do not understand, then you shall have to gain understanding through experience."

Kale laughed.

"You find that amusing?"

Not your advice, Father, but that I have received the same admonition from another source at another time. I suppose I should heed the suggestion.

Her father only harrumphed and glanced toward the returning doneel.

"Our doneel cook is approaching, and he's decided to trust us."

The cook placed his tankard on the table, then jumped into his seat. He took a swig of his ale.

"It's this way," he said. "Many years ago I lived in Wittoom. I know what it is to have the authority of Wulder deeply ingrained in the culture. Here, we think of Wulder when it is convenient, if at all."

"It is this way in many parts of Amara," said Sir Kemry. His tone did not condemn the people of Black Jetty. "And there are parts of Amara who have forgotten Wulder altogether. They choose to follow their own pleasures."

The doneel gazed at his drink, his face solemn. "I know of those depraved places. I used to be a traveling man like most of the folks in this room. But I came upon this small town and decided to stay." He took a long draw from his cup. "We're not a bad lot. But we are not as good as we could be either."

Kale's father rested his hand on the doneel's shoulder. "There are very few of us who are as good as we could be. I don't claim that distinction."

Doxden leaned forward. "Maybe it's because I was raised in Wittoom." He glanced around the room. When his eyes came back to Sir

Kemry, he paused a moment, then nodded as if he'd made a final decision. "I seem to notice things the others don't. Things that speak of evil encroaching upon the region. You know, situated as we are, we have great good to the north of us, the urohm and kimen lands. And we have great evil south of us where Crim Cropper and Burner Stox have dominated those lands for years."

"Yes, I know."

Kale twisted her hands in her lap. Would this cook ever get to the point?

"Patience, my daughter. This is not only hard for him, it is dangerous as well."

He's stalling.

"We have time. Let him tell his story in his own way."

Kale stifled a sigh of exasperation. She didn't want to distract the man and give him an excuse to further delay the telling of his tale.

Doxden leaned back in his chair. "Dragons have always been scarce in this part of Amara. But there were rumors of egg clutches hidden away. Men went into the mountains, searching like they would search for rich ore—gold or silver or the like. But there were no stories of anyone finding the dragon eggs."

He took a drink, looked around the room once more, then leaned forward. "About two years ago, the men who went looking for the clutches no longer came back. They vanished."

Kale's hand went to the row of six small bulges at her waist. She could find eggs hidden in those mountains. Would she vanish as well? She looked at her father, and he winked at her. His head moved slightly, indicating he understood her fear, and no, she would not disappear.

Again, Doxden glanced around. This time he smiled his pleasure at those who conversed in the tavern's common room. "As you see by the company tonight, we are rarely troubled with the lower races." He frowned. "About the same time the seekers of dragon eggs started disappearing, bisonbecks and grawligs were spotted in Greenbright Valley. Then it became impossible to penetrate the passes into the valley from any direction. A haze fell over that area, so you could not view the land between the ridges."

"And the people believe…?" asked Sir Kemry.

"That a great and powerful wizard has taken over the valley, and it is not any of our business what goes on there. No one here would appreciate my giving you information. We keep away from those in the valley and pretend they don't exist. The traders found alternate routes and do not even mention Greenbright Valley, as if to do so would bring bad fortune down upon them."

"And the rumors of the dragons? There were sightings?"

"Not that I know of. Nothing substantial behind the rumors. But the whispers were persistent a year ago, and then they ceased. I don't think these tales would have stopped abruptly for a natural reason. I believe there is something behind the gossip. And I believe that something is evil."

"We wish to investigate, perhaps turn the tide of this invasion. Will you tell us where the valley is?

The doneel sighed. "Yes."

25

Unpleasant Surprises

"I'm surprised it took you so long to get here," Bardon told Regidor.

Gilda placed a hand on her hip and protested, "We haven't been wasting our time."

Regidor drew her close with an arm snuggled around her waist. "That isn't what he meant, sweet woman. And if you take note, he looks as harried as a rabbit with no hole to hide in."

Bardon's head jerked, and he grimaced at his old friend. "I do not."

"You do," said Regidor.

Gilda smiled and dipped her elegant hat with a nod of her head. "I agree. He does." She wrinkled her long nose. "And I'm afraid the news we bring you will not brighten your day."

"Great!" Bardon motioned them toward one of the tents set up on the hillside. "Come with me, and I'll see if I can commandeer some refreshments. We've been organizing a network of supplies to get salt to strategic places along the coast."

They passed a marione youth wearing huge boots and a too-tight jacket.

"Lad," said Bardon, "see if you can hijack the cook and bring him to my tent with food and tea for our friends."

"Yes sir." The boy saluted with more precision than the soldiers who had arrived from Paladin's forces.

Bardon led Regidor and Gilda into the headquarters he shared with Sir Dar.

"How long have you been here?" asked Regidor.

"A week."

"You've established quite an outpost in such a short time."

"As everyone keeps reminding me, we have no time to spare. Stox and Cropper are up to something we haven't been able to discover. And who knows when Pretender will pop up to add confusion and chaos."

"Are our countrymen finally seeing the malevolence that surrounds them?"

"To some extent. Dar's away being a diplomat, trying to make people realize that all this hardship is the result of the devious plans of Burner Stox and Crim Cropper." He motioned for his company to sit. "Lady Lyll is off saving children."

"Saving children?" asked Gilda as she arranged her beautiful gown around her and sat on a camp stool.

"In one of the seaside towns, she found a workhouse where children labored from dawn to dusk and dined on weak soup."

"Again," said Regidor, "a sign of our society's degenerate state."

Gilda patted his arm. "Not our society, Regidor. Their society."

Bardon raised an eyebrow at her, and she fluttered a fan in front of her face.

"I'm sure," she said, "when we find the hidden meech colony, we will find a much more civilized social order."

In response to Bardon's inquiring look, Regidor shrugged his shoulders. The meech dragon's voice entered his head. *"Gilda's philosophy of life is sometimes tainted by her early association with Risto. We're working on these lapses. But prejudice instilled at an early age is hard to extract."*

Regidor smiled his toothy grin at his bride and winked. "Yes, my wife longs for more of a higher culture. Since Gilda has been released from her bottle, she no longer allows me to go to rowdy dens of iniquity."

"You never!" exclaimed his wife.

Regidor grinned with the sardonic twist that always made Kale double over in laughter. Bardon wished Kale were here now. She could help him sort out this mix of signals he got from Regidor and Gilda. His wife assured him that Regidor only enjoyed looking worldly-wise, but in actuality, the meech preferred a tamer lifestyle than he pretended.

Bardon shook his head as he thought. Kale knew Regidor better than anyone, and with the bond that had formed even before the dragon hatched, she certainly should be able to discern his core code of ethics. Gilda, on the other hand, could be either as shallow as she seemed or a river running deep. Only time would tell.

"Tell him what we saw," demanded Gilda. "Explain why we took longer to get here than he expected."

Regidor leaned forward, resting his elbows on his knees and his chin on his interlocked fingers. "We saw a migration of sorts."

Gilda rolled her eyes. "We saw bands of grawligs all headed toward a central spot. Of course, we investigated."

Regidor steepled his forefingers and tapped them against his lips. "They looked very much like herds of wild deer gathering at a winter pasture."

"But, of course," interrupted Gilda, "grawligs are not herding animals."

Bardon shifted uncomfortably on his stool. "They aren't animals at all."

"Technically," said Gilda. "But I see little reason to belabor the point."

Regidor cleared his throat and sent Bardon a warning glance. "Gilda, customarily the people of Amara give the low races the benefit of the doubt until facts prove otherwise. With quiss, blimmets, and schoergs, the evidence indicates they are nonrational beings with no sense of right and wrong. Bisonbecks, grawligs, and mordakleeps have shown themselves to have intelligence and the ability to choose to obey orders."

"They also," said Gilda, "show a propensity to choose to do evil."

Regidor sat up straight and stretched. "That's true."

"And ropmas?" Bardon asked, knowing that studying the different races fascinated his meech friend.

Regidor smiled and stood up. His head almost brushed the tent's roof. "Ropmas are like big speaking dogs. They can be intensely loyal, but they can't reason out whether their actions will hinder or help in the long run. They are guided easily and have an unpredictable stubborn streak."

He crossed to the tent flap and held it open as the cook and two boys came in with trays of delicacies.

Regidor sniffed, smiled, and turned a knowing eye on Bardon. "Oh my, you are roughing it, aren't you? Is that *pâté sot grunmere* I smell?"

"If you mean that ground-up meat that Leemiz spreads on bits of bread, yes."

"I'm starved," said Gilda. She pulled off her gloves and motioned for the servants to place the teapot near her. "I'll pour."

"Thank you, Leemiz," said Bardon. "Thank you, boys."

Gilda did not acknowledge their departure, but Regidor tapped each lad on top of his head and gave them the coins he "found" there.

"Wheezers! Thank you, sir," said the older boy.

Regidor reached in his pocket and tipped the cook with a larger coin. He smiled, bowed, and followed his young workers through the tent flap.

Gilda offered a cup of tea to Bardon. "This is refreshing. We've eaten in poor country inns since we started our journey to join you." She took a bite of a daggart. "Mmm. Delicious!"

"I agree," said Lady Lyll from the entrance to the tent, "but I, for one, want to sit in a real chair, at a real table." She advanced into the small headquarters and gave Gilda a peck on the cheek and Regidor a warm hug.

Lady Lyll leaned back from the tall meech dragon and patted his leathery cheek. "In celebration of your arrival, I suggest we go into town and eat a real meal, complete with napkins and a tablecloth." She smiled at Gilda. "You'd like that, wouldn't you, dear?"

"Yes, and if there is a decent inn, I prefer to sleep in town as well."
Regidor bowed to the women. "Consider it done, sweet ladies."

Late that afternoon, Dar returned from his most recent sojourn among the people of Trese and agreed to a trip to the nearest settlement. The seaport of Grail had three taverns and four inns to choose from. Dar knew which one had the most elegant dining hall and delectable cuisine.

Bardon had to admit that even sitting in the crowded room didn't dampen his enjoyment of the dinner. He leaned back, sipped his drink of mulled cider, and listened to the others talk of fashion, modish places to visit, bazaars, and excursion trips. He longed for Kale to be with him and could imagine her animated face as she asked questions and laughed at their sillier tales.

Always, though, their stories had a tinge of regret. The places that used to give so much enjoyment now seemed to have fallen under the tawdry influence of an immoral world. They could think of no place in Amara that had remained untouched.

Gilda discreetly pointed to a table in a dark corner across the room. "That's typical of the degeneration we see everywhere. There's an emerlindian girl keeping company with a bisonbeck. I admit he dresses better than most, and his table manners are more refined, but still…"

The others followed her gaze and watched as the lithe young woman leaned toward the bulky man and whispered something in his ear. Bardon sat up and exchanged an incredulous look with Dar.

Lady Lyll spoke up. "Don't judge by appearances, Gilda. There may be more to that story than we can see on the surface."

Bardon worked to bring his expression under control. *I certainly hope Lady Lyll is right. I can't imagine a legitimate reason for Leetu Bends to be flirting with a bisonbeck.*

26

Mountain Encounter

Kale and Sir Kemry set out on foot early the next morning. They had a generous packet of food from Doxden and a map sketched on a brown piece of wrapping paper. Several miles out of town, they spotted Pat and Filia flying fast in a direct line toward them.

Sir Kemry shaded his eyes. "I may be out of practice with my dragon-keeping skills, but aren't your dragon friends rather high?"

"Yes." Kale scurried toward a rock outcropping and climbed up to see better. "Something must be wrong."

The two dragons circled, one a splotchy brown and the other a multitude of pink hues. They spiraled down to land on Kale. All the minor dragons had come to welcome the two travelers back and to exclaim over their adventures. Kale winced at the ruckus their excitement inspired. While they chattered rapidly, she stroked first Filia's side and then Pat's tummy.

"Oh, I'm so glad you made it back. I never would have sent you had I known what danger you'd be in." She turned to her father to relay what the dragons had said. "They had to dodge rocks from slingshots and—"

He held up his hand. "I am a Dragon Keeper, Kale. I understood."

"I forget. Bardon has trouble understanding when they're excited."

Her father smiled, and she felt his irritation dissipate. "At least with this bit of news, another piece of the puzzle has fallen into place. Confirmation of our suspicions. The ropmas are anxious to capture dragons to keep Burner Stox from raining her devastation upon their community.

Their instinct for self-preservation has made them slaves. Rather than die, they serve Stox."

He put out his hand in invitation, and Pat flew to roost on his finger. Sir Kemry stroked the brown dragon's stomach. "We must get into this valley of dragons. I regret that your little friends had such a harrowing experience. And I am glad they got back to us without being captured."

He paused, concern etching deep lines in his face. "Who would have believed that ropmas could be so devious? It would seem that they're more resourceful than we've given them credit for."

Kale climbed down from her vantage point. "I suspect their traps and weapons are like Bug's little box he gets into to disappear—devised by someone else and given to the ropma to use. Each of the devices Pat and Filia describe has an element of cruelty that just doesn't line up with the ropmas' nature."

"Correct, and a further indication that Burner Stox is behind this movement."

Kale moved closer to her father. "Bug and his friends have great motivation."

She frowned at the thought of the good-natured creatures being tortured or threatened by death. "This must stop, Father. It is right to turn away from our main quest to investigate the valley, isn't it?"

"Definitely, and I believe we will find many dragons to release. Our hope must be that they will join our side."

Kale could barely hear over the prattling of the dragons perched on her shoulders. She fluttered her hands at them, effectively shooing them. They chittered their disgruntlement as they fluttered to a bush.

Kale turned her attention back to her father. "Why wouldn't freed dragons be grateful and eager to serve Paladin?"

"I'm not sure what the effects of having been subjugated to Burner Stox will be."

Kale shook her head until her hair slipped from the knot at the nape of her neck. She reached to redo the bun. "What do you mean?" With quick fingers, she secured the twisted hair with two long hairpins.

"Any number of things. Their spirits could be broken. They could have bonded to their evil overseers. They may be loyal to Stox."

"No!"

"Not all dragons are good like the ones among your acquaintance."

Kale bristled. "I've known bad dragons. Well, not actually known them. We were attacked once by fire dragons. And Celisse made a very bad choice when under emotional strain. I am not naive, Father."

He smiled and cupped the side of her face with his hand. "Of course not, but it's hard for an old father to remember the baby he lost years ago has had time to grow up."

With his palm pressed to her cheek, she felt the great emptiness in his soul that told of the sorrow of not being her father for too many years. She gulped back sympathetic tears.

The minor dragons raised an outcry. Kale and her father recognized the change in tone. Both pulled their swords from their scabbards and scrutinized the area around them.

"Five bisonbecks coming up the path," Sir Kemry exclaimed and turned to face the direction the warriors would come.

Kale stood next to his shoulder, as ready as he was to face the enemy. "How did they know we're here? They are looking specifically for us."

"It would seem one patron of the tavern last night was a spy."

She twirled, attiring herself in her best fighting outfit.

Her father chuckled. "Your mother certainly has influenced you in your short acquaintance."

"Humph!" said Kale, placing her feet apart for balance and raising her invisible sword. "It just so happens that Bardon thinks I look good in a vibrant pink."

Sir Kemry cocked an eyebrow at her.

A small grin lifted the corner of her mouth. "He also says it's easier to keep track of me in a fight and not mistake me for one of the villains when I'm in this outlandish costume."

Sir Kemry tilted back his head and laughed. "That's exactly what I told Lyll many years ago." His expression sobered, and he looked around. A high rock cliff rose behind them. A drop off to one side would keep the enemy from surrounding them. "This is an easily defended spot." He tipped his chin toward the aggressors. "They have no idea we've stopped and are waiting for them. When they come around the bend, we'll be at a distinct advantage." He lowered his sword and gestured for Kale to change places with him.

"Why?" she asked while following his direction.

He pointed at the drop-off with the tip of his blade. "Don't want you falling off the mountain."

Kale rolled her eyes. "Father!"

"No time to chat. They're here."

Kale kicked the first bisonbeck in the chest. He fell backward, flailing his arms. He landed against the bisonbeck behind him and socked the soldier next to him in the face as he went down. The soldier he punched stumbled toward the edge of the chasm, colliding with his comrade who had just pulled his battle-ax from its leather strap. The battle-ax arched around the front of his body to a strike position slightly over the warrior's shoulder. Ordinarily, the centrifugal force of his action would not have unbalanced him. But when his fellow soldier slammed into his side, he toppled over the edge.

"Two down!" exclaimed Sir Kemry. "See here, girl, let me at least look like I'm fighting."

Kale aimed her next blow at the warrior whose arms still held the first man she had knocked over. She planted her heel in the middle of his face. Blood spurted from his nose as he collapsed.

The fifth man rushed around the corner and fell over the two men on the ground. The first injured man roared, tossed the sizable bisonbeck off his lap, and scrambled to his feet. Growling with his teeth gritted, he swung a fist at Sir Kemry. The knight stepped back against the stone wall. The bisonbeck swung again, and Sir Kemry ducked.

"Are you not at the top of your form?" asked Kale's father as he easily dodged another blow. "Perhaps it is because my daughter hit you." He kept up the chatter as the man continued to swing and miss. "She's not all that strong, being a small female, you know. But every once in a while, she gets in a smashing good kick. I wouldn't be embarrassed if you're feeling woozy."

The warrior said a few unsavory words under his breath and pulled a knife from inside his waistcoat. He waved it in front of Sir Kemry's face.

The knight smiled. "That's an eating utensil, isn't it?" He peeked around his adversary and dodged the blade at the same time. "Now where *is* your weapon? You had a battle-ax, didn't you? No, that was your friend. The one that went into the chasm. You had a sword, didn't you? Must have dropped it in the confusion when three of you were piled up on the ground."

Sir Kemry focused again on his opponent, although he had avoided being struck even when he wasn't looking. "It's all right," he said. "I've spotted it. Your comrade is using it against my daughter. Nasty blade, curved like that."

The bisonbeck's eyes widened, he licked his lips, and a wicked grin stretched his mouth wide. He swung about to observe the fight between Kale and the only other soldier still on his feet. The minor dragons belabored Kale's opponent. With swift thrusts and lethal swings, he clearly indicated he meant to make mincemeat out of the young woman in pink. His energetic defense against Kale and six spitting dragons gave no indication he might sometime soon grow tired of the fight. Covered with colored dragon saliva, he held one hand to an eye that stung from one of the dragon's direct hits and fought on.

Sir Kemry grinned at the back of his own opponent. He'd won the battle except for the final blow. The fighting prowess of a bisonbeck was hard to beat, but they had weaknesses that could be easily used against them. Sir Kemry raised the hilt of his sword and brought it down on the unprotected head of the man he had taunted.

"I don't like being bullied," the knight said as the man fell. "And for some odd reason, I'm just not in the mood for a fight right now."

He sat down on the nearest boulder and propped one polished boot on the back of the downed soldier. "Do hurry, Kale. We have a valley to visit."

Kale's opponent glanced toward the voice. His next look was up, but his eyes were not focused. He fell with a thud.

"Good blow, Kale. You excel in the fighting craft, my dear."

She bowed in acknowledgment of his praise, and then surveyed the mountain pass. Her father came to stand beside her, his arm draped casually over her shoulders. She panted, smiled weakly at him, but didn't speak.

"Three dead." Her father gestured to the chasm and to the man on the ground. "I believe you kicked his nose into his brain. He didn't suffer." Sir Kemry looked at the other two bisonbecks. "Two wounded." He shrugged and rubbed the back of his neck. "All of them a problem."

"Why?" asked Kale. She still sounded a bit winded.

"We don't really want them found."

Kale nodded. "We don't want the enemy alerted to our presence on their doorstep."

"Precisely. Can you do that temporary trapped-in-metal-clothing trick?"

"I suppose I could. But they might be found before the metal disintegrates and the victim awakes."

"True, and that doesn't solve the problem of the two at the bottom of the cliff." He shook his head. "We'll have to travel down to recover the bodies and hide them. That will take up far too much time."

"Necessary, though, if we are to keep our whereabouts unknown."

"I wonder who else this spy told about us. If it were only one of these men, then our troubles in that regard are over. But if he is blabbing to every one of our enemies he meets, then we can expect a great deal of interference."

"I suppose we won't know until later." Kale sighed.

Sir Kemry shrugged again and patted her on the shoulder. "I suppose not. Well, let's get busy. You go over the edge and climb down to the chasm floor."

"What?"

"I said—"

"I know what you said, Father. I'm wondering what I am supposed to do, how I am supposed to do it, and why it is me that will be doing..." She flapped one hand around. "Doing...whatever?"

Sir Kemry looked exasperated. "I haven't got it all planned out yet, Kale. I just know the plan I come up with will require one of us to be on the chasm floor."

"I'm the one descending a steep, almost vertical mountain wall."

"Yes."

"Yes? That's it? Just yes?"

Sir Kemry furrowed his brow. "Yes, I believe that's it."

27

Another Surprise

Bardon studied his mother-in-law. She knew Leetu Bends, had trained her to take her place in Creemoor, and trusted the young emerlindian to continue her work. The work had been her way of dealing with the loss of husband and daughter. Now she had her family back, but had Leetu Bends destroyed her labor of all those years?

Lady Lyll looked down at her plate. Using her fork, she pushed one large tubular pasta through the creamy sauce. She twirled it to and fro but did not pick it up.

Bardon's mother-in-law mindspoke to him. *"Keep Gilda busy while I communicate with Leetu Bends."*

Bardon cleared his throat and drew the attention of the others. "What are the chances of finding the meech colony if they don't want to be found?"

Gilda took the bait. "Once they know that two meech dragons are looking for their own, I imagine they will send out an emissary to lead us home."

"Why do you call this nameless, hidden location your home?"

Gilda shook her shoulders and lifted her chin as she sat up straighter. "I find most society a little crude. Even my dear Regidor mingles too much with the mundane."

Bardon chanced a peek at Lady Lyll. She did not look happy. Was she listening to Gilda or Leetu Bends?

Regidor gave Gilda a half smile but looked Bardon in the eye. Bardon watched his expression for a moment and determined the meech dragon had picked up on the tension between Dar, Lady Lyll, and himself.

Bardon tried focusing a thought to Regidor's mind. It would be pointless unless the meech were already eavesdropping. *Are you listening to me, my friend?*

"*I am, indeed.*"

One of our allies, Leetu Bends, is the emerlindian girl Gilda pointed out.

"*I had surmised that much.*"

Either she's in trouble, and we should help, or she is doing her job and would not appreciate our interference.

"*I'd say neither.*"

Why?

"*Do you forget that I see auras around people and can discern their general standing, whether good-hearted or a black villain?*"

Bardon's eyes widened. It had been a long time since he had seen his friend use that particular talent.

"And?" Bardon forgot and spoke aloud.

"And what?" asked Gilda.

"And," said her husband, "Leetu Bends and her friend, Latho, are companions. Friends. Nothing more sinister and nothing immoral."

Sir Dar cocked his head, his ears perked forward. "The bisonbeck isn't under Pretender or the evil wizards?"

"No." Regidor shook his head and turned to study the couple. "The lights dancing around him tell of peace, generosity, and a deep sadness."

Lady Lyll leaned forward so she could see around Gilda. "Have you ever seen the like of it before, Regidor?"

"No, never."

"Well, it doesn't matter now, does it?" Gilda arched a shoulder and smoothed her sleeve. "He's still a bisonbeck and not to be trusted."

"I've had enough of speculation." Sir Dar stood. "Excuse me."

The doneel's eyes were locked on Leetu Bends.

Bardon decided he'd better go along. "Excuse me." He followed his friend as the doneel zigzagged between the tables.

Sir Dar approached the table where Leetu and her friend sat. He swept his arm in front of him and gave a court bow. When he straightened, a pleasant smile brightened his eyes and turned his thin black lips upward in a smile that almost stretched from ear to ear across his furry face.

Leetu jumped up from the table and hugged the doneel.

"I want you to meet my friend." She turned to the bisonbeck who had awkwardly risen and stood behind her. "This is Latho."

He stretched out his hand and shook with Sir Dar. Dar's hand closed around two of the bigger man's fingers.

Latho grunted. It might have been a word, but Bardon didn't catch it. Leetu Bends looked at him and back to Dar.

Dar stepped to the side, and with an open hand, gestured to Bardon. "This is Kale Allerion's husband, Sir Bardon."

"We've met." Leetu Bends saluted Bardon with a fist tapped over her heart. "The introduction was meant for you, Latho."

Bardon returned the salute, then put his hand out to shake with the bisonbeck. For the first time, except in a fight of some kind, Bardon touched one of Pretender's chosen race of warriors. Bardon's hand almost covered the big man's palm, but his fingers didn't extend far enough to wrap around the hand.

"What brings you to Grail?" he asked Leetu Bends.

"Latho. His family lives here." She gave a quick glance around the room. "Look, let's sit down. We're attracting attention, and Latho hates it."

"Hates what?" asked Bardon.

"Don't be thick," she said, pushing Dar and Bardon toward the alcove table. "He doesn't like people staring at him. It happens all the time because he doesn't wear the uniform."

They crowded in around the little square table, Latho in the back next to the wall, Leetu Bends next to him, and Dar on the outside. Bardon sat opposite the knight and the emerlindian. The last side had no bench, and servants passed by with their trays and pitchers.

The emerlindian's hair had darkened since Bardon had seen her last. Instead of the soft honey color, her straight locks held a red undertone that caught the light of the lanterns. A light tan had tinted her skin. He couldn't see the color of her eyes in the gleam of the scattered lamps. However, Bardon suspected her sky blue eyes were darker now.

Leetu Bends fingered her spoon, turning it over and over where it lay next to her plate. "We heard about the quiss attacking some sea vessels last week and came up because one of Latho's brothers is a sailor. We couldn't get any reliable information down south. Some people even said that the boats were transporting the quiss."

"Ridiculous rumors," said Latho and shuddered.

Bardon thought it a very believable shudder. He looked across the room at his mother-in-law, and she dipped her head, just enough to relay she perceived the bisonbeck's reaction to be true and not a sham.

"Why," asked Bardon, "does Latho not follow the usual path of bison-becks? He obviously isn't a warrior."

"He's a merchant," explained Leetu Bends. "He trades goods." She ducked her head and lowered her voice. "He provides the market com-modities for Burner Stox's army."

"It's not as if I have a choice," Latho said. He shrugged his massive shoulders. "It was either develop a career that aided her cause or mysteri-ously disappear. And I don't mean that I would arrange this inexplicable vanishing act."

Sir Dar patted Leetu Bends's hand and gently removed the spoon. He laid it on the table out of her reach. "And tell us about your friendship. You know that it is odd, to say the least."

Latho studied his dirty plate. All the food had been eaten, but the remnants seemed remarkable enough to capture his full attention.

Leetu Bends chose to answer the inquiry. She lowered her voice to such a whisper that Bardon had to strain to hear her. "Latho has abandoned his oath to follow Pretender. He has vowed allegiance to Wulder."

Bardon opened his mouth to say that the emerlindian's revelation was impossible. He stopped, sealed his lips together, and looked to Sir Dar to make some remark.

"And you believe him?" asked the doneel.

Bends nodded.

"Why?" asked Bardon. He couldn't help the frown on his face or giving the quiet bisonbeck another look of examination.

"Because he transported me when I was wounded to a safe house. He paid for my keep while I got well, and…" She lowered her voice even more. Bardon leaned across the table, then realized she mindspoke the final words. *"He gives me information about the enemy troops that I pass on to Paladin's generals. He's a spy."*

28

Snakes

Kale lowered herself down the side of the cliff, holding on to a long rope her father had anchored to a boulder on the path above. The minor dragons accompanied her, making useless suggestions. They didn't really understand how an o'rant navigated the world. She grumbled as her knee scraped against the rock wall.

"*What was that, my dear?*" asked her father.

Nothing. Just remembering your last instructions.

"*Find the bodies and dispose of them.*"

You know this isn't what I normally do, objected Kale, trying to keep her mindspeaking voice light. She didn't want her father to know the depth of her annoyance. *I haven't disposed of a body yet in all my experience as a warrior, and I'm not so sure I'll think of something to do with them.*

"*I have confidence in you.*"

Dibl landed on her head, and she almost giggled. "Get off. I don't need you telling me this is humorous. This is not humorous, and I don't need the added complication of carrying you down this cliff."

The orange and yellow dragon hopped off and did a fancy acrobatic maneuver before soaring above her head.

"That did not cheer me up. It certainly does not show me that I need not be nervous. I don't have wings!"

Sir Kemry's voice in her head interrupted. "*Are you down yet?*"

Kale snorted. *What have you done with the bisonbecks on the path?*

"*Still working on it.*"

Well, I'm still working on rappelling this sheer drop of over one hundred feet. She looked up to judge how much she had already accomplished and caught her breath. She looked the opposite direction and smiled. *I'm nearly to the bottom.*

"Do you see the two warriors?"

Yes. It's pretty hard to miss three-hundred-pound, seven-foot-tall corpses.

Kale's feet touched the floor of the gorge. She unwound the rope from between her legs and stepped away from the cliff. She looked up to see her father's head as he peered over the edge.

Any ideas as to what I should do with these goons?

"Bury them?"

Kale stamped her foot. *In solid rock?*

"You'll think of something. And, Kale?"

Yes?

"Do watch out for Creemoor spiders. We're very close to their territory."

His head disappeared from view, and Kale scowled as she examined the area. Her dragons provided the only color in the scene aside from a few scraggly bushes. She studied the ground, looking for the telltale scratch marks that Creemoor spider legs made. She saw nothing to alarm her except the two inconvenient bodies of the bisonbecks. Something must be done with them.

Maybe she'd find a cave or deep crevasse to shove the bodies into. Then she could cover the entrance with rocks to keep wild animals from dragging them out again. She communicated to the dragons what she wanted to find and began the search.

As she walked, she ran over every wizardry ploy she might use to conceal the dead enemy. The fact that her father couldn't think of anything was some consolation. After all, he'd been a wizard and a knight much longer than she had been a wizard. If he couldn't pull an idea out of his experience, she shouldn't be faulted. But she had to admit, she'd like to be the one to come up with a plan.

She passed the bisonbecks and avoided looking at them. Too much blood and gore turned her stomach. Bardon said she would never get used to it. He hadn't. Wrinkling her nose against the coppery odor of blood, she focused on finding a cave.

She explored close to the opposite wall, peering into cracks and behind scrubby bushes, traveling north for two hundred feet. Not wanting to carry the bodies any farther, she started back, examining the other side of the chasm. She returned to the fallen warriors without uncovering a hiding place. Her dragon helpers had strayed from their task. Pat had discovered a delectable insect in abundant supply. The others had joined in the feast, chittering to one another about the unexpected sweetness and enjoyable crunch of the bug.

"Would you six lollygaggers get back to work! We're supposed to be disposing of bisonbecks, not beetles."

Hoping for better results as she moved south, she continued up the gorge. Just as she contemplated crossing to the other side and searching the opposite wall, she spotted a dark shadow that could be a cave. She called to the dragons, who joined her and exclaimed over the find. It was a cave.

She sighed. "I wonder if I can raise those corpses off the ground and float them this far. What was that called? Levitation. I think I've remembered correctly. Fenworth taught us years ago. I do remember I wasn't very good at it. I needed Bardon to complete the task then. And Regidor. Well, Regidor, of course, could do it on his own. Ah, it would be nice to have Regidor here."

She approached the shadow and saw that it was, indeed, more than just a large crevasse. "I wonder how deep you are?" She spoke to the cave as if it would answer.

With a gesture to Ardeo, she stepped inside the opening. "Come on, friend, light the way." The small dragon flew ahead of her. As soon as the light faded from the entry, Ardeo's mottled white skin began to glow with a beautiful moonlike luminance.

"Ah, this is plenty big," said Kale, looking around. "But I don't see many loose rocks to cover the bodies. What are those black lumps ahead? Are those—"

One of the mounds moved.

Kale stopped in her tracks and hissed, "Let's get out of here."

A head on a skinny neck arose and hissed back. A red forked tongue flicked, tasting the air. Ardeo swooped over the cluster of dark, roundish creatures. More heads popped up and voiced their disapproval with a sound somewhat like a kettle letting off steam.

Kale stretched out her hand and a globe of light appeared on her palm. She hurled it to pass over the nest. She gulped as the light revealed what she and Ardeo had stumbled upon. A hundred heads swerved above a mass of intertwined bodies. Beady eyes stared back at her. Crimson tongues licked the air.

"I don't like snakes," murmured Kale as she inched backward. "One tiny garden snake is tolerable." She took another step back as the heads swayed, but none of the creatures slithered from the nest. "One medium-sized water snake is acceptable." *How much farther is it to the opening? I have to keep calm.* "One large and lazy tree snake can easily be avoided." She narrowed her eyes and glared at the reptiles. "This...this is ridiculous."

The snakes uncoiled and followed. Kale gasped again. Not quite as many snakes threatened her as she had thought. Each body had five heads. So only twenty or so serpents slithered across the rock floor. Their heavy bellies rasped across the stone.

The warmth of the sun hit her back. A few more feet and she would be out of the cave. Would these creatures follow? She drew her sword and called mentally to her dragon friends, *Come help me. Snakes!*

Kale backed into the open, sunlit area. The snakes slithered out and stopped a moment to blink their eyes.

Were they grinning? A shiver went up Kale's spine. These serpents were unnatural. Her dragons dove from above, spitting caustic saliva. The smirking reptiles dodged most of the hits and countered by striking upward. Several times they almost connected with the swift dragons.

The snakes fanned out and surrounded Kale. She swung at them with her sword, but the devious creatures kept out of range.

Father!

"What is it?"

I'm surrounded by snakes. Come help me!

"You've fought bisonbecks and grawligs, mordakleeps and quiss, blimmets and schoergs. You can handle a few snakes."

There are more than a few, and each one has five heads.

"Five heads?"

Yes! I think that one over there has six, no seven, but most of them only have five.

"Unnatural. Sounds like Crim Cropper's work to me. He's always experimenting. Then when he tires of a project, he dumps them into the wild."

I don't care how they got here. I want help protecting myself.

A snake lowered all five heads and sped forward. When it reached her feet, Kale swung downward with her sword, scooped the beast up, and flung it against the stone wall. It hit with a cracking thud and five lesser thuds, then slid to the chasm floor.

"Are the minor dragons gone? They aren't protecting you? Oh, blast! They haven't been eaten by these nasty snakes, have they?"

They're here, spitting. But the heads are hard to hit, and the dragons are going to run dry soon.

"You can do this, Kale. You don't need me. Five heads, you say? If we judge by Crim Cropper's other experiments, they've only one brain between them. Not literally, of course, but figuratively. They should be slow and stupid."

They are not slow, and I have no way to determine how intelligent they are.

One serpent charged Kale. She lopped off a couple of heads, and it retreated. *I can say they are persistent.*

"Well, if you insist, I'll come down. It'll take a minute or two."

Kale bit back the plea to hurry and busied herself keeping the troop of snakes at bay. She caught movement in the corner of her eye. Surprised that her father had accomplished the climb so quickly, she glanced beyond the circle of reptiles to greet him.

Four short, stocky ropmas glared at her. She sensed more newcomers and turned to see five of the hairy beasts standing behind the other group of snakes.

Father!

"I'm coming," he snapped. *"I'm not as young as I used to be, and I'm a lot stiffer."*

Nine ropmas have joined the fight against me. I could really use some help.

"The ropmas are attacking?"

Not yet. So far they're just standing around, making faces.

"They aren't likely to attack. They're generally very placid creatures."

One of the snakes flashed a head at her leg and struck. She yelped and hopped backward. The leather of her boot showed a mar, but the fangs had not penetrated.

Pardon me if I am a little skeptical, Father. You're the one who told me the snakes would be slow.

"Throw some ice on them. They are reptiles. Cold will slow them down."

I'm short of water to make ice.

"I can't think of everything, Kale. Use some initiative."

Kale let out an exasperated growl. She dropped her sword, balled her fists, and began to throw orbs of energy. She took three seconds to gather a charge of power in her palm, opened her hand, and hurled the weapon into the squirming snakes. In a few minutes, most of the creatures were dead. Around the circumference of the slithering circle, the ropmas stamped the remaining injured and retreating snakes.

Kale heard a noise behind her and swiveled to throw another blast of energy. Her father stood with his hands on his hips.

"See? I told you so. You didn't need me in the least." He nodded toward the ropmas. "And the hairy beasts were not here to attack you but to help." He shook his head. "You really must have more confidence in your father, Kale. I've been around quite a while."

He knelt beside one of the slain serpents and picked up its head. He screwed up his mouth and wrinkled his nose. "Poor workmanship. Definitely Crim Cropper's design." He used his thumb to open the creature's mouth. "The fangs are not hollow. No poison here." He dropped the beast, dusted his hands against his britches, and stood. "I supposed it would smart some if one received a hit from one of the foul creatures."

A spot ached on Kale's leg where her boot had protected her from a "foul creature's" strike.

One comment came to her mind, and she didn't bother to disguise it from her father. *I want my husband.*

29

Enlisting Aid

The congregation of so many grawligs worried Sir Dar and Bardon.

"Who's bringing them together?" asked Sir Bardon as they sat in their headquarters tent. "And why?"

"We need a spy." Dar cocked an eyebrow at Bardon.

"You're thinking of Leetu's friend, aren't you?"

Sir Dar's ears twitched.

Bardon tapped the papers he held in one hand on the side of the table. "These are notes from the far reaches of Amara. They all say the bisonbecks are becoming outrageous in their defiance of district laws. Their troops openly mock Paladin's authority."

"Leetu has known Latho for two years."

"I don't trust him." He tossed the papers on his mentor's desk.

Dar didn't move to pick them up. "He can't fool Regidor, you know."

"That should be reassuring, but trusting a bisonbeck is like putting your head in a mountain cat's mouth and saying, 'Don't bite.' It's against the cat's nature not to bite."

"You are leaving Wulder out of the equation."

Bardon shrugged. "Wulder rarely changes a bentleaf tree into a fruit tree."

"Ah, but He could if He wanted to. And He changes caterpillars into butterflies all the time. Thousands, millions, billions of butterflies, and they all started as lumpy worms."

Bardon shifted his lower jaw to one side, then let it ease back into a normal position. "Wulder planned for caterpillars and tadpoles and grippets to change."

Dar nodded. "And you don't think that He might have planned for one measly bisonbeck to change?"

Bardon stood, arched his back, rolled his shoulders, and picked up the papers he'd tossed on the table. "A principle: 'It is generous to believe your enemy capable of doing good, and prudent to watch his actions.'"

"So we use him to spy on this collection of grawligs?"

Blowing out a stream of pent-up air, Bardon scowled. "I don't like it, but you're in charge."

Dar's eyes twinkled, and he twisted his lips into a wry grin. "There is that."

＋━━＋

The ride into town on Greer's wide back lifted Bardon's spirits. He left the dragon in a field of sweetgrass while he searched for Leetu Bends and Latho. He found them walking back from the docks. The big bisonbeck's head drooped, and his slumped shoulders added to his air of dejection.

"Did you find out about Latho's brother?" Bardon asked Leetu Bends.

She bit her lower lip. "Yes, he was lost at sea during the quiss fiasco."

Bardon looked at the forlorn man by her side. Latho didn't wear leather armor, but a cloth suit with a pale yellow shirt and brown tie. He didn't wear boots, but laced-up leather shoes. He didn't glare at Bardon with haughty scorn but shuffled his feet in the dusty street and studied the ground.

"I'm sorry for your loss, Latho." Bardon wondered what else to say. "I'm afraid our attack on the quiss caused the uninjured quiss to go berserk."

The bisonbeck didn't look up. "If my brother had crossed your path in battle, you would most likely be dead." He took a deep breath and released it. "My sorrow is that my people live by hate. When they die, they will live in the same condition. Anger builds in them, and they release it by hurting something or someone. After death, I believe the same rage will boil but be contained, burning and devouring the one who is angry."

Leetu patted the big man's arm. "It does not sound to me like a pleasant way to spend your existence."

Bardon waited, wondering if the man would further unburden his grief, or if Leetu Bends would offer words of comfort or encouragement. Neither spoke.

"Well." Bardon searched for something to say. "Were you going somewhere?"

Leetu Bends pointed up the street. "To that hotel."

"I have something I need to talk to you about. Something that should not be overheard."

"Then we will go to The End of the Day," said Latho.

Bardon guessed, "A tavern?"

"No, the place where the ashes of the dead are hurled into the air. In this town it's overlooking the bay."

He started walking, and Bardon fell into step beside him, stretching his stride to keep up. Leetu Bends trotted along on the other side of her bisonbeck friend. Bardon had never heard of The End of the Day. In The Hall he'd learned more about the bisonbeck's military tactics than their cultural habits.

"Why do you call it The End of the Day?" he asked.

For a moment he thought he had offended Latho. The merchant's face grew grim. He answered after they'd traveled a few yards farther up the road. "It is the point where one leaves this existence and enters the night." He grunted. "Most bisonbecks believe there is no morning after this night. But Leetu revealed the truth to me. It is hard to adjust one's thinking. I am fortunate that Wulder stretched out His hand and pulled me into His dominion."

When they reached a cliff overlooking the choppy waters, Latho stopped. Leetu Bends sat on a large boulder to catch her breath.

"I am sorry, my little friend." The bisonbeck merchant cupped his big hand over her reddish blond head. "My mind was on something else, and I didn't remember your short legs."

"I'm disgusted," wheezed Leetu Bends.

"I am sorry."

"No, not with you. With me." The emerlindian panted between words. "I am out of condition. I would fail the physical tests at The Hall. I used to be able to run for miles."

Bardon smiled. "Too long sitting in houses, making polite conversation."

"Ha!" said Leetu Bends. "I spent about five years in a dungeon—very little room for exercise. Still, I could have done my forms more conscientiously."

Bardon's eyebrows rose high on his forehead. "You didn't do your forms?"

"Don't judge me, Bardon. I know I would have done better if I had maintained the discipline. But instead, I got very good at making excuses. 'The guards will see me. The other prisoners will wonder. I'll do forms tonight in the dark.' Then I fell onto my mat when night arrived and slept like a black-nosed sloth."

"I'm not judging."

Leetu Bends grinned. "No, the well-trained knight in service to Paladin does not judge me. It is the lonely, abandoned schoolboy underneath who does."

Bardon started to protest, shrugged, and said, "You've become more perceptive during your work among the people of Creemoor."

"There's very little entertainment in prison. Listening to people was part of my job. Studying them became my hobby. I learned exactly where they hurt and offered the knowledge of Wulder to soothe their wounds."

"And," said Latho in his deep voice, "she was very good at it." He faced Bardon. "You said you wanted to talk to me."

"I do."

Bardon explained the necessity to discover what caused the grawligs to gather and what they were planning to do next. Latho agreed to help.

Bardon's suspicions mushroomed. "Why do you offer to help even before I ask?"

"Being born a bisonbeck was my curse. Now that I follow Wulder, being a bisonbeck is a gift. I can go where you may not."

"Let him do it," urged Leetu Bends. "I keep telling him he doesn't have to prove to Wulder that he is loyal, but he keeps doing it. He says it makes him feel good."

"I don't do these things to show Wulder I am His servant. I do it to show myself that I have this honorable position. I didn't deserve it. How can it be mine?"

Leetu shrugged. "Just because Wulder wanted you."

The bisonbeck's frame sagged. He breathed in and out twice and then seemed to inflate. His head came up, his spine straightened, and he lifted his head. "I will do whatever He asks. He knows I will do this, and I know."

The bisonbeck charged down the hill toward the seaport.

"Hey!" called Bardon. "Where are you going?"

"I must find who sends supplies to these grawligs."

Bardon ran to catch up with him. "Grawligs don't buy supplies. They scavenge from the countryside and farmers."

Latho clamped a hand on Bardon's shoulder and gave it a crushing, but friendly, squeeze. "This is why I am the spy. You do not know how the armies of Burner Stox and Crim Cropper work."

Bardon rotated the arm and shoulder that had been squashed in the big merchant's grip. "I've never even seen Crim Cropper's troops."

"That does not surprise me. He has only a token military. The evil wizard enjoys his work and isn't pursuing ruling the world."

"But Burner Stox is?"

"Oh yes. I think that was the root of their argument. She wanted him to come out and storm through the country, conquering all. He wanted to do one more experiment."

"You know this?" asked Bardon, barely keeping the skepticism out of his tone.

"It is a speculation founded in multiple reports, some more trust-worthy than others."

Leetu Bends dashed up beside them. "What are you talking about?"

Latho grunted. "I am teaching your friend. He says grawligs forage food and steal from the farmers. But when you have this many of the oafs in one place, purloining can't support them. So whichever personage gathered them will feed them. And I will deliver supplies myself to get into their camp."

"Won't you stick out as the only bisonbeck in a horde of grawligs?" asked Bardon.

"There will be bisonbeck soldiers there," Latho assured him.

"No one reported bisonbeck soldiers to me."

"Still, they will be there. Whoever gathered the grawligs, whoever feeds them, will watch them. I must get there and discover who sends them, where they are to be sent, and to what purpose."

"I'll go with you," said Bardon.

"Me too," said Leetu Bends.

The bisonbeck stopped and put his hands on his hips. "Why?"

"This situation smells of a major enemy push of some kind," Bardon said. "It's not something we can ignore. It may be something that must be countered immediately without the delay of reports gathered and studied. Leetu Bends and I will assess the significance on the spot."

"And you were worried about me being conspicuous?" Latho laughed and started off for town again. "Come," he said, "if you must. I shall disguise you as a loaf of bread, a side of beef. No, I have it—as a barrel."

30

A Ropma Village

Kale eyed the ropmas gathered around. Under normal circumstances she would not be afraid of the gentle folk. But these ropmas had been under the influence of Burner Stox. Two of the bigger beasts growled as they glared at the ground in front of Kale.

A small ropma grabbed a dead snake, whirled the carcass around his head like a whip, then with a warlike cry let the creature loose. It landed amongst the rocks. The other ropmas grunted. Kale backed up, closer to her father. The band of hairy beasts turned to watch her.

Their fierce expressions had been replaced by smiles. Kale wondered if the lopsided grins were friendly or menacing.

One stepped forward. "Snakes bad."

The voice sounded familiar. "Bug?" asked Kale.

The speaker tiptoed gingerly through the dead snakes. "Yes. Bug." He pointed to himself, then motioned to his friends. "Come, look. I say she pretty."

With Bug's hairy, stubby finger pointed at her nose, Kale blushed.

Another ropma hopped through the scattered snake corpses and knocked Bug's arm down.

Kale smiled at the female. "Are you Rain? Bug told us you cook good food."

The ropma's face broke into a grin, and she tapped a fist against Bug's arm below the shoulder. "Bug eat good."

With a scowl returning to her face, Rain eyed Kale. She pinched

Kale's arm and felt her brown curly hair, ending her examination with a pat on the cheek. "You skinny. No hair where hair belongs."

Kale glanced at her father. A smirk on his rugged face told her he enjoyed the inspection she had endured from Bug's jealous wife.

"Your frown is showing, Kale." His voice in her thoughts soothed her agitated nerves.

She relaxed the muscles in her face and smiled at Sir Kemry.

He smiled back, a small smile that showed his approval. *"Rain likes you. Your skinny body and hairless face will be invited to the village. It's what we want."*

Rain bestowed a toothy smile on her fellow ropmas, nodding her head with enthusiasm. "Wizards come to our hut. I give food." She beamed her yellow grin on Kale. "You eat. You sleep."

Kale quizzed her father with a raised eyebrow. But Bug took hold of her arm, distracting her.

She shook him off. "What are you doing?"

"You come. Go home. Go valley."

Sir Kemry stepped forward. "You're taking us to the valley of dragons?"

Bug jerked his head in an emphatic yes.

Rain smoothed the hair on her husband's arm and looked up at him with admiring eyes. "Bug say we have two wizards. Becks have one. Wizards fight." She pointed to Kale and her father. "You win. We free."

Rain and her companions laughed at the plan, and Kale probed their minds. Proud of concocting a design to end their slavery, the ropmas were giddy with relief. The simple scheme reflected their uncomplicated thinking. To them, the end of the long period of terror under the evil wizard's rule was an accomplished fact. The ropmas' wizards would defeat the woman wizard. The band of ropmas would take Kale and her father home, feed them, guide them to the valley, and then leave the wizards to wage war against the adversary. Their minds hid no plot to turn the wizards over to Burner Stox.

Her father patted Kale on the shoulder. *"A neat plan, don't you think?"*

If it works. They've neglected to factor in scores of bisonbecks and dragons who are loyal to the opposing force.

"The dragons are an unknown."

Some of the ropmas scampered off together. Bug gestured for the two o'rant wizards to follow, pointing in the direction his friends had gone.

"Yes," said Sir Kemry, rubbing his hands together. "Let's see where this path shall lead us."

⊰━━⊱

After a long, arduous walk through rough terrain, Kale looked forward to the plain comfort of the ropma village. She only knew of the lower race from a few minor encounters in the past and from what she found in books.

Bardon's aunt had raised his cousin N'Rae in a ropma community. N'Rae's insight into the way these people really lived had changed Kale's perception of the ropmas. Where grawligs were unintelligent bullies, the ropmas were simple homebodies with a knack for caring for beasts like cows, chickens, goats, and sheep. Now it would seem dragons could be added to the list.

Bug led them through twisting, narrow crevasses until the ravine they followed opened into a spacious, green valley. The stunning contrast of the emerald grass and flowering trees against the black rock formations took Kale's breath away.

Her words came out in a reverent whisper. "It's beautiful."

Rain took her hand and pulled her forward. "Home." The ropma took off, dragging Kale along. Sir Kemry followed with Bug by his side, and the other ropmas hopped about, doing a jig.

The minor dragons cheered at both the physical beauty and happy spirits. They flew in ever-widening circles to examine everything they could see. They sent Kale a barrage of images. She shielded her mind from too much sensory input and concentrated on enjoying what her own eyes could see.

In the distance, nestled under pink and yellow flowering bingham trees, twig huts fashioned like upside-down nests stood in the shade. One round circle close to the ground provided an uncovered entry, and three smaller round holes, erratically spaced, allowed light and air into the homes.

Bug trotted ahead with Kale and the others following. They passed through what looked like an area where the homes had once stood. Evidence of a fire showed through sprigs of new green grass. Next they passed by some decrepit huts that leaned precariously or had collapsed.

Sir Kemry explained what she saw. "The first settlement burned down. By accident or because of an attack, I can't determine. These huts are the old town." He pointed at the ramshackle homes.

"Ropma don't construct sturdy dwellings. When their home begins to deteriorate, they abandon it and move to the other end of the village, which is set up in a rather linear pattern. They leave behind the hut, which returns to nature by the process of decay.

"The men and women in the band build a new habitat for the displaced family in exactly the same manner as the others. All this takes place in a rather celebratory attitude. The home is new, the area clean, pristine. And neighbors have changed so that the group remains fluid in the relationships between families." Sir Kemry sighed with a wistful expression on his face. "I would love to study the process."

Out of the newer huts, the entire village came to greet them. The ropmas hugged their returning friends and eyed Kale and Sir Kemry with guarded expressions. Those returning whispered in the ears of those who had stayed. Excitement replaced the troubled look, and the ropmas came closer.

A dozen young children approached by folding their hairy limbs over their stomachs and rolling in smooth somersaults until they bumped gently into the visitors' legs. The ropma ball sprang open to reveal a giggling child sprawled on his or her back at the wizards' feet. The youngster hopped up, ran away, and repeated the greeting over and over, sometimes rolling into one another or their parents instead of their target.

The force of each impact made Kale stagger, even when she saw the approaching child-ball. She grasped her father's arm and tried to avoid getting knocked over like a piggledy pin. Even though she laughed at their antics, she grew tired of the game. Kale called to her minor dragons to help distract the ropma bas.

The colorful dragons swooped through the clearing, attracting attention with their chatter and aerial acrobatics. The youngsters ceased the rolling sport and began an impossible chase of the dragons in the air. By design, the dragons lured the children away from the others. Still their laughter and shrieks filled the twig town.

When their exuberance settled to a quieter frenzy, Sir Kemry spoke to the older crowd in general. "We will do all we can to help you. Paladin wants us to be your servants. Wulder cares for your sorrow."

The ropmas hushed, the children quit their game, and puzzled expressions replaced the happy countenances of the villagers.

Kale lifted one ropma child who had stayed at her feet into her arms. "We will help," she said to those gathered around. "Paladin will help. Wulder will help."

The ropmas nodded solemnly. The child squirmed, and Kale handed him to a mother who came forward with arms outstretched.

Kale glanced at her father. *Why would the mother not let me hold her son? What is the current I can't quite put my finger on?*

"Something evil has happened here, and there is a warning to keep outsiders from discovering the event."

Sir Kemry gestured to the gathering. "I have seen bas this big." He held his hand low, indicating the height of most of those who had rolled into them. "And I have seen big bas." He pointed to the fringe of the crowd where adolescents hung back, observing rather than participating. Sir Kemry moved his hand to show the height of a child in between these two age groups. "Where are the other children?"

In an instant the friendly chattering ceased. With eyes closed and faces screwed into masks of misery, the ropma men, women, and children pulled air into their lungs and let out a keening wail.

The weight of sorrow almost pushed Kale to her knees. She placed her hands over her ears to protect herself from the physical assault and blanketed her mind to stop the flow of utter despair coming from the villagers. The children ran back to stand beside their parents and joined the strident lament. The minor dragons flew to seek refuge in the pocket-dens of Kale's moonbeam cape. She cradled the unhatched eggs with one arm wrapped around her middle.

Sir Kemry raised his hands in the air and shouted, "We will help. We will help," until the noise subsided with only a few sobs and sniffles breaking the silence.

Kale's father let his arms sink from an expression of command to one of supplication. In a softer tone, Sir Kemry said, "Let us help."

Lowering her hands from her ears, Kale gazed into the eyes of each ropma, sending them a message of reassurance. Yes, she and her father would help. Ignoring the ropmas' plight was unthinkable.

Kale looked at the gentle creatures and could not imagine anyone harming them. But the images she gathered as she communicated with the band of ropmas told her otherwise.

In their recent past, they had endured the cruelty of Burner Stox as administered by her army of bisonbecks. Grawligs had ravaged the small settlement, beating the populace and destroying their property. Bisonbecks ambushed the band and carried off their children.

In their abortive attempt to flee, Burner Stox herself had come to the valley. Standing before them with a staff in her hand that shot out a stream of pain-inflicting energy, she had explained her demands. The ropma slaves would do as she said, or their children would die.

Her instructions: seek dragon eggs and bring them to the Greenbright Valley. Capture smaller dragons and give them over to her men. Locate larger dragons and keep watch as one runner went to the valley to bring warriors back to trap the dragon.

Stox with her brutal warriors had bestowed upon the ropmas a heart-rending situation. The becks allowed the youngest ropmas in the village to remain because they were too much bother to keep alive. The warriors left the adolescents to help with the capture of dragons and the gathering of eggs. The middle-aged youngsters were held hostage to keep the ropmas from fleeing or rebelling. Old enough to forage for themselves and not be an additional burden to Stox's army, the children were kept in Green-bright Valley to tend the dragons.

When Kale tried to get an inkling of how long this servitude had been enforced, she could not interpret the images in the ropmas' minds. She looked to her father for an answer.

He shrugged, answering her unspoken question in the same manner she had communicated it. *"In one form or another, I believe Stox has been accruing this dragon force since the days before Joffa and I were trapped in the sleeping chamber."*

That could be a very large number of dragons subjugated to a horribly evil woman.

"I think we have been handed quite an impossible task, my dear."

What should we do?

"Go on, of course."

Of course.

31

On the Hunt

Bardon and Leetu Bends rode with the bisonbeck merchant through a pass between two high hills and into a valley. At the bottom of the incline, Latho stopped to hide his two passengers, not disguising them as barrels, but stuffing them into two barrels designed to carry dried longfish. The containers stank, and the rough insides scraped against them in spite of the thick blankets Latho had given them to wrap up in. But the staves had gaps between them, sufficient enough for them to breathe easily and to peer out. The wagon bumped over every hole and rock in the road.

When they got to the camp, Bardon heard harsh voices loudly inquiring about Latho's business.

"We aren't expecting supplies until next week," hollered one.

"Have you got papers to verify this shipment?" asked another.

Latho was correct, thought Bardon. *These men are bisonbecks, not grawligs.*

"Can you see anything?" asked Leetu Bends.

Not a thing.

"I have one tiny crack, but I've picked some slivers of wood out of it to make it bigger."

The wagon jolted and moved.

I guess they accepted Latho's papers.

"He's also known among the soldiers. Some of them show a great amount of disrespect for 'the bisonbeck coward.' Others have just heard his name, because it's so unusual for his kind not to be in some type of fighting force."

The wagon lurched to a stop.

"Now we'll see if this plan works."

At Leetu Bends's words Bardon's mind leapt to the last time he'd seen Kale. Her mouth had puckered in a pout, her eyes welled with tears, and she'd looked altogether adorable in a spoiled-princess sort of way. *Wulder, give me the chance to make her smile again.*

Several grawligs gathered around the wagon.

"You," said Latho, "take these crates over to the captain's quarters. You, unload these baskets and take them to the cook."

Latho kept the workers scurrying. Bardon listened intently, trying to determine what was going on around him. The big bisonbeck merchant ordered the grawlig recruits to unwrap some of the bundles and carry off the goods. He unpacked some of the merchandise himself and handed it to one of the grawligs to carry off.

After a few minutes of observation, Leetu Bends said, *"Aha! Very clever."*

What?

"He's directing them to different sides of the wagon. When a grawlig comes back, he doesn't know what has been moved or which containers have already been emptied."

Bardon remembered his puzzlement when he saw the dried fish wrapped in canvas. Now he understood. *So Latho can claim he already unpacked the longfish from our hiding place. I agree, very clever.*

The problematic point in time passed with Latho distracting the workers and maneuvering the six-foot-long dried fish into position as if he had just taken them out of the barrels. He directed the rest of the unloading with no incident and haggled with a bisonbeck officer about the bill.

"Fine," said Latho, when he finally got his money. "I'll be leaving at sunup."

"We don't want you around here tonight," said the officer.

"I'm not going into those hills after dark. I won't be in your way."

The man left, and Latho busied himself around the wagon but never came near the barrels containing Bardon and Leetu Bends. They had food and water in their hiding places, so he didn't have to provide anything for them. Latho had done everything possible to keep from drawing attention to the supposedly empty cargo crates left on his wagon.

An hour after dark, two soldiers came to the wagon.

"You're to come with us," one said.

"Why?"

Bardon heard one of the men growl. "Come and don't give us any trouble."

Bardon and Leetu remained silent.

"Bardon?"

Yes?

"Don't worry. I'm keeping track of them. I'm mindspeaking with Latho. He'll let me know if he needs us."

Well, let's hope he doesn't. This place is getting crowded with grawligs. I can smell them over the stench of the longfish.

"You're right." She paused. "Oh my!"

"What?"

"They're expecting Pretender himself to be here. He's going to talk to them." She paused again. "I don't like this."

I'm hoping we get to stay in our little cocoons and aren't asked to join the party.

"I won't be able to mindspeak with you. I don't want Pretender to pick up on our being here."

Can't you cover your mind the way Kale does? She asks Wulder to protect her thoughts and keep them guarded.

"I can, and I will. You better do the same. And keep repeating it. There's going to be a lot of evil going on here tonight. I don't want us vulnerable for even a moment."

A chant rose from the gathering. A drum beat a steady rhythm, and Bardon surmised a wild dance had begun. He squirmed around until he could get out his small dagger. With the point, he broke open a niche between two staves, so he, too, could have a peephole.

He placed his eye against the crack and sighed with frustration. A row of mountain ogres stood in a line, obstructing his view of the main participants. He could see the taller grawligs within the circle and those who leapt high enough during their chaotic celebration.

A clap of thunder stilled the grawligs. The loud crack indicated a nearby lightning strike and should have been preceded by a flash of lightning.

As if they understood this as a signal, the grawligs sat on the ground in a large circle. Bardon could see more but had no way of estimating the number. *I hope Latho has an idea when we climb out of these stinking barrels. No reason to think we won't get out of here. Hopefully in one piece. Wulder, order our way.*

The hush that fell over the throng seemed unnatural. Bardon found he was holding his breath and deliberately let it out. The sound of his heart beating echoed in his ears. A murmur ran through the gathering, and then that unnatural silence again. Bardon recited the words that would keep him connected to Wulder and protected from evil.

A cloud formed in the center of the grawlig circle. Lights sparked within, sending off refracted flashes of different colors. The flickers ceased. The cloud pooled on the ground. In the center stood a man, twice as tall as any bisonbeck, covered with a shimmering black material, and producing a constant outpouring of vapor that sunk to swirl around his feet. Coarse dark hair covered his bulky head, including the face. A hefty nose like a bull's; a mouth, giant but looking like an o'rant's; and enormous eyes with undersized, black pupils combined to make a hideous visage.

Quite a show. I'm sure the grawligs are impressed. Bardon swallowed. *I think I'm impressed. Wulder, guard me as I seek Truth.*

The figure raised his arms and lightning streamed from his fingertips, spreading out into the night sky.

Now, that was spectacular. I wonder if he'll rain brimstone for an encore.

The performer turned and looked Bardon's way. Bardon caught his breath. The man's prominent eyes sparkled for a moment and seemed to focus on the wagon, then on the barrel where a shiver spread through Bardon's chest.

Wulder, protect me, for I am a dolt. Keep me ever mindful of Your strength, Your honor, Your presence.

The man looked away and lowered his arms to his sides.

"I am Lord Ire." His announcement boomed over his listeners. The grawligs cowered. "I have chosen you for my subjects. It is your honor to serve me. Together we shall dominate the world. You will be revered, not spurned. You will be great, and those who pass before you will cower and cry with fear."

Bardon expected a mighty cheer. But the awed grawligs only mumbled in their throats and nodded their massive heads.

"This will be my challenge to you." Lord Ire drew from his pocket a red cloth that dripped scarlet drops onto the ground. He held it above his head. "Do you smell it?"

His audience grunted and growled and stirred in their seats.

"It excites you, doesn't it? The smell demands that you run. The smell insists that you hunt. You are urged to your feet."

The mass of grawligs rose as one. They fidgeted as if they could not keep still, nor could they move from the spot until released by the speaker. Their feet shifted in the dirt.

"You *need* to hunt. You *need* to track. You *need* to ferret out all those who carry this smell. You *need* to kill."

Bardon felt the swelling desire churning among the grawligs. They craved to be set free, to break loose from this confining circle.

Lord Ire waited just one moment longer, restraining them, making them all the more eager to be off. He allowed the cloth to drop. When it hit the ground he said, "Go."

The wagon shook as the multitude stampeded away from the camp. Dust rose in the air. Bardon peered through his small crack and watched. The air became still. The cloud of grime settled. Lord Ire stood for a moment and then vanished.

The bisonbeck soldiers started as if awakening from a trance. They moved around, straightening overturned barrels, putting out the fires, and collecting cooking utensils and abandoned food supplies. Soon even that activity stilled.

Bardon waited.

He listened.

He heard a whimper and then a sob.

"Leetu?"

A mangled word came back to him through the staves of the barrels.

"What is it?" he asked.

She choked and moaned and managed to speak. "Kimens. He has sent them to hunt kimens, as hounds would track down a fox. They will tear apart each kimen they find with their teeth and their claws." Another sob escaped her. "He has commanded it so."

32

TODAY OR TOMORROW?

Practicality stalled the choice to go on. Kale and her father couldn't proceed without the cooperation of the ropmas. Without being deliberately obstinate, the ropmas threw up one obstacle after another. To them, the threat of Burner Stox and her army had already been removed, so there was plenty of time to do enjoyable things like eating and sleeping. Nothing Kale or her father said could change what the band of ropmas decided to do.

The villagers expected music and stories from the visiting o'rants. They provided dinner, a place to sleep, and breakfast in return.

"When will you take us to the valley of dragons?" Sir Kemry asked.

"Tomorrow," each would answer when quizzed.

After inquiring of all the ropmas who seemed to share a loose leadership role, Sir Kemry shrugged and wandered over to sit on one of the crude benches clustered under a shade tree. He pulled out his flute, cocked an eyebrow at Kale, and whispered, "I hope they have a clear concept of tomorrow becoming today. Otherwise, we will have to go on without their guidance."

"We could do that, couldn't we? If we scanned their thoughts, we would get a picture of the path to the valley."

"That's doubtful. Their thought patterns are not orderly. Jumbled in with the course we should take would be memories of fishing spots and berry patches. It would be like trying to follow a map that had inserts of foreign countries with no explanation."

"Oh."

"We need Bug to guide us."

Kale grinned. "Pretty humbling, isn't it?"

Sir Kemry's eyes twinkled. "Being dependent on these simple creatures? Yes, it is."

He raised the flute to his lips and blew a brisk, cheerful melody. Metta flew to the bingham tree and sat in its branches while she sang her accompanying chirps. She looked like a giant purple flower set among a backdrop of dainty pink blossoms. Kale picked up the lyrics of the winsome ballad from her dragon and sang the words. The villagers ceased their activities and gathered around. The entertainment would have gone on indefinitely had it not been for growling stomachs.

Kale learned ropmas' bellies produce a very loud complaint when empty too long. She also discovered their evening meal of stew was very tasty, although it could have benefited by a pinch of salt.

As the day ended, the village turned in for the night. Kale watched one ropma duck into the small door of his home. He came out with a sturdy stick, waved it in the air as if he were warning an invisible foe, then disappeared into his hut. Each ropma performed the same routine. Even the small children came out and repeated the little ritual with smaller sticks.

"What are they doing?" Kale asked Bug.

"Who?"

She pointed to two adolescents standing in front of their tent and threatening the sky with their sticks. "Them."

"Say to night, 'I have weapon.'"

"So your enemies see you are ready to defend your homes?"

Bug surveyed the mountains surrounding the valley. "Bad no come. Bug sleep." His chin dropped to his chest. In the moonlight, tears glistened on his cheeks.

"What's wrong, Bug?" As always, Kale surveyed the ropma's mind as he spoke, to aid in interpreting what he meant. Frightened by the images she picked up, she turned to her father, wondering if he, too, saw the raid upon the settlement: fire, clubs battering terrorized ropmas, women and children fleeing, men slashed with long swords.

Bug sobbed, and Sir Kemry placed his hand on the ropma's hairy shoulder. Kale saw his fingers tighten and relax, tighten and relax.

"We will face your enemy, Bug. Wulder willing, we will destroy them."

Bug nodded and shuffled to a nearby hut. He motioned for Kale and Sir Kemry to follow.

Bug pointed at Kale's father. "You sleep." He pointed to the door.

With his back to the round opening, Sir Kemry raised his staff and shook it at the sky. His fierce expression must have impressed Bug. The ropma's face lightened with hope. Kale's father kissed her on the forehead, went down on his knees, and crawled into the hut.

Bug motioned Kale on. The next hut was to be hers. He offered her the stick he carried.

"No thank you, Bug. I have a weapon." She drew her sword.

Bug looked at her empty hand.

"It's invisible," she explained.

Bug tilted his head, squinted his eyes, and obviously saw nothing.

"Watch." Kale drew a circle in the dirt with the tip of her blade. She added two eyes, a nose, and a smile.

Bug reached for the space between her hand and the ground. Kale pulled the sword back just in time.

"No, Bug. It's sharp. It would cut you."

"Sleep!" commanded another voice. Rain stepped out of the shadows.

She brought Kale a big stick and pushed it into her free hand. The female ropma took the o'rant wizard by the shoulders, forced her to turn, bend, and enter the round opening.

"Lie down! Sleep!" she ordered.

From the dark confines of the hut, Kale answered, "Yes ma'am."

In the morning, Kale tasted the breakfast gruel, expecting it to be as savory as the evening meal. She fought to keep from spitting out the lumpy, sticky mass of flavorless goo. She chewed with her eyes scrunched shut. The blob clung to her teeth, the roof of her mouth, and the insides of her cheeks. As she chewed, the gob developed a sour taste.

Her eyes watered. She felt a hand on her shoulder and heard her father say, "Drink this."

She reached blindly for the offered cup and washed the gruel down. As the liquid mixed with the porridge, a sweet, nutty flavor covered the horrid aftertaste until her mouth felt fresh and her stomach full.

She opened her eyes and gazed into her father's sympathetic face. "Thank you," she whispered.

He winked.

"Think nothing of it." He gestured to the communal table. "Try the bread. It's safe. Don't touch the green stuff in the wooden bowl."

Kale nodded and went to pick up a small round loaf of bread, no bigger than her palm and as hard as a rock. Two small ropmas sat on a boulder under a tree, sucking on the end of their bread. Kale scraped her front teeth over the smaller end of her roll and tasted a honey-sweet surprise.

Her father smiled and leaned close to her ear. "I thought you would like it. The bread lasts for hours, and if you tire of the delicacy, you can always use it to render someone unconscious by knocking him on the head with it."

Bug and his family ate under a tree close by.

Sir Kemry tilted his head in their direction. "I think I'll go ask when we're leaving. I may find out that today is the tomorrow from yesterday, or tomorrow is still a day away."

Kale could easily hear her father's exchange with Bug.

"Good morning, Bug, Rain." He smiled and patted the head of a small child sitting in her mother's lap. "When do we leave to go to the valley of dragons?"

"Now," said Bug and continued to chew.

Sir Kemry beamed. "Fine, Kale and I will get ready to go."

Bug nodded, tipped his bowl, slurped up the contents, then smacked his lips.

An hour later, Kale and her father sat in the commons and watched Bug unhurriedly do his chores.

" 'Now' doesn't mean now," said Sir Kemry.

"I hope it means today," said Kale.

Kale and her dragons entertained the youngest ropmas. Each new activity distracted the older ropmas. They stopped working and came to observe the antics of the visitor. Sir Kemry sidled up to her after she finished acting out a children's story with puppets stored in a hollow of her cape.

"You'd best find something to do that doesn't draw attention to yourself."

"Why?"

"Because Bug and the others will never finish their work, and we will be stuck here another day."

Kale and her father then attempted to blend in with the community. They spent time mingling with the ropmas and making friends, gleaning tidbits of information, and helping with the simple chores.

Two hours later, Bug had finished his chores, played with his children, and started more chores.

"Do you think Bug is procrastinating?" asked Kale when she passed her father.

"I doubt he would know the word or understand the concept, but he might be doing it out of some innate instinct of self-preservation."

"What can we do?"

"Let's go talk to him."

They approached Bug as he wove together sturdy weed stems. Kale puzzled over what he was making and came up with no answer.

"Bug," Sir Kemry spoke firmly. "We must go now."

Bug nodded. "We go now." He continued working.

Sir Kemry pondered the busy ropma. "Ah!" he said. He patted Kale on the back. "Not to worry, dear. 'Now' means today. We shouldn't have to wait much longer."

After the noon meal, which was more like breakfast than the wonderful stew they had had the night before, Bug kissed his wife and children, and said, "We go."

For a moment it appeared that one of his older bas would come along. The young man pleaded, but Bug would not allow it.

"So they do argue," said Kale as she observed the interchange.

"The Tomes say, 'Water moves the rock until the rock stops the dam.'"

"I never understood that one and never remembered to ask when I was with someone who might tell me."

"You can figure it out for yourself if you understand that *plug* is another word for 'stop.'"

"I had figured that out. I still don't get it."

"A force in nature affects what surrounds it. Since another force is also affecting its surroundings, there will, at times, be conflict." He looked at her face. "Here's another one. 'The weed and the oat want the same ground.' Neither the weed nor the oat is evil, but they need the same thing. Thus, conflict."

Bug walked past them, and they fell into step behind him.

"Why," asked Kale, "can't Wulder just say in plain language some of the things that are 'hidden' in the Tomes?"

"Because the high races learn better when they struggle to wrap their minds around a concept. 'Hard lessons are best learned.'"

"I've heard Bardon quote that principle."

"A child learns not to touch a hot rock beside the fire, not because he heard his parent say, 'Don't touch,' but because there are tears in his eyes and a blister on his finger. Hopefully, he also learns to listen to his parents' admonitions."

"Why do I so quickly grow tired of talk like this?"

Sir Kemry threw back his head and laughed. "Because you are one of the high races. You wish to be in charge, and the principles point out that you are not. You chafe against hearing proof of your own weakness, and therefore avoid it, much like Bug avoided beginning this trip. Self-preservation. In his case, he hoped to preserve his life. In your case, you hope to preserve your self, your autonomy."

Kale hunched her shoulders and relaxed them, sighing.

"The odd thing, my dear," said her father, "is that once one has ceased trying to protect self, one finds one's self in a very comfortable position."

"Where?" asked Kale.

"In Wulder's care."

They walked for hours, following a trail Kale could barely make out. At the top of a ridge, Bug stopped and pointed.

"There."

Across a small, dismal valley, an encampment stood at the opening of a canyon. Bisonbeck tents lined up in rows. Perhaps two dozen warriors dwelled in the outpost.

"You go there. Bug go home." He turned to leave.

"But you said you would take us to the valley."

Bug nodded in his usual, jerky style. "Becks, gorge, valley." He waved his hand in the direction of the camp. "Bug no go."

He marched off, and neither Kale nor her father tried to stop him.

Sir Kemry sat on the ground and leaned against a large boulder under a shade tree. "Time for a respite."

"Are we going to go on?" Kale knew the answer. They would make sure they were connected to Wulder by the simple task of resting and refreshing.

"Yes, but not now." He shielded his eyes against the setting sun and studied the small stronghold that blocked their way. He lowered his hand, placing it in his lap. "Yes, later. Impossible tasks always look easier after a nap and some tea."

33

†HE FRENZY BEGINS

Bardon's hand tightened on his dagger even as his eyes opened, and he became aware of his tight position inside the longfish barrel. One of the staves pulled back with a screech and revealed the morning sun.

"It's me," said Latho. "The camp is deserted."

"Deserted?"

The round top of the barrel popped off. Latho's big, hairy face blocked the opening. "They left about an hour ago. Kept me down the road apiece all night long. Didn't get much spying done. Two guards eyed me and grunted at every twitch I made."

He moved away, and Bardon heard him talking to Leetu Bends. With considerable wriggling, Bardon managed to extract himself from his confined hideout.

He walked around the camp. In the sunshine, the setting didn't seem fraught with malice, but still, as he remembered the scene from the previous night, the hair on the back of his neck stood up.

Leetu Bends came to stand beside him as he stared down into a small black pit that had been a cooking fire.

"What are your plans?" she asked.

"Get out of here as fast as possible and send warnings to the kimens plus a report to Paladin."

"Nothing will be fast enough."

"I know."

The trip down from the grawligs' meeting place bumped and swayed

over the same road, but Bardon and Leetu sat on the empty crates instead
of being scrunched in longfish barrels. At the bottom of the pass, they
came to a small house nestled among a scattering of armagot trees. A marione mother held her two children tightly in her lap as they wailed.

Bardon and Leetu Bends jumped down from the wagon and ran to
her side.

She couldn't speak but pointed to her open doorway.

With weapons drawn the two warriors went into the humble home.

The ransacked room stank of grawligs. Their odor lingered over the
havoc they had created. On the floor in the center of the room, an elderly
man sprawled with a club in his fist. A pool of blood circled his head.

"He's still alive," Leetu Bends whispered to Bardon.

She tilted her head in the same manner Kale did when she surveyed
an area with her talent instead of her eyes and ears.

"The grawligs are gone." Leetu Bends returned to the door and called
to the marione mother. "He's not dead. Come and help me."

The woman stood, and the children slipped to the grass. She ran
inside and knelt with Leetu Bends. The two small girls hovered near the
door. The emerlindian examined the injured man. "Bardon, help me get
him to his bed."

"Da," the woman said under her breath. "Oh, Wulder, preserve life."

Bardon left his task of restoring order to the room and lifted the father
in his arms. "Tell me what happened."

The woman answered in a rush of words. "They broke down the door
and came into the house without warning. There were three. Grawligs.
I've never even seen a grawlig before. Da grabbed his club and swung at
one. The monster hit him across the chest, and Da fell against the table.
He hit his head. I thought he was dead."

She reached out to touch her father's hand. Reassured, she hurried
around Bardon.

Bardon followed the woman into the next room, where a rumpled bed lay on its side. The children scuttled into the house and trailed behind their mother. She and Leetu Bends set the bed on its feet, and Bardon placed the fragile old marione on the mattress. Leetu Bends held a cloth against the bleeding head wound.

Bardon straightened and put a comforting arm around the woman's shoulders. "Did they say anything?"

She shook her head. "Nothing. Not a word. They snorted and sniffed and growled like animals. They pawed through every nook and cranny in the house. Then one gave a shout, and they all ran out the back door, running as if they had a curry-wolf chasing them."

"They weren't running from something. They'd caught the scent of a kimens."

Leetu looked up from her patient. "He's going to be all right. The blood flow is slowing."

"You're an emerlindian." The woman twisted her fingers together. "Can you heal him?"

"I don't have that talent, but I can leave you herbs to help him."

Bardon looked around the cottage and saw a man's jacket, a pair of trousers, and a pair of boots, all too big for the father of this woman. "Where's your husband?"

"He's out in the fields, working." She gestured toward the south. "His name is Bocker. Mine is Eraline."

"I'll go fetch him while you get your da comfortable."

"Take Latho with you," suggested Leetu Bends.

"Yes." Bardon left by the front door. He approached Latho, who stood leaning against his wagon.

The bisonbeck straightened. "The grawligs were searching for a kimen?"

Bardon nodded.

"Why in a marione home?"

Bardon swiped his hand across his chin, feeling the stubble that the lack of a morning shave had left. "Many people do not realize that some-times kimens coexist with the other races. I'm not sure I understand, but they dwell in homes like that one." He gestured with a thumb over his shoulder. "Kale, my wife, always thought we might have a couple at our home in The Bogs."

"They can make themselves invisible?"

"There are two things I don't think anyone has ever figured out about kimens. One is, do they run incredibly fast, or do they fly? And the other is, do they become invisible and mingle among the other high races as sort of guardians?"

Latho jerked his head toward the house. "So those people never saw a kimen?"

Bardon shook his head. "But even if the grawligs couldn't see one—"

"They could smell it."

Bardon looked over the field in the direction he thought it had gone.

"Shall we go after it?" asked Latho. "Maybe help the little fellow?"

"We wouldn't catch up, and…" He heaved a sigh. "I'm hoping the kimen can take care of himself. They truly are fast."

Latho and Bardon walked to the acreage where the marione farmer tilled his soil. From a distance they saw the husband Bocker talking to another man. As they drew nearer both marione farmers took a wary stance. Bardon assumed the man closest to the horse-drawn plow was Bocker. He pulled a shovel off his rig. The other man held a pitchfork ready.

Bardon put his hands up in front of him, palms out. "We're friends. We came to fetch the man whose house is just over that knoll."

"Why?" asked Bocker.

"Your house was attacked by grawligs."

The second man shot a look at the first. "See?"

"My family?" The husband lost some of his guardedness and anxiety flooded his face.

"Your wife and the girls are all right. Your father-in-law took a blow to the head."

He ran past them, shovel in hand, with the obvious intent of reaching his home as fast as he could.

The other farmer stepped forward. "My name's Graick. I live back of those trees." He pointed.

"I'm Sir Bardon, and this is my friend, Latho."

Graick shook hands with Bardon but looked askance at Latho. "You travel with a bisonbeck?"

Bardon chuckled. "He comes in handy in a fight."

The farmer frowned.

"He's a merchant, not a warrior. But his size is enough to scare many opponents off." Bardon gave up trying to explain the unexplainable. "You seemed to know the grawligs are rampaging."

"They came by my place. I don't think it was the same bunch as did this." He waved toward the farmhouse Bardon and Latho had visited. "They tore up my barn and went on. I heard of them stealing livestock from time to time. Never happened to me, but I heard others say it." He shook his head, bewildered, and pushed his hat back on his head. "They didn't take any kind of food. They wrecked the place like they were looking for something. Then left. They were frothing at the mouth for whatever it was they wanted. I just kept my family hid. They're still hiding." Again he pointed over the knoll. "I came to see if Bocker knew anything."

Bardon and Latho said nothing.

"You're a knight?"

"Yes."

"You're gonna fix this? I mean, you're here to right a wrong or something?"

"I vowed to protect. The grawligs aren't after mariones. They're after kimens. Pretender sent them on a hunt for our little friends."

"Oh well, then. Those grawligs will be long gone. There're no kimens around these parts."

"I think you're mistaken."

"Oh?"

"I think one or more dwelt in your barn, or at least, visited it frequently."

The farmer puffed up his cheeks and blew the air out his lips. "I don't know how I feel about that. You think kimens have been trespassing on my property? Maybe even living in my barn?" He scratched his arm and then his head. "Well, I guess it don't hurt. Some people even say a kimen around is lucky."

He thought for a minute. "But it ain't good luck if it brings grawligs."

Bardon fought the urge to give this man a lecture. Wulder's Tomes were laced with principles that said to take care of others. One's own personal safety came second when danger threatened. He sighed instead. "Just remember, the grawlig threat is even worse luck for the kimens."

34

THE NEXT MOVE

Sir Kemry made himself comfortable and closed his eyes. Pat found a bush harboring ring beetles and called to the other dragons to join his feast.

Kale gathered wood and built a small fire. She put a kettle on and assembled a light tea, pulling everything she needed from her cape hollow. After having a cup of tea, she put together dough for fried mullins but didn't cook them. She'd wait until her father awoke.

She knew the knights took great care in giving importance to sleep and sustenance. Sleep represented resting in Wulder's care. Slumber served as a tribute to Him who cared for them. And sustenance signified the nourishment received not only in the food and drink, but in the study of the Tomes. In days of old, many households read a principle from the pages of one of the volumes. The little ones were led in a discussion of the meaning and application of the truth they had just heard. Kale had missed that in her upbringing, but she'd learned a lot since she'd come into Paladin's service.

Sipping another cup of sweetened tea, she watched the minor dragons' antics. Once his tummy was full, Pat curled up next to Sir Kemry, looking like a very round, bumpy stone next to the knight's elbow. Filia and Gymn soon joined him. Kale knew by the way the green healing dragon draped himself across her father's shoulder that Sir Kemry would awaken from his nap with more energy and fewer aches.

Kale's feet hurt, so she took out her medicine bag and mixed up an ointment. She put it next to the fire to warm while she pulled off her boots and socks. When the balm felt warm to her fingertip, she scooped up a dab and rubbed the arches of her feet and then her ankles and heels. The medicine tingled as it soothed.

Dibl landed in front of her and flipped onto his back. He wiggled his feet and slapped her leg with his tail.

"You want your muscles soothed as well?"

The minor dragon blushed with anticipation, changing his yellow skin to orange and his orange skin to red.

"Oh, you always look so pretty when you do that." Kale reached for another dab of ointment and picked him up. He purred with contentment, not as a kitten purrs, but as a dragon does. The vibration trembled even the tips of his wings.

She massaged the balm into his arms, legs, and body. When she finished, Ardeo and Metta had lined up for a turn. She rubbed Metta first, and then while she smoothed the ointment over Ardeo's mottled gray skin, Metta sang. Dibl bopped about in a comical, clumsy dance. Kale had to be careful not to laugh too loud and wake her father.

"You know, Ardeo," she said as she finished his tail and put him down, "this reminds me very much of traveling with Wizard Fenworth. I hope my father wakes up with a brilliant plan. Fen would sleep and dream and sometimes concoct the most outrageous scheme. I miss him."

She poured hot water into her cup to warm up her tea and finished it while the three dragons stretched out on a log to soak up what was left of the afternoon sun.

Paladin had charged her with six minor dragons, and soon there would be more. Kale lifted her tunic and unwound from her waist the bulging blue scarf. She had tied six dragon eggs into the long length of material. Of course, not enough time had passed for the eggs to hatch, but they might have quickened. Kale wanted to feel that thrum emanating from each one of them. She'd been too tired last night and the night before to check.

At this stage of hatching the dragon eggs, she didn't have to be careful. The stonelike shells would not break even if she threw them against a boulder. Later, the developing babies would be secure in a leathery shell. On the last day, the shell became brittle, and the newborn would kick and peck its way out.

Kale had never quickened more than one egg at a time. How would she ever handle so many? Good thing they didn't require as much care as infants did. They walked at once, flew soon after, and slept a lot. The second day they searched for their first meals. Keeping the chickens happy in River Away had required more work and was much less fun.

The small creatures even came with a name. As soon as she held the hatchling, she knew its name. Kale thought that was one of the most amazing parts of being a Dragon Keeper. She also thought that it must have something to do with Wulder. She would have to remember to ask her father. After all, he had been a Dragon Keeper for decades.

With care reflecting her awe of dragonkeeping, Kale untied the thin ribbons that secured the eggs, unwrapped the six orbs, and laid them in a row on the soft blue material. The old cloth still held its bright azure color, and the eggs looked deceptively fragile on their long bed. Kale picked up one after another and smiled at the slight pulse she felt from each one.

How am I going to give each of these dragons the attention it needs?

"You aren't their sole caretaker." Kale's father stretched. "I'll be there to help you. The older dragons will mentor the younger ones." He rubbed his hands together. "This is going to be one grand adventure."

He sat beside her and helped rewrap the eggs, securing them with bows that would untie easily. "You know, Kale, I had an interesting thought when I left off sleeping and reentered the wakened state. An image rose out of a fog. The picture may have been left over from a dream, but it sharpened to the point that when I opened my eyes, I thought I might see in reality what I knew was just my wishful thinking."

Kale nodded, watching her father's face, enjoying the sound of his voice. This was something she knew about. Dreams that almost seemed real came to her as well. "I've done that. What did you see, Father?"

"Before I got myself entangled by that sleeping spell, I had a fair amount of dragons in my keep. Two riding dragons, Benrey and Alton. Six major dragons, Poe, Dobkin, Streen, Clive, Wardeg, and Veryan. I wonder if any of my old friends are in this valley of dragons we seek. That is what I saw. My dragons, hale and hearty and waiting for me to come rescue them."

"That would be wonderful." She put her hand on his arm and leaned against his shoulder.

Kale had rarely considered how her father must feel. He woke up from the long sleep induced by Wizard Risto to find his daughter grown, his wife changed by the hardships she had endured, and his dragon friends dispersed, their whereabouts unknown. Her heart contracted at the thought of Celisse, Greer, and all her minor dragons she knew disappearing. Their lives were interwoven with her own. How she would miss them. It pained her just to think about what a loss their absence would create.

She squeezed her father's arm. "I'm sorry. I didn't think about how sad you must be."

Sir Kemry wrinkled his brow. "Sad? I'm not sad. I'm hopeful. Why, it's unheard of that a Dragon Keeper be without dragons."

Kale leaned back to examine his face. He did not look morose, after all, but a bit excited. Her own doubts expressed themselves in her words. "It's been three years."

"Yes, and busy years. Your mother and I returned some order to the Northern Reach, specifically the region surrounding the castle."

Kale shivered. "Mother told me about some of the wild animals that had overtaken the land, nearly consuming all the small creatures and making it unsafe for the high races."

Sir Kemry chuckled. "I have to admit, after years of inactivity, it felt good to hunt down packs of icebears and thin a herd of fanged portucads. Those portucads, if they are young, are very tender and tasty."

She loved to hear her father relate tales of his adventures, but rather than encouraging him to go on, she asked a question to get him to talk of the task ahead. "Have you decided how to get through to the valley?"

"We'll wait until dark and then walk through the center of the camp. I also thought it would be a good time to give those bisonbeck soldiers a scare. They're altogether too cocky for my liking."

"What's the plan?"

"I'm going to teach you a few tricks using your talent to control light."

<hr />

Kale thought they would pull off their major hoax as soon as full dark spread over the land. But her father took her back into the ravine where they were less likely to be seen and made her practice the manipulation of light he had explained. At first she didn't see the necessity, but after trying to maneuver energy particles, she saw she needed to be able to change the intensity quickly and without having to think through the procedure. After they ate supper, they experimented again.

The moon came up, a sliver of waning light. Stars glittered through the chilling air. Kale and her father watched from a distance as the soldiers wrapped themselves in woolen blankets and crawled into their single-sleeper tents. Three guards walked the perimeter of the camp.

"Wait here," said Sir Kemry. He disappeared into the darkness.

Kale knew what he intended to do and that he was capable of the tactic, but nonetheless, her nerves jangled at every little sound. "Oh, Wulder, protect us and help Father bring back two of the guards alive."

By using her talent, she kept track of her father's location. She gritted her teeth when he approached a guard and breathed out a sigh of relief when he stunned the soldier and took command of his mind. Influencing a person with a suggestion placed in his thoughts was not such a difficult thing. Requiring the person to do something contrary to his will was harder. Kale kept tabs on her father as he met up with the second bisonbeck guard and brought him under his power. He returned to Kale, followed by the two subdued soldiers.

"Are you ready to do this?" he asked.

Kale wanted to sound more confident than she felt, so she stood straighter and gave a firm nod. "Yes, let's get into position."

They stole through the tall grass that edged one side of the camp and waited until the third guard was at the farthest point of his route. Kale stood in the middle. Sir Kemry positioned the pair of captured soldiers on either side of her and then took his place directly behind his daughter.

"All right, Kale. Let see what you've learned."

Kale cloaked the two soldiers with a green light that shifted and swirled like a mist. She and her father were enveloped in the edges of the light as it came from both men.

Sir Kemry gave the mental command to begin walking. Kale maintained the quality of the light's performance. Around the men, the luminescence was thin enough for anyone to identify the soldiers. The combined light between them hid the o'rant wizards. As the four walked forward, the light pooled around their feet and drifted away in tendrils of thick green luminosity. To the observer the light snaked away and dissipated while the central illumination remained the same.

The first soldier to see the apparition yelled out a warning. "Attack! We're under attack!"

Bisonbecks roused from their beds and hurled themselves out of their tents with their weapons drawn.

"What wizardry is this?" shouted a voice.

"Isn't that Agore and Illar?" asked another.

"It may be their bodies, but something unnatural has a hold of them."

"Your orders, sir?"

The first gruff voice responded, "Destroy them."

Kale heard her father's cheerful laugh. "Good thing we planned for this."

A pike came flying at them. It hit the green light barrier and appeared to ricochet. Kale knew her father's spell was more complicated than that. Whatever hand had held the weapon was now the target. The pike would return to its owner. Unfortunately for that bisonbeck warrior, the pointed end of the long stick zeroed in on him. The soldier jumped aside in time, but the pike made a wide turn and came hurtling back. This time he tried to catch it. He did but not in the manner he desired. The pike pierced his hand. He screamed.

Kale flinched and marched on, keeping her part of the show operating smoothly. The bisonbecks flung more weapons. Knives, arrows, pikes, and clubs all returned, attacking their owners, usually hitting the hand. If the warrior ducked at the last moment in the wrong direction, his weapon hit him on another part of his body. But then the instrument of destruction would pull back and again try for the hand that had last touched it.

Soon the orderly military encampment dissolved into utter chaos. The beleaguered soldiers ran helter-skelter trying to avoid their own flying weapons. They crashed into one another, knocked over tents, and hollered for help. Kale and her escorts plodded along. When they reached the inside of the canyon beyond the camp, Sir Kemry turned the bisonbecks around and sent them trudging back. The greenish, flowing light clung to them.

"How soon will your suggestion to keep walking wear off?" asked Kale.

He shrugged. "Maybe six or seven miles on the other side of their outpost. But without you to sustain the light energy, that will fade in just a few minutes."

"I hope they don't run into any wild animals in the night."

"Kale, this is the enemy. You aren't supposed to be wishing no harm comes to them."

"I just like to think they'd have a fighting chance if, say, a fanged portucad attacked."

"We are too far south for one of those beasts. They're more likely to run into a Creemoor spider."

Kale shuddered. The huge, poisonous spiders gave her the creeps. She'd seen the ugly monsters close up and been poisoned. If not for the combined efforts of Bardon, Gymn, Paladin, and Wizard Fenworth, she would have died. Even now when she heard the sound of a twig scritching against a rock, she remembered the noise made as the hideous creatures advanced.

The hair on the back of her neck stood up. Was it because she was thinking of the spiders that she heard that scritch? Perhaps a tree limb scraped the side of the canyon wall.

"Speaking of which," began her father.

"Which 'which'?" interrupted Kale.

"Creemoor spiders," said her father, pulling his sword. "I believe we have encountered the first obstacle in our trip through the gorge to the valley. I count eight. How about you?"

Kale surveyed the area as her father had done, with her mind and not her eyes. "Yes, eight, but a half dozen are very young."

"That's not to our advantage, daughter. The young ones are not as heavy and therefore jump farther."

"Of course," said Kale. With a sigh, she pulled her weapon from its sheath.

35

Madness

Leetu Bends and Bardon left Latho at the first town they reached and went ahead, riding horses. Bardon wanted to get back to Sir Dar, report what they had seen, and get started on some sort of defense for the kimens against the grawligs.

They traveled a straight trade-route road to the seacoast. Crops covered the rolling hills on each side of the wide lane. Some of the fertile fields had yet to be harvested. Others showed the stubble left after the summer's yield had been gathered. No other part of Amara had more productive farmland.

When they stopped to water the horses, Bardon surveyed a stretch of land beside the stream. On the other side of the brook, an orchard stood in straight rows with plump parnot fruit dangling from the branches. "I don't see any evidence of the war between Pretender and Stox and Cropper here."

Leetu petted her horse's nose. "Maybe they're smart enough not to damage the crops that keep their armies' bellies full."

"I doubt that they waste much time thinking about the comfort of their minions." Following the emerlindian's example, Bardon rubbed his horse's face. He preferred a dragon and was uncomfortable around these animals.

Leetu tilted her head. "What's that noise?"

Bardon strained to hear something unusual, but only the slight breeze whistling through the leaves above them sounded in his ears. His mount snorted and shuffled his hooves.

Leetu Bends sprang into her saddle. "Come on!"

Bardon's horse danced away as he tried to put his foot in the stirrup. "Be still, beast."

The horse circled him, unable to get away since Bardon held the reins. Bardon calmed his voice. "All right. I'm talking to you nicely. I really do like horses. I think you're beautiful. You're very useful." He crept closer and stroked the animal's neck. "I don't know what I'd do without you. Now, you're going to be a good boy and let me get in the saddle, aren't you?"

A whuffling noise came out of the horses nostrils, and Bardon took that as a yes. He put his foot in the stirrup and heaved himself onto the horse's back. "Now, we have to catch Leetu Bends and see what she's up to. No more tricks, all right?"

He dug his heels into the horse's flanks. His mount arched his back and crowhopped twice.

Bardon yelped but kept his seat. "That's right. You don't like to be touched on the flanks. Greer is not that picky. On the other hand, my legs don't reach his flanks. Let's try this again. I promise to be more considerate."

Bardon's ride took off at a full run with only a tap of the knight's heels on his sides. He caught up with Leetu Bends as she entered a line of trees. Weaving through the skinny trunks of a gordon grove, Bardon nearly lost her again. Her agility on horseback astonished him.

Now he heard the grunts and growls she must have heard earlier. Leetu burst through heavy underbrush into a clearing, Bardon right behind her.

Five grawligs gathered around a tree, snarling at their prey in the upper branches. A kimen, pale and panting, sat on one of the thinnest limbs at the top of the gordon tree. Slick bark covered the trunk and peeled away easily, making it hard for the mountain ogres to climb.

Bardon and Leetu Bends pulled their bows from where they were strapped to their backs. Bardon cocked his arrow and shouted, "Hold!"

The grawligs didn't acknowledge the command. Their present pursuit thoroughly occupied their attention, a madness that prevailed over reason.

The tree shook under their assault. Three ogres clawed at the tree trunk. One tried to clamber onto the back of another to reach a lower branch.

Leetu Bends's arrow whistled through the air and sank into the fleshy ear of one of the ogres. The grawlig screeched, grabbed his ear with one hand, and pulled out the arrow with the other. He stamped his feet and let out a horrific wail, then to Bardon's surprise, returned to his battering of the tree trunk.

Bardon joined Leetu in sending a barrage of arrows at the frenzied grawligs. Leetu killed two. A skilled shot pierced the eye of one grawlig on the opposite side of the tree as he leaned toward his comrade. The arrow penetrated its brain. The second shot in the head entered through the ear.

Bardon aimed to wound. After annoying the beasts with well-aimed shots to their tender ears, he realized he hadn't deterred even one.

Leetu took that moment to lower her bow and scowl at him. "Shoot to kill. If they turn on us, we've got very little defense."

"That's just it," Bardon said. "Look at them. They aren't fighting back. All their concentration is on that poor kimen. Nothing deters them."

"Right! Nothing! Only death. We have to kill them to make them stop." She sighted down her arrow once more.

It bothered Bardon's sense of ethics to shoot at the backs of the enemy. He got down from his horse, laid down his bow, pulled out his sword, and approached the three remaining grawligs. Leetu felled another one as he advanced.

He slapped the broadside of his sword across the muscular back of one beast. This creature stood at least seven feet tall and outweighed Bardon by a hundred pounds. Bardon gagged at the stench rising from his matted hair. He stepped back.

The mountain ogre ignored him.

Bardon swung again, this time leaving a line of blood across the back of the beast's arm and slicing through the material of his ragged shirt. The pain got the grawlig's attention. He turned, raised two massive hands to smash this pest. Bardon thrust his sword into the attacking grawlig's chest. The weight of the falling enemy struck Bardon, knocked him down, and pinned him to the ground.

With the air pressed out of him and his nose buried in sweat-soaked, greasy hair, Bardon thought he might expire from the simultaneous need to breathe and vomit. He heard Leetu's scornful laugh and felt the weight of the grawlig shift.

Bardon rolled twice, once to get out from under the ogre, and the second time to lie face upward in the wonderful, fresh air. He sat up and scooted backward, away from the grawlig corpses. The atmosphere surrounding them was not as fresh as he wanted. He scooted back some more, sucking in cleaner air with each effort. He saw the fifth grawlig lying peacefully next to the gordon tree trunk.

Bardon pulled a handkerchief from his pocket and covered his nose.

Leetu Bends sat down beside him and shaded her eyes to peer up between the lacy leaves. "Are you hurt?"

Tears welled in Bardon's eyes. He hoped he wouldn't further disgrace himself by emptying his stomach. "No, I'll be all right."

"I wasn't talking to you." Leetu cupped her hand to her mouth. "Do you need help? Do you want me to come up and get you?"

A squeak answered her query.

Bardon could not make out the words, but Leetu did. "She's coming."

"The kimen is a female?"

Bardon's eyes roamed over the five hefty grawligs who had hounded one tiny kimen. His queasiness passed as anger roiled in his veins. He jumped to his feet and strode over to the tree in time to offer his arms to the small woman who had descended from its heights. She leapt from the last branch into his kind embrace.

"I'm so sorry, m'lady." Bardon held the shivering form gently. "Can you tell us where to take you? Do you have friends or family nearby?"

"You're sick," said the kimen. "I can feel the fever in you."

"My concern right now is to find you sanctuary."

She quivered, making her dress flutter. The material woven of light lifted and swirled and settled over Bardon's coat sleeve.

She tsked. "Those hounds chased me for a hundred miles."

"We're going to our headquarters outside of Grail. Would you like to accompany us, and perhaps give your statement of what is happening to our commander?"

"No, no. I want to go home."

Leetu Bends came closer. "I don't believe it's safe."

She shuddered. "You're right, but I'm not sure what to do."

Bardon jerked his head around and stared into the sky. A small black dot grew larger. "Greer."

He patted the kimen awkwardly on her tiny shoulder and handed her to Leetu Bends. "My dragon has arrived."

Joy swelled in his heart as he walked to the nearby stubbled field. *What brings you, my friend?*

He listened to the thoughts pummeling him from his dragon, and then answered. *Yes, there* has *been a battle but we're all right… No, I have not been grousing and grumbling all day… I certainly did not yearn for your presence. It's convenient to have you here. I've been riding a clod of a horse. Leetu always seems to pick the better animal… I doubt that my handling of the beast is a deterrent to good behavior… I am not sick. I just became overwhelmed by the stench of a grawlig while it was lying across my face… Well, I was glad to see you. Now, I am not so sure.*

Greer landed, and Bardon jogged out to him. The big dragon rested his chin on his knight's head, rubbing back and forth.

You're messing up my hair... Well, yes, I guess I am a bit of a mess as it is... I know I smell like grawlig, and I need a bath. Bardon reached up and patted Greer's chin. *I'm glad you're here.*

Leetu Bends agreed to Bardon's plan. He would take the kimen with him on Greer, and she would take his horse with her.

"You do look peaked." Leetu Bends placed a hand on his forehead. "And you have a fever."

"I'll be all right."

Leetu picked up the kimen and handed her up to the saddle on Greer's back. "You keep an eye on him, Izz. Kale, his wife, says he's the sweetest berry on the bush, but I think he is *not* the sharpest thorn in the patch. He's likely to think he can do anything instead of taking care of his body first."

"All I could do is nag him." Izz laughed, sounding like the gurgling of water over stones in a creek.

"Nagging is acceptable."

"Pardon me, ladies," Bardon interrupted. "I'm right here, and we'll be back at Grail before Izz has an opportunity to nag me."

They flew off, and Bardon expected an uneventful trip. However, three times in the short distance, they swooped down out of the sky and rescued more tiny victims. He delivered six of the kimen race to headquarters early that evening. He escorted them into Sir Dar's presence without delay.

"Oh my," said Dar when he saw their condition. "I shall send for Lady Allerion immediately."

Sir Dar's sense of hospitality took over, and he treated the rattled victims like visiting royalty. Over tea and daggarts, they calmed down and told their tales. Each resembled the other. A sudden onslaught of slavering grawligs, a harrowing chase, and the last-minute rescue by Sir Bardon and Greer.

Leetu Bends came through the flap of the tent. Her disheveled appearance testified to the hard ride she'd made to reach headquarters swiftly. Dar served her and introduced her to the kimens she hadn't met. A ripple of amusement momentarily lifted Bardon's spirits as he watched the military-minded emerlindian try to be socially adept. Leetu Bends was worse at social amenities than he had ever been.

Lady Allerion arrived and escorted the refugees to secure and cozy lodgings.

Dar, Leetu Bends, and Bardon sat in silence for a while. Bardon found it hard to swallow. His throat felt raw and swollen, so he poured himself another cup of tea.

Leetu Bends gave an account of what she and Bardon had witnessed at the grawlig camp. She also gave an account of why Latho was not with them and what they had encountered that bore out the tales of the kimens being hounded. Bardon merely nodded when necessary.

Sir Dar's ears lay back as he frowned at Bardon and Leetu. "This explains some of the incidents we've heard about in the last twenty-four hours."

He sighed and looked at a chart behind his desk. "We can move some of our men off the quiss defense and have them patrol Trese. Any rampaging grawligs shall be arrested. If they resist, our troops have permission to shoot to kill."

Bardon swallowed the last bit of his beverage and wished there were more. "They will all resist, sir."

"And sooner or later," added Leetu Bends, "they will sniff out the kimens we have brought here.

Dar's ears perked up, and a bright gleam entered his eye. "Another trap, perhaps? We shall house the kimens away from the main camp and be on guard. When the grawligs arrive, we shall have the upper hand."

Bardon shifted in his seat, wishing his bones did not ache so. "That doesn't sound too comfortable for the kimens."

"You're in charge of their security, Sir Bardon. Set up a periphery and guard it well. Perhaps build a holding pen you can drive the grawligs into when they attack."

"Yes sir."

"Are you all right?" Dar cocked an eyebrow at his comrade.

"I'm fine."

36

In the Canyon

Kale put her back to one wall of the narrow gorge, and her father positioned himself against the other wall. The minor dragons came out of their pocket-dens to help in the upcoming battle. Ardeo illuminated the area enough for Kale and her father to advance without falling over rocks along the path. They edged forward, sidestepping against the base of the cliffs.

"This is our strategy," said Sir Kemry. "You take the six immature spiders."

"Me?" Kale's voice squeaked. She cleared her throat.

"Yes. Throw a blanket of light over them, much like you did for our bisonbeck friends back there."

"All right." She congratulated herself that she sounded confident.

"Draw the spiders together so that eventually you have them under one covering. Maintaining a shield will be easier for you when it is one rather than six. Reverse the flow of the energy. Instead of things hitting the outside and being reflected, when the creatures strike the inside wall, their momentum will bounce back at them. Any questions so far?"

"No. Well, yes. What do you want the minor dragons to do?"

"What they do best."

"Spit."

"Yes, spit. And tell them not to get entrapped in your light barrier." He paused for a moment, and Kale knew he was reevaluating the combat zone ahead. He nodded. "They haven't changed positions. Once you get all six of your targets under one radiant shell, squeeze them together by decreasing the size of the holding pen. Hopefully, they will become agitated and fight among themselves."

Kale thought the plan sounded solid, but she had to admit approaching the giant insects made her nervous. "Shouldn't we be sneaking up on the spiders?"

"They already know we're here and are waiting. But they don't know we know they know. If we were to stop talking, they might come investigate, and we want to use their instinct to ambush us to our advantage."

"Right." Kale inched along the wall. She put her sword away, knowing she'd rather have her hands empty while she controlled the light shield. It didn't make much sense, since she used her mind to manipulate the energy particles. But she did use her body to channel energy, and sometimes she used her hands and arms because it felt comfortable to act out what she configured mentally.

"Father?"

"Yes?"

"What are you going to be doing?"

He chuckled. "Taking a vacation. No. I am going to cast a fireball on the spider that will be closest to you when we come upon them. Be careful you don't get caught by surprise. It should be a nice toasty explosion."

Kale laughed. "I've seen one before, thrown by Wizard Fenworth."

"Ahem. Well, I daresay mine will be a little more defined around the edges. If I remember, his used to splat on the target."

"It did, indeed, splat."

"After I have annihilated the first spider, I'll lengthen my sword and battle the second."

"Sounds like a good strategy."

"We're almost there." He hefted a shiny black orb in his hand. It began to glow. "We'll soon know."

Sir Kemry stepped into the middle of the passageway, took three more paces, and threw his fireball to a space ahead of Kale. She shielded her eyes, then lost no time in propelling six light nets over the immature spiders.

The fire consumed the ambushing spider, burned out in a matter of seconds, and left a charred carcass that crumbled into a black pile of ash. Kale stepped around it and focused on bringing the six separate bubbles of light together. Through trial and error, she discovered she could move one to join another and then move that one more easily to swallow up a third. The larger the circumference of the barrier, the easier it was to manipulate. She worked alone. All of the minor dragons bombarded the larger Creemoor spider with their acidic saliva.

The brief battle ended as Kale hoped it would. Sir Kemry vanquished the spider and joined her to help tighten the container that trapped the smaller spiders. The crowded spiders began to clash. They snapped at one another with pincers. Kale turned away as one beast tore off the leg of another.

"All right. That's enough." She thickened the opaque quality of the light until she could see nothing but faint shadows. Then she and the others waited until lack of movement within indicated the fracas had ended.

"Do you suppose they're all dead?" Kale asked her father.

"Maybe." He continued to be vigilant, eyes on the light shield, chin jutted forward.

Kale knew that he was monitoring more than the isolated spiders. They didn't want to be attacked from behind while their attention focused on the captives. She did a mental reconnaissance, but her hold on the container slipped. It would be best for her to concentrate on one thing.

"Do you think we can lower the shield?" she asked.

"I think that would be a good plan, but be prepared to slay any who may have survived. Wait a moment. I want to put a protective shield in front of us. No sense in being poisoned after the fight is finished."

He worked for a full three minutes weaving a protective wall. Kale noted he used a technique similar to binding the edge of a gateway. The process enthralled her, as this method offered more possibilities than the one she had been taught. When he finished, he put his hands on his hips as he inspected his handiwork.

"That should hold," he said. "Kale, let the little beasties go."

First, Kale thinned the light so they could see the shapes within the enclosure. Two still twitched.

When she let the barrier drop, Sir Kemry pitched a fireball into the spiders' midst and incinerated them all.

"I wish all conflicts went so well," he said as he cleaned his sword with a cloth. "Shall we go on and face our next challenge? Or do you need a rest?"

Kale tilted her head and scrutinized her father. The exertion of channeling energy had worn her down. Gathering the force to develop a fireball, contain it until dispensed, and minimize the collateral damage required a great deal of fortitude. Building the reflective shield to protect them drained her father further.

If one were not a wizard, one had no idea how much strength performing "magic" entailed. Magic involved recollection of minute details, envisioning a shift in actual circumstances, then the ordering of many small pieces of the puzzle. Finally, the release of the created force required timing. And if the wizard accidentally bumped up against one of Wulder's irrefutable laws, the "spell" could backfire and injure the instigator. Fenworth used to call these conflicting components H-2-oil.

"H-2-oil," Kale said.

"What?"

"Fenworth used to say, 'H-2-oil, water and oil do not mix.' He was warning Regidor and me not to try to do something that Wulder did not allow."

Sir Kemry sheathed his sword and spread his hands in a questioning gesture. "And that applies to what in this situation?"

Kale shook her head, her hair slipping out of its binding. "Nothing really, except that I'm very tired. I don't know if I could handle another attack without some rest."

"Fine, then. We shall set up a protective shell around us, snuggle down into some warm blankets, set a dragon to watch, and sleep."

"Oh, Father, that sounds first-rate."

Kale fixed supper out of food she had packed in her hollow. Sir Kemry produced blankets, pillows, and a pair of thick body-length cushions out of his. After they ate, he played a few sweet melodies on his flute. Metta sang, and they all relaxed. Tomorrow would be soon enough to face the trials and tribulations Burner Stox had in store for them. The minor dragons would guard the camp during the night.

Kale slept almost as soon as her head rested upon the pillow. She dreamed of Bardon, Sir Dar, and Regidor. The men sang in a tavern and didn't miss her at all. In her next dream, her mother and Toopka played benders and didn't notice that her chair was empty. Finally, Kale roused herself from slumber to get away from her pining to be with the other members of her family.

She rubbed her eyes. She should be able to see the skylights, but something obscured the stars and moon. Had clouds gathered while they slept? She sensed she was alone, yet her father should be within reach, and five dragons should be cuddled close to her. The sixth one guarded them. Or did he?

Kale remembered Leetu Bends's description of being inside a mordakleep. Her breath caught in her throat. Where was she?

37

GRAWLIG BRAWL

Bardon stood watching as men built sturdy walls out of log poles. Izz glided through the trees. He watched her coming and noted her dress of a yellow hue. The lighter color indicated hope.

"I have a plan," she said without preamble. "The other kimens and I have been discussing our predicament."

"I'm willing to listen. This enclosure will hold the grawligs for a short time. If the brutes become frenzied, I'm afraid they'll be able to break out."

"Yes. We thought so too." Izz waved at a group of men who were covering a finished wall with branches, camouflaging the trap. "The ogres will race in, you'll swing the gate shut, then what will happen?"

"I've asked Lady Allerion to work on something that would either sedate them or extinguish this mad desire they have to annihilate all kimens."

"We want you to leave them to us after you have them trapped."

Bardon jerked. A sharp pain stabbed his temple, and the ache in his neck and shoulders reminded him he still had a fever. "I'd like to know what you're planning. I can't hand over a half dozen wild monsters set on killing you. For some reason, that doesn't sound like you would come out alive. Please explain to me the part I must be missing."

"From what I understand," said Izz, "the grawligs hunt us because of our scent. What do you suppose would happen if we shot them with our arrows? Our arrows would be like small darts to the grawligs, but they smell of us. And we will rub the arrows in our hair to make sure the scent is strong."

A devious smile lifted the corners of Bardon's mouth. If they were plotting against the bisonbecks, the plan would not work. But grawligs were known for their lack of intelligence.

"It's a good plan, Izz. Tell your friends we're grateful for their help. You realize if something goes wrong, your people will be in the middle of the chaos."

The truth of that statement settled on the little woman's face. "Our whole race is in danger." Her shoulders squared. "We can do this."

By the time the men finished with the enclosure and tested the swinging gate that would trap the grawligs, Bardon felt like he'd been in battle for a day and spent the night rowing a boat across turbulent waters. Sweat soaked his clothing. His head spun with every step he took.

"Would you bring me a drink, Lo Kyl?"

"Another one, sir? Are you all right?"

"I'm fine." He ruined the declaration by succumbing to a coughing fit. The soldier ran to get his drink.

Bardon lay on his cot, thinking that he should send for Kale and Gymn. Not that she would be able to come, even if he did locate her. But Lady Allerion's herbal tea had done nothing to alleviate his misery. "Or maybe it did." He groaned. "Maybe I'd be dead if I hadn't swallowed that awful concoction."

Sir Dar snored in the cot across the room. Bardon tossed his covers aside and turned over. Cold air hit his feet, and he scrambled to straighten the blankets.

"Sir!" a voice barked outside the door. "We've reports that grawligs are closing in on the trap."

"Good!" Bardon sat up, swinging his legs over the side of the cot. He made the move too quickly. Clutching the side of the bed, he waited a moment for a wave of dizziness to pass.

He managed to get out of the tent right behind Dar. The little doneel scurried toward the dragon field. Both officers mounted their dragons and flew into the star-studded sky.

Greer immediately cross-examined his rider.

Bardon huffed. *There's nothing wrong with me but a sore throat and headache… Yes, I'm fit enough for this mission. Quit nagging me.*

Bardon and Dar circled low and saw the small band of grawligs crashing through the woods, headed for their trap. The dragon riders landed in a field on the opposite side of the trees, then jogged to the enclosure and climbed to the lookout platform above. The crude structure had half-walls around the sides except for the entrance at the top of the ladder.

Four kimens stood with their bows ready. The fifth kimen ran in circles within the enclosure. The baying of the grawligs drew nearer. Bardon shook, trying to release the tension all in one shake rather than shiver continuously.

The mountain ogres smashed through the last break the men had constructed. As they entered the trap, the lone kimen on the ground scurried up the wall to safety. Soldiers pushed the gate closed behind the grawligs. The kimens let loose with a barrage of arrows.

The grawligs froze in bewilderment, then spun back and forth, trying to figure out what had happened. Some slapped at the pricks caused by the tiny arrows.

Just as the words formed in Bardon's mind that their trick was not working, a grawlig growled and attacked one of his comrades.

Izz turned to the back of the platform. "I'm not staying to watch this." She disappeared over the edge, and the other kimens trailed behind her.

The noise from below reminded Bardon of stray dogs in an alley, fighting over a scrap of meat. Occasionally, he heard an oath, but for the most part there were no words, just animal grunts, snarls, and yelps.

"Go back to headquarters," said Dar. "You look awful. Take some more of that tea Lady Allerion gave you and sleep."

Bardon rose from his crouching position, clenching his jaw to hold back a moan. The aches had intensified in the cold treetop. "You wouldn't call it tea if you'd had a sip."

Dar, with his face turned away from the savage contest going on below, managed a chuckle. His expression turned somber. "Go home. Sleep. The men and I will clean up after this is over."

Bardon thought of the climb down the ladder made of tree branches, the tramp through the woods, and the ride back to camp on Greer. He shivered, pulled a wool blanket out of his knapsack, and curled up on the rough floor of the lookout platform.

Sir Dar watched him make his bed. "Well, if you are determined to stay, I'm going." He pulled a wad out of his carrier. "Here's my blanket to add to yours."

Dar gave orders to some men about the procedure he wanted followed. Within minutes Bardon fell into a deep sleep and heard no more.

Something bumped against his leg. "Oh, excuse me," said a soft, high voice.

Bardon stirred and heard grawligs below. He sat up.

"I'm sorry," said a kimen. "I tripped over you. They sent word for us to come back."

Bardon shook the haze from his mind and leaned over to view the mayhem below. A marione lehman passed beneath on the outside of the barricades.

"Soldier, report!"

The man snapped to attention and looked around.

"Up here."

The soldier lifted his gaze to the lookout platform. "Three more grawligs, sir. We're having trouble getting them into the pen. They smell the kimen on the dead brutes and are confused."

Bardon released the man. "About your business, soldier." He turned to the five kimens waiting with their arrows notched. "Shoot arrows into the trap far away from the door. See if we can lure them in."

The little warriors shot. The strings pinged, and the arrows swished through the air.

"Five more," said Bardon.

The kimens complied.

One grawlig stumbled through the opening. He pulled in air through his nose and gave a roar. The other two ogres lurched into the trap. The door swung shut as the kimens drew bead on the milling monsters. Less than a minute after they had delivered the scented arrows, the grawligs turned on one another.

Bardon sank to the floor, his back against the lookout's wall. "We should set this sort of trap up in other parts of Trese."

"You're sick." Izz place her hand on his forehead. She turned to speak to one of her comrades.

Bardon heard what sounded like birds chirping to one another. *Birds wouldn't be singing in the middle of the night. They certainly wouldn't be this close to a grawlig brawl.*

"Drink this," a voice commanded.

Bardon sipped.

"Lie down."

He allowed his body to collapse. Something squirmed beside him.

"Not on me."

Another voice drifted through the fog of his mind. "What do you think is wrong with him?"

"I think he has stakes."

"That's a childhood disease."

"Not if you get it as an adult."

"He's pretty sick, isn't he?"

"He's deathly ill."

Bardon tried to open his mouth. *I'll be fine. Just let me sleep.*

38

CAUGHT

Kale reached farther into the darkness, trying to locate the dragons. Her hand touched nothing, no blankets, no cushion, no ground below. From a distance, Sir Kemry's voice echoed. "Take my hand."

She sat up. "Father?"

"Take my hand."

She stretched her arms in circles around her and encountered nothing. "I can't find you."

"Concentrate on my voice." He sang a melody she knew from her brief time at The Hall. This hymn announced the morning vespers and had been sung by a baritone from one of the towers each dawn.

Was she moving, or was the gloom around her moving? Something swirled against her cheeks, but it did not feel like air.

Metta's clear tones joined her father's song.

Kale attempted to stand. She had nothing to push against. She seemed to be hanging in mid air. She rolled onto her stomach and tried to "swim" toward the sound of her father's voice. Again, she could not push or pull with her hands or feet.

Terror shivered her spine. *Mordakleeps! Am I inside a mordakleep?* "Father?"

Metta kept singing as her father answered. "No, not a mordakleep, but a Burner Stox replication of one. While mordakleeps live and breathe, I detect no organic form in this abominable abyss."

"So we can't whack off its tail and escape?"

"I'm afraid not. Keep following my voice." He joined Metta, harmonizing with her alto.

Kale kicked and thrashed her arms about. Since she couldn't see anything, she didn't know if she had moved past anything. Since she couldn't feel anything, she couldn't tell if her body traveled any distance due to her maneuvering. As far as she could tell, she moved not one inch.

Kale sighed, crossed her arms, and rested her forehead on them. The song ceased.

"Kale," Sir Kemry called.

"What's wrong?"

"Nothing. Metta found me. She says the singing linked us so that we could come together. Sing, Kale!"

Metta and Sir Kemry now crooned a reverent ode to Wulder. Kale lifted her head and her voice. The atmosphere around her changed—warm and damp. Kale sang louder. The air altered back to the stagnant, lifeless state. Kale concentrated on blending her voice with the others, so that she harmonized with each note. Metta helped her with the words and tones. Again the heavy darkness ebbed and flowed in a pleasant, moist current.

Now she felt as though she was floating. The other singing voices became more distinct. Air brushed against her like a warm breath. Her father's voice drew nearer. She reached toward the song. In the dark, Metta landed awkwardly on Kale's back. She gave a trill of joy and flew off. A moment later, Kale heard the same trill from a short distance away. Metta returned, still singing. Her cry of joy burst from her throat as soon as her feet touched Kale.

Both Dragon Keepers understood that the other had reached the same conclusion. Metta was flying between them and calling out each time she connected. Each trip between father and daughter shortened until the singing dragon hopped from Sir Kemry's shoulder to the top of Kale's head. Her father pulled her into his arms. The song broke off as they laughed and embraced.

"I can feel the floor beneath my feet," said Kale.

"Feels good, doesn't it?" Her father tightened his hug. "And I can feel the material of your cape." He touched the crown of her head and brought his hands down to cover her ears, then rest on her neck. "And your hair. It's fallen down again, just like your mother's. She can't keep up a bun for the life of her."

Kale giggled. She might not have the stately beauty of her mother, but they shared unruly hair.

"How are we going to get out of here?" asked Kale. "And where are the other dragons?"

Metta answered. The other dragons had been snagged by Burner Stox and trapped in Greenbright Valley. Metta and the others had searched. She saw the black dungeon and heard Sir Kemry's voice.

"You deliberately flew into this horrible darkness?" asked Kale.

Metta assured her she had. How else would she have found her o'rant wizards?

"Father, can we follow Metta out the same way she came in?"

"I don't believe it is that simple. Metta's as stuck in here as we are."

Kale felt the little dragon slide down her hair and perch on her shoulder. Metta rubbed her head under Kale's chin.

"Then what do you suggest, Father?"

"We are fighting darkness, and you are the light wizard. I think this one is up to you."

"Oh dear."

"Try something small first."

Kale held out her hand, and a tiny glimmer illuminated her palm. "That's not much."

"Don't talk," said Sir Kemry. "Concentrate."

Kale intensified the glow enough to shine on the faces of the three standing there.

"You *are* untidy," remarked her father.

Kale frowned at him. "I was sleeping."

He scowled in mock disapproval, and then their faces broke into grins. Metta chirruped.

Kale turned her head. "Look, there's a small light coming our way. Ardeo!"

Sir Kemry barked a laugh. "Ha! A second minor dragon gives up his freedom—well, relative freedom—to come to your aid."

"Your aid too," insisted Kale. "And, I think possibly, Metta. Metta is his favorite sister."

Ardeo perched on Kale's other shoulder. She laughed at his assurance that now that both he and Metta were here, they would soon be free.

"I'm sure that will be so," she commented and then gazed at the flickering light in her hand. "But this small offering is not enough to dent this massive shadow."

Metta flew to Sir Kemry's head. "We'll sing," he said.

Ardeo scampered down her arm to sit next to the insignificant light. It instantly brightened.

With the song as a backdrop, Kale imagined a tendril coming out from the orb. In her palm, the sphere bulged on one side and popped out a feeler as a vine would reach out with new growth. This branch shot out, burst, and produced more tendrils. Another bulge formed on the orb and let out a long string of radiance. The light plant glowed through the stem, branches, and tiny leaves. Light streams stretched into the darkness and pushed back the gloom. The branches grew until the plant filled the dark dungeon and continued to grow.

"Look," said Kale and nodded toward the farthest limb.

A crack shone in the solid black, allowing a stream of sunshine to pierce the inside. Another crack appeared and another. Soon the outer shell of the abyss shattered and crumbled, exposing a beautiful countryside with mountains all around.

Sir Kemry cheered, and the dragons chirruped their delight.

"Well done, daughter." He surveyed the land beyond the dense vines of the light-shining plant encasing them. "I believe we're in Greenbright Valley. I see several dragons, major and riding dragons. Are those minor dragons in that tree? It seems to be a whole flock of them." He clapped his hands together. "Good, good. Now let's explore and see what we are up against."

"The vine should wither in a day or two," said Kale.

Sir Kemry gave her a sharp look. "What are you saying? Now we are trapped inside this twisted light vegetation?"

Kale shrugged. "Sort of."

"Sort of?" Sir Kemry barked. "What kind of a sentence is that?"

Kale shrugged again and bent her head to hide the grin that tickled the corners of her mouth. The relief of being out of the clinging darkness made her lightheaded. Surely, it wouldn't be that hard to get through a jungle of vines made of light.

39

Mordakleeps
in Your Dreams

Bardon lay on wrinkled, sweat-soaked sheets in a cool room with the sound of gentle waves lapping at the pier. The hostel where Lady Allerion had deposited him sat half on land and half on the wooden wharf. He couldn't recall when he came, how he came, or how much time had passed since he came.

His mother-in-law entered his quarters with two people behind her, a chambermaid and a leecent.

The young woman carrying sheets scooted behind Lady Lyll, keeping out of Bardon's sight. "Is he going to die, m'lady?"

"No, he's passed the dangerous days, but he'll be uncomfortable for a good while longer."

The leecent spoke up. "That's why I've been assigned to him as personal batman."

The maid giggled. "Sounds like you belong in a cave or an old barn."

"It means personal servant to one of high rank."

"La-de-dah. Sounds like a chambermaid position to me."

Lady Lyll tsked at them. "You two hush and get busy. We've a lot to do, and if he wakes, we don't want to tire him by hustling around the room."

"I'm awake," Bardon croaked.

"Oh, good. You'll be worn out when we're through, but you'll feel fresher and more alive."

The gleam of her teeth in a wide smile told Bardon that he was not going to like her plans. "Time to clean up, drink some broth, and get a little exercise."

Bardon groaned and turned to the wall.

"I know you're weak. Leecent Voet will lift you out of the bed, and he and Mistress Traysian will help you walk to the chair."

With a monumental effort, Bardon turned over and sat up on the side of the bed. No batman was going to pick him up like a baby. He couldn't get his legs to cooperate and had to accept help to his feet and then to the chair.

"Fine," said Lady Lyll, signaling Traysian to fetch the tray. "You must eat and drink."

Leecent Voet dragged a table close, and Traysian put the tray down in front of Bardon. His dinner consisted of hot chicken broth and cold cider. He tried to protest that there was not even a crust of bread, but he was too weak to make the effort of a jest. He moved his hand to pick up the spoon and nearly fell over. Leecent Voet rescued him.

"Aren't you...," began Bardon.

"What, sir?"

"Afraid of..."

"Of catching the stakes? No sir. I had 'em as a baby." He tucked a napkin under Bardon's chin and lifted the spoon to feed him.

"I can..."

The batman deftly tipped the broth into Bardon's mouth while he protested. He leaned forward and whispered, "Come on, Sir Bardon, eat this up. I've seen the brew Lady Allerion wants you to drink after, and believe me, this is much more tasty. If you take enough of this, we can say you're full-up for the time being."

Bardon submitted to the humiliation of being fed. While Leecent Voet poked the spoon in his mouth and held the glass to his lips, his mother-in-law and Traysian changed the sheets. Bardon concentrated on cooperating with Voet. In his head, he knew the nourishment would be beneficial, but his body wanted to burrow into the covers and be left alone. Under Lady Lyll's direction, the chambermaid opened the windows to air out the room and brought in something spicy-sweet smelling that stewed in a ceramic bowl over a short candle.

"Potpourri," Traysian told Voet when he asked.

Bardon knew he should be grateful for the food and the care, but the activity in the room annoyed him. Halfway through the broth and cider, he could no longer hold his head up. His chin rested on his chest, and his neck muscles refused to lift such a heavy burden as his big head.

Lady Allerion came and placed a hand on the nape of his neck. "No fever at present. We'll just leave you men to do the rest."

She and Traysian bustled out and closed the door behind them.

"Rest?" Bardon croaked.

"A bath, sir."

"No." He tried to shake his head but couldn't.

"You see, sir, it's this 'chain of command,' sir." The batman crouched beside the chair so he could look Sir Bardon in the eye. "Now strictly speaking, Lady Allerion is not in the position to command me or to over-ride one of your commands to me."

Bardon felt a moment of relief. No bath.

"But I took my orders from Sir Dar, and his orders were that I was to do what Lady Allerion told me to do."

Traysian came back in with a large earthenware bowl of water. She put it down on the table, then pulled a bar of soap and a washrag out of her apron pocket. She turned without a word and left.

Leecent Voet slapped his hands on his knees and stood. "Right, then.

Let's get this over with, sir, and I'd appreciate it, if you ever find me under your command again, that you either forgive me for this indignity, or forget my face altogether. My name, too."

Bardon alternately stewed over the process of getting sponge bathed or slipping into an uneasy sleep, sitting up in the hard chair. The warm water relaxed him, and Leecent Voet sang under his breath in a very decent tenor as he worked.

Lying back down on the clean sheets felt like a soft bed after a hard campaign. And Leecent Voet got him tucked in before Lady Allerion came back with her medicinal tea.

Bardon kept his eyes closed when he heard her enter, and if he'd been able, he would have cheered for the batman when he said, "I wouldn't wake him now, m'lady. He's exhausted and needs to sleep. Leave that tea here, and we can reheat it later when he wakes."

The door closed. The table scraped across the floor. "Sir, I'm putting this glass of water and this cup of tea right next to you. When I come back tomorrow, if you haven't drunk it, I'm going to have to heat the tea up again. That is, unless you knock it over during the night. So be careful when you reach out." Leecent Voet paused. "Sir, did you need anything else before I go?"

Bardon winced and opened his lips enough to get the word out. "No."

"I'd stay, sir, but we're short of men, and I'm pulling double duty."

Bardon wanted to ask why they were suddenly short of men, what kind of duty Voet would be going to, and why they had billeted him in town instead of at the camp. Instead, he drifted off to sleep.

Bardon woke up chilled. He glanced at one of the windows, but someone had closed it. He turned his head to see the other window and caught sight of a dark shadow moving across the wall. He reached for his sword, but his hand closed only on rumpled sheets.

He looked again, but no shadow loomed against the wooden panels.

He sighed, reached for the glass of water, and managed to drink it all, spilling less on his pillow than went into his mouth. He lay back and stared at the ceiling. His weighted eyelids hung open by a sliver.

The shadow passed above him. Bardon's eyes popped open. What was that batman's name? No matter. He was gone somewhere.

Bardon shifted to his side. The empty room mocked him. He let his head collapse against the bedding.

Fever. I have a fever again. I must be better, though. They got me up. They left me alone. I'm better. Where's my sword? Where's my dagger? What kind of people leave a man unattended and unarmed?

Slowly and deliberately, he examined the room, every shadow, every nook, every piece of furniture. The danger stirred only in his mind. His chambers held no threat. He closed his eyes.

A shout from below woke him. His eyes focused on red glowing orbs set deep in a black bulk.

"Here!" came the frantic voice from beneath the hostel. "Here's another one!"

The tramping of many feet on wooden planks resounded through the walls, shaking the pillars and causing a cold sweat to break out on Bardon's brow.

The creature hovering over his bed breathed deeply. It smelled of stagnant water and rotting vegetation. He and Kale had cleared The Bogs of these monsters.

The mordakleep sagged toward him. He couldn't see the gray shades of the room. He couldn't smell the potpourri Lady Lyll had left. His sheets were gone. The bed was gone. Darkness.

Wulder!

"I see the tail, but no monster!" One voice from the other world penetrated the gloom enveloping Bardon. "It must be inside. Cut it! Cut it!"

Bardon breathed in. Fresh, cool air penetrated his lungs. He tightened both hands into fists, holding the sheets, feeling the texture. He opened his eyes and saw the room lightened by the pale peach hues of sunrise. He pulled air in through his nose and sighed over the heavy smell of spices.

Rolling onto his side was again a painstaking adventure. He propped himself up on his elbow. Dizziness washed over him. Eventually, he reached for the tea and drank.

I must get well, Wulder. Amara needs me to fight Your foes. He took another sip and made a face. He put the cup down and leaned back into the bedding. *Did you save my life last night? Was it a dream of Your saving my life? Either way, I know my life is spared for the purpose of being Your servant. Strengthen me. Use me.*

He sighed, and his eyelids fluttered shut. He opened them again, fighting lethargy. The room brightened. The streams of pinkish sunshine turned golden.

"Thank You for the morning, Wulder."

Bardon could see the words written in the Tomes. These words he had recited often while he studied at The Hall. The words were repeated at morning vespers.

"And it was morning, and the man said, 'What will You have me to do with the day as it is given?' And Wulder answered, 'Serve Me in each minute, through each encounter, through all time, this day, and into eternity.' And the man rejoiced, for he had work to do. 'Nay to the idleness that devours the soul. Wulder has Himself declared the minutes of my day to be valuable in His sight.'"

Bardon smiled. He remembered Kale's face when he recited that bit of the Tomes to her. She would put her hand on her hip and say, "That's all fine, but I like a pat on the back in the evening just to know for sure I've done well."

He longed to tell her she'd done well. He'd sleep, and maybe in his dreams, he'd be able to say the words, and she would hear them.

40

Out of the Frying Pan

Sir Kemry grabbed an illuminated vine and yanked it downward.

"Ouch!" He let go and shook his whole arm. "It bites."

Kale grabbed the injured hand. He had his fingers tightly coiled.

"Let me see."

A red line the same thickness of the stem he'd seized ran across his palm.

"Well, this is going to make things a tad more difficult," Kale said.

She peered through the jungle of a plant, grimacing at the tangle that kept them from walking into the valley. Ardeo and Metta could fly out. Their tiny bodies would fit. But the dragons sat on her shoulders and chittered useless advice. Pat would have been more help in the situation.

"You're the light wizard," said her father. "Touch it, and see if it sears your hand."

Kale raised her eyebrows at him. "Good idea." Her voice couldn't quite hide the sarcasm.

She reached out one finger and tentatively tapped a leaf.

She smiled. "Nothing."

"Not quite." Sir Kemry nodded at the vines.

Where there had been one tiny leaf here and there among the branches, now leaves were sprouting and filling out, making palm-sized bright lanterns among the foliage.

Kale and her father squinted.

He shook his head and peered down at his daughter. "I don't think we need this much radiance, my dear. After all, it is the middle of the morning."

Kale screwed up her mouth and scowled at him. "Do you have any suggestions?"

He shrugged. "Try going backward through the configuration."

Kale closed her eyes and concentrated. Decreasing the foliage by obliterating the leaves turned out to be difficult. She didn't know exactly how the leaves had proliferated in the first place.

She heard her father's voice. "Good, good."

Her eyes popped open, and she saw the leaves that had just sprouted, dropping to the ground, their lights extinguished.

"Don't stop now," her father urged.

She closed her eyes again and gave a frustrated sigh. So often this wizardry stuff worked or didn't, and she had no idea how or why.

"You're slowing down now. Are you concentrating?"

"Yes, Father, I'm concentrating."

"You couldn't be. You're talking to me."

"Only because you're talking to me."

"Hush now, and work."

Kale growled. Her father laughed.

She set her mind to unwinding the vines and to lowering the energy level flowing through them.

"Ah, that's better." She heard her father murmur. "I don't have to squint so much."

Sir Kemry touched her arm. "Look." His voice sounded wobbly.

She opened her eyes and peered through what was left of the withering vines. A major dragon stood outside the enclosure. He blinked his huge eyelids and crooned a long, drawn-out, solitary note in his throat.

"Dobkin," said Sir Kemry, and his voice definitely broke.

Kale looked at her father's face. Tears ran down his cheeks, but his bright eyes and smile told a tale of joy.

"Dobkin, you old scalawag. Are the others here as well?"

The dragon stamped one enormous foot. Major dragons were the biggest of all the different varieties, and the ground shook. The branches of the dying light vine shuddered, and some collapsed.

Dobkin opened his mouth, and Sir Kemry yelled, "No!"

The big beast didn't heed his warning and lunged for the illuminated vegetation, biting into a huge chunk and ripping it out. He spit the leaves and branches out and smacked his lips as if trying to get rid of a bad taste.

Kale gasped. "He's burned his mouth."

Dobkin stamped his foot again, looked intently through the brambly bushes, and pulled his lips back from his long teeth.

"He's going to use just his choppers to rip this hedge down," said Sir Kemry.

The dragon grasped the next branch in his teeth and hauled back his neck, effectively breaking a massive piece of the plant away from the main stems.

"How clever of him!" remarked Kale.

Sir Kemry chuckled.

"What?"

"Wait until you've known my friend Dobkin longer."

"Why?"

"He always means well, but calling him clever is rather a juxtaposition of terms. You could never put clever, intelligent, cunning, or any such word in the same sentence with Dobkin. He's mammoth and has a gigantic heart to match, but his brain must be very, very tiny."

Three more chunks, and the dragon had a path cleared so Kale and her father could walk out of the lifeless plant and into the grassy meadow of the valley.

Dobkin bobbed his head until Sir Kemry reached up a hand. The dragon placed his chin on Kale's father's shoulder. The broad jaw took up the shoulder space and all the room on his arm down to the elbow. Sir Kemry stroked the big animal's cheek, and Dobkin hummed.

Ardeo and Metta soared around their heads. Metta's voice rose in a triumphant aria. Soon, dragons of all sizes streamed into the meadow, surrounding the two Dragon Keepers. Sir Kemry found all of his friends from before the sleeping-chamber episode. Kale rejoiced with him, her face as wet with tears as his. She greeted her minor dragons and listened to their scrambled tale of how they had been captured.

Shock struck her when she heard her father's stern order.

"Away with you. Hide."

She looked around but could see nothing unusual. The air chilled around her. The sky darkened, even though not a cloud coursed overhead.

"Be gone. I don't want you hurt." Her father's voice rang out.

The dragons departed, some on foot, but most took to the air.

On the hillock, near a cluster of dark trees, a woman held out a staff aimed at Sir Kemry.

"Burner Stox," whispered Kale.

"Amazing," the evil wizard said, staring at Sir Kemry. "Amazing that you should decide to visit my domain on a day I am in residence. And unfortunate," she sneered, "for you."

She paced down the hill, her back straight and proud; her head held aloft like royalty; her chin jutting with arrogance at her visitors; and the look in her eye, dealing death. At the bottom of the slope, she stopped, stood with her feet apart, and raised her staff in front of her. One end pointed to the leaden sky. Lightning crackled out of the tip and spread into the air above, leaving the smell of sulfur. She clasped it with two hands, and when she pulled her hands apart, the staff separated into two whole rods of equal size.

"Run," Kale's father commanded. "Let me deal with her."

"I've fought her before," protested Kale, but she moved away from her father's side, racing to the other edge of the meadow. She realized they would stand a better chance if Stox had to divide her attention.

Sir Kemry moved to the opposite side. Burner Stox now had to shift her head back and forth to view her opponents. Still she smirked, confidence in her powers radiating from her person.

She raised her two staffs and pointed them at Kale and Sir Kemry. "Shall I reduce you to ashes in one blow, or linger over the moment with a slow, smoldering blaze?"

Kale felt an invisible shield materialize in front of her.

"Hold this!" her father demanded.

She grasped the handle with ease. As soon as she felt comfortable with the weight, it became heavier, indicating that her father had let go.

Kale whispered, "Wulder protect me from evil. In the same way this shield guards my body, defend my mind so that Burner Stox cannot enter my thoughts. Strengthen me for combat, give me wisdom for this contest, and may Your power be shown."

Even prepared, Kale staggered back a step when the first blast from Stox's rod struck the shield. While Kale held the fabric of the invisible armor in place, she gathered energy in her other palm. When the power reached an apex, she cast it through the air and slammed Burner Stox with a devastating blow. Only, the evil wizard did not falter. She threw back her head and laughed. It seemed to Kale that she glowed.

She absorbed that energy, Kale called to her father.

"Use the shield to deflect her stream of fire and send it back at her."

Kale gauged the flow of flames, and as it hit the barrier she held, she turned it. The torrent backtracked along the outgoing barrage and struck Burner Stox in the chest. She expanded, and the glow intensified.

"Stop," ordered Sir Kemry. *"We're feeding her energy."*

That doesn't make sense.

"We'll stop and figure it out later."

What are we going to do now?

"We'll try dousing her blaze."

Kale's father gathered moisture and concentrated it in a small dense black cloud. The cloud scuttled over their adversary and dumped a deluge on her head. She sputtered but did not cease throwing the steady surge of powerful flame their way.

"All right. Plan A and Plan B didn't work. Plan C, if you please, Kale."

What?

"I came up with A and B. It's your turn."

You sound just like Regidor ribbing Bardon in the middle of a duel.

Her distraction allowed her shield to droop.

"Kale!"

Her father's sharp tone caused her to jerk. Her hand turned upward just in time to send a blast from Burner Stox ricocheting into the sky above.

"Good move, daughter of mine. You didn't feed her power, nor absorb the shock of the impact." He angled his shield to ward off Stox's next discharge and send it upward. *"Let's hope no birds choose to fly over at this time."*

No dragons, either.

"Dragons are too wise to fly over this battle. They are keeping themselves well out of the way. Well, most dragons, anyway."

Along the edge of the wood, at the top of the hill, Dobkin slinked as if a backdrop of dark trees could camouflage his massive body.

Kale's eyes widened. *Is he tiptoeing?*

"He thinks he is. Don't look directly at him. I don't want Stox to become aware of his presence and toss fire at the simpleton."

Dobkin lumbered down the slope, his eye fixed on the evil wizard. When within reaching distance, he stretched out his neck, opened his mouth, and picked her up with his teeth. His mouth covered her entire head, but he didn't bite down into her neck. He held her, squirming, ten feet above the ground.

She dropped her staffs and reached to take hold of his jaw.

Kale heard her infuriated screech. The dragon's giant mouth muffled her string of profanity.

Burner Stox must have done something with the fist clutching Dobkin's right jaw. His lip curled as if hurt. He shook his head and clenched his teeth. Her body fell to the ground minus the head.

Kale gasped and kept her eyes on the poor dragon's face. She felt a wash of confusion from the large beast. Her father walked calmly up the hill. "You can spit it out, Dobkin. I know it doesn't taste very good."

⊱ 41 ⊰

Good News, Mostly

Kale and her father walked among the dragons, making their acquaintance and accepting their congratulations at defeating Burner Stox. Everywhere they turned, father and daughter heard the dragons' sweet wordless songs of victory. Although their o'rant ears could not decipher the words, through mindspeaking the lyrics came across clearly. Kale blushed at the praise leveled at them. Her father just beamed and continued to socialize with the dragons, big and small.

Sir Kemry delighted in introducing those dragons who had been his special friends before his unfortunate period of sleep. He also explained over and over that he had not deserted his comrades, but had been under a spell created by Risto. Most of the dragons understood, but a few were prickly and wanted Sir Kemry to fawn over them a bit before they forgave him.

From a distance, the bisonbeck guards kept an eye on the newcomers to the valley.

"Are they going to attack?" asked Kale.

"No, I don't think so." Her father stroked a green minor dragon on his shoulder. "They saw what happened to their leader and are probably not anxious to do battle with two mighty wizards and a ferocious major dragon.

"Dobkin isn't ferocious. I think he was embarrassed when he accidentally bit the wizard's head off."

"Yes, I'm sure you're right. He only intended to hold her until we could do something. She shouldn't have hurt him. It was a reflex action on his part, not an intentional decapitation."

Kale put her hand on her stomach. "Let's not talk about it." She gazed off into the surrounding hills. "The ropmas don't know what to do, do they?"

"No, they don't," Sir Kemry agreed. "They're watching to see what happens. They're probably fond of the dragons and enjoyed taking care of them. But they're afraid of the bisonbecks and don't know what their guards will do in the wake of Stox's death."

"What can we expect from Crim Cropper?"

Sir Kemry shrugged and bent to scoop up a red minor dragon. "Hello, fella." He rubbed under the creature's chin. "He's a fire dragon, Kale, rare in the major dragon species, even rarer in this size."

"I know. How do you think Crim Cropper will get the news?"

Sir Kemry picked up a yellow dragon with his other hand. "What's your name, little miss?" He tucked the dragon under his chin, then spoke to Kale. "I don't know. Why are you so interested?"

"She's his wife. He'll feel something. Sorrow? Grief?"

"I thought they weren't on speaking terms. Maybe he'll feel relief."

"Father, look." She nodded toward the woods. A group of bisonbecks made their way from the trees to the place where Dobkin had slain Burner Stox.

"Coming to collect the dead." Sir Kemry pursed his lips. "That's probably your answer, Kale. Those bisonbeck soldiers will relay the message to Crim Cropper."

"Aren't they part of Stox's army?"

"Yes, but now there is no 'Stox's army,' so they'll have to seek employment elsewhere. I doubt Pretender would welcome soldiers who have fought against him."

"So they'll join Cropper's army?"

"*If* Cropper bothers to expand his army." Sir Kemry squinted, still watching the movements of the ropmas and bisonbecks. "He's always been more interested in his experiments and let Stox do all the outside work."

"He might just send them away?"

"Possibly. And if they can't be a part of either army, they don't have any choice but to go abroad. There are wars on other continents that give mercenaries something to do."

Kale sat in the sweet-smelling grass and allowed the smaller dragons to race over her, chasing one another and singing softly. "This nightmare could be almost over, couldn't it, Father?"

"No, I don't think so. Crim Cropper may never come out of his sanctum, but Pretender isn't going to disappear and leave Amara alone."

"I choose to be optimistic. We've gone from three armies ravaging the countryside to maybe one. That seems to be an improvement."

"Umm." Sir Kemry brought his gaze back from a gordon tree grove. "The ropmas are coming closer."

"What do you suppose they want?"

"Why don't you use your talent to find out?"

"Do you really bounce back that quickly?" Kale sighed deeply. "I still feel drained from our encounter with Burner Stox. I'm finding it difficult to communicate with these dragons close at hand, let alone with ropmas a half mile away."

Sir Kemry laughed. "I'm drained too. I was hoping that your youth provided more resilience."

"Have you ever run yourself completely dry?"

"No, and I don't want to. They say it takes an eon to recover."

Sir Kemry stretched out in the grass beside her. They rested in the camaraderie of the dragons. Kale kept watch as the bisonbecks picked up Stox's body and carried her away. The ropmas came closer after that but still kept their distance.

Kale tried to count the number of dragons in the vicinity. She couldn't count the minor dragons. They flitted about, and from a distance, those of the same color could not be distinguished. She counted twenty-eight riding dragons, eleven major dragons, and fifteen fire dragons, who were just a bit smaller than the riding dragons. The rare fire dragons kept to themselves, in their own circle, away from the others.

Her father's soft snore pleased Kale and eased her tension. She actually enjoyed his company, now that she'd gotten used to some of his peculiar ways. *Not nearly as peculiar as Wizard Fenworth. I miss him. I miss Bardon more. I wonder what my husband is doing. Wulder, keep him safe in battle.*

Gymn curled around Kale's neck, and she leaned back in the grass. "The only thing that would make this more ideal would be to have Bardon here as well." She sighed and slept.

———

Sir Kemry's muttering filtered through Kale's dreams. She sat up and rubbed her eyes. Gymn stretched, unwrapped himself from her neck, and skittered down to sit in her lap. Her father still slept, two green dragons curled on his chest. In his sleep, he smiled.

He sat up so suddenly, Kale started. Alarm rushed through her. "What is it?"

Sir Kemry stood. "Alton and Benrey." He pointed to the west end of the valley. Under the low-lying cloud cover, two dragons flew toward them.

Her father's joy swept away the anxiety of only a moment before. Kale rose to her feet and cheered as the dragons landed. The two great beasts lumbered over to where the o'rants stood and took turns stroking Sir Kemry's head with their chins.

Benrey's red wings extended behind him as he arched his back, head pointed at the sky. The riding dragon let out a musical warble that sent shivers of delight down Kale's spine. At the end of Benrey's exclamation of praise, a column of fire shot from his mouth into the air.

Kale laughed and clapped her hands. Benrey bent his head to look her in the eye and then touched her lightly on the top of her head with his chin.

Sir Kemry stroked the side of Alton's neck. "I see you've been keeping fit."

The purple and black dragon hummed his pleasure.

"Let's get down to business, Alton, Benrey." He nodded at each. "How many of these valley dragons are enslaved to Burner Stox, and how many will follow Paladin?"

He listened for a while to his favorite dragons' mindspeaking, then turned to his daughter. "How much of that did you get?"

"Your two dragons have headed a movement to keep Wulder apparent in the lives of those in the valley. They've introduced those born here to His principles, reminded those who became despondent of His care, and tried to keep rabble-rousers in line." She frowned at her father. She didn't like admitting that a gaping hole in her education had just revealed itself. But pretending just wouldn't work. "I don't know the story of Wulder saving the dragons from a grave by opening a river of time and letting them go through. So, I didn't get the references to that."

Sir Kemry rested a hand on her shoulder. The yellow dragon on his arm leapt over to the back of her. "The important thing is that about three-fourths of the dragons in the valley are predisposed to follow us. They didn't bond to Burner Stox. Some bonded to their ropma caretakers, but none to the bisonbeck guards."

"That's good news!"

"Benrey thinks that the fire dragons, who are the most reluctant to join with any other group, can be persuaded to fight with us as long as one of their kind is their leader."

"That's good news."

"Alton doubts the ropmas will go into battle with us, but he thinks they can be trained to provide off-field assistance."

"More good news."

Sir Kemry rubbed the back of his neck with a hand callused by weapons of war. "Burner Stox's spell, which prohibits flight out of the valley or leaving through the mountain passes, still stands even after her death. Alton and Benrey have searched for over thirty years and never found a way out."

"Hmm?" Kale looked at the hills rising to mountains around them. "Not such good news."

⇒ 42 ⇒

STiff AS STAKES

Bardon knew the stages of stakes, but since he had skipped the disease as a child, he hadn't expected to be walking along peglegged as an adult. All of his joints were stiff, but his fingers and toes ached the worst. Flexible toes had not been toward the top of his to-be-thankful-for list. Now, if he got past this uncomfortable and inconvenient stage of the disease, he would express his gratitude for flexibility daily.

Five minutes with his dear wife and Gymn would undo all the swelling and also unbend his joints. But he didn't know where she was. She and her father's mission wouldn't lead them to a specific place where he could send a message. He had no specific destination that he could use a gateway to reach. So frustrating when a brief visit would certainly be welcome.

He hobbled through the nearly deserted camp. Troops had been assigned to help with the eradication of quiss as they came ashore. Others had been sent with volunteer kimens to build and secure grawlig traps. Sir Dar and Lady Allerion had gone off to investigate a report of Burner Stox's army of grawligs deserting her forces and joining Crim Cropper. Leetu Bends and Latho took on the same mission, only working from within the enemy camps.

Bardon's load had lightened briefly when he saw Leetu disguised as Latho's wife. The embellishments to the emerlindian's trim figure were arranged by courtesy of Lady Allerion's wizardry. But even laughter at his friend's expense cost him the pain of jarring muscles.

No laughter lit his eyes now. He'd been left behind and "in charge" of the base.

Most of his work consisted of shuffling paperwork. As far as commanding the troops, this morning he had ordered his unfortunate batman to tie his shoes. Bardon couldn't even tie his own laces in the aftermath of stakes. And no one knew if this condition would be permanent or not. "It depends upon the individual," Lady Allerion had said, with a voice too full of sympathy.

To get away from the depressing reports coming in to headquarters, Bardon decided to take a walk. Perhaps the exercise would be good for his stiff joints. Leecent Voet trailed behind him.

"Do you think I don't know you're back there?" Bardon asked. He couldn't turn his head enough to toss the question over his shoulder.

"Of course not, sir."

"What are you going to do? Pick me up if I fall over?"

"Something like that, sir."

"Well, come up here and walk beside me. I'd rather see you than hear your footsteps behind me."

"Yes sir."

They passed the domestic tents and wives of the men out on patrol. Most of the women stopped their chores to give the passing knight a curtsy. Children halted in their running and jumping to give stiff bows and wobbly curtsies. Voet waved and grinned at the tykes, even reaching out to tousle the hair of boys who ran up for a closer look. Bardon tried not to grimace as he bowed slightly to acknowledge their greetings.

He sighed with relief when they passed the last tent.

"My knees and elbows are better, Leecent."

"I'm glad to hear it, sir."

"Perhaps you won't have to mollycoddle me forever."

"I never thought that would be the case, sir."

"Do you have to call me 'sir' in every sentence?"

"Yes sir."

Bardon glanced over to see a big grin on his batman's face. "You enjoy giving me a hard time, don't you?"

"Well, sir, it's just that I have brothers, sir. And giving you a bit of a tease comforts my soul, sir."

"I see." Bardon turned down a path that would lead them to the river. "I wouldn't want to stand in the way of your soul's comfort."

"Exactly, sir."

They walked toward the water's edge. At this point of the river, the water flowed slowly between wide, grassy banks. Large bentleaf trees created cool, shady groves. Bardon shivered as they entered one stand that stood back from the water.

"The most disturbing news I hear," he said, "is the reports of mordakleeps. We have plans in motion to handle the quiss and grawligs, but the mordakleeps are attacking at random, and there's no way to predict where they'll strike next."

"Yes sir. And therefore, no way to put up a defense."

"And our men are stretched and scattered as it is. If we could have more men enlist from other parts of Amara…"

"Paladin has sent out recruiters, sir."

"I know."

"That's how me and my brothers heard. That's why we signed up."

Bardon wanted to clap the boy on the shoulder but could not make his arm obey his desire. "Not all men see the need as you and your brothers do. Many think the danger will pass. Or that someone else will take care of it."

The batman shook his head. "We had a battle between Pretender and Burner Stox in our own fields and pastures, sir. The armies killed each other and our animals as well. What they didn't destroy during the battle, they carried off as plunder. It broke my da's heart. He would have gone off to fight, but he's too old and crippled, sir." The boy's voice faltered on the word "crippled."

"Just as I am, Leecent?"

"No sir. Yours is temporary because of an illness. His is permanent due to old age. You'll get better, sir."

"I certainly hope so." They took a few more steps along the path. "And I'm sorry for your loss, Voet."

"It's all right, sir. We couldn't go back to farming right away, seen as how the damage of the battle worried the soil some. But Da says to give the land a rest of a season or two, and the ground will be better than ever for planting."

"Your da sounds like a wise man."

"Yes sir. He also said he'd be raising no livestock for those monsters to come by and steal."

"Another wise move."

"Yes sir. So my ma's flock of chickens and poultry-birds are living out in the woods, going wild, but still producing eggs and meat for the family that's still at home."

They passed out of the trees in silence and ambled along the path on the broad bank of the river. Fatigue began to nibble at Bardon's strength. He needed to return to camp and rest. Perhaps he would take a nap.

What an excellent warrior I am! What a marvelous leader of men! He realized his self-mockery. *"Do not favor Pretender with the honor of quoting his lies."* The principle calmed his exasperation.

The batman's sword rasped lightly as it came out of the sheath. Bardon jerked at the sound, sending a wave of pain through his neck. The sight of three mordakleeps standing in the shallow water gave his heart a twist. He and Voet stood feet away from the river's edge and imminent danger.

The middle mordakleep raised the lower part of his body and put what almost looked like a foot on dry land. Voet slashed downward and pierced the appendage. The dark flesh sizzled and drew away from the cut. The monster lifted his body out of the river.

The leecent waved his sword in front of him. "To arms, men. Attack!"

Bardon gave him a sharp look that went unseen. He marveled at the batman's naiveté but didn't want to distract his only protector. Instead, he groused to himself over their predicament.

Our men won't hear you, boy. Or, was that for the benefit of our visitors? Do you think they would assume that more soldiers will arrive any minute? Do you think the prospect would scare them? You are so young. Too young to die.

Bardon looked again at Voet's earnest expression. He would be a leader for this raw recruit. "You know to slice off their tails?"

"Yes sir. Of course, sir." He paused. "Their tails are on the wrong side, sir."

"I'll bait one and draw it past you. You make your move right after it passes."

"Yes sir."

"And watch your back while you're doing it."

"Yes sir."

"Wulder, protect us."

"Yes sir. I mean…well, I do mean, 'Yes sir.'"

"Step back three paces."

The leecent followed the command, and before the mordakleep could advance, Bardon hobbled in front of his batman. The dark beast turned to follow the crippled prey. Voet sliced downward and severed the tail. Its body dissolved, leaving a splotch of goo on the grassy bank.

Leecent Voet stood staring at the spot as it quickly soaked into the ground. "I'm going to be sick."

Bardon panted as he shambled back. "Nonsense. It's no worse than wringing a chicken's neck. You've done that before, haven't you?"

"Yes sir, I have. But I'm wondering if you have. The two don't compare at all." He paused. "Sir."

"Get ready. Here comes the next."

Bardon made his tottering run in front of the water monster. Voet took in a deep breath, held on to the air in his lungs with a grimace on his face, and released the breath in a great rush when he made the deathblow to the second mordakleep.

Wheezing with one arm pressed against his side, Bardon returned. "One more." He gasped.

"I don't think so," a gruff voice interrupted.

Bardon and Voet turned. Five bisonbeck soldiers in a semicircle cut off their escape. Bardon checked the water's edge to be sure the mordakleep was not taking advantage of the distraction to sneak up on them. The water rippled where the monster had submerged.

"Drop your sword, boy."

Voet looked at Bardon. Bardon nodded. The weapon thudded on the grass.

"Your weapon, too, Sir Bardon."

"I can't reach it," he said.

The bisonbeck motioned Voet to remove the sword from Bardon's belt sheath. The batman complied.

"Now, you're coming with us."

"Where?" He chafed at the situation. *I don't suppose I could talk you pretty-faced messengers out of this little trip, since I surely can't fight my way out of this mess.*

"Master Crim Cropper wishes to speak to you."

Ah no, there will be no talking you out of disobeying Master Cropper. There's no escape, and I don't want Voet playing the hero. He'd just get killed.

He stepped forward, indicating he would come peacefully.

Voet came too, staying at his side.

A soldier raised the blunt end of his weapon. "Not you." He brought it down, whacking Voet's head. The boy sank to the ground.

Bardon objected, "That's—"

Pain exploded at his temple, and he fell. He knew he hit the ground. He knew Voet's body lay beside him. He knew he was losing consciousness and fought to keep his senses. But in another moment, he knew he couldn't keep the darkness at bay.

43

From the Wizard's Lair

Bardon became aware of the stench first, the scuttling of animals next, then the haze in the room that diminished the lights, and the muttering man last. Bardon's head hurt, and he couldn't move. He slid his eyes to one side, and even that caused pain.

The muttering man stood by a wooden worktable cluttered with papers, books, jars, boxes, and a vase full of feathers. He wore a shabby wizard's robe and a pointed hat that drooped around the brim. As Bardon watched, the tip of the point fell over and hung down in front. The wizard brushed his hand upward through the air, and the point stood up again. Although he'd never seen him before, Bardon guessed this was Crim Cropper.

A short servant shuffled toward the wizard on overlarge feet. The man could have been a tumanhofer, but something odd about him made Bardon believe he was not. He wore a good suit of clothing, befitting his station, but of finer cloth and better condition than the wizard's.

He stopped a few feet away from Crim Cropper and clasped his hands behind his back. He laced one hand's fingers with the other hand's. His knuckles turned white. "Master Cropper, I've sent the messages you requested."

The man didn't look up from where he wrote in a book. "You've had answers already, Prattack?"

"No, Master."

"Then go away until you have."

The servant didn't speak, and his face didn't show that he had any reaction, ill or fair, to this rude response. He turned and started away. His eye fell on Bardon. "He's awake, Master."

"I know."

Prattack shuffled out of the room. Bardon heard his dragging gait, then the creak of a door opening, then closing, and the bolt click as it was set.

He waited. He couldn't move. He couldn't speak. He ached, but not as much as when he first woke. He forced his eyes to move in a full circle, trying to determine the various factors of his situation.

No bars surrounded him. No guards stood over him. No windows offered a clue as to the time of day. And he suspected the deplorable smell came from a series of three vats along one wall. Each one bubbled, and the two outside vats gave off a colored steam, one green and the other a purple brown. Bardon figured this accounted for the haze in the room.

The man at the bench underlined something, closed the book, and put his pen in a holder with assorted other writing instruments. "You won't be much use to me."

He picked a box out of the disarray before him and walked to a row of cages. He didn't bother to look Bardon's way. Bardon, however, was pleased that he could shift his eyes more comfortably and follow the wizard's movements. As the man turned, Bardon viewed his profile. Crim Cropper's full beard reached almost to the floor. He'd braided his mustache from the corners of his mouth down to where the tips brushed the hem of his robe.

Crim Cropper opened a small feeding door in the side of the cage and poked something from the box into the opening. He hastily withdrew his fingers and shut the wire-woven flap, then moved on to the next enclosure. "But it feels good to have you helpless and in my power. Revenge."

Bardon tried to process this information. Why would having him imprisoned give Cropper the pleasure of revenge? He wanted to ask the question out loud, but his mouth still refused to open. He realized he was thirsty.

"I shall make sure that your wife knows I have you and that you are dying slowly and in a most humiliating manner."

Oh, Kale isn't going to like this. I don't think I shall like it either.

Having fed whatever animal dwelt in the next cage, the wizard moved to the third in the row. "I've thought of rodents nibbling away at you while you can't move. But you would die too quickly."

Wulder, protect me from death at all, quickly, slowly, whatever. But if it is my time, I prefer quickly.

Crim Cropper finished feeding the animal in the last cage, the thirteenth by Bardon's count. "Then I realized I didn't have to put all of my mutant rats in with you. Just three or four."

Not comforting information at all.

A second and third row of cages were stacked on top of the first. The wizard walked slowly back, feeding the creature in each enclosure, sometimes speaking to them, saying, "Soon, soon. Be patient."

He continued to talk to Bardon as he strolled through the feeding routine. "You're wondering why I would seek revenge? Why I would target your wife? Because your wife took my wife, and it is only fitting that I should take her husband."

He fed an animal that hissed. "Be quiet. You don't impress me."

He sighed and put his hand under his beard in the general vicinity of his heart.

If he has a heart. This all seems melodramatic to me. I no longer wonder if this man is sane.

"Burner Stox," said Cropper, with another sigh. "No female compares to her. Intelligent. Cunning. Masterful. When she walked into the room, the air crackled with her power."

He stood still with a faraway look in his eye and a smile brightening his dark visage. "Burner Stox understood my work. She, and only she, knew the depths of my secrets. She went with me to the lower levels and marveled over my creations.

"She laughed and named them for me. I never bothered to name them, but she delighted in finding just the right-sounding words to describe each and every creature, every living, breathing, functioning organism developed purely and simply from my handiwork."

Bardon found it odd that Crim Cropper talked to him but never looked his way. He pointedly avoided the sight of Bardon, the man he held trapped in his laboratory.

That's all right, Wizard Crim Cropper. I'd rather not be looking at you.

The tip on the wizard's hat again fell forward. He waved it into its proper position once more. "You're wondering about our latest difference of opinion. A minor disagreement. Normal husband-wife tension." He scowled and spoke through clenched teeth. "She would have come back. She always came back."

Crim Cropper stared at the door for a moment as if he thought she might actually appear. He took a deep breath, closed his eyes, and continued his soliloquy.

"My Burner Stox. Such a dominant, vigorous, formidable personality required some measure of freedom. Her beauty, her attraction, rose out of her vibrant character. Burner Stox could accomplish anything she desired. And she chose me to be her partner. She supported me and my research. She put aside her personal ambitions to nurture my amazing talent."

Crim Cropper opened his eyes, and his face became tense, his voice rising in pitch. "She was my inspiration. The months she's been away have tortured me. Now, your meddlesome wife has murdered my guiding star. Kale Allerion has made the unbearable separation permanent."

The wizard's head jerked around, and his eyes fell on his victim at last. "Do you know what I'm going to do? Something very practical, I think. I have no further need of my laboratory animals, the mutants I've created, the resulting specimens of my genius. Every experiment I've conducted had one ultimate purpose—for me to hear my Burner Stox exclaim with delight. So what should I do with the creatures I no longer need?

"In the past, I've taken one or two and deposited them here and there in regions of Amara. Burner Stox and I used to be entertained by the havoc that our little friends could create in just a few days. But this time, I shall open all the doors."

He placed his hands behind his back and wove his fingers together. Staring up at the ceiling, he rocked back and forth on his feet. In rhythm to the swaying, he clasped and unclasped his hands. Bardon thought the wizard had entirely forgotten his prisoner until a small smile tipped his mustache.

Cropper's words flowed from his mouth in a soft coo. "And then, just because my star would have laughed at the resulting panic, I am going to incite my dark minions, the evil sprites of the earth."

Crim Cropper again looked at Bardon. He cocked his head and grinned, white teeth showing through the dark beard. "My blimmets and schoergs. Under my command, because Pretender didn't bother to culti-vate them. But I am not so shortsighted.

"I've won the respect and the obedience of the schoergs. I've trained the blimmets to follow a sound and surface where I want them to. I've fiends for messengers. Evil fiends who relish in doing mischief." He turned away and turned back. "And the mordakleeps. Let's not forget the mordakleeps. We know how helpful they can be now, don't we?"

He strode to the door, his body quivering with energy. "Prattack!"

The stunted servant appeared as if he had been just around the corner.

"We're taking our guest down to our lower levels. I want him to see the creatures who will destroy his world."

Prattack trudged across the stone floor, grabbed Bardon, and hoisted his dead weight onto his broad back.

With one arm slung over the servant's shoulder and one leg held in a viselike grip against the other shoulder, Bardon watched the floor as they traveled to a stairway. His knuckles scraped against the rough stone, but Bardon could not lift his arm any more than he could turn his neck to see ahead.

The odor of animal waste increased with each jarring step down the stairs. Cages rattled, creatures barked, howled, and snarled. Prattack's breathing wheezed in and out with increasing difficulty as they proceeded down the stairwell.

They reached a dimly lit dungeonlike chamber.

"Open the portals," Wizard Cropper commanded.

Prattack dropped his burden and shuffled away. A draft of cold, clean air swept over Bardon. He breathed in deeply. The movement freed his neck from the stranglehold of stiffness.

Bardon forced his knees to straighten, then pulled them back to the curled position in which he had landed on the floor. *I thought this rigidity came from some spell by Crim Cropper. Perhaps it is part of the stakes.* He worked to get his arms to move but with little success.

The sound of metal latches lifting, crate doors opening, and the scurrying of feet drew Bardon's attention. A slight shift of his neck accompanied the movement of his eyes. A blur of creatures passed before him. Fur, feathers, and scales. Claws and talons. Sharp beaks and pointed teeth. Growls, snaps, howls, roars, snarls, and screeches. Scuttling, slithering, racing toward the outside. Following the flow of fresh air.

The stampede lasted longer than Bardon could fathom. Then he realized that Prattack must have gone down to another layer and opened cages there, for some of the creatures came out of a dark stairwell.

Thank you, Wulder, that I was dropped on the sidelines. I would hate to encounter even one of these monsters.

A laugh cackled over the noise of mass exodus. Bardon shifted his neck enough to view Wizard Cropper sitting on a raised dais on a throne-like massive chair.

"What do you think?" The question shrieked over the clatter of hooves as a herd of larger animals climbed the stairs and headed for freedom. "Do you think my pets are merely going outside to play for a while in the sunshine and then return? No! I've built gateways to each region of Amara. They are dispersing throughout this miserable land."

Another wave of creatures passed. "Do you think I want to rule the world? Ha! What good would it do me to gain the world, since I have lost my Burner Stox?" Cropper's voice dropped to a mutter as smaller animals skittered through the chamber. "Rule the world? No. Destroy the world? Yes." He laughed again. "What do you think? I will tell you what to ponder upon, Sir Bardon. My genius has bred into my creations only one common characteristic."

He sneered, his curled lip lifting one side of his mustache. Bardon shivered.

"None of my creatures are friendly. They all revel in killing, in blood, in screams, in choking and rending the life out of their victims. A suitable gift for me to leave your world, isn't it, Sir Bardon?" He enunciated each word with obvious satisfaction. "Don't you agree, Sir Knight in service to Paladin, unfortunate husband of Kale Allerion?"

Bardon closed his eyes and tried to block out the maniacal laugh of the demented wizard.

He whispered, "Wulder?"

44

WHO ARE THE ALLIES?

Under a bentleaf tree, Kale paced back and forth. Her father played with two baby dragons who would grow up to be taller than the tree and twice as long. Two minor dragons rode on Sir Kemry's shoulders, and one clung to his hair as he dodged the bigger dragons in a game of tag.

Kale stopped and gazed at the perpetual cloud cover. "Burner Stox and her bisonbeck guards were able to go in and out of the valley. There must be a way."

"I agree," said Sir Kemry. "Why don't you see if you can find it?"

"Did you want to help me?"

"Not right now, dear. I'm saving my energy for later." He tackled the smaller of the two dragons. The minor dragons took to the air, chirruping their glee.

When I know my father better, will I understand him? Right now I haven't one idea of what he is up to. If it was Bardon, I'd say, "What in all of Amara are you doing?" Are husbands easier to deal with than fathers?

Kale sent her six minor dragons out to gather information. What were the ropmas doing? Approximately how many dragons lived in this valley?

Kale stood before Benrey and Alton. Communicating with a dragon other than one with whom she'd bonded required extra concentration. She hoped her father's two dragons would be receptive to her. "Will you show me the exit used by the bisonbecks?"

Alton consented and invited her to mount.

She looked at his slick purple scales and the black ridges down his spine. "I can't ride you without a saddle."

Alton swung his head toward the western slope and then ambled off in that direction. Kale followed him.

She looked back over her shoulder. Sir Kemry sat cross-legged under the tree with a dozen minor dragons scampering all over him. The older wizard laughed at their antics.

This would be much easier if Father were more cooperative.

Alton led her to a shed that smelled like bisonbecks. No trace of the fetid odor of grawligs nor the pasture-and-wildflower smell of ropmas lingered in the air. Bisonbecks left behind the scent of leather, canvas, and the particular oil they used to clean their weapons. In the wooden hut, Kale found dragon saddles and riding gear in all shapes and sizes.

She dragged out equipment she thought would fit Alton and be suitable for their aerial surveillance.

Oh, how I miss my Celisse. I'm glad Alton isn't much bigger. This saddle is heavy!

When all the straps were in place and secure, she imitated Bardon's trick of running up the dragon's tail and jumping into the stirrups. She heard Alton's chuckle and liked him all the more for his sense of humor.

They were aloft for only a few minutes before Kale spotted exactly what she needed to see. An obelisk, centered in the valley, provided energy that severed connection to the outside world.

Kale would not have to locate whatever gateway the bisonbecks and Burner Stox had used. She would not have to enlarge some portal to allow the larger dragons to go through. Once she disabled the obelisk, the impenetrable cloud cover would disappear, and the natural passes through the mountains would again be useable.

She and Alton set down near where her father dozed under a tree. She ran to tell him the news, but he only sat up and smiled at her.

"Come with me," she said. "Let's unravel the obelisk spell and get out of here."

Sir Kemry leaned back against the tree trunk and closed his eyes. "You can do it, my dear."

Kale kept her booted foot from stamping her dissatisfaction. "Of course, I could do it, Father. But you are a much more experienced wizard, and between the two of us, we could have it done in no time."

"I'm saving my energy, Kale. I believe I told you that before."

This time she did stamp her foot. "For what?"

He opened one eye and gave her a stern look that reminded her vividly of Wizard Fenworth. "For later, my dear."

Kale took Pat and Filia with her when she and Alton went back to the obelisk. It took the three of them all afternoon to discern the pattern of Burner Stox's spell and then unweave it. During the first few moments of work, resentment toward her father thwarted her efforts to concentrate. Once her mind engaged in the intricate puzzle, she forgot about his annoying attitude.

The weaving reflected an inside-out gateway with strands that confined instead of opening up a corridor. The tapestry expanded from the tip of the obelisk into a huge covering. Kale suspected that should she pull the right string, the whole fabric would unravel.

She, Pat, and Filia untwisted and unwound the filaments until they found the one thread that held the framework intact. Then they pulled until every last wisp of the spell lay in disorder. Kale destroyed the remnants of the spell by shining a light so bright that the tangled heap of elements faded away to nothing.

When finally finished, she sat on the ground next to Alton and leaned back against his side. He unfurled his wing and covered her for an instant.

"Thank you, my father's friend. I am pleased that you're proud of me, and welcome your friendship extended directly to me instead of through my father."

At dusk, she came back to find her father had set up a camp, with dinner ready and two tents with comfortable bedding inside. Fatigue kept her from being talkative. The mental labor she had done that day with the two minor dragons had left her drained.

◆━━◆

Sir Kemry ladled soup into a bowl and handed it to her with a chunk of bread. "Did you fix the problem?"

"Yes."

His gaze went skyward. "No stars yet. I imagine it will take a few hours for those clouds to dissipate."

"Probably."

"I've sent Benrey out to explain to the dragons that you will want to talk to them in the morning. So you'd better get a good night's rest."

Kale stopped her spoon halfway to her mouth. "What am I going to talk to them about?"

"Joining the forces of good to vanquish evil."

"I'm to mindspeak to all the dragons in the valley at one time?"

"Simultaneously. Yes." Sir Kemry nodded and placed a large spoonful of soup in his mouth.

"A lengthy discussion with even one dragon is tiring."

"Yes, but you have youth on your side."

"And I am to *persuade* them?"

"I did some preliminary work for you today, Kale. It won't be that difficult. Most will back you without much effort on your part."

"Just communicating with that many will require a great deal of effort on my part."

"Kale, you are a wizard, are you not? You are pledged to Paladin's service, are you not?"

She nodded to each question.

"This bellyaching is not becoming to an Amaran with your privileges. Just do the job."

Years of training at keeping a respectful tongue in her head kept Kale from firing off a few choice words about "just doing the job."

She carefully guarded the thought, because she didn't want her father to hear her opinion. But she understood that Wulder knew what she was thinking whether she reworded her thoughts to sound more polite, tried to hide them, or spoke to Him as she really felt.

It seems to me that I'm the one doing the jobs around here, and my father is saving his energy. He's saving his energy a lot! What is he saving it for?

The question made her pause.

He's saving it because he's old. And he's much more experienced than I am, so he knows what the battle will be like once we meet Crim Cropper or Pretender.

The reasoning behind her thoughts soothed her irritation. The line of thinking hadn't come out of her own heart. She knew Wulder had inserted the thoughts to redirect her determination. Wulder helped her even when she least wanted the assistance. She needed to cooperate, not chafe at His instruction, and at this point, He guided her through her father. *All right, I understand. Therefore I better admit I need the right words for when I talk to those dragons tomorrow. And I guess I need some sleep, so I'll have the energy.*

Bardon's voice echoed in her memory. *"The best way to learn to play an instrument is to play that instrument. The best way to learn to be patient is to be patient."*

Oh, Bardon, I miss your quoting principles at me. Wulder, keep him safe, and keep me patient.

She finished her soup and bread. "Good night, Father. Sleep well."

"And you, as well, my daughter. You have a big day ahead of you."

Kale awoke in the morning with the feeling of a great weight upon her. But with every breath, a small fraction of the heaviness departed. Awareness of the dragons' departure from the valley launched her out of her bed.

"Wait!" Although she shouted, she felt like her voice whispered in a canyon where no one heard.

She scrambled out of her tent and stood with the first rays of morning shining on her. "Stop! Dragons, come back!"

Her words flew into the trees and the cloudless sky.

She fell on her knees, clamped her lips together, closed her eyes, and used her mindspeaking talent.

You cannot go! We need you. Please, dragons. Those of you who know either me or my father, tell the others. We aren't asking you to fight for our own glory. We will fight too. The struggle is to return Amara to the way our homeland used to be when Paladin was strong and the seven high races looked to Wulder.

The air buzzed with voices. She cringed. This reminded her too much of when she was a young girl and first approached the capitol city of Vendela. At the time, she had been overwhelmed by the thoughts and feelings of the great populace of the metropolis. She had learned to guard her thoughts and fine-tune her talent so that she no longer listened to all those around her.

But now she had to be open to all the dragons. She had to reach beyond those she could see with her eyes to those who, even at this moment, were making their way out of the valley.

Wulder has given us Paladin. Follow Paladin!

She heard voices in a tumult of noise that almost knocked her over. *"Yes! We will serve. Tell us where. We will go."*

But there were other voices. *"I do not follow Paladin. I care nothing for Wulder. I stand alone."*

The positive voices trailed away. Kale could hear their affirmations as a backdrop to the few who protested with loud cries.

Each naysayer shouted, *"I stand alone."*

Kale's throat hurt with the agony of finding words to persuade this stubborn faction of the dragon populace.

You stand alone. Do you know how alone that really is?

She sent out a picture of one dragon. Kale sobbed. She couldn't control the image as she wanted. The main figure switched between a lone dragon and a lone marione. No, it was an o'rant. No, a tumanhofer.

Kale squeezed her eyes shut. She must project the picture. She tried again. One dragon—the image broke—one kimen. Did it really matter?

Look! She cried. In her mental picture, black and evil creatures swarmed the ground, rushing over the lone figure. When the horde had passed, the figure lay as a pile of bones.

A long moment of silence passed, and then, the voices returned, loud and confident. *"I have a brother. I have a friend. My neighbor stands with me."*

Two! You think two can stand?

"I'll watch his back. He'll watch mine."

See with your heart what your mind won't.

Again the mixed-up image left Kale frustrated. She could not hold the picture of two dragons overcome by the wicked stampeding beasts. The evil devoured a flickering array of the high races as well as the dragons. Always two figures in the scene and never a survivor.

But Kale's assignment was to speak to the dragons, and she wanted them to see themselves in this peril. She didn't think they would fight for anyone but themselves.

Again the awed silence pulsed through a moment. Kale felt the petulant dragons throw off their dread, denying the possibility. Abruptly her mind filled with voices, but this time an edge of desperation crept into the words the dragons forced to sound assured. *"We can fly. We can hide. We can run. There are many of us. We must flee. But there are many of us. We must hide."*

This time Kale didn't bother to try to hold the central figures to that of dragons. She worked to make the image clear as a black mass chased down, pulled out of cracks, and smothered anyone who tried to withstand or flee the attack.

†〓〓†

"You've done it, Kale." Her father's voice drew her back from a very cold place. She lay in his lap. One of his arms cradled her. One hand stroked her face. "You've reached the dragons, Kale. And you did more. Every citizen of Amara who has had any allegiance to Wulder also heard your plea. Each saw the images you sent as if you put that person in the picture."

He squeezed her to his chest and kissed her forehead. "You've done more than I imagined you could."

She felt droplets splash on her cheeks.

Her father wiped away his tears from her face. "You must rest."

"I'm all right."

"Are you?"

"Yes, just tired."

"Try to summon Gymn, or Metta, or Ardeo. Summon just one of your dragons."

He waited.

"I can't." She struggled to sit up. Her body did not cooperate. She returned to a limp rag-doll state in her father's lap. "Help me."

"I can't call the dragons for you."

"Then help me sit."

With her father's aid, she brought her head up and rested her back against his chest.

Her muscles refused to hold her. She started to slide to one side. Her father repositioned her in a more stable spot with his arm around her.

She blinked back tears. "What's wrong with me?"

"You're exhausted, but you're young. Soon, physically, you will be as strong as ever."

"Physically?"

"You've exhausted your talent, Kale, and I don't know if that will return."

⇥ 45 ⇤

WHO IS THE ENEMY?

Kale wore a belt that would help keep her in the saddle. She thought it unnecessary, but Sir Kemry insisted. She looked down from Alton's back to her father's worried face. "I'm all right."

He smiled and winked. Then, patting Alton on his shoulder, he said, "Take her to her mother, friend. And remember she can't hear you."

Kale forced a brave smile on her face as the dragon spread his wings and jumped into flight. But as soon as no one could see, she let it slip. Of course she could hear the dragon's wings beat against the air, but she couldn't hear him mindspeak.

All six of her minor dragons were with her, but she couldn't communicate with any of them, either. Gymn traveled in a sling under her tunic so that he would be next to her heart. She knew he was giving her more healing, but not the speedy recovery that used to come when her talent cooperated with his. The rest of the dragons tucked themselves into their pocket-dens. The eggs rested in the scarf wrapped around her waist.

Her father's plan met with Kale's wholehearted approval. He would organize the dragons. She would return to her mother. Kale didn't have any talent to help her locate Lady Allerion, so she and Alton would have to set down often to ask for news and directions. That might prove to be dangerous, but Kale tried not to worry.

Father said I would be as strong as ever physically. All the training I've done to fight didn't rely on my talent. I can still defend myself.

She and Alton flew north, away from the Dormanscz Mountains and over Ordray. Far below, indistinct shapes moved in mobs. They swarmed a house or barn, then ranged the open spaces until they detected another target. Kale wanted to ask Alton to fly lower so she could investigate, but none of her efforts to mindspeak to the dragon resulted in anything other than frustration.

She knew that what she saw below were animals, but without a closer look she could not tell what type they were. From the way these creatures moved, she surmised that they were not ordinary wild beasts.

The agreement had been for Alton to set down outside the first town they came to. He didn't. Kale felt certain that he had a reason, but it was a reason she had no way of understanding.

Alton picked up speed and soared to a higher elevation.

"Is something wrong?" Kale called out. But if he answered her with mindspeaking, she had no idea.

She craned her neck to scan the skies around them. Nothing in the air. She surveyed the land. Squinting at a dark smudge on the horizon before them, she realized she'd spotted a military camp.

"I bet it's not ours."

Alton veered to the north rather than fly directly over the encampment. The activity below stunned Kale. Troops of soldiers marched down every road. Ordinary citizens engaged in battles with swarms of strange, scrawny animals. From her position, Kale could not see that any of the farmers and villagers won against the onslaught.

She was so busy watching the tableau beneath her that she carelessly forgot to pay attention to her dragon's body cues. Alton changed directions and flew faster. The sudden shift caught Kale off guard, and she was thankful for the belt that helped her keep from falling. She clenched her knees into the stirrups and fussed at herself.

You've lost your talent, not your brain. Pay attention. It doesn't require wizardry to keep your seat on a dragon's back.

She glanced around and saw two dark shapes in the sky. *That's why*

*you've changed directions, isn't it, Alton? Dragons, and I'll bet they're fire drag-
ons sent to kill.*

She didn't expect an answer and didn't get one.

The dragons behind became larger as they drew closer. Red scales glistened in the sun. She could see smoke curling from their nostrils. Her
heart beat faster, and she willed Alton to find the strength to escape.

Alton had not lost hope. She marveled that he continued the steady
beat of his wings. His long flight since dawn that morning prevented him
from exerting more effort. He'd been in the air for hours. They could not
speed ahead. But Kale recognized the wisdom of flying higher. The thin-
ner air would not provide the necessary zoic to fuel the fire dragons' flames.
But the high altitude also meant Alton had more difficulty breathing.

Kale pulled one of her spears from its quiver. Most of her strength had
returned before her father would allow her to make the journey. Healing
had taken more than a week when, with Gymn, it should have taken less
than a day. Her aim had always been good. And if the fire dragons passed
beneath them, she had a good chance of striking her target.

The muscles along Alton's shoulders quivered. Kale put her hand on
his scales. If she shouted, he might hear. But would he understand? Different dragons had different capacities for understanding spoken language. Her own Celisse had lived with a farming family before coming to
her. Celisse comprehended speech proficiently. Kale couldn't encourage
Alton with words, but maybe her touch would tell him she appreciated
his efforts to save both their lives. She patted the purple scales and left her
hand to rest on his shoulder until the fire dragons drew closer.

The enemy dragons bore no riders. Kale knew this was often the case.
The dangerous beasts were pointed at their prey and told to hunt. Once
the fire dragons brought their victims down, they often feasted on the
flesh of the dead opponent. Of course, more civilized dragons thought
this practice abominable, and the fire dragons who served Paladin held
their cannibalistic cousins in disdain.

Kale waited until the distance and angle of her target lined up with what she knew would be her best chance. She heaved the spear and glowed a little with satisfaction, knowing she had made a good shot. She'd chosen the fire dragon's weak spot under a shoulder blade, but the lance struck something first. The spear bounced off an invisible barrier two or three feet from the dragon's flesh.

Kale gasped with outrage and drew out another javelin, determined to impale this flying beast. She aimed for a less deadly target and hurled the spear at a point exposed on the dragon's side beneath its wing. Again, her weapon bounced off before reaching flesh.

Someone had put a protective shield around each of the dragons. Now that she realized it was there, Kale could see the markings of a wizard's spell around the neck of her targeted dragon. The complex wizardry spoke of a seasoned expert. Probably Crim Cropper.

Her hopes soared. She could see the evidence of a spell. Her talent must be returning. Then she looked more closely and fought tears of disappointment. The markings were tattooed on the fire dragons. This would be so laborers in the wizard's camp would know which dragons needed special care.

Alton dove between the fire dragons with such speed, Kale grabbed the horn of the saddle, clung with her knees, and prayed for safety.

What is he doing? He's going to land? Why? To save me. Oh, Alton, I'm so sorry I cannot fight with you. I've nothing to offer. Isn't there some other way?

She knew there was not.

Alton's surprise maneuver had worked for a moment. The fire dragons flew on in confusion and then turned back. Without a rider to help with strategy, the beasts had to rely on learned tactics that did not adapt well to an unusual ploy.

Kale watched the ground rise to greet them. Alton swooped in a precise curve and zoomed along the treetops until he came to a clearing. He plopped down in the small space.

Kale did not want to endanger her mount any further. She released the belt and slid off his back. He took off before she was clear, and she fell to the ground from the rush of powerful wings.

She got to her feet and watched him rise into the sky. She knew he could maneuver more easily without a rider. He could make more dramatic turns and lead those fire dragons on a merry chase, but still she felt deserted.

"My weapons!" She stamped her foot and twirled around. "Aargh! How could I have been so stupid?" She felt at her waist and found her dagger and fingered the lumps in the scarf. Her eggs were safe. She opened her cape and called for the little dragons to emerge. They came out and examined the immediate area.

Kale explored the hollows of her moonbeam cape. With each forgotten weapon she pulled from the deep pockets, she sighed her relief.

It's been a long time since I've practiced with some of these, and some I have never used. But it's good to have something to lay my hands on if attacked.

A growl from the woods stood the hair on the back of her neck on end. She rose to her feet with a knife in each hand. The minor dragons came back to guard her. Gymn and Metta landed on her shoulders, Dibl on her head. The others perched on a branch, ready to dive at an enemy.

Out of the bushes came a lone animal. Not wolf, not bear, not mountain cat, but somehow each of these in a twisted body. With teeth bared, the beast circled Kale. She flipped her right hand knife in the air, caught it by the pointed tip, and launched it at the animal's neck. As the blade sank in, the creature screamed and lurched backward. Shaking its head, it swiped at the injury with a front paw, knocking the blade out. Blood spurted from the wound.

The animal charged. Kale dove toward the beast but to one side, hit the ground, rolled over the bloody knife, and came up in a fighting stance with both hands wielding a blade. The minor dragons harassed the wounded animal with their caustic spit. They aimed for its eyes and its wound.

The creature turned. Kale threw another knife. The blade struck its broad side and penetrated. Again the animal screamed but did not halt. It lowered its head and ran back at Kale.

She had only a second to pull another, longer-bladed knife from her arsenal. With one arm extended down and the other up, she waited to perform the ice-tong maneuver Regidor had taught her. She almost smiled, remembering her friend's impatience with her clumsiness, and his determination for her to master the "simple technique." But the snarl of the injured animal did not allow her to make light of the situation. Kale hoped she had the strength to drive both knives in from opposite directions.

The beast struck as Kale sidestepped. She closed her arms around it as if giving the beast a sudden embrace, only this embrace held the bite of two blades stabbing into its ribcage. The animal fell, taking Kale to the ground with it.

She lay with one arm pinned by its weight.

Is it dead? No breathing. I don't feel it breathing.

The minor dragons roosted in the trees nearby.

They wouldn't be resting if this brute wasn't dead.

She pulled herself away from the body, shaking with the aftermath of exertion and fear. She made herself retrieve her weapons, clean the blades, and put them away. Without another look at the hideous beast, she started into the forest.

I must find my way out. I need to see what's happening with Alton.

A few feet into the tangle of underbrush convinced her she needed more protection. She willed the transformation of her clothing and then realized nothing would happen. Her talent was gone. Instead of using wizardry, she delved into the hollows of her moonbeam cape, relying on someone else's gifts and talents. She found leather gloves with extended cuffs like gauntlets.

This will do.

She put them on and forged through the thicket. Just above her the minor dragons flew, keeping watch. From farther above she heard the screeches of the fire dragons. They battled Alton above the treetops.

Only a small patch of sky was visible through the leafy branches. Alton passed with a deadly opponent right behind him. The fire dragon breathed out a blaze that caught the small, high branches in flames. The fire leapt to surrounding trees. Kale redoubled her efforts to push through the woods.

A crash of limbs breaking warned her that one of the flying dragons had fallen. She came upon the body after another twenty minutes of pushing and shoving through tangled bushes.

Alton's only defenses against the fire dragons were claws, teeth, and his mighty tail. This dragon had received a blow to the head. His neck twisted as if broken. Kale hurried on.

Fire raged behind her. She heard another dragon fall, smashing trees as it plummeted toward the ground. This was farther ahead, and it would take her a few minutes to reach the place.

I must get to a clearing so Alton can pick me up. I hope he isn't injured. Perhaps we can hide somewhere while he recovers. He needs to rest. Do I have the right medicine in my hollows if he's burned?

She choked on the smoke from the rapidly spreading fire.

Those stupid fire dragons probably torched more than one section of the woods.

The minor dragons chittered a chorus of distress. Even without her talent she knew they expressed great agitation. She grasped the branches of two bushes and pushed them aside so she could scramble through. Her heart stuck in her throat. Ahead of her, a dragon's body hung from the thick lower branches of the trees.

A sob tore from Kale's throat. "Oh no! Alton!"

46

BETRAYAL

Heavy smoke stung Kale's eyes and lungs. She struggled to make her way to Alton. Broken branches littered the ground directly under him. His head hung downward, ten feet above hers. The minor dragons circled him, making mournful sounds deep in their throats.

"Is he dead? Oh, I wish I could understand you." She ran to the closest tree and shinnied up the trunk to the first unbroken branch. The smell of burned flesh assaulted her nostrils. She saw the damage a fire dragon had done to her friend. Red flesh showed through singed scales. She crawled over smaller limbs growing out from the main branch. Inching out to a place where she could reach Alton's wing, she tried to see signs of life. Her fingers touched the soft leather that spread between thin ribs of bone.

"Alton?"

A tree in the distance exploded as the sap burst into flame. She heard the blast. "Alton! We have to get away. The fire is coming."

The minor dragons surrounded Kale, pulling at her clothes with their tiny, clawed hands. Clearly, they wanted her down from the heights of the tree. Stubbornly, she crept farther out on the branch, reached with her foot to another limb, and crossed over. Now alongside his flank, she felt for Alton's heartbeat in the hollow where the wing joined his body.

She hung over to a lower branch so that she was only a few feet from the dragon's head. "Alton."

The morose tone of the minor dragons' chirrups told her Alton was beyond help.

She clambered back to the main trunk of the tree and looked over her shoulder. Flames shot above treetops not more than a mile away. Crying, she scrambled back down the tree.

Holding the edge of her cape over her mouth and nose, she followed Ardeo's soft glow through the haze of smoke. Soon the other dragons took refuge in their pocket-dens. Kale stumbled on.

Other animals crashed through the undergrowth, trying to escape the blazes. Kale didn't see as many as she heard. Most of the fleeing creatures looked like ordinary forest wildlife. Occasionally, an odd shape would pass too quickly for her to identify.

A breeze cleared away the smoke. She hauled in a lungful of fresh air.

Good for us, Ardeo. But not good as far as the fire goes. The wind will push the flames into more trees. I read that a forest fire makes its own wind. I wonder if that's true.

You don't hear me, do you? Of course not. But it feels good to think I'm speaking to you. Did that make sense?

A cloud of smoke dropped over them and concealed the trees a few yards ahead.

"Let's go." Kale followed Ardeo's shimmering body.

Another animal slammed through the bushes and into Kale's leg, knocking her over. The creature kept going. Kale struggled to her feet.

We must be going in the right direction. Don't the animals know the quickest way to safe ground? Didn't I see a couple of small lakes and a river from Alton's back? Were they this way? I think so.

The air cleared again. The sound of burning woods drowned out the cries of terror from the woodland creatures. Kale followed Ardeo. The smoke thinned, then thickened. Kale made herself hurry even more. She refused to think of the flames reaching Alton's body. She refused to believe that safety was more than a few more yards away.

Plowing through the clawing limbs of the bushes, she prayed Ardeo would be all right. He had no protection for his lungs. She held the cape over the lower half of her face and still felt the sting of poisoned air.

An animal screeched like a nocturnal bird that calls out as they hit their prey with sharp talons. The cry came again, above her and some distance behind, but closer than the first call.

Something landed on her back. Claws dug into her scalp. Searing pain tore through her flesh. Had she been struck by a burning branch? Kale twisted. Thin, hairy arms wrapped around her head. Small hands with long yellow claws scraped down her forehead and pulled the moonbeam cape away.

Kale fell forward. Still the animal dug its hands into her hair, pulling and scratching. She batted at it and tried to shield her head. Teeth sank into her hand. She shook her whole arm to dislodge the small beast. The last hard shake flung the creature into the bushes. Kale rolled in the opposite direction and got to her knees.

The animal came out of the thicket and stood glaring at her. Coarse brown hair covered its wiry body except the face that looked oddly like a face belonging to any of the high races. It pulled back its lips, showing long, pointed teeth. Screeching, it launched itself into the tree limbs and swung away, catching each branch with hairless hands at the end of long arms.

Kale sat back. Every scratch and bite burned like fire. Fire! She had to make herself move. "Ardeo! Ardeo!" The smoke made her voice scratchy. She stood and swayed. "Ardeo!"

Walking on trembling legs, she continued to call. "Ardeo!"

She stumbled and fell. A gray rock caught her attention. She reached out. Her fingers touched not cold stone, but Ardeo's leathery skin. Tenderly, she scooped him up and once more got to her feet. Opening her cape, she placed him in the sling with Gymn.

She didn't think she could go on, but if she didn't, they all would die.

The woods thinned. A field stretched just beyond the last trees. A bisonbeck throng milled over trampled meadow grass. The fact that this was an army took a minute to sink into Kale's mind.

There isn't anyplace else to go.

She fell out of the last bit of underbrush. Rough hands picked her up.

"It's Kale Allerion, the Dragon Keeper."

"The master will be pleased."

She'd fallen into the hands of enemy soldiers, and all Kale could hope was that they had some ointment to soothe the burning wounds inflicted by the strange animal.

Kale regained consciousness on an elevated canvas cot in a large tent.

"Send for Latho's wife." A deep voice, but Kale felt certain it was a female.

"They say she can deal with this vermin." A different voice, lower than the first, but still having the sound of a woman.

The rustle of cloth. "I can't wait to get these lizards out of my medic tent." The first voice. "They hiss at me every time I go near this Dragon Keeper person. Go, now, Urssa. Don't stand there talking. Go get Latho's wife, Bends."

That's funny. I know a woman named Bends. Leetu Bends. If she were here now, we'd be on our way out of this camp.

Her mind drifted. People moved in the tent. She heard moans but sometimes couldn't tell if the moans came from her or others. The claw marks from the beast burned. A cold, wet rag draped over her forehead and hair. Occasionally, someone would come and pour fresh cool water on her head. She tried not to move. She tried not to cry out.

Kale opened her eyes and stared into the face of a bisonbeck woman.

"She's awake." The woman straightened and gestured to someone.

"Come, Bends, take these beasts so I can tend her wounds. Crim Cropper wants her alive."

Another woman came to the side of the bed. Kale stared at the face. She did look like Leetu Bends. Kale blinked. No, it was a bisonbeck woman. Someone's wife. The bisonbeck woman named Bends held a large woven container.

Kale watched her pick up the minor dragons and place them in the basket. She tried to protest. Her dragons shouldn't be going with this woman. Why didn't they resist?

Again the woman briefly resembled Leetu Bends, and then her features shifted back into the face of a stranger.

The woman frowned. "There should be a green one somewhere. Have you seen a green one?"

"Under that cape, if you can touch it. It burned my hand. But there's a bulge under her tunic."

The dragon gatherer pulled back the moonbeam cape with no trouble and located Gymn.

"You've got the touch, now, don't you? I'm wondering where you picked up a way with dragons and the ability to handle things like that awful cape."

The woman shrugged and picked up Ardeo. "I lived with Pretender some. This one's dead. You can toss it in the trash."

"I'm not putting that in my trashcan. It'll stink by morning. Crim Cropper sent orders you were to take care of the dragons. You take care of them. That dead one as well as the live ones."

Tears formed in Kale's eyes and ran down her temples.

The woman hovering over her bent closer. She looked like Leetu Bends and then didn't.

"Hurry up, Bends. I want to go to bed sometime tonight."

"One such as this would have eggs on her. Did you look for a pouch with an egg?"

"Didn't I just tell you I couldn't touch her much with the cape burning me and the dragons hissing and spitting and snapping?"

Bends's rough hands poked and patted Kale's clothing. "Here they are. Give me scissors to cut this cloth."

The other woman handed over the shears, and with a few snips, the eggs were taken from Kale's beautiful blue scarf and put in the basket.

"Take that cape off her. Take it with you. Can you do that?"

"Sure I can. Help me raise her up."

"Do it yourself. I'm not touching her till you've carried that thing away."

The Bends woman pushed Kale onto her side. Searing pain overwhelmed her. The last thing she remembered was the moonbeam cape being pulled out from under her.

Shadows filled the tent. One lantern shone. Smoke clung to the air. Deep breathing set a rhythm in the background. Few noises seeped in through the canvas walls. Footsteps. A man's voice in the distance. A scornful laugh.

Kale's face and scalp burned. Someone had placed her on her stomach with her face over the edge of the cot. A rolled towel under her chin kept her face from falling forward. The bed was raised a good distance off the ground. She tried to lift her hands but couldn't. Her wrists were tied to the wooden slats of the cot. She pulled. The binding held.

"You were clawing your wounds."

Kale gasped. "Regidor?"

Black boots appeared before her. A man knelt, a black cape swirling around his bent legs. Regidor's strangely handsome meech face appeared in her view. He smiled.

"Regidor, how did you get here? Did you come to rescue me?"

"You're in no shape to travel, and the roads are clogged with people fleeing the fire, coming to help extinguish the fire, and going back to their homes now that the fire is under control."

"It is? Under control? How?"

"Kale, there is an army of men here. An army belonging to Crim Cropper who were terrified when Pretender showed up. They have earned the wrath of Lord Ire by pledging their loyalty to Cropper. Face to face with Cropper's superior, they realized the folly of their ways and jumped to do his bidding. He ordered them into the burning forest to extinguish the flames."

Kale's mind had wandered away halfway through his explanation. "Is Bardon here? Is he close? Is he coming?"

"No, he's on another mission."

"I need him, Regidor."

"I know."

"Where's Gilda?"

"Safe. Where she belongs and safe."

Kale gulped back a moan. The scorching heat of the wounds tormented her. "Regidor, I hurt. Can you fix it?"

Compassion softened the meech dragon's mouth. "No, I'm sorry. I can't."

"But I can."

Kale saw a hand rest on Regidor's shoulder. The fingers squeezed, then gave a pat. Regidor stood, and another man took his place. Kale nearly breathed Paladin's name before she realized her mistake. Pretender could look a lot like her beloved leader. But harshness around his mouth and coldness in his eyes made the resemblance incomplete.

"I can help you, Kale."

The pain washed deeper into her soul at the same time she heard her own voice saying, "No, no, no!" She couldn't make deals with Pretender. Wulder would take care of her needs. Wulder would send someone to ease the pain and the fear that welled in her heart.

"I can help now, Kale."

Pretender put a hand on her shoulder and his touch felt warm and comforting. The throbbing eased as if he had drawn off some of the poison.

"Please." Kale didn't know what to ask. Right now she wanted reprieve. She sobbed. She would beg for some relief. But was that what Pretender offered?

He moved closer. Leaned over her so that his warm breath tickled her cheek. "The creature who attacked you carried a venom. Poison devised by Crim Cropper. But as always in Crim Cropper's designs, there is a flaw. I have the antidote."

"Please."

He pulled an orb from a pocket in the lining of his jacket. It was no larger than the end of his thumb, yet Kale had the impression it loomed large in the tent, even invading the entire camp with some mystical power. She trembled, thinking she should avoid this orb at all costs. Something inside the glass ball swirled and glowed, spun and faded, then glowed again.

"I will give you the salve that will take away the pain, but I must ask you to carry this. The potion will not work unless you carry this to energize the ingredients."

Suspicion rose in Kale's mind, but a surge of agony blocked it out. She stared into the orb, saw brilliant colors whirling, and some of the tension eased from her shoulders. Some of the pain ebbed away as well. Pretender lowered the pretty bauble out of sight, and the throbbing swept over her open gashes.

She drew in a sharp breath. "Yes, please."

Pretender unwrapped the gauze binding that held her right hand to the cot. He placed the cold orb in her palm and wrapped her fingers around it. Then he bent her elbow, lifted her side slightly from the bed, and guided Kale's hand underneath her. The orb rested within her clutched fingers tight against her chest.

"Keep it close to your heart, Kale, and you will soon become strong."

Long into the morning, Kale stirred again. She lay on her back in the raised cot. Her wounds felt cool and slightly itchy. She reached a hand up to touch her cheek, and someone caught it at the wrist.

"Ah, none of that. You'll be undoing all the good we did." The gruff bisonbeck woman of the day before stood beside her. This was the woman who ran the medic tents, not the one who looked like Leetu Bends.

A bisonbeck who looked like a small, pale emerlindian? I must have been in the throes of a powerful poison to imagine that. Poison? Pretender used that word. Said he'd help me.

"I'm better?"

"You're not going to die."

"Where did you get the salve to cure my wounds?"

"What salve? You just needed a tincture of time and the same old ointment I use on every hurt that comes in here."

Perhaps I dreamed… "The smell of smoke is gone."

"Some. We had a rain during the night."

The nurse moved away from Kale's cot. Kale followed her eyes, moving her head with very little pain. The woman bent over another patient on a raised cot.

It was a dream. Why would Regidor be here? I thought a bisonbeck woman was Leetu Bends. Then I dreamed Regidor was here. And Pretender in Cropper's camp when they're at war? I dreamed it.

She shifted to her side and became aware of an object in her hand. She drew her hand out from under the covers and slowly uncurled her fingers. In her hand was the orb.

47

DISCOVERY

"Ouch!" Bardon jerked away from the sharp pain on his chin. He opened his eyes to see a small rodent, sitting on its haunches and watching him.

Where am I? Stone floor. Dungeon. Cropper's lower levels. Not a dungeon. But not a good place, either.

He looked around, surprised that his neck had some mobility.

They've left me alone.

His eyes went back to the beady-eyed rodent.

Not completely alone.

"Shoo!"

The little animal didn't move.

I suppose this is one of Cropper's mutants. Unafraid of people and designed to inflict pain.

The beastie put his front paws down and took a tentative step forward.

Oh, no you don't.

Bardon forced his muscles to move. He rolled.

Ah, not quite as incapacitated as Cropper thought.

He tested his arms and legs. Some movement. Not much, but some.

I've got to stand.

He surveyed the room and decided the stairs going down presented his best option. He managed to get his arms in front of him and then raised up on his forearms to pull himself across the floor. He reached the doorway to the stairs and took a great deal of time to shift his body so his legs would go down first. With his concentration on reaching the steps, he hadn't paid attention to the rodent. He glanced its way and moaned.

So you have friends, do you? Lots of friends.

One rodent had become at least a hundred. They mingled in their pack, not seeming to be interested in him. He scootched back until his whole body lay on the hard stone stairs. He bent his knees so that he knelt. Then he placed his hands on the step beneath his shoulders and pushed. After a tremendous struggle, he stood, sweat dripping off his brow and breathing as if he'd run a race. He leaned against the stairwell wall to recover.

When he opened his eyes, the horde of rodents had moved to the top of the stairs.

Why are you so interested in me?

The rodents stared. The fact that they all stared, all sat on their haunches, and all had ceased any squeaking made Bardon nervous.

It would be most convenient if you rodents turned out to be minnekens sent to rescue me. But, pardon me for thinking this, none of you look intelligent.

Bardon eased down to the step behind him. Without hesitation, the rodents poured over the edge until the next step held no more room.

I don't like this.

He took another step down. The rodents advanced one more step. Bardon sucked in a breath. The number of rodents seemed to be increasing. The micelike creatures still filled the doorway to the stairs, yet at least a hundred had moved down.

I don't think I could outrun these creepy little monsters, but I'm sure going to try to get away.

As if they understood Bardon's decision, the rodents surged down the stairs and surrounded him. They clawed and chewed his pant legs. He felt them gnawing on his boots.

Bardon tried to go up and discovered his knee would not bend enough to manage the step. He moved down, knocking rodents away and stepping on a few. Bardon shivered. The image of the beasties crawling up his legs sent a tremor of panic through his body.

Steady, Sir Bardon. This is no time to lose your discipline. "Think clearly. Act rationally. Wulder has given you a choice as to how you behave. Choose well and you will prosper."

He continued down the stairs. He reached a landing and made the turn. At the bottom of this flight, he saw that a heavy wooden door blocked whatever level he approached.

Wulder, I need that door to be unlocked.

He continued down, one painstaking step at a time, trying not to let the rodents trip him, not caring how many he injured in his clumsy descent.

When he reached the door, he lifted the latch and pulled it open. With speed generated by fear, he jerked his body around the door's edge and slammed it shut. At his feet were a fraction of the rodents that had come down the stairs with him. The hem of his pant legs hung in tatters. Sharp, tiny teeth had scarred the leather of his boots. The rodents still plagued his feet, and he didn't have enough suppleness in his legs to shake them off.

He examined his surroundings. On either side of the small platform where he stood, two doors stretched from the floor to low ceiling. He tried each one, but the locks held fast. If an escape route existed behind one of the doors, he wasn't going to be able to use it. He hobbled across the square of stone floor and started down another flight of stairs.

With each step down he injured several of the rodents, but the tenacious beasts still harried his feet and lower legs. The boots kept him safe from their gnawing teeth. At the bottom of this set of stairs, he found an unlocked door that provided a way to diminish the number of beasties plaguing him. He stepped through and faced two frustrating doors, locked and unyielding. And another stretch of steps led downward.

Bardon sighed and started down again. He looked at the two dozen or so mice still trying desperately to demolish his boots. They'd chewed his pant legs until the fabric was higher than the distance they could leap. He chortled and caught the anxious edge in the tone of his own laughter.

Oh, Wulder, this would be funny if I were not so exhausted, hungry, and full of aches. I have been chased by a horde of ineffectual monster mice. Did Crim Cropper ever develop a truly functional beast? Yet, I'm glad these creatures are horrendous at their appointed task.

He came to another door and slipped through. He'd become more adept at getting on the other side and leaving behind the rodents. Now he could count the rodents that remained after he slammed the door. With his eyes downward as he looked to see how many had been eliminated, Bardon sensed the space around him was different.

He stood at the edge of a great hall. Scattered around the room, large globes rested on pedestals. The ivory columns were uniform in width but of different heights. The orbs atop each one varied from the size of a head to the very large spheres that could not possibly roll through the door. Bardon wondered briefly how Crim Cropper had managed to get these inside the room. Within each translucent glass sphere, small shards of lightning crackled. An uneven rhythm of pops, sputters, and hisses emanated from each large ball. He ambled around the room with his awkward gait, examining the different sizes of the globes and colors of the encapsulated energy.

I know these instruments. I've seen them in Kale's rooms in our own home. I've seen them when we visited other wizards and in the books Kale reads. I wonder what Cropper does with all of these. If Kale were here, she could discern their uses and fill me in. As it is, I can only make guesses.

Bardon yelped as a sharp tooth met his toe. One of the rodents had finally pierced the leather of his boot. Bardon stumbled and knocked against a pedestal. The sphere toppled and hit the floor with a crash. Holding on to the rocking pillar, Bardon regained his balance. He looked down at the shattered glass and then at the pesky rodents. They had lost interest in him. They scuttled around the floor, whiskers twitching and tails dragging like ordinary mice.

A door on one of the side walls crashed open.

The stubby servant Prattack rushed in. "What are you doing here? You can't be in here! What have you done? Master Cropper will be furious." He shuffled to a closet and grabbed a broom and dustpan.

"What do these globes do, Prattack?"

The servant bustled over to the broken glass and began cleaning up. "Nothing important. Nothing you'd be interested in. It's the master's business, not yours. These are important to him, not you."

Bardon deliberately knocked another globe to the floor.

It shattered, and Prattack came scurrying over with his broom. "Look what you've done. The master will be so annoyed when he sees his creatures aren't obeying him. I'm telling him you did it. He's going to be angry, and I won't take the blame."

Bardon pushed two more to the ground. Prattack turned to him with tears in his eyes. "You might as well do them all, and then shatter me as well."

"I have a better idea. Why don't we both knock them over, and we'll escape together?"

"Oh, I couldn't do that." Prattack fixed his eyes on a globe that sparkled with green and blue lightning. "I can't defy the master."

Bardon hobbled across the room and picked up the sphere that held Prattack's attention. The little man gasped. Bardon threw it to the stone floor. Prattack's eyes grew big, and his face turned purple.

"Breathe, Prattack," Bardon commanded and shambled over to thump the man's back with his hand.

The servant took a deep breath and charged forward. He hit one pedestal after another, smashing all the remaining globes.

He turned to Bardon with a gleam in his eye. "Where do you want to go, sir? There's gateways to anyplace in the world!"

48

One Battle

Clattering sounds, clanking and banging, intruded on Kale's peaceful slumber. She stretched and opened her eyes. All the other occupants of the medic tent had disappeared. A tall woman swept into the tent.

"Gilda!"

The meech dragon hurried to her side. "Come, Kale." She helped her sit up. "We have to get out of here."

"What's happening?"

"As soon as the forest fire was out, Pretender turned on Cropper's army of bisonbecks. He rode overhead on his black dragon and hurled bolts of lightning at them. His scourge of an army came over the hills and attacked this bedraggled crew of Cropper's finest. Compared to those under Pretender's authority, they were the runts of a litter of kittens."

Gilda threw an underrobe around Kale's shoulders. "Help me here. I'm not accustomed to dressing anyone other than myself."

Kale shoved her fist through the sleeve. Her hand still held Pretender's globe. "I thought the armies were evenly matched. I thought that's why the war had gone on so long."

"Stox's army stood up to Pretender fairly well, but since her death, her men have no leadership."

"Crim Cropper?"

Gilda's fingers worked to button a tunic over the first garment. "A lunatic hermit. He knows nothing of military tactics, nor how to lead men. Drive animals, maybe. But lead men, no!"

The meech dragon leaned back and inspected Kale. "Bah! I'll do this the better way."

She squinted her eyes, and Kale felt the material of her clothing shift, twist, and expand. She examined her arms and found the sleeves to be of an elegant cream-colored silk. She stood and yards of soft fabric swirled around her legs. The green fabric shimmered as she took a step.

"Not exactly my style, Gilda."

"More's the pity. Come on." She grabbed Kale's arm and tugged.

"Where are we going?"

"We're escaping! Isn't that obvious?"

Kale stopped in her tracks. "I can't. My dragons. I have to find the dragons. The eggs. I have to find the eggs, too."

Gilda turned and put a fist on her hip. The meech dragon's disgust curled her lip and raised an eyebrow. "Didn't Leetu Bends come and collect them for safekeeping?"

"No, it was a bisonbeck woman who...looked...a little...like Leetu Bends."

"Right." Gilda grabbed her arm again. "It was Leetu Bends."

Kale still dragged her feet. "She took my moonbeam cape, too."

Gilda stopped again and didn't disguise her anger. "Don't you realize that anything you own, once you enter an army medic tent, is fair game for anyone who can still walk?"

"She took them for safekeeping?"

"Yes."

"No! I don't believe you."

"What?"

"Why should I? What are you doing in the enemy camp? Why did Pretender treat Regidor like a good friend?"

"What are you talking about? When did Lord Ire treat my husband like a friend?"

"The night they were here. Regidor came first to soften me up. I know how it works. Then Pretender came and patted him on the shoulder and took over."

"Took over? Took over what?"

"Winning my confidence. Bringing me over to his side."

"Whose side? Regidor's side? Lord Ire's side?"

"I was weak and in pain, lots of pain. Pretender offered to take the pain away. All I had to do was—"

Gilda's voice became calm. "All you had to do was...what?" She came close to Kale and put a gentle hand on her arm. "What? Do what?"

"It's nothing."

"Oh, I very much doubt that. What are you supposed to do, Kale?"

Kale drew her clenched fist closer to her heart. She needed to be strong to stand up to Gilda. Gilda's gaze shifted from Kale's face to the closed hand. The meech dragon opened her own hand and held it in front of Kale, palm up.

"No." The word came quietly out of Kale's strangled throat. Though nothing touched her, she could barely breathe.

"Let me see it."

"No."

"He gave you something to carry."

"No."

"You just lied to me, Kale. Is it like you to lie?"

"No."

"Now, that was the truth. What did Pretender give you to carry?"

"I can't."

"You can't what?"

"Open my hand."

"Oh." Gilda studied her for a moment. "I don't know what to do about that." She gently pulled on Kale's arm. "Come on. Let's go find Regidor."

"What's he doing?"

"Besides fighting Cropper's crazed troops and Pretender's forces, who don't seem to care what they destroy as long as they crush every bisonbeck in the wrong army, Regidor is battling a swarm of vileness that has broken loose. We believe Crim Cropper freed every poor malformed creature from his experimental lair and thrust them out upon the world. Perhaps to even his odds against Lord Ire. Regardless, my husband is fighting against whichever evil steps into his presence. At any moment, it might be any one of the above. He blew our cover as spies."

Kale followed Gilda to the tent flap. They both peered out at the chaos. A dragon roared in the sky above them.

"I almost forgot," said Gilda. "Your father is here, as well, with a battalion of fighting dragons."

Kale felt a surge of love. Her fingers loosened their grip on Pretender's globe. She gasped and clenched it tighter. She'd almost dropped the gift.

Gilda no longer looked out of the tent but studied Kale. Kale tried to make her face look calm, unbothered by the panic and confusion churning inside.

"What does the orb do, Kale?"

"It took away the pain. Gilda, you can't conceive how excruciating the burning was."

"I think I can. The marks of it are still on your face and through your hair."

Kale's fingertips went to her cheek. She felt new skin healed over her wounds. The skin was ridged, lumpy, and tender. Gilda pulled a hand mirror from her pocket and held it in front of Kale. Tears filled Kale's eyes. She grabbed the mirror from Gilda and held it closer. Jagged red lines ran across her face. Gaps in her hair exposed the same ugly scars in her scalp. The tears blurred her vision, but not enough to block out what she saw in the looking glass.

Gilda eased the mirror from Kale's trembling fingers. She put it away and with her hands formed a hat with a veil, using material she pulled from her pocket. She kissed Kale's cheek and settled the hat on her head, pulling the veil down to completely hide the scars.

She put an arm around Kale and squeezed. "We have to go." Her head swiveled as she surveyed the scene. "Now, Kale."

Kale looked at the stragglers rushing through the deserted camp. Most of them were bisonbecks, but a few were from the high races. The panic on their faces masked the differences in races.

"Yes, we have to go. But where?"

49

Another Battle

Kale and Gilda ran toward the river at the edge of the camp. Once they reached the bank, Gilda turned upstream and ran through the trees. Kale followed. A bluff rose out of the bank, and when they reached it, Kale realized it was honeycombed with tunnels and small rooms. Gilda led her into the network of caves. The place teemed with women and children, refugees from nearby farms and villages.

"You'll be safe here." Gilda avoided looking directly at the crowd but waved her gloved hand in their general vicinity.

"Where are you going?"

"To fight beside my husband. He's a mighty warrior, but even a hero gets tired."

"I'll go with you. I can still fight."

"No, Kale. Stay here."

Kale started to protest, but Gilda cut her off. "Your dragons are here."

"They couldn't be. They would have flown to me as soon as I entered."

"You don't have your talent anymore, Kale. They don't sense your presence. You'll have to look for them." With a swirl of her fashionable dress and cape, Gilda left, calling over her shoulder, "I'm needed, dear. I have to go."

Kale wandered from one room etched out of sandstone to the next, through wide corridors and narrow passageways. At every turn she met other displaced people, people who couldn't be at home and couldn't help the fight for their homes.

She followed the sound of children giggling. In a larger room far into the bluff, she found a bright atmosphere with many lightrocks encrusting the walls. Kale recognized several of the games being played as ones she'd seen children play when she was a slave in River Away.

I've come such a long way since then. But here I am watching, not really part of the community.

She hovered in the arched doorway and gave herself up to being an observer. She wanted to leave and not see this little picture of fellowship. She certainly did not want to be seen. It hurt that it wasn't her place to become involved.

Her dragons played with the children.

I should leave them here. They're doing something good for the young ones. I don't have any great commission in this battle, and even if I did, the dragons and I couldn't help each other because we can't communicate.

She counted the dragons. Five. Ardeo, of course, was not with them. Kale batted tears back. If she'd been able to mindspeak with Ardeo, would he still be alive? And if she had not burned out her talent, she wouldn't have been on Alton's back. She wouldn't have been the reason he came into harm's way. She hadn't done much right on this quest. *I'm not even sure I'm on a quest anymore.*

A granny got up from his spot on several cushions and crossed the short space. Kale stepped aside, thinking the man wanted to leave.

"No, no," he said, holding out a woven container. "Leetu Bends gave me these to keep safe until you could come to get them."

Kale recognized the basket, but she was reluctant to take it. "You don't know who I am."

"Yes, I do. Maybe at this time I know who you are better than you do yourself." He patted her arm. "Do you need a reminder? You are Kale

Allerion, Dragon Keeper of Amara, in service to Paladin." He pushed the basket into her hands.

She glanced inside and saw her eggs nestled in the folds of her moon-beam cape. Closing her eyes against the sight, she moaned. She'd have to find someone who could protect and nurture this precious clutch of dragons.

A familiar chorus of happy chittering filled her ears. The minor dragons had recognized her, even covered as she was in borrowed clothing. Gymn landed on the front of her dress and climbed under the veil to rub his face against hers. Metta sat on a shoulder and sang one of Kale's favorite morning songs as if this were the beginning of a day. Dibl landed on her waist and ran round and round her middle. She knew if she could hear him, he would be laughing at the ridiculous dress Gilda had chosen for her. After their greeting, Filia and Pat perched on the handle of the basket, examining the eggs.

"We're back together." She sniffed. "Except for Ardeo. Brave Ardeo who was determined to lead me to safety. Do you all know what he did for me?"

"They do," said the granny, "and they believe you will do the same for others. You have a giving heart, child, whether you can use your talent or not."

"I lost my talent."

"At present, you cannot use your talent." He patted her arm again. "Go, go with your dragons and your dragon eggs. You have work to do."

Kale started to tell him she had no work, that she had been told to stay here out of the way. The dark granny gave her a piercing look.

"We who wait in these caves are not useless, Kale Allerion. We are waiting for our turn to serve."

"Of course, you are not useless, Granny."

"Go now. You've come to get what you require, and you have." He smiled a white toothy grin. "And as a little extra, you've heard what you need as well."

Kale stroked Pat and Filia with two fingers. Her other two fingers and thumb kept the small globe tightly in her hand. The granny squinted at the orb, gave Kale a scowl, and then went back to his seat.

"Are you taking the dragons?" asked a little marione child.

"I'm not taking them. They can choose to stay or go with me."

"I hope they stay."

Kale caught herself just before saying, "I hope they do, too."

Why would I say that? It's ridiculous. Of course I want them with me.

She turned and ran away from the happy gathering place. The minor dragons flew with her. She bumped into someone and said, "Excuse me," without stopping. Getting out into the open, away from all these people, became her only objective. She came up to a group of women talking.

"Which way is out?" she asked.

Several pointed down a corridor. Kale raced on. She came to another intersection of tunnels and again asked those nearby to direct her. Finally, she saw blue sky at the end of a passageway and ran straight for the opening. She found herself on a ledge, high above the entrance Gilda had used. From here she could see many aspects of the battle.

Alone on the ledge, she sat down with her back to the cliff and lifted the veil off her face. It took her a minute to puzzle out who was who and what they were doing. Crim Cropper's bisonbecks fled across the southern hills with Pretender's forces right behind them. The dark animals that she had seen from Alton's back no longer hunted in packs but were scattered. They attacked anything or anyone they came across, including one another. Her father's dragons fought these beasts, spotting them from the air and swooping down to do battle on the ground. A marching army appeared on the eastern horizon. Kale thought for certain she saw Paladin's flag. Reinforcements were on the way.

Where are Regidor and Gilda? Where's Leetu Bends? My mother? My father? Sir Dar? My husband? Could Bardon be near?

A sudden ache clutched her heart. She lifted a hand to touch her scarred face.

Shuddering away the melancholy, she scanned the sky. Miles from where she sat, two dragon riders battled. Her father rode Benrey, and the two of them faced Crim Cropper on a small, quick fire dragon. Kale jumped to her feet. Blasts of power hurled from one wizard to the other rippled the air with heat waves. Sir Kemry deflected the hits, but the smaller fire dragon's agile moves meant that most of her father's strikes missed.

As the men maneuvered in the sky, their conflict moved closer to the river and the bluff. She could now hear the crack and sizzle of the wizards' attacks.

The struggle became more uneven. Sir Kemry had more experience in battle and that kept him alive. But Cropper put strength into his weapons that far surpassed anything Kale's father could muster.

She spoke aloud to the minor dragons perched on her shoulders. "All those years Crim Cropper spent experimenting must have included weapons as well as animals."

If I had my talent, I could do something. I could throw a blast of light energy at Cropper from this angle. I could mindspeak to his dragon and confuse him. I could meld my energy with Father's and give Cropper one stunning wallop. If I only had a source of energy, perhaps I would have enough wizardry left in me to direct it.

She put her hands to her head, pressing against her skull, willing the lost power to come back.

In her hand, the hard globe pressed against her fingers. She brought her hand down and looked at the orb closely.

"Energy," she whispered. *The pain may come back.* Kale looked from her hand to the two combatants in the air. *It might not work. It probably won't work. You have no talent, remember?*

As she watched, the smaller fire dragon dove, then reversed directions and climbed, coming up under the bigger, slower Benrey. Her father moved to deflect the expected blast of fire, and the spell sputtered. The attacking dragon opened his mouth, and a stream of fire shot upward. Bits of flame penetrated, and Benrey jerked. As the fire dragon soared upward, passing Sir Kemry's mount, Cropper discharged a powerful blast. Her father had not re-centered his shield, and they took a hit. Benrey's wings folded, and his head tipped downward. His huge body spun.

"No!" cried Kale.

Benrey's wings extended, and the great dragon righted himself. His injuries slowed his flight. Sir Kemry sat askew in his saddle.

"Father! Oh, he's hurt. He's hurt!"

Crim Cropper circled around. The angle and speed at which his fire dragon flew declared his intentions.

"He's coming in for the kill!"

Kale looked once at the globe of energy. Her eyes went back to her failing father. She squeezed the orb with tight fingers against her palm until it hurt, then threw it to the ground. With one hand extended so that the cupped fingers pointed to the shattered fragments, she stretched the other arm toward her father. Energy flowed in a visible current from the broken orb into her hand, then reappeared as it streamed out of the other. The transference lasted only long enough for Kale to breathe deeply five times. She sank to the rocky ledge after the last tingle left her fingertips.

Her gaze went back to the battle. She saw her father's shoulders straighten, and she raised to her knees. Cropper and his mount's reckless approach demonstrated their overconfidence. They did not expect a counterblow. They believed their enemy all but taken.

Sir Kemry raised his hand, and Kale watched the energy flow she had provided directed at the enemy. The power streamed, not as a flash, but as a steady torrent washing over Cropper and his dragon. The barrage stunned both man and beast. They fell from the sky, plummeting without one effort to save themselves.

Cheers rang out from all around. Others had been watching the battle. Benrey circled, obviously struggling with his injuries. He came to land with less grace than usual and far away from people. Kale guessed he hadn't the strength to make the short flight to a more suitable spot.

She gathered up her dragons and hurried down through the twisted tunnels. She wanted to see her father soon. He must be all right. He had to be.

50

Final Battle

Kale remembered to put the veil over her face the first time she heard someone gasp as she went by. She came out of the entrance next to the river and realized her first obstacle was crossing to the other side. She stopped to pull the moonbeam cape out of the basket and went through the hollows to find several gold pieces. She put her plain moonbeam cape on over the fancy dress.

"I'll take you," said the third boatman she asked. He took the gold from her hand and pocketed it. "You got everything you need? Because I'm not waiting while you run back to get trunks and parcels and the like."

"I have everything." Kale stepped into the skiff and sat down on a wooden plank that served as a seat.

The marione looked askance at the minor dragons as he gathered his docking lines. "Plenty of strange creatures around these days. It's good to see a normal beast."

"Usually people are astonished to see minor dragons."

He sat down, put his oars in the oarlocks, and used one to push away from the pier. "I've seen pictures of dragons. The things that are creeping about have never had their likenesses put in a book." He pulled on the oars, and the skiff slid out into deeper water. "Have you got a weapon on you?"

"Yes."

"Better have it ready, then."

Despite the man's dire predictions, they made it to the opposite shore with no incidents.

"You're going out there alone and on foot?"

"My father's out there."

The marione pulled the bill of his cap down farther on his forehead. "Wulder's protection on you then."

Kale's head jerked up. "Thank you. It's been a long time since someone thought to give me that blessing."

He ducked his head in an awkward nod and shoved off.

"Good-bye, and thank you."

He didn't acknowledge her farewell.

Kale surveyed the landscape. The grass that hadn't been scorched by dragonfire had been crushed by many feet. She didn't have time nor did she care to determine what types of people and animals had done this damage. She pushed the veil off her face and marched across the broken stubble toward the place she'd seen Benrey land. It seemed to her that a rush of people should be going out to greet her father, offer him aid, and congratulate him. She saw not a living soul.

As she trudged through a scorched field, ash blackened the hem of her skirt. Passing a burned-out farmhouse, she couldn't help but miss Celisse. She'd found her dragon in a barn where bisonbecks from Wizard Risto's army had torched the home. Was Celisse all right or dead like Alton? She blocked the image of his body from her mind, swallowed hard, and continued on.

Just beyond that line of trees, I think. It isn't much farther.

The vicious fighting had somehow left this patch of woods unscathed. With anticipation spurring her on, Kale dashed between the trunks and came out the other side. Benrey's long body stretched across yellowed grass. With his eyes closed, her father sat with his back resting against his mount's side. Burn marks scored most of the dragon's hindquarters.

Kale ran to kneel beside Sir Kemry. Gymn leapt to his chest and began to explore, checking for injuries.

Kale placed a cautious hand on Sir Kemry's cheek. "Father!"

He opened his eyes. "Kale. I had to save my strength, and even then, it wasn't enough."

"Where are you hurt?"

He shook his head with effort. "Just a twinge. I don't know if Benrey's going to make it, though."

Kale jumped up and went to the head of the dragon. She knelt beside him and put her cheek on his forehead. She placed one hand next to his nostril and felt no breath. She listened and heard no beat of blood coursing through his veins. Tears streamed down her cheeks. Benrey would never fly for her father again.

"So much sadness." A man's voice rumbled with sympathy, but an underlying tone of mockery scraped over Kale's nerves.

Kale looked up to see Pretender standing a few feet away. He looked as if he'd just walked out of a palace. No grime, no wrinkles, no smudge of battle stained his elegant attire.

"I can make it better, Kale."

"Bring back Benrey, and Ardeo, and Alton? I don't think so." Kale dampened the fire of anger in her chest. She knew from Wulder's Tomes that "a heart that boils over with rage blisters the mind and scalds reason."

Her father stirred. "Who are you talking to, Kale?"

"Pretender."

"Tell him to crawl back in his hole."

Pretender laughed. "Why do people always react to me like that?" He spread his hands in a "what can I do" gesture, then laughed again. "Well, actually, not all people do. Some find my friendship the best thing that has happened to them in this life." He moved a few feet away from the side where Kale's father rested. "You have so many problems right now, Kale, and I can help you with quite a few of them.

"For instance, you want your talent back. I can arrange for that to happen. Did you know that Celisse is quite near? She's approaching with that army you saw from the bluff. If you had your talent, you could call to her, and she would come."

"If she's coming, I need only be patient and wait."

He studied Kale for a moment. "Still sad? What else can I do for you? Your face? I have the expertise to smooth those scars and wash out that ugly red discoloration. Your husband will be so distressed when he sees what Cropper's hideous beast has done to his once-exquisite wife."

"Being your 'friend' would scar my soul. I think that would distress Bardon more."

"What about the pain, Kale? You accepted my gift without any qualms when the pain held you in its grip."

Kale steeled herself. "The pain is gone."

Pretender arched his eyebrows. "Gone for good. Are you sure?" He looked pointedly at her hand. "Where is the little bauble I gave you to energize the healing salve?"

Kale said nothing.

"You broke it. And I'm not even angry with you, Kale. I understand. And I am most glad you were able to assist your father. It was very clever of you. And you assisted me, as well." He performed a formal bow. "I thank you for your part in Crim Cropper's demise."

Kale clenched her fists, tightened her jaw, and refused to answer his taunts.

"Kale," her father called. "What's all that muttering? You aren't still talking to that villain?"

"He's still here, Father."

Lord Ire smiled and cocked his head to one side. "But the pain, Kale. I'm afraid it will return."

The worst of the scars on her face twitched. An ever-so-slight sensation of tightening muscles and discomfort made Kale wince. With the wince came a burst of searing pain. Kale dropped to her knees and held her face in her hands.

"Just come with me, Kale. Live in my palace. Enjoy my company. You will have your talent. You can have whichever one of your friends you want to be there with you. No pain, and your beauty back. And one more thing, Kale. I was most irritated with your father for leading the dragons against me as well as Crim Cropper. I came here to kill him. For you, Kale, if you come with me, I'll let him live."

Still holding her burning cheek, Kale looked up at Pretender. "If I go with you, it would kill my father. A slow death of disappointment and despair."

"Kale!" Her father's voice sounded near.

She twisted to see him standing with his sword drawn. She stood. "You can't fight him. You're too weak."

Sir Kemry smiled. "Never underestimate a father's love." He strode forward. Only a little wobble ruined the effect.

Another voice interrupted the scene. "I think it's time I stepped in."

All eyes turned toward the newest arrival. Kale, Sir Kemry, and Pretender each reacted differently.

Kale grinned. "You're well!"

Sir Kemry bowed and said, "Your servant, sir."

And Pretender rolled his eyes. "Not you again."

Paladin grinned at his knight and his Dragon Keeper, then turned a solemn face to Pretender. "Are we going to fight?"

Kale took her father's arm and held on. At the moment she didn't know if she was supporting him or if he held her up.

Pretender sneered. "You mean as in a duel to the death? You know He won't allow it."

Kale turned to her father and whispered, "What does he mean?"

"Wulder has said that Pretender may not kill Paladin. And even Pretender must abide by Wulder's mandate."

"No." Lord Ire's cold voice sent shivers down Kale's spine. "I can't kill him, but I can wound him, humiliate him, destroy those he loves, and take away all his possessions."

"And in the end, Pretender?" asked Paladin. "What is the end?"

Pretender ground his teeth. "The end is not written yet."

Paladin's eyebrows shot up. "Isn't it?"

A clap of thunder, a puff of smoke, and Pretender vanished.

"Dramatic exit," muttered Sir Kemry and collapsed.

Kale went down with him. "Father, are you all right? Paladin, I think he fainted."

Paladin came to her side, put one hand on her shoulder and one on Sir Kemry's. After a moment, he said, "He's all right, Kale. You are too."

Her father opened his eyes and winked. She smiled at him and then at Paladin.

"So here you are," Gilda said. "I thought I told you to stay in the caves. What have you gotten into this time?"

Kale laughed and glanced over her shoulder. Regidor, Gilda, and Bardon stood in a row. They looked exhausted but unhurt. Her husband had a nick on his chin. Kale ducked her head and turned away. She frantically grabbed the veil and tugged it in place.

"What are you doing?" Bardon's boots were firmly planted beside her. When she looked up, he smiled. "Get up. I want to kiss you."

She didn't move. She heard him hiss out, "Kale, are you hurt?"

She began to cry but shook her head.

"Please, lady of mine. I'm still stiff as a stake from that awful disease, and I can't come down there to you. Stand up."

Kale stumbled to her feet, stifling sobs but not hiding her sniffles at all. "You've been ill? I wasn't there to take care of you."

"And inconvenient it was, too. I could have used you and Gymn." He softened his voice. "I could have used you."

His hand reached up to lift the veil, and she stopped him. "Don't."

"Why? I want to kiss you."

"I don't have any talent left. I exhausted it. A Cropper creature attacked me during the forest fire, and Alton and Ardeo are dead, and the creature scratched my face, and it was poison and my face is scarred." She hiccuped. "And my head."

Bardon lifted the veil. She watched his eyes, waiting for the reaction. She saw only love and amazement.

"I don't know what you're talking about, Kale. You're beautiful."

She sniffed twice, hiccuped, and dissolved into tears. He gathered her in his arms, knocking the silly hat off. That seemed to please him. He kissed the top of her head.

Kale felt the smooth skin of her cheeks. "Paladin must have healed me." She hiccuped again.

"When?" asked her father from behind her.

She turned around with difficulty because Bardon didn't let her go. "When he healed you."

"But that was later. There was nothing wrong with your face when you first found me."

"But the scars were still there. I felt the pain course through them again when Pretender spoke to me. He said he'd take them away if I went with him."

Gilda sashayed over on Regidor's arm. "The scars were there. I saw them. And they aren't there now." She turned to Paladin. He sat on a log, playing with the minor dragons.

"Well," said Gilda, sounding her most demanding, "are you going to explain this?"

He laughed. "I think Sir Kemry explained it. He said, 'Never underestimate a father's love.' Through eyes of love, he saw the beauty even before the beauty was restored."

Kale put her fingertips to her temples.

Bardon hugged her tighter. "Are you all right?"

She tilted her head. "Yes, I hear voices." She looked up at him and beamed. "I hear Dar and Celisse and Greer and all the minor dragons."

Her eyes widened. "And I know what you're thinking, Sir Bardon."

With a twinkle in his eye, Bardon leaned down, a bit stiffly, and kissed his wife.

EPILOGUE

"Forgive me for doubting you, daughter." Sir Kemry offered Kale a plate of food.

She scooted over on the log she used as a seat and balanced the dish on her knee. Her moonbeam cape slipped, and she used one hand to resettle it on her shoulder. The chilly night air brushed her cheek. Kale glanced at Sir Kemry as he settled on the log. "How did you doubt me?"

Her father gestured with his fork. "Look around. We've walked into your mural at Black Jetty."

Kale's head swiveled as she took in her surroundings. Regidor and Gilda stood by the fire with Dar. Paladin stood off to the side, talking to Bardon. But her husband was almost invisible in the shadows of a bentleaf tree. The minor dragons decorated a bush where they'd found a horde of night beetles.

"The grave?" Kale peered toward the other bentleaf tree.

"Not there." Sir Kemry took her hand in his. "Perhaps it's a figurative grave and not a resting spot for one individual."

Kale's throat closed as she thought of those who had died. Three dear dragons came to mind first. Then the homes she'd seen ravaged by armies and obliterated by the flames of fire dragons. The blackened forest on the other side of the river was just one spot scorched by the war. More than property and livelihoods had been destroyed. Each of the high races had lost many people.

Where others had lost sons, fathers, mothers, friends, and spouses, Kale sat by her father, could see her husband, and knew her mother helped in a field hospital. Very soon, her dragon eggs would hatch. She had the promise of new life tucked in the scarf at her waist. Even her injuries had been cured.

She stood and handed her untouched dinner to her father. "I have to talk to Paladin."

Sir Kemry nodded.

She trudged toward the clump of trees where she had seen him last. He still talked to Bardon. Did she want Bardon to hear what she had done?

She'd have to. She walked across the camp site. Paladin might be needed someplace else and be gone before she had a chance to ask him if certain things were her fault. If she were guilty.

She felt guilty.

Bardon put his arm around her as she came up beside him. The stiff muscles felt odd across her shoulders.

Kale managed a curtsy while encumbered by her husband's embrace. It made all three smile.

Paladin looked hale and hearty with the grin on his lips and a twinkle in his eye.

Kale blinked back tears and made her voice sound cheerful. "I'm glad you are well, sir."

"When you mindspoke to the dragons and it carried on to the citizens of Amara, they shook off the stupor that had blinded them to their true desire. Our people knew they wanted to follow Wulder more than they wanted to avoid conflict. With the renewed life in their hearts, I grew stronger. Strong enough to lead the army."

Kale swallowed. "I'm sure everyone was happy to see you."

"I didn't lead them all. Small factions rose up and defeated the enemy forces in their own regions. But the rightly focused commitment expressed by individual members of our society strengthened the whole." Paladin tilted his head as he looked down at her. "What's wrong, Kale?"

"Dar told me about the battles that raged after I spoke to the dragons in the valley. So many were killed."

The solemn expression on Paladin's face did not change. Bardon's arm curled inward a bit to embrace her as best he could.

"If I had not given that speech, there would not be tears and grief in more than half the homes of our people."

Paladin still didn't speak.

Bardon shifted beside her. "Kale, if the people had not defended their homes, the scourge of Pretender would still have a stronghold in their lives."

Kale shook her head, and tears flowed down her cheeks. "If I hadn't drained all my energy, Ardeo, Alton, and Benrey would have lived."

"Kale—"

"No, Bardon. Ardeo and Alton died trying to get me to safety when I couldn't fight to help protect us. Benrey died in the fight against Crim Cropper because I had no energy to pull together a wizard's defense."

She leaned against Bardon, and he brought his other arm up to encircle her. He placed his forehead on her temple and whispered. "In a battle, we do what we can. We aren't always in the correct position to do the most good."

Paladin touched Kale's arm. "She understands that, Bardon. She also knows she did what she did in obedience to Wulder, so the resulting consequences are His responsibility, not hers. She had to expend her energy without her father's aid so he would have the resources to fight Crim Cropper or Pretender, whichever one showed up to do battle."

Kale's eyes came up to look at Paladin's face.

"Tell me, Kale. There's something else. What distresses you? Why do you feel such guilt?"

"Pretender's orb. I took Pretender's orb. I knew I shouldn't. I knew if I held it, I would not be able to put it down. I gave in just a little, but I knew this moment of weakness would mean that Pretender had gained power over me. Once I allowed him to manipulate me, the next time it would be easier for him to tempt me and for me to give in."

"And still you took his gift?"

"Yes."

"What did you do with the orb?"

"You know, don't you? You know it all."

"Yes, but you need to tell me."

"I held it, and it made the pain go away. But I knew holding it was wrong. In the caves, I didn't want to be with the people there. I didn't want to be with my own dragons. I felt worthless and as if my presence would damage those around me."

"But you broke the orb. Why?"

"Because I needed the energy within it to help my father."

Paladin gently squeezed her arm. "Your love for your father was stronger than the hold Pretender had on you."

Kale wanted Paladin and Bardon to understand. They couldn't possibly know how wretched she'd been. They had to fully comprehend to forgive her. "I took the orb because of the pain."

"Wulder would have provided another remedy, had you been able to hold on."

Kale studied Paladin's expression.

He nodded so slightly she almost didn't see it. "I believe," he said, "that Gilda had a potion with her to help ease the pain."

Bardon rubbed his face against Kale's head. His stubble caught at the fine hair. To Kale, the scratchiness felt wonderful.

"I thank Wulder," said her husband, "for bringing you through all that. When I stepped out of the gateway and into Paladin's palace, I had no idea if you were still alive. The last I saw of Cropper, he was determined to annihilate the world, starting with you."

Kale's mouth twisted into a frown. "I don't understand that. It was father's dragon who bit off his wife's head."

"Maybe he didn't have the facts straight."

Paladin chuckled. "That sounds like a possibility. Not having the facts straight can cause all sorts of havoc."

"I have one more question, sir," said Kale.

"Yes?"

"Why was I able to use something created by Pretender for evil to do good? I didn't think through what the consequences might be. I just threw it down to break it open."

"The orb?" guessed Bardon.

She nodded.

Paladin put his hand up to his chin and rubbed as he thought. "Pretender did not make the energy. He contained it in the glass sphere. Energy is no more bad than water is. You could use water to refresh a thirsty man or drown him."

He put both hands on his hips and stared up into the sky. "Now that the threat of evil is at bay, we will have the rebuilding of Amara ahead of us. And we must be sure at the foundation, our citizens are choosing to share what water they have and not drown their neighbors."

"What will you have us do?" asked Bardon.

Paladin clapped a hand on his knight's shoulder. "Just what is right in front of you."

Glossary

Amara (ä´-mä-rä)
Continent surrounded by ocean on three sides.

armagot (är´-muh-got)
National tree, purple blue leaves in the fall.

armagotnut (är´-muh-got-nut)
Nut from the armagot tree.

ba
Ropma baby.

batman
Soldier assigned as personal servant to an officer.

bentleaf tree
Deciduous tree having long, slender, drooping branches and narrow leaves.

bingham trees
Flowering trees found at high altitudes.

bisonbecks (bī´-sen-beks)
Most intelligent of the seven low races. They comprise most of Risto's army.

blimmets (blim´-mets)
One of the seven low races, burrowing creatures that swarm out of the ground for periodic feeding frenzies.

Bogs, The
Made up of four swamplands with indistinct borders. Located in southwest Amara.

borling tree (bôr´-ling)
Tree with dark brown wood and a deeply furrowed nut enclosed in a globose, aromatic husk.

cygnot tree (sī´-not)
A tropical tree growing in extremely wet ground or shallow water. The branches come out of the trunk like spokes from a wheel hub and often interlace with neighboring trees.

da
Father.

daggarts (dag´-garts)
A baked treat, a small crunch cake.

doneels (dō´-neelz)
One of the seven high races. These people are furry with bulging eyes, thin black lips, and ears at the top and front of their skulls. A flap of skin covers the ears and twitches, responding to the doneel's mood. They are small in stature, rarely over three feet tall. Generally are musical and given to wearing flamboyant clothing.

Dormanscz Range (dôr-manz´)
Volcanic mountain range in Bange southeast Amara.

druddums (drud´-dumz)
Weasel-like animals that live deep in mountains. These creatures are thieves and will steal anything to horde. Of course, they like to get food, but they are also attracted to bright things and things that have an unusual texture.

emerlindians (ē´-mer-lin´-dee-inz)
One of the seven high races, emerlindians are born pale with white hair and pale gray eyes. As they age, they darken. One group of emerlindians is slight in stature, the tallest being five feet. Another distinct group are between six and six and a half feet tall.

feather-petaled bonnie
A flower with a large crown of densely placed delicate petals. The blossoms come in a wide variety of colors.

fire dragon
Emerged from the volcanoes in ancient days. These dragons breathe fire and are most likely to serve evil forces.

forms
A regimented set of exercises.

gordon tree
Named after the marione who cultivated them, the gordon trees are tall, thin, and shed their bark. The bark makes a superior paper and can be harvested each spring.

grand emerlindian
Grands are male or female, close to a thousand years old, and black.

granny emerlindian
Grannies are male or female, said to be five hundred years old or older, and have darkened to a brown complexion with dark brown hair and eyes.

grawligs (graw´-ligz)
One of seven low races, mountain ogres.

greater dragon
Largest of the dragons, able to carry many men or cargo.

guard
A fighting unit made up of a captain and four loes.

icebears
Carnivorous bears living at the northern and southern extremes of the planet.

kimens (kĭm´-enz)
The smallest of the seven high races. Kimens are elusive, tiny, and fast. Under two feet tall.

leecent
Lowest-ranking officer in military service.

lehman
Lowest rank in military service.

lightrocks
Any of the quartzlike rocks giving off a glow.

lo
Rank between leecent and lehman.

longfish
An extremely long and slender fish that is easily smoked and cured.

ma
Mother.

major dragon
Elephant-sized dragon most often used for personal transportation.

mariones (mer´-ē-ownz)
One of the seven high races. Mariones are excellent farmers and warriors. They are short and broad, usually muscle-bound rather than corpulent.

meech dragon
The most intelligent of the dragons, capable of speech.

minnekens
A small, mysterious race living in isolation on the Isle of Kye.

minor dragon
Smallest of the dragons, the size of a young kitten. The different types of minor dragons have different abilities.

moonbeam cloth
Cloth made from the moonbeam plant.

moonbeam plant
A three- to four-foot plant having large shiny leaves and round flowers resembling a full moon. The stems are fibrous and used for making invisible cloth.

Morchain Range
Mountains running north and south through the middle of Amara.

mordakleeps
One of the low races, shadowy creatures with long tails.

mullins (mŭl´-lĭnz)
Fried doughnut sticks.

nordy rolls
Whole-grain, sweet, nutty bread.

o'rants
One of the high races. Five to six feet tall.

ordend (or´-den)
A basic unit of Amaran currency. Twenty ordends equals one grood.

owlwing fern
A plant that grows in the shade and has broad, feathery fronds.

parnot (pâr´-nŏt)
Green fruit like a pear.

piggledy pin
The clublike target that stands on end in a children's ball game called piggledy.

poor man's pudding
A mound of custard with carmelized syrup or ale poured over the top, so it looks like a white island sitting in a brown lake.

portucads (por´-tuh-cadz)
A porcine creature whose fangs grow too long to be useful in a fight. The animal provides excellent meat.

quiss (kwuh´-iss)
One of the seven low races. These creatures have an enormous appetite. Every three years they develop the capacity to breathe air for six weeks and forage along the seacoast, creating havoc. They are extremely slippery.

ring beetles
Beetles with a target-ring pattern on their backs.

ropmas (rōp´-muhz)
One of the seven low races. These half men–half animals are useful in herding and caring for beasts.

schoergs (skôrgz)
One of seven low races, much like grawligs, shorter, less playful.

Sniffer
Official at court responsible for enforcing hygiene.

stakes
A disease that leaves the victim stiff for weeks after the fever has passed and can recur when the patient becomes overtired. For children, the symptoms pass. In an adult, the side effects can last ten to twenty years.

tumanhofers (too´-mun-hoff-erz)
One of the seven high races. Short, squat, powerful fighters, though for the most part they prefer to use their great intellect.

urohms (ū-rōmz´)
Largest of the seven high races. Gentle giants, well proportioned and very intelligent.

Vendela (vin-del´-luh)
Capital city of the province of Wynd.

Wittoom (wit-toom´)
Region populated by doneels in northwest Amara.

wizards' conclave
A cloistered gathering of a chosen group. The agenda is kept secret and the discussion within is undisclosed.

writher snake (rī-ther)
A water snake, long and slender. The snake wraps its body around a victim, drags it under the water, and eats the body as it decomposes.

About the Author

DONITA K. PAUL enjoys writing, but she enjoys her readers more. Her Web site, www.dragonkeeper.us is a place where she can interact with readers, old and young.

Mrs. Paul is a retired teacher and still spends a great deal of time with young people. Although she lives in the shadow of Pikes Peak, she does no mountain climbing, preferring more sedate hobbies such as knitting and stamping. And she likes to make things she can give away.